A PASSIONATE CHOICE

As the city hummed into life below them, Nancy lay protected in Ramon's arms. She stirred, and he kissed the pulse beating in her throat. "Come away with me," he said.

Unbeknown to her, it was the first time he had ever asked for anything. She shook her head. "Not yet. I have things to do. I have to think."

He kissed her, and her fingertips touched his cheekbones wonderingly. Leaving him would be the hardest thing she had ever done. "I'm going back to the Cape. Today," she said, trying to convince herself of her own certainty.

"What is it?" Ramon pressed. "What's the matter?"

"I'm frightened," she whispered.

His arms encircled her, his body granite hard. And his expression was almost ferocious as he said, "I'm going to teach you never to be afraid again. Not of anyone or anything."

Then he tilted her chin upward. "And I'm going to love you," he said as his mouth came down hard on hers. . . .

THE FLOWER GARDEN

BY

MARGARET PEMBERTON

ZEBRA BOOKS
KENSINGTON PUBLISHING CORP.

ZEBRA BOOKS

are published by

Kensington Publishing Corp.
475 Park Avenue South
New York, N.Y. 10016

Printed in the United States of America

For Mike, who made Madeira so memorable.

Chapter One

To tell a patient they are about to die is never the easiest of tasks. When the patient is thirty-five, a woman and exceptionally beautiful, the task is even harder. Dr. Henry Lorrimer furrowed his brow and drummed well-manicured fingers on the leather-topped surface of his desk as the minute hand moved steadily up towards the hour.

It was the winter of 1934 and the sidewalks were piled high with snow. Henry Lorrimer thought longingly of Florida and The Keys and the giant marlin he had hooked way back in September. From his window he could see the frosted citadel of the Chrysler building soaring against a leaden sky that indicated more snow to come. He sighed, wishing himself back in Florida; wishing himself anywhere but in his opulent surgery about to face Nancy Leigh Cameron.

In the icy streets below chaotic traffic made way for a Rolls Royce Phantom II. It slid to a standing halt outside the discreet entrance of Henry's surgery. No brass plate adorned the entrance. There was no need of one. Dr. Henry Lorrimer was the most respected consultant in New York State. A world expert on rare blood diseases. His patients came from places as diverse as South Africa, Switzerland and Japan. They all had two things in common. They were ill and they were rich.

Over the years he had perfected his method of breaking bad news. Ninety-nine times out of a hundred he simply did not do it. If the disease was fatal he saw no reason to mar his patients' last months of life by telling them so. Smoothly he would talk of treatment, of blood transfusions, of rest. Something in the demeanour of the remaining one per cent caused him to give them the highest accolade of his respect and tell them the truth. Nancy Leigh Cameron possessed that undefinable trait of character. Dr. Lorrimer wished heartily that she did not.

Three floors below, an epauletted chauffeur opened the door of the Rolls and a slim figure stepped out. The growing group of spectators inched forward, blowing hard on mittened hands. Even the down-and-outs, emerging from the shelter of the doorways, knew to whom the Rolls belonged. Jack Cameron's initials were emblazoned in gold on the doors of all his automobiles. It gave them class and Jack Cameron liked class. It was the reason he had married Nancy.

A neatly shod foot emerged from heavy folds of ankle-length sable as Nancy Leigh Cameron stepped on to the sidewalk that Dr. Lorrimer's minions had cleared of snow.

"I shan't be long, Collins. Leave the engine running."

Her voice was low and well modulated. It had husky undertones that brought an intimacy to the most banal of conversations. Nancy Leigh had disturbed more men's peace of mind than any other woman in New York. The fact that she seemed oblivious to it only added to her fascination.

"Yes, m'lady." Collins touched his peaked hat deferentially, enjoying the envious glances as he sauntered back to the front of the Rolls.

A nurse in a starched white overall held open the door so that Mrs. Cameron was exposed to the Arctic air for a minimum of time. She escorted her into a deeply carpeted lift and they rose in silence towards Dr. Lorrimer's inner sanctum. The sable coat shimmered and gleamed and the nurse resisted the urge to reach out and stroke it. It had a deep shawl collar and lavishly high cuffs. A matching hat was tilted coquettishly over one eyebrow, exposing dark hair that feathered in small curls around a perfectly oval face. Nancy Leigh Cameron had inherited the dramatic colouring and superb bone structure of her Irish forebears. Her skin was milky white and flawless. Her eyes sloe-black and thickly lashed. Her nose was straight, her cheekbones high. Her mouth was the only feature that was less than perfect. It was a mouth that smiled easily and often, but it was too wide and full for classical beauty. It added a dimension to her face that her rivals could not hope to emulate. That of effortless sensuality.

She smiled at Betty Duggan as the lift doors opened and she indicated with a slight movement of her hand that she did not wish to be accompanied. Betty hesitated. She had strict instructions from Dr. Lorrimer on the way his patients were to be treated and escorted. Her role was to open the door for them and then leave silently. She had no wish to incur Dr. Lorrimer's wrath. She moved forward but Nancy Leigh Cameron was already entering Dr. Lorrimer's room and saying throatily, "How gloriously warm it is in here. It's absolutely *freezing* outside."

Dr. Lorrimer stared in dismay as the door closed behind her.

"Where is Mr. Cameron? I expressly asked that . . ."

Nancy sat down and began to remove gauntletted gloves. "My husband runs to a very tight schedule, Doctor," she said pleasantly. "He doesn't have time to hold my hand while I have medical check-ups."

"But this is more than a check-up, Mrs. Cameron," Henry Lorrimer could feel the sweat break out on the palms of his hands. Where was Cameron, for Christ's sake? He had stressed the seriousness of the situation to him a week ago. He had no right to allow his wife to come unaccompanied and unprepared.

"Dr. Lorrimer?" Velvet-black eyes held his queryingly. "Will you please give me the result of the blood test. I have to be at the Yacht Club by two."

With difficulty Henry Lorrimer curbed his anger and, steepling his fingers, leaned across his desk.

"Mrs. Cameron, I would really appreciate it if another appointment could be made when I can speak to both you and your husband together."

The lightness in her voice died a little. "But why? Surely a simple thing like a blood test . . ." Her words hung in the air.

Henry Lorrimer cursed Jack Cameron heartily and began his usual repertoire of polished assurances. Nancy cut him short.

"If the blood test shows I am anaemic, then I need pills. Why does my husband have to be here for you to tell me that?"

Dr. Lorrimer took off his rimless glasses and polished them carefully. "Because it's a little more involved than that, Mrs. Cameron."

Nancy looked perplexed. "I fainted. People faint every day. It isn't the end of the world."

"And your doctor sent you to Professor Walton?"

Nancy nodded.

"And he referred you to me?"

Nancy nodded again.

Now was the moment of decision. Either he told her or forever held his peace.

"Mrs. Cameron," he said, replacing his glasses. "Let me tell you something about anaemia. It isn't the simple disease you seem to think. In many cases it can't be treated with a handful of pills."

Nancy listened to him attentively, her head slightly to one side, a small frown furrowing her brow.

"Roughly, anaemia falls into four classifications: microcytic hypochromic anaemia, megalabastic anaemia, aplastic anaemia and haemolytic anaemia."

"And which have I got?"

"Aplastic anaemia."

"Then I need iron?"

Dr. Lorrimer shook his head. "If you had microcytic hypochromic anaemia then we could treat it by giving iron. But you haven't. It's aplastic anaemia and that's a different thing altogether."

There was no mistaking the gravity in his voice. Nancy sat very still. "Tell me about aplastic anaemia."

Dr. Lorrimer leaned back in his leather swivel chair and studied her face long and hard. At last he said, reluctantly, "Aplastic anaemia is a disease in which the red blood corpuscles are greatly reduced, Mrs. Cameron. For reasons we don't know, there is no attempt by the bone marrow to regenerate them. The symptoms are often slight. A fainting attack, in your case. A number of sufferers are completely unaware of their condition."

"Then it isn't serious?"

Dr. Lorrimer's eyes held Nancy's. They were pansy-deep, dark and trusting. She believed implicitly that he would tell her the truth and the strength in the delicate line of her jaw and chin indicated that she would be able to cope with it. Nancy Leigh Cameron was not a woman who liked deceit and Dr. Lorrimer knew that he was dealing with the rare one per cent of patients to whom he would tell the stark truth.

"I'm afraid the condition *is* serious, Mrs. Cameron. It was for that reason I wanted your husband to be here with you today."

Nancy sat motionless: the face she had always thought of as benign was frighteningly sombre. There was a dreadful stillness in the centre of her being. She knew instinctively that his next few words would send her plunging down a precipice from which there would be no return. She could step back from the precipice: smile, thank him and leave the office. She sensed that he would not detain her if that was what she wanted to do. The words hovering ominously would never be uttered. And she would never know what they were. Her hands remained still in her lap.

"And what happens?" she asked.

"The red blood corpuscles diminish steadily over a period of time."

"And . . . ?"

His voice was grave. ". . . and are not renewed. There is no treatment, Mrs. Cameron. Regular blood transfusions will help stave off the inevitable consequences but are no cure."

She was over the precipice now and there was a sound in her ears like the roaring of waves. She opened her mouth to speak but no words came. Dr. Lorrimer reached out for his bell to summon Nurse Duggan.

Nancy's voice seemed to come from a great distance as she said shakily, "No. Please don't call the nurse. I'm perfectly all right. If I could just sit for a few minutes . . ."

Dr. Lorrimer poured two generous brandies and walked around his desk to her, pushing a glass into her unprotesting hand.

"You will, of course, receive the very best care and . . ."

"How long, Dr. Lorrimer? How long have I got to live?"

Dr. Lorrimer was not a man to allow emotion into his professional life. Only hours earlier he had told the parents of an eight-year-old that there was no hope for their son. Now he could hear the pity in his voice as he said quietly: "I can give you no accurate length of time, Mrs. Cameron. It could be anything from three months to a year.

"In very rare cases it has been known for a sufferer to recover, though why and how we still do not know. You mustn't give up hope entirely. We are discovering new drugs daily . . ."

The rest of his words flowed over her, unheard. Three months to a year. Slowly, she rose to her feet and walked across to the giant window. Below her, taxi cabs and limousines hurtled backwards and forwards. The clock on the building opposite showed ten minutes past two. She thought inconsequentially: I'm late for my meeting with Consuelo at the Club: and then, in wonder: Consuelo will still be entertaining every Friday afternoon at the Yacht Club, flirting with Commodore Stuyvesant, chatting about her last vacation to Europe, and I won't be there. Everything will go on as normal and I won't be a part of it. I will be dead. It was incredible; unbelievable. With painful clarity she wondered what it was about human nature that thought itself indestructible. That could see people dying daily and yet still live in a kind of wonderland where death would never strike.

"My nurse will accompany you back to your apartment," Dr. Lorrimer was saying.

Nancy shook her head. "My chauffeur is waiting. I would prefer to be alone."

She turned and picked up her gloves from his desk. Her skin was marble-white but there was no other outward sign of shock or distress. Her voice was perfectly composed as she said:

"Thank you for your honesty with me, Dr. Lorrimer. As there is no treatment it will be unnecessary for me to see you again."

"But the disease must be monitored!" Dr. Lorrimer protested in alarm. "We must have regular blood samples . . ."

"So that I may know how rapidly or slowly I am approaching death? I think not, Doctor. Goodbye."

Before Henry Lorrimer could regain his shaken composure she had left the room, and as he hurried protestingly after her the lift doors closed. To his utter amazement he discovered he was trembling as he seated himself once more behind his desk and reached out for his unfinished brandy. Her calm had been unnatural. For the first time in his career Dr. Henry Lorrimer wondered if he had made an error of judgement in telling a patient the unpalatable truth.

"Three months to a year". The words rang in Nancy's head like an incantation as the lift slowly descended. "Three months to a year". Jesus Christ. She had imagined she was going to be given a box of pills and advised to rest. How could she be going to die? She was fit and healthy. Fainting at the opera didn't qualify one for an incurable disease, for God's sake. She didn't see the bewildered expression on Betty Duggan's face as she ignored her request for a convenient date for her next appointment. She never knew who opened the door for her. All she felt was an incredible relief as the icy air blasted her face. She wanted it to blow the unreality of the last half hour away. To wake her from the nightmare. Three months to a year. Her brain would not function beyond that. It chanted the words like a repetitive hymn, blocking out all further thought.

Collins stood at the open door of the Rolls, waiting for her to enter. The interior was warm, safe and familiar.

She could enter it and be swept away from Dr. Lorrimer and his claustrophobically hot surgery. She could have a Gin Sling with Consuelo and go with her and Stuyvesants to the Met. She stood motionless, staring at the open door for so long that Collins asked hesitantly:

"Is everything all right, m'lady?"

She looked at him unseeingly. "Yes, Collins. I don't need the Rolls. Thank you."

In stupefied amazement he watched as she began to walk on ridiculously high heels down the icy street, the hem of her sable trailing in the snow. Collins had inherited a certain amount of British phlegm from his previous employer. He exercised it now, imperturbably waiting until Nancy was a hundred yards away and then followed at a discreet distance, hugging the kerb.

Nancy walked blindly, flurries of snow coating her hair and clinging to her cheeks. Down 42nd Street and into Fifth Avenue. Across Broadway and down to Canal Street. Passers-by, scurrying for the warmth of one and two-room apartments on the lower East Side, eyed her warily and gave her a wide berth. The leaden skies began to darken and gas lamps flickered into life as she turned into the warren of streets fronting the docks. At last she came to a halt, standing motionless and staring out over the grey-green waters of the river. Five minutes passed, and then Collins left the engine running and approached her cautiously.

"The Rolls is waiting, madam." And then again, this time touching her lightly on the arm. "The Rolls is waiting, Mrs. Cameron."

Nancy turned, blinking the snow from her lashes and looking around her for the first time. The tenements were dark and high and strangely threatening in the gathering twilight. She had no idea where she was.

"Of course. Thank you, Collins." She allowed him to help her into the blessed warmth of the car.

Collins let out a guarded sigh of relief and accelerated through the battered streets and into areas in which he felt more at home.

Nancy leaned back against the monogrammed upholstery, feeling for the first time the intense pain that seared her face and legs, her hands and her feet. She tried to reach down and ease them from the sodden and ruined crocodile shoes, but her hands were too numb to obey the instructions her mind gave. She abandoned the attempt and leaned back once more as Collins sped smoothly up Park Avenue. She would have to break the news to Jack and her father and Verity. She flinched physically. Not Verity. There was no need to mar Verity's happiness. And her father . . . ? She closed her eyes. Chips O'Shaughnessy was campaigning vigorously for re-election as Mayor of Boston, riding exuberantly on a new tide of political popularity. At Verity's wedding he had looked like a man twenty years his junior, as he flaunted Nancy's young stepmother on his arm, daring Verity to make him a great-grandfather before his seventieth birthday.

She shivered convulsively. First and foremost she needed her husband. It was 6:45 and by 7:00 he would have left his Washington apartment for the evening round of cocktails and parties and endless government gossip. She reached for the speaking tube and asked Collins to hurry.

What would Jack do? Motor up? Catch the late train? Fly? Anything as long as he reached her quickly. The thought of the evening stretching out into lonely darkness was suddenly terrifying. She didn't want it to be dark and she didn't want to be alone.

The Rolls slid to a halt outside the brownstone mansion that had been the Cameron home for three generations. Nancy didn't wait for Collins to emerge and open the door. She flung it open herself and broke into a run.

Ramon Sanford tapped a black Sobraine impatiently on his cigarette case. He wasn't accustomed to being kept waiting and Nancy Leigh Cameron was nearly an hour late. Only the fascination of the photographs had detained him. They scattered the room in oval silver frames, Camerons and O'Shaughnessys, past and present. Ramon ignored the Camerons with their jutting chins and firm-set mouths. Several times he came back to a photograph of Nancy taken aboard the Cameron yacht. She leaned against the rail, her dark hair blowing in the wind, a long chiffon scarf fluttering against her throat, her head tilted back slightly as she laughed. It was an unusual photograph, sharply different to the stylized poses affected by her husband. Ramon wondered if the senator ever laughed with the spontaneity and naturalness so obviously displayed by his wife. He doubted it. Everything Jack Cameron did had a purpose. If he ever laughed it would only be if it was advantageous for him to do so.

Two photographs stood side by side on a rosewood secretaire. Roman studied them with interest. One of them was an aged sepia portrait of an elderly man. The other the familiar face of Boston's mayor. Ramon had never met Patrick O'Shaughnessy, Nancy's grandfather, the dominating, still-straight figure with the mane of white hair eyeing the camera with pride. Yet he knew the face. An identical portrait had graced his grandfather's desk for over forty years. Sanford and O'Shaughnessy. A slight smile touched Ramon's lips. Friends and enemies. It was an old story and past history. He wondered if Nancy was as well acquainted with it as he was. Leo Sanford had been a great talker and reminiscer. As a child Ramon had sat on his knee on the terrace of their Oporto *quinta* and heard time and time again of how his grandfather's great friend, Patrick O'Shaughnessy, had saved his stepson from drowning. Of how, with only a little help from the grateful Leo, he had turned a small grocery store in Boston's North End into a multi-million dollar business empire. With his grandfather's death the photograph had disappeared. His father, the child Patrick O'Shaughnessy had saved from the grim waters of the Atlantic, had no love for his rescuer. Or, more precisely, none for his descendants. He hated Chips O'Shaughnessy so implacably that, out of respect for him, Ramon had never made the mayor's acquaintance. Only now, with Duarte dead and at his mother's request, was he renewing the ties that existed between them. And in a way his father would have approved. His rare smile deepened as he looked in vain for a photograph of the mayor's second wife. None was on view. Gloria was conspicuous only by her absence.

His eyes flicked to his watch. It was 6:55. He stubbed out his cigarette and moved towards the door. As he did so they were flung open and a dark-haired woman hurtled into the elegant room, stopping short in stupefaction when she saw it was not empty. Ramon's dark eyebrows rose. Her hat was clutched in her hands, her disarrayed curls filmed with snow. Her face was white; her eyes blue-rimmed. Her lavish sable was wet, the hem muddied and coated in slush, her delicate crocodile shoes were cracked and on the point of disintegration.

"Ramon Sanford," he said. Whatever he had expected, it was not this. Intrigued, he moved towards her and held out his hand.

She stared at him, blinking as if she had just come in from intense sunlight.

"I'm sorry, I . . ."

He raised her hand to his lips and kissed it. It was icy cold, the fingers frozen together. He kept hold of it, warming it between his own. Dazed, she made no effort to remove it. He could see her visibly striving to gather her scattered wits and reassume her social poise.

"I'm sorry. I'd forgotten . . ."

"There's no need to apologize. I amused myself by studying your family portraits. The one of your grandfather is very familiar. Leo Stanford had a likeness to it on his desk until the day he died."

Nancy forced herself to think. Sanford. The grandson of her family's benefactor. A man she had never met but with whom she had promised to have cocktails at six. Was it his father who had just died, or his mother? Her head was pounding. She only knew she had to be rid of him.

"I'm sorry. As you see, I had completely forgotten we were to have drinks together and I'm afraid it's terribly inconvenient . . ."

She was breathing rapidly and he could feel the race of her pulse as her hand remained firmly trapped in his. Her eyes darted around the room as if looking for a way of escape. They focused on the telephone and then on the drinks tray.

"Excuse me . . ." She withdrew her hand and Ramon was sure that she wasn't even aware that it had been held. As she crossed to the gleaming cut-glass decanters of whisky and brandy she knocked a cushion off the arm of a chair, her hands were shaking visibly as she reached out for a glass.

Ramon watched her, all thoughts of the waiting Gloria forgotten. Nancy Leigh Cameron's social circle was centered mainly around Boston and Palm Beach. She avoided Washington whenever she could, was seldom in New York and only in Europe for the Paris Collections. On his own well-worn playboy circuit of Cannes, Deauville, St. Moritz, New York and London, they never met. Their last meeting had been in 1909, with their respective parents, aboard King Edward's yacht at Cowes. He wondered if she remembered it.

"A shame our fathers hated each other so intensely," he was saying. "The feud broke my grandfather's heart and he and my father were irreconcilable for years."

Nancy felt the room spin. My good Christ. Another few months and if her mother's belief in the after-life was proved correct, she'd be able to hear the Sanford/O'Shaughnessy story from the original participants! Her hand shook so violently as she lifted the decanter to pour a drink that it cracked sharply against the rim of her glass, sending golden droplets scattering on to the tray and carpet.

Ramon moved quickly across to her and took the decanter from her grasp, pouring two stiff drinks and handing her one. He understood now the reason for her dishevelled appearance and disorientation. He was well acquainted with the habits of alcoholics. Most of his rich and famous friends belonged to that particular club. For the first time he felt a grudging respect for Jack Cameron. He would have to be more of a man than he had thought him to have the audacity to proclaim himself a future candidate for the presidency when he had an alcoholic wife.

"I'm really sorry that I have no time to spare you . . ." Nancy began again, trying to regain her composure, "but I have a personal telephone call to make. If you will excuse me . . ."

"I'll excuse you to make your call," Ramon said easily, "but not from our dinner date."

They didn't have a dinner date but Nancy didn't protest. She didn't hear him. She was already dialling Washington.

Ramon crossed the room, noticed two Vermeers that were worthy of closer attention, heard Nancy ask for her husband and closed the panelled doors behind him. A little maid in a dusky pink uniform moved forward to enter. Ramon shook his head.

"Mrs. Cameron is making a personal call."

Maria hesitated. She never listened in to private conversations. Mrs. Cameron knew that, and according to the butler she was cold and wet. Although she had not been summoned she would surely be needed. She opened her mouth to protest and then thought better of it. Mrs. Cameron's guest was not a gentleman who would appreciate impertinence from staff—or anyone else for that matter. She had seen his photograph in papers and glossy magazines but couldn't remember his name. She would ask the butler. She wondered what his connection was with Mrs. Cameron. He had never visited before and didn't fall into the usual category of Cameron guests. He wasn't a politician: he wasn't even American. A little shiver ran down her spine. He was very handsome. Very male.

She put back the high-necked evening dress that she had laid out on Nancy Leigh's bed and replaced it with a stunning Schiaparelli that plunged back and front and clung silkily over the hips. In Maria's eyes it was a more suitable dress for an evening out with such a man.

"This is Mrs. Cameron speaking," Nancy said, as the familiar voice of Jack's personal assistant answered the telephone.

"I'm afraid Mr. Cameron is in conference with Mr. Rogers of the State Department," Syrie Geeson said smoothly.

"At the apartment?"

"Yes, Mrs. Cameron. Mr. Cameron and Mr. Rogers are dining later with the attorney general and . . ."

"Please put me through to my husband."

There was a fractional pause. "I'm sorry, Mrs.

Cameron, Mr. Cameron expressly asked that . . ."

"*Immediately*!"

There was a long silence, then Jack's voice said brusquely, "Nancy?"

"Oh Jack! Thank goodness I caught you before you left . . ."

"For Christ's sake, Nancy. I've got Rogers in the next room. What the hell is it?"

"I've just come from the clinic and . . ."

"I can't talk about that now, Nancy. It's important that I make Rogers see my point of view. The son of a bitch has been queering everything these last few weeks . . ."

"This is *important*! More important than Rogers or Roosevelt or the New Deal or . . ."

"Have you been drinking? You sound hysterical. I'll give your love to Mrs. Rogers and . . ."

"To hell with Mrs. Rogers! Don't you want to know what Dr. Lorrimer said? Don't you *care*? Has it ever crossed your mind that he wanted to see me urgently and that you should have been with me when he did?"

In the background Syrie Geeson's voice could be heard. "It's seven-fifteen . . ." Another word followed faintly.

"And don't you even have the decency to talk to me in private?"

"Look, Nancy. I don't know what the hell's got into you but I've got a heavy evening ahead of me. I'll phone you later tonight and you can tell me what Lorrimer prescribed."

Nancy's anger suddenly evaporated. Her voice was dangerously quiet.

"I telephoned because I needed you. Are you telling me you haven't time to listen?"

"I'm telling you I'll listen to you later. This meeting with Rogers and the attorney general is crucial. Hell, if you knew some of the stunts he's tried to pull . . ."

"It's seven-twenty. Mr. Rogers is getting edgy."

"Take him down to the limousine, Syrie. I'll be right with you."

There was no goodbye, only a purring sound as the line was disconnected.

Nancy slowly replaced the receiver and stood motionless. She hoped FDR appreciated Jack's devotion to duty. And that Syrie Geeson enjoyed his company at the high-powered dinner table. He would telephone her later; when it was convenient.

She eased her throbbing feet from the remnants of her shoes and stared with surprise at the pool of water she was standing in. She wouldn't tell him. The moment, if there ever had been one, had gone. Snow fell from her coat on to the Aubusson carpet and rapidly melted. They had talked together once, a long time ago. Before Verity's birth and before Jack's absorption in government. She remembered Dr. Lorrimer's surprise when she had attended the surgery alone. He had expected Jack to be with her. He had specifically and privately asked Jack that he should be. Jack had been too busy. Too busy even to telephone Dr. Lorrimer and say that he would not be accompanying her. If he had done so the doctor would surely have emphasized to him the seriousness of her condition. Nancy was glad he had not done so. For the first time since she had left the surgery she was thinking clearly. If Jack knew she was going to die he would feel obliged to spend the next few months with her and he would resent it. The grim-faced attorney general had done her a favour. She would keep her secret to herself. There was nothing to be gained by sharing it.

She picked up the receiver again and re-dialled Jack's number. There was just enough time to catch him before he left and tell him not to ring the New York apartment. She had already made up her mind what to do. She was going back to their home at the Cape.

The number rang unanswered for a long time and Nancy was just about to replace the receiver when an unfamiliar voice answered.

"Mr. Cameron, please. Mrs. Cameron speaking."

"I'm sorry, Mrs. Cameron. The senator has just left for a dinner engagement."

"Then may I speak to Miss Geeson?"

There was the slightest of pauses. "Miss Geeson has accompanied the senator, Mrs. Cameron."

"I see. Thank you."

She replaced the receiver slowly, knowing now what the whispered word had been that Syrie Geeson had spoken to her husband. "Darling. It's seven-fifteen, darling." So now it was the smoothly efficient Syrie Geeson who was keeping his bed warm on his long absences from home. And because of her position as his personal assistant, Jack could afford to be less discreet than usual. No one would think it odd that the bright Miss Geeson accompanied him occasionally to dinners or luncheons. She stared out through the windows at the glittering panorama of the New York skyline and shivered. If Jack sought sexual comfort elsewhere, she had only herself to blame. At least the nature that had so disappointed him had protected them from disaster. One after another of her friends had hurtled into passionately torrid love affairs. She had been immune. Her tragedy was not that she was dying. It was that she had never lived. She picked up the half-full whisky tumbler and flung it violently against the darkened window that mocked her reflection.

"Goddamn it to hell!" she shouted. "It isn't fair! It isn't bloody *fair*!"

Chapter Two

Ramon heard the raised voice, the shattering glass, judged that the ill-timed telephone call was at an end and entered the room. Nancy swung around furiously.

"What the hell do you think you're doing? I told you to leave!"

Ramon's eyes flashed. "I'm a Sanford, not a servant. If I make a dinner date the lady keeps it."

"This lady does as she pleases and we didn't have a dinner date. My secretary booked you for cocktails at six."

"An appointment *you* didn't keep! Take that fur off before you catch pneumonia."

"I'll take it off when I choose and I'd be obliged if you would see yourself out!"

"You'll take it off now and I'll leave when I choose!"

Nancy marched across the room with all the dignity her stockinged feet could afford, and pressed the bell by the fireplace, hard and long.

"The gentleman is leaving, Morris."

Ramon did not even bother to turn his head in the butler's direction.

"The gentleman is staying. You're dismissed."

Nancy gasped, angry colour stinging her cheeks. "How dare you override my orders to my staff. Morris, escort this . . . this . . . *gentleman* to the street."

"I wouldn't advise it, Morris," Ramon said pleasantly.

The butler gazed from one to the other despairingly. In all his years of service he had never been faced with such a situation. The eviction of gatecrashers and underlings, yes. But not a gentleman of Mr. Sanford's stature—or physique.

"Madame, I . . ."

"Thank you, Morris," Ramon said with deadly finality, smiling suddenly at Nancy and moving towards her.

He was tall, much taller than Jack, and there was something powerful and dangerous in the way he moved. Beneath the exquisitely-cut suit his body was hard-muscled with broad shoulders and narrow hips. His hair was thick and black and tightly curled. It tumbled low over strong brows and clung decadently to the nape of his neck. His hawklike nose and jutting chin were those of a man to be reckoned with, and there was a sparkling "damn you" insolence in the dark eyes that Nancy found profoundly disturbing.

The butler, taking hurried advantage of Nancy's momentary silence, hastily retreated and closed the door behind him. It would take a Gene Tunney to tangle with the likes of Mrs. Cameron's unwelcome guest and he was no Gene Tunney. Neither were Collins nor the footman. He doubted if the whole lot of them combined could have removed him against his will.

"You're mad," Nancy said, unable to move any further as she came into contact with glass-fronted bookshelves.

Ramon grinned. "Maybe, but I don't walk snow-covered streets in shoes suitable only for a palm court *or* bury myself in sodden fur."

With cool deliberation he reached out towards her, grasped the sable by the collar and threw it back from her shoulders so that it slid down her arms on to the floor.

"Now your stockings."

Nancy found that her breathing was coming hard and sharp. "Get out! Get out this minute or I'll call the police."

"Rape and murder are all they're interested in and I have neither in mind. Your stockings, if you care to look, are saturated."

He rang the bell and, as a nervous Morris entered, said curtly, "Send Mrs. Cameron's maid along with warm towels, please."

Morris was beyond surprise. If Mr. Sanford wanted warm towels he would get warm towels. What his mistress was doing shivering and in her stockinged feet was a mystery he had no intention of trying to unravel.

"What are you going to do?" For Nancy the whole proceedings had taken on an air of unreality.

"Look after you, though God knows why. You're the most ill-mannered woman I've ever met."

"*I'm* ill-mannered?" Nancy found herself rallying. "*I'm* ill-mannered! You burst in here when you've been asked to leave. You're rude to my staff! Rude to me! You . . . you . . . *manhandle* me."

His white teeth gleamed in amusement. "The removal of a coat can hardly be classed as manhandling. However . . ."

"Lay one finger on me and I'll ruin your reputation!"

"An impossible task. It's ruined already."

His dark eyes laughed at her. She was incredible. Instead of the boring half hour of cocktails and small talk that he had anticipated, he was being entertained in a way he hadn't been for years.

Maria entered the room, bewildered by Morris' explanation of the events taking place in the drawing room, two thick warm towels in her hands along with a pair of maribou-trimmed mules.

Ramon turned to her, smiled in a way that made Maria's legs weaken, swept the towels and mules from her unprotesting hands and said easily, "Mrs. Cameron requires a hot scented bath. Let me know when it is ready."

Dazedly, Maria nodded and wondered if the formidable stranger was intending to bathe Madame himself. Mr. Cameron never ventured either into Nancy's bathroom or dressing room. The olive-skinned stranger obviously had no such inhibitions.

"This is not Europe, Mr. Sanford," Nancy's voice quivered with rage. "I don't care how high-handedly you treat your servants in Portugal, you'll treat mine with a little more respect. When I want a bath to be run, *I* will ask for it to be run. Now that you have humiliated me and given the staff enough to gossip about for a month, perhaps you would kindly leave. The fun is over. I have no intention of being treated like a peasant in my own apartment."

"I doubt if you have the slightest idea of how a peasant is treated. Now, remove your stockings and sit down."

"I will do no such thing! I . . ."

"Then I'll do it for you."

He tossed the towels and mules on to a deeply cushioned couch and took a step towards her.

Nancy's voice was suddenly faint. "You wouldn't dare!"

"I would."

Nancy saw the sudden hardening around the sensual mouth and knew that he spoke the truth.

"Now be a sensible girl and take them off."

Dazedly she looked down at her damp feet and freezing legs. They were so cold that they burned. Or at least her legs did. Her feet had long since lost any semblance of feeling.

Meekly she turned her back to him, unhooked her stockings and rolled the sheer silk downwards. As she did so Ramon moved away from her to the drinks trolley, pouring a large brandy. The stockings were thrown on to the discarded sable and he said in a voice that was surprisingly gentle:

"Sit down and have a brandy while I rub some life back into your feet. They're bad enough to need hospital treatment."

The pain in her toes was excruciating. Obediently, she moved to the deeply buttoned couch and sat down. Ramon swirled her brandy, warming it in his hands before handing her the glass. Then he sat beside her, ignoring her gasp as he swung her naked legs up off the floor and across his knees and began to rub them with the softness of the towels.

Nancy swallowed deeply from her glass and closed her eyes. The whole day had been a farce. From the moment she had stepped into Dr. Lorrimer's surgery nothing had been real. Least of all this. Ramon Sanford was not known for acts of kindness or geniality. The press had dubbed him the Panther of the Playboys and it was a title that suited him. He had been born into a family of vast wealth and impeccable breeding. The knowledge sat easily on him. He moved through life with the careless arrogance of a man who had never had to ask for anything.

She opened her eyes and in the dull light his handsome face was a study in bronze. The towel had been dropped and his strong hands moved rhythmically, massaging and kneading, warming and relaxing her. She felt a glow spreading through her, replacing the numbed cold with a sensation of heat as the blood began once more to circulate. His hands mesmerized her with their combination of strength and gentleness. A ruby the size of a nut flashed blood-red on the little finger of his left hand. Small dark hairs disappeared beneath the lace-frilled cuff of his shirt. She gazed at them and knew that his broad chest would have the same olive flesh tones: the same dark springing hair that curled so unfashionably and originally low over the collar of his evening shirt. The heat that warmed her feet and legs changed character, spreading higher and upwards.

With a cry of protest she swung her legs from his grasp, leaping to her feet with such momentum that she stumbled and nearly fell.

Immediately he was on his feet, his arms steadying her, dangerously close. The alien feeling he was arousing in her intensified at his nearness. His mouth was only inches away from hers. She wondered what his kiss would be like and raised her hands to his chest, pushing him away viciously. She was going mad. The shock of the diagnosis had unhinged her mind.

"What the hell . . ."

"Don't touch me! Don't ever touch me!" She was trembling and there was a note of rising hysteria in her voice. "I can't bear to be touched! Not now! Not ever!" Her voice broke and she began to sob, hugging her breast as though holding herself together against an inner disintegration.

Ramon's eyes narrowed. He had thought her behaviour nothing more than the disorientation of a perfectly possessed public figure caught out in the midst of a drinking bout. But the tearing, racking sobs were those of a woman either deranged or hurt beyond comprehension. She had rushed into the apartment wanting desperately to speak to her husband. Whatever the conversation had been, it had obviously been unsatisfactory. Ramon wasn't surprised. He couldn't imagine the glossily smooth senator being a comfort to anyone but his bank manager.

His hands gripped her shoulders hard and she shrank away. His grip tightened and he pulled her against his chest. This time she submitted, clutching the lapels of his jacket, burying her head against the ruffled lace of his evening shirt, crying and crying as she had wanted to do ever since the dreadful interview in Dr. Lorrimer's surgery. At last, exhausted, her breath coming in shuddering gasps, she eased herself away from him, his handkerchief clutched tightly in her hand.

"I've ruined your shirt." Dear God, what a fool she had made of herself. Never let your guard down. As the daughter of a political man and wife of another, this dictum had been drummed into her for years—and assiduously obeyed. She never had; not until now. For years she had stood beside her father on the hustings and had accompanied him to official functions when his election was successful: had captivated the hard-headed Washington crowd without one careless slip of the tongue. Never one foolish word that could have been used against either her father or Jack. In the last few hours all those years of careful self-control and caution had been thrown to the winds. She had not just let her guard down, she had thrown it away. And in front of a man she had never met before. A man whose father had been one of her father's most implacable enemies, and a man her husband had only ever spoken of with contempt.

Jack had publicly proclaimed long and often that a man born as he had been, into a family of great wealth, also had social obligations. In his case, he would explain disarmingly, he intended fulfilling them by dedicating his life to public service. It made his intention of running for the Democratic nomination in 1936 seem almost a self-sacrifice. He had no time for the Ramon Sanfords of the world. Once, while listening to her husband's condemnation of Ramon's latest affair with the Russian Princess Marinsky, she had wondered if he were jealous. The princess' husband had insulted Ramon at the Savoy Grill and Ramon had laid him flat with one blow, fastidiously adjusting his cuffs and continuing with his meal of quail and champagne while the staff carried the prostrate body of his companion's husband to the nearest hospital. Flashbulbs had popped and reporters had scurried to their news desks. It had filled the world's press for three delicious days. Jack's moral outrage had been deeply appreciated by their guests, a fiercely Baptist senator and his wife.

Nancy was not so convinced of her husband's moral outrage. His latest affair with the wife of a New York judge was well into its sixth month. The only difference between the two affairs that Nancy could see was that one was furtive and the other was not. She suspected that the reason for Jack's venom was that Sanford could, and did, choose his mistresses wherever his fancy took him. The need for circumspection narrowed Jack's choice alarmingly. The judge's wife was eight years older than Nancy. It had been an affair that had hurt her intensely.

She was aware of a distinct desire to ask Ramon if the Russian princess still figured in his life, and stilled it. She was behaving like a child. She had needed comfort and he had given it: therefore she felt grateful, nothing more.

"Aren't you going to tell me?" The dark, almost black eyes, were questioning.

She shook her head, wiping her cheeks with her hands, taking on the outward appearance of Nancy Leigh Cameron again as she said lightly, "It was nothing. Some bad news, that's all. I'm all right now. Really I am."

His eyes were unreadable as he watched her push her bobbed hair from her face, smooth her dress, changing her manner to that of a polite hostess.

"I'm most awfully sorry for throwing such a scene. I can't think what got into me. I hope I haven't made you late for your evening engagements."

It was nearly eight o'clock. Gloria would have been tapping her heels for almost an hour. He said, "I don't have any engagements this evening."

Her composure was tinged with embarrassment. The sable coat lay in a crumpled heap; clear evidence of the brutal way he had thrown it from her shoulders. The ruined stockings littered the elegant room, giving it the intimacy of a bedroom. She remembered his insistence that she remove them and felt her cheeks tinge with colour. She wondered if he had watched and knew instinctively that he hadn't. Ramon Sanford would be too accustomed to the practised undressings of his mistresses to be titillated by her amateur fumblings.

The silence stretched uncomfortably between them and Ramon did nothing to break it. He watched her steadily, seeing her newly found composure crumble as he failed to make the expected polite assurances, the convenient "goodnight," the speedy exit.

He flicked open his cigarette case and offered it to her. Nancy rarely smoked and her hand trembled slightly as she reached for a cigarette. As Ramon slid the gold monogrammed case back into his pocket he knew that her apparent calm was nothing but the thinnest of veneers.

The lighter flared and as Nancy bent her head towards its glow, his hands steadied hers, holding but not releasing.

"You're a bloody liar," he said softly. "What happened to you this afternoon?"

She was trapped. There was no avoiding his eyes or his nearness.

"Nothing . . ." She faltered. "Everything."

"Tell me." His voice was one that was used to being obeyed.

She shook her head soundlessly, knowing how easy it would be to tell him and knowing that if she did he would not offer meaningless platitudes.

"No," she said at last. "If I can't tell my husband then I can't tell anybody."

Ramon remembered the short, sharp telephone call; the violently thrown glass and the angry sobbing words. His dislike of Senator Jack Cameron deepened. There was a finality in her voice that deterred him from pressing her further. He had no desire to break her fragile defences and reduce her to the tears that he felt instinctively were only just below the surface.

He grinned. "That's a very Bostonian sentiment."

She stared at him for a second and then a smile hovered at the corners of her mouth. "I'm a very Bostonian lady."

"So I've heard. Go and take that hot bath and we'll have a quiet dinner somewhere together and you can tell me what else you are."

Ramon Sanford, Panther of the Playboys. If any columnist saw them dining together *à deux* they would be choice items in the next day's gossip columns. Jack would be furious. Mentally she could see him flinging his morning newspaper angrily across his Washington breakfast table. He would be on the telephone within seconds, demanding an explanation. She would tell him she was too busy to listen to him.

"I'd love to have dinner," she said and Ramon noticed, with a sudden contraction of his stomach muscles, that when she smiled she was extraordinarily beautiful. Thickly-lashed eyes tilted tantalizingly upwards, giving her the mischievous look of a kitten. He had seen her at her worst—cold, crying, dishevelled—and she had aroused feelings of tenderness in him that he hadn't experienced since his childhood. He wondered what effect she would have on him when she had bathed and changed and her eyes had lost their blue-ringed shadows.

The doors closed behind her and he poured himself another brandy, moving across to the vast windows that looked out over night-time New York. One thing was certain: she was not the sort of woman he had expected. She was definitely not the sort of woman Gloria had so maliciously depicted.

Gloria had been waiting for him now for more than an hour. He scrawled a brief line on the back of one of his cards, crossed to the secretaire, extracted a "Cameron"-embossed envelope and slid the card inside. He smiled as he did so. Gloria's fury at his non-appearance would be nothing to her fury when she saw the family name on the envelope. He sealed it and rang for Morris. Gloria's passion was always heightened when she was enraged. The weekend would be an enjoyable one.

"Have this delivered to the Algonquin immediately," Ramon said as Morris entered.

The butler eyed the scrawled name and his eyebrows rose fractionally as he withdrew. In his opinion Mr. Sanford was rapidly reducing the Cameron household to the fairground antics of the Park Avenue set.

Nothing was as Nancy had expected. They didn't go to the El Morocco or the Persian Room or the St. Regis or the Waldorf. Instead, they drove to a small restaurant some twenty-five miles outside the city. It was the first time Nancy had ever been driven by her escort. His handling of the car on the icy streets was expert and confident. They sat in silence, the road streaming beneath them. The snow-covered sidewalks gave way to trees and fields of ghostly white. His hands on the Daimler's wheel were sure and strong. Nancy looked quickly away, staring out into the darkness, aware of the unbidden drift of her thoughts. Their silence was without strain. It was as if the intimacy of being alone together was entirely natural.

Ramon had not booked a table but the head waiter deferentially gave them the best one in the room, and was to be seen later apologizing profusely to an astrakhan-clad gentleman who vowed he would never patronize the restaurant again. The waiter was polite but unmoved. The patronage of Ramon Sanford was worth far more than that of an overweight, elderly railroad baron.

"Would you like a drink?"

Silver gleamed on white napery. They had been seated on a red velvet banquette surrounded by freshly imported flowers from Florida. She could feel the slight touch of his body against hers.

"A Martini, please."

He raised his head the merest fraction and immediately there was a waiter beside him.

"One Martini and one bourbon and soda. Bring the menu please, and we'll order."

"Certainly, sir. At once, sir."

"Here's to the end of prohibition," he said as his drinks arrived, and he raised his glass to her. Nancy smiled. The nightmare was receding. Tomorrow she would go to the Cape and think. Tonight her prayers had been answered and she was not alone in the dark.

There was no long perusing of the menu as there would have been with Jack. He ordered oysters and a chilled bottle of Sauterne; saddle of venison and a bottle of 1870 Chateau Lafitte.

"You've hardly changed since last we met," he said as the oyster shells were borne away.

Nancy looked across at him, bemused. "We've never met," she said.

The Sauterne had had the desired effect. He could see the tenseness that had been in every line of her body receding. Her skin in the revealing gown glowed luminously. Her breasts were small and high, in perfect proportion to a petiteness that had surprised him. He had expected her to be tall and studiedly elegant. Instead, even with the evening shoes, she scarcely reached his shoulders and her gown was worn with natural grace.

Never once did she check her appearance in the restaurant's large mirrors. Her attention was given wholly to him. She didn't primp into her powder compact, fiddle with her jewellery or hair, or display any of the female mannerisms that irritated him beyond endurance. Her hands were milky white; her only rings a wedding ring and a cabachon emerald surrounded by diamonds. Her nails were free of the blood-red enamel he so disliked. They were short and perfectly shaped, buffed to a pearly sheen. He wanted to touch her more than he had ever wanted to touch any other woman in his life. He put down his wine glass and took her hands in his, covering them completely.

At his touch she felt an impulse of sensuality flare within her. She tried to pull away, but his thumbs caressed her wrists restrainingly.

"It was at Cowes," he said. "It was 1909 and I was eight years old. You wore a pastel blue frock and had ribbons in your hair."

"It was my birthday," Nancy said, her hands remaining in his as the years slipped away. "I thought that was why we had been invited. I remember thinking it awful bad manners that there wasn't a birthday cake."

He laughed. "My mother said I was to be nice to you and I thought you the most frightful nuisance."

"You had a sailor suit on and you sulked because you had a hoop and weren't allowed to bowl it."

His eyes held an expression she wasn't familiar with. "I'm glad you remember."

"I remember everything about that day." She was back in the past, her nightmare shelved to a far recess of her brain. It had been a hot, sunny day and she had been forced to wear white gloves that had irritated her skin.

"You must address the king as 'Your Majesty' if he should speak to you," her mother had said, holding on to her lavishly trimmed hat as their launch approached the *Victoria and Albert.*

"Of course the king will speak to her," her father had said, tossing his cigar stub into the sea. "I'll make sure of that, honey. Don't you worry," and his arm had tightened around Nancy's shoulders.

Nancy's mother had shuddered. "It's the King of England you're about to meet, Chips. Not a steel magnate."

Chips O'Shaughnessy had grinned. He knew damned well whom he was going to meet. Hadn't he just paid a hundred bucks to have the event photographed? He could see the man now, balancing camera and tripod on a rocking boat rowed as close to the royal yacht as protocol allowed. They'd be damned good pictures and would send up his stock in Boston. The city would like a mayor who hobnobbed with Britain's king.

"That's my girl," he had said to Nancy as their launch pulled alongside and then, as they stepped aboard, Nancy saw the colour drain from his face.

She had giggled, thinking it funny that her ebullient and rumbustious father should be so disconcerted at meeting an elderly, stout man with a beard and laughing eyes. But Chips O'Shaughnessy was looking at one of the other guests aboard the yacht and not at the king. It had been ten years and she had not changed.

Her hair was a deep, burnished bronze, swept upwards in thick waves beneath a broad-brimmed hat decorated by a single, full-blown rose. The breeze from the Solent blew her silken skirts back against her body. The seductive gold-green eyes met his and the expression in them was agonized. He wanted to race across the deck and crush her to him.

It had been just such a hot summer day ten years ago when they had parted. Then the breeze blowing her hair and skirts had been the stiff breeze from Boston Harbour. She had cried and cried and he had cursed heaven and her and known that he had lost her for good. Ten long years ago and the pain in his chest was like that of a knife wound. The man beside her stepped forward. He was unmistakably European: a tall man with swarthy skin and meticulously trimmed beard and moustache. One hand rested lightly and proprietorially on his wife's shoulder, a blood-red ruby glowing in the sun. Chips could not see, but he knew that Zia's body had tremored. The lines of pain around the soft, curving mouth were so acute that Chips wanted to cry out in protest.

Chips could feel his wife's fingers pressing tightly on his arm. He was aware that he was being stared at and, with a supreme effort, he collected himself. He turned his head to his wife and child, flashed the broad smile that was his trademark, and stepped confidently forward to be presented to Britain's sovereign.

Nancy liked the king. He was enormous and sat in a wicker chair that looked as if it would give way under his weight. He wore a blue sack coat and his white trousers were creased at the sides—which Nancy thought very strange. He smoked cigars like her father and he laughed a lot. A little boy in a sailor suit was sitting on his knee, tugging at his beard. The king was telling him jokes and roaring with laughter. Nancy didn't understand the jokes and she didn't think the boy did either, but it didn't matter. When Nancy forgot to call him "Your Majesty" and called him "Kingie" instead, he had laughed even louder and ruffled her curls, and Nancy knew that no one could be cross with her because of her mistake.

Later on there were flutters of excitement as the news

spread that the Kaiser's launch was approaching. Nancy was very disappointed when she saw him. He wasn't at all like the king. Instead of being jolly, he was dour and stern-faced and she was sent to play with the dark-haired boy in the sailor suit.

"I don't like girls," he had said rudely, and Nancy had been just about to give him a sharp kick on the shins when his mother approached.

Nancy forgot about the boy's rudeness. The lady smiling down at her was like a character from a fairy tale.

"I'm Zia Sanford," she had said, holding out her hand to Nancy as if Nancy was a grown up.

"And I'm Nancy O'Shaughnessy," Nancy had said shyly.

"I know."

The boy stepped closer to his mother and Nancy saw them briefly touch hands. The gesture had surprised her. She realized she had never seen outward displays of affection between mothers and sons since her arrival in England.

"I come from Boston too."

Nancy stared at her, round-eyed. She wasn't at all like her mother or her mother's friends. She didn't smell of lavender or rose-water but carried with her a mysterious Eastern fragrance. There was powder on her cheeks and her eyes had been exotically lined in black pencil, the lids touched with gleaming colour.

"You don't look as if you come from Boston," Nancy said naively.

"I'm from the old North End," Zia had said with a smile.

Nancy's incredulity deepened. She knew the North End well. It was where her father did his hardest campaigning, but the North End was poor. Ladies like Zia Sanford didn't live there.

"It must have been a long time ago," she said at last.

Zia's smile deepened. "It was. When your grandparents lived in Hanover Street."

Nancy hadn't even known that her grandparents had done so. She wanted to know more, much more, but her parents were approaching and there was a strange expression on Zia Sanford's face.

"We're taking our leave," her father had said to Mrs. Sanford and Nancy had thought his voice sounded odd, as if he was coming down with a cold. There was a whiteness around his mouth that she had never seen before. She hoped he wasn't going to be ill. They were going to the Riviera the following week and she was looking forward to it.

Her hands were still trapped in Ramon's. The untasted venison had long since been removed. Because she liked ice cream the sweet trolley had been waved away and a ridiculous tutti frutti graced the table.

She said reminiscently: "Your mother was so beautiful. I thought at first she was the queen."

"She's still beautiful." The sensuous mouth with its hint of savagery was suddenly gentle. Nancy remembered the open affection between mother and son.

"She told me she came from Boston and I didn't believe her."

"I find it very hard to believe myself. To me my mother is totally European."

In the candlelight he looked very foreign. "As you are."

"Yes, as I am. My father was wholly Portuguese."

She didn't want to talk about his father.

"Did you go to Cowes again?" she asked, slipping her fingers from his and running them around the rim of the glass.

"Yes, but it wasn't the same. There was a new king,

thinner and quieter. And instead of the Kaiser there was the Tsar. He seemed even less like a king than George V, very quiet and subdued. There was no more royal gaiety after Bertie."

"I never met him. My father was mayor of Boston by then and I never went to Europe again. Not until my marriage."

There was a tiny silence. Ramon had no intention of darkening the conversation with the spectre of the distant senator.

"I could never quite understand *why* you were invited aboard the *Victoria and Albert*. I was an awful snob for a boy of eight."

"You probably heard your parents wondering the same thing," Nancy said, smiling. "My father was barely tolerated by most of the aristocracy. They considered him brash and vulgar: which he was. He was also the most loveable eccentric and the English are tolerant of eccentrics. I think that was his saving grace. My mother's pedigree was impeccable. William the Conqueror was quite a latecomer in her family tree, so the combination of English blue blood and American wealth gave them entry practically everywhere."

"Despite your father's Irishness?" Ramon asked, quizzically.

Nancy's smile deepened. "My father's Irishness wasn't quite so blatant in those days. You forget that he's a politician."

"From what I hear, your father never lets anyone forget that. Will he get the mayoralty again? He must be close to seventy now."

The ice cream had been removed and coffee and liqueurs littered the table. She gave him no opportunity of reclaiming her hands. They cradled her liqueur glass as she said, "Sixty-nine—and he'll get it. If he fails he intends to run for governor."

"Then let's hope he gets it," Ramon said feelingly. "The thought of your father as governor is terrifying."

"His supporters wouldn't agree with you. They're loyal to a man."

"And are you?"

"Of course," Nancy said simply. "He's my father."

There it was again. Their fathers and the implacable hatred that had existed between them.

She said hesitantly, "I never understood it. Why our grandfathers were like brothers and yet your father and mine . . ."

He shrugged. "It doesn't matter. It's past history. Dead and forgotten."

"Your father owed his life to an O'Shaughnessy. O'Shaughnessys owed the seeds of their wealth to a Sanford. Yet your name is forbidden to be spoken in my father's presence. It doesn't make sense."

"It doesn't have to." He had no intention of telling her what she most wanted to know.

"How was your father wholly Portuguese when the Sanfords are an English family?" she asked after a while.

"My grandfather was the Visconde Fernando de Gama, a minister in Queen Maria's government. My grandmother was twenty years his junior and very beautiful. Leo Sanford fell in love with her and didn't play the Englishman. Instead of a discreet *affaire*, he abducted her. The scandal rocked Portuguese society and they had to flee to America until my grandfather died some years later. Being a maternal woman, my grandmother took her son with her. That was my father. He was two or three at the time."

"And that was when my grandfather rescued him from the sea?"

"Yes. The lovers had no time to wait for a more luxurious vessel. The outraged visconde was hard on their heels and they sailed for the New World on a ship crowded with Irish emigrants."

"It's a very romantic story."

He wanted to kiss her so much it was a physical pain.

"They never had a child," he said. "Leo Sanford left my father everything. The wine shipping company of Sanfords; his American business interests; his European business interests. But all on condition that he took the Sanford name. He sent my father to public school in England and did everything in his power to turn him into an Englishman." A smile touched his lips. "He failed utterly."

"But Sanfords have lived in Portugal for over three hundred years," Nancy protested. "Surely they must regard themselves as Portuguese now, not English?"

"Your mother may have been English but you don't know them very well," Ramon said drily. "Oporto is like an outpost of the British Empire. All the great wine shippers have been there since the 1700s. The Cockburns, the Sandemans, the Sanfords: yet they still don't speak Portuguese. They play cricket on their exclusive playing fields, commandeer the beach at Fox, send their sons to public schools in England and marry the daughters of other wine shippers."

"Your grandfather didn't."

"No, and it cost him years in exile."

"And your father married an American."

"For which I am very grateful." He reached across and removed her fingers from her glass, wondering why he was talking such nonsense when all he wanted to do was make love to her.

With the touch of his fingers the ease and spontaneity of the conversation died. Nancy had never been so acutely aware of another person's body or presence. She felt her throat tighten as she tried to continue the conversation.

"I saw your mother several times after that first meeting."

"In England?"

"No. In Boston. She first visited us when I was thirteen and then, after my mother's death, she came once or twice a year. She never stayed long and I was always sad to see her go."

His shock was palpable. She realized that neither he nor his father had known of Zia's visits to Boston.

"Of course," he said impassively, "Boston was my mother's home."

His eyes were once more an inscrutable mask. She had an overwhelming urge to see the mask slip; to see a flicker of anger or jealousy.

"Jack and I honeymooned at *Sanfords*."

"All the best people honeymoon at *Sanfords*," he said smoothly.

The lines around his mouth had hardened. She suddenly felt foolish. His hands released hers and he lit a cigarette.

"Does Zia still spend all her time in Madeira?" she asked, trying to recoup the ease and spontaneity that had suddenly evaporated.

He passed a cigarette across to her. "Yes, she's always loved the island and has lived there for the past twenty years." His voice was polite: disinterested.

"And is *Sanfords* still more like a royal court than an hotel?"

The conversation had deteriorated into the small talk of strangers.

"The last time I was there, three months ago, there were no guests with a rank lower than that of an English duke."

"Then there must have been some very high ranking guests," she said spiritedly. "An English duke regards himself as ranking far above the exiled royals who now litter Europe."

A smile tugged at the corners of his mouth. "And where does a German count from the pages of the *Almanach de Goetha* rank?"

A slight tinge touched Nancy's cheeks. "I'm too much of an American to care very greatly. It is enough for me that he loves Verity."

"And his politics?"

"Are his own."

Ramon saw her knuckles tighten and knew that her son-in-law had not converted her to his political beliefs.

"Your daughter doesn't look like you," he said.

The wedding photographs had filled every paper from the *Boston Globe* to *The New York Times.*

"Verity is very pretty."

"She isn't beautiful." It was not the careless compliment he had meant it to be. His voice had betrayed him. He looked at her in growing bewilderment. She was thirty-five years old: two years his senior. He hadn't made love to a woman in her thirties since he was fifteen and his father's mistress had seduced him. Princess Marinsky was twenty-five; Lady Linderdowne was a mere eighteen and Gloria, for all her sophistication and world-weariness, was only twenty-three.

Her beauty was nothing exceptional. All the women that had figured in his life were beautiful. He studied the line of her cheek, the thick sweep of her lashes. She had an air of vulnerability that he had never encountered before. That, with her ability to amuse him, and the tantalizing glint of a temper never far below the surface, was undoubtedly what was attracting him so strongly. He had known from the instant he had first seen her that he would make love to her. The only thing that was unexpected was the urgency he felt. He didn't want to go through the usual play acting; the expected routine of chase and capitulation. He wanted her more desperately than he had ever wanted any woman before in his life. His longing for her was so intense that his bones ached with it.

He knew she was not the sort of woman to embark on an affair easily. Her husband's ambition would be one powerful deterrent. There was also another: her passionate avowal that she hated to be touched. Her words had rung true and he had believed them, yet the generous curve of her lips, her every movement, indicated that she was a woman of deep sensuality. It was intriguing. He would have given a lot to know what sort of honeymoon she had spent on Madeira.

The restaurant had slowly emptied around them. Tired waiters stifled yawns and waited patiently. Nancy glanced about her, aware that the evening was drawing irrevocably to a close. The happy memories of childhood had faded. Outside the moon shone on fields blanketed with snow. She shivered. She was in New York: not Cowes or Boston. Not even Madeira. Twenty-five miles away in Dr. Henry Lorrimer's office a buff folder carried her name in thick black type. Nancy Leigh Cameron. Diagnosis—Aplastic anaemia. Life Expectancy—3 months to a year.

The dark had terrified her as a child. Now the terror came back in full force. Was that what death would be like? An endless black void from which there would be no return.

"Are you all right?" he asked sharply.

She stared at him, seeing his lips move and hearing nothing.

Her fur was around her shoulders, his arm around her waist and she was once more out in the snow as he opened the Daimler's door. Snow and death. They had become synonymous. She hated snow. She began to laugh hysterically. She would never see it again.

They were in the car and his hands were gripping her shoulders hard.

"What is it? What's the matter?"

She was shaking, her eyes huge in her whitened face.

"I'm frightened," she whispered. "Oh God, I'm so hideously, unbelievably *frightened.*"

His arms were encircling her, his body granite hard, his expression almost ferocious as he said, "I'm going to teach you never to be afraid again. Not of anyone or anything."

He tilted her chin upwards in the darkness. "And I'm going to love you," he said as his mouth came down hard on hers.

Chapter Three

They drove back into the city in silence, Ramon's right hand gripping hers so tightly the knuckles showed white. Briefly, he would release it to change gear and then he would cover it again, his powerful left hand manipulating the wheel with the skill of a man accustomed to the race tracks of Europe. A small pulse beat at his jawline. He felt as if every sexual nerve ending in his body were raw. Her vulnerability and pain had triggered off an emotion that shook him in its intensity. It was one completely alien to him. He wanted to protect her; to drive the look of fear from her eyes; to submerge her in so much love that her inner hell would drown and cease to exist. He felt his body tingle at the memory of her kiss, the way her lips had parted beneath his. She had clung to him with the passion of fear, and he had crushed her to his chest so tightly that when they had parted the marks of his fingers had bruised her flesh.

The city roared out of the darkness. Lights and noise and traffic and people. The nightclubs were emptying and singing revellers piled into fur-blanketed Packards and Rileys. He skirted the park and sped down West 79th Street with scant regard for its icy surface.

She didn't ask where they were going and she didn't care. His mouth had been hard, almost brutal, and as she submitted it was as if all his strength passed into her. The wave of fear had receded. She had surfaced from her inner torment and had done so with savage joy. For the first time in her life she wanted to touch and be touched; to feel his skin beneath her fingers; his hair springing in the palm of her hands. To have his hands caress her, touch her. She felt faint, her nails digging deep into his hand as they careened into Riverside Drive. Dear God! She had never known anything like his touch. The slightest pressure of his fingers and a fire leapt within her.

Was this what Jack had expected of her? This shameless physical response? If so, no wonder his disappointment had been so bitter.

She hadn't thought of him for hours. Her throat tightened and she felt suddenly dizzy. She was Nancy Leigh Cameron, not a jumped-up tart from the Cotton Club or a nymphomaniac socialite. Others might be able to conduct a scandalous love affair for the benefit of the world's press. She could not. She was being groomed to become the next First Lady of the United States. She began to laugh hysterically.

"This is crazy. Insane. Please take me home."

"I will. After."

There was an edge to his voice that sent her pulses racing.

"No." The hysteria had died. She felt as if she had been caught in a whirlwind and tossed ruthlessly to earth.

"No." She was calm; utterly deflated. "I owe you an apology, Ramon. I don't indulge in casual love affairs. I was emotionally distressed this evening and allowed you to take advantage of it. I'm sorry."

"Don't be." His hand left hers as he changed gear and the wheels screamed as the Daimler swerved to a halt outside a glittering apartment block. His face was impassive; his eyes unreadable.

"I do indulge in casual affairs," he said as the engine died and a uniformed doorman approached the great glass doors from the warmth of the interior. "I've indulged in them for the last seventeen years. Tonight, for the first time, I realized I was capable of something deeper. Something unimaginable. I'm not going to sacrifice it for the sudden panic of propriety on your part. You want me as much as I want you. I can see it in your eyes and I can feel it in your body."

He touched her bare shoulders and she jumped as if it had been a live switch. "I don't know how the hell it happened." His voice thickened as he pulled her to him. "But I love you and I'm damned if I'm going to lose you now."

"I can't . . ." She was held captive against his chest and she could feel the heavy slam of his heart against hers.

"You can," he said softly. His lips touched her eyelids, the corners of her mouth, her throat. He lowered his head, kissing the crevice of her breasts. "You will."

She pressed her lips to his thick black curls, burying her face in his hair.

"No . . ." she whispered and it was the primeval protest of invitation.

Silently he opened the Daimler's door and escorted her through the brightly lit lobby to a sumptuously gilded lift.

She was trembling. She had never been unfaithful to Jack. She had never wanted to be. Words from a fifteen year old row rang in her ears as the lift slowly ascended.

She had just discovered that Jack was having an affair. It was the first one she had been aware of. She had cried and expected him to beg forgiveness. He had not done so and her tears had turned to bewilderment and then to anger. "I don't sleep with other men!" she had shouted. He had turned to her and there had been pity tempered by resignation in his voice as he had said, "Of course not, Nancy. You don't enjoy sleeping with me so why should you sleep with anyone else? There's no virtue in abstaining from a vice you have no desire for."

The lift gates were thrown back by a hand accustomed to control.

"It's not going to be how you think . . ." she said desperately.

"It's going to be everything I think." He smiled as he opened the door. "Why is it I'm always contradicting you?"

She didn't answer.

The whole vast room and the rooms opening from it were covered in ankle-deep white carpet. The walls were white, the ceiling, the leather chairs in strangely geometric silver frames. Even the flowers were white: orchids and lilies and freesias flown in from Florida. On the far wall there was one single violent blaze of colour. Red and orange and screaming pink seared a huge canvas. Nancy had never seen anything like it before. It was of nothing recognizable and yet it portrayed all the things she lacked: passion and wildness and joyous abandonment.

Not looking at him she said simply, "I'm no good in bed. I'm sorry."

He said, amused, "You told me that when you told me not to touch you." He was dimming the lights, moving smoothly and leisurely. "Since then, I've touched you several times and you haven't objected."

"That was different. I was upset and you were comforting me."

"I'm not expert at comforting women," Ramon said gravely and with more than a measure of truth. "But I doubt if the action usually has such results on the comforter or comforted!" His smile was tender. "Stop being afraid, Nancy. There's nothing to be afraid of," and gently and easily he lifted her in his arms and carried her through to the bedroom.

She buried her face in his neck and her feelings of shyness and inadequacy ebbed away. Her longing for him was so intense that there was no room for any other emotion. His dinner jacket had been discarded. Only one lamp gleamed and as he moved towards the giant windows his frilled shirt was opened to the waist, exposing a strong chest with a pelt of darkly curling hair.

He pulled the cord, the heavy white drapes swishing back, revealing stars and moon and a scattering of lights. He didn't want to take her in the darkness. He wanted to see the fear chased from her eyes.

He moved across to her unhurriedly and her heart began to race. Slowly he slid the straps of her evening dress down and over her shoulders, letting the golden material slip over her breasts and hips till it dropped lightly to the floor. With superhuman control he continued to take his time, handling her with the soothing gentleness with which he would approach a frightened horse.

His hand travelled up the length of her leg, skimming her hip bones and cupping her breast. She shivered, but not with the revulsion she was accustomed to. His mouth came down on her hairline, brushing it with feather-like kisses. Her fingers burrowed deep in his hair. She wanted his mouth on hers and moved her head voluntarily so that their lips met and parted and left her filled with longing.

"Love me," she whispered.

He only smiled, his hands caressing the high roundness of her breasts. "I will love you, Nancy. I do love you."

"Oh God," she said, and arched her body to his.

This time his kiss was deeper, his tongue exploring hers, his hands sliding down to where she waited willingly.

With every passing second her senses were heightened as he undressed without haste. In the moonlit room his skin gleamed bronze, his muscles hard. She drew in a quick breath. It had never occurred to her before that a man's body could be beautiful.

"Now," she said urgently and he laughed softly.

"I thought you didn't like to be touched."

"I didn't," she said, "not before."

He touched her with his hands and his mouth, and when his body pinned hers down and he entered her, she was as ready for him as he was for her. She flew higher and higher until, in the same split second, they reached a mutual ecstasy of momentary disintegration. They were no longer two separate entities, but one. She heard her own cries and her face was wet with tears. He kissed them away, trembling, murmuring words of love he had never uttered before. It was a long time before he parted from her. When he did they lay in each other's arms, close and not speaking. At last, almost as a gesture of homage, he kissed her forehead. "Nothing will be the same, Nancy. Not for either of us."

"No." There was nothing else to say. She felt no need to ask about Princess Marinsky or Lady Linderdowne or any of the other women he was so often seen with. She felt no insecurity or jealous doubts.

After a while he gently disentangled himself from her arms and walked naked out of the vast bedroom. When he returned he was carrying a bucket of ice containing a bottle of Dom Perignon. As he poured the champagne it splashed on her breasts and he kissed the droplets away.

She held him close. "I feel like a girl of seventeen."

He smiled the slow, lazy smile that turned her heart over. "You looked it before. You don't now."

"What do you mean?" Her eyes widened in apprehension.

He laughed and reached for his glass of champagne. "I mean you had an untouched look that sat oddly on a woman of thirty-five. Innocence is for the young. Maturity is for something a little better."

"Was it so obvious?" She drank from her glass, her body pale against the satin sheets.

"To me, but I doubt if anyone else realized the reason for your continued girlish prettiness."

He cupped her face in his hands and kissed her deeply. "Immaturity often has that effect."

"And was I immature?" It was a startling thought. She ran three homes, she was the mother of a seventeen-year-old daughter and the wife of a prominent man . . .

He laughed. "Sexually, though God alone knows why. You've all the easily stirred passions of the Irish."

Her soft lips curved into a smile of utter intimacy. "They've never been stirred before."

He took the glass from her hand. "You're only just beginning to learn."

Later, lying together in the darkness, she said, "You still think I'm pretty, don't you? My finding myself hasn't changed that, has it?"

Unseen by her, he grinned. "Every last trace has vanished," he said gravely. "You'll never have that virginal look again."

She bit her lip and involuntarily tightened her hold on

his hand.

He laughed softly and rolled across her, winding her hair in his hands. "No more immature, girlish prettiness, Nancy. Only beauty."

Desire ran through him like a hot, swift current. "Incredible, devastating beauty."

This time he abandoned the unbearable restraint he had previously exercised. His lovemaking was passionate, savage in intensity. She heard herself utter cry after cry and marvelled at her own joyous abandon. Her response to him was without inhibition. It was deep and wild and the cool, passionless Nancy Leigh Cameron was dead for ever.

"I never knew it could be like this," she said as Ramon poured the last of the champagne into their glasses. She gave a small, self-deprecating smile. "Do I sound an awful fool?"

"You sound totally honest. It isn't a quality I've met in a woman before."

They sat in silence for a little while, the night sky slowly turning to a pearly grey.

"I've never slept with anyone apart from Jack. But then, you know that."

He did, and he remained silent. He could quite easily have pointed out to her that her previous feelings of sexual inadequacy were entirely her husband's fault, but it would be far better if she reached that conclusion herself.

"I remember once, not long after our marriage, I skated around the subject with a woman friend. Loretta had been married twice and was notorious for her lovers. She obviously didn't object to something that was a complete mystery to me and I thought that talking to her might help me. I could already sense that Jack was becoming dissatisfied with what he called my passivity."

Ramon's face was inscrutable. He remembered Loretta

Dettarding clearly. It was ten years ago, and she had been as near to a nymphomaniac as any woman he had ever met.

"She merely patted me on the cheek and said that all women found sex the most frightful bore and that I must do what other women did, and pretend."

Ramon's lips twitched. If Loretta had been pretending then she deserved an Oscar.

"Did you believe her?"

"Yes I did, but I was only eighteen." She began to giggle. "After I read the details of the Dettarding divorce I wasn't too sure. Entertaining two men in one bed seemed to be taking pretence to unreasonable limits. Only by then it was too late. Jack had already written me off as absolutely hopeless."

She leaned back against the pillows and tucked her hands behind her head. It was a spontaneous gesture that raised her breasts in a way that made Ramon catch his breath.

"It was only a month after Verity was born. A week after our first wedding anniversary. Jack wasn't a politician then. He was still heading the family bank in New York. Jack's valet had emptied the pockets of one of his suits and had left the contents on a bedside table. Whether intentionally or not, I never knew. I didn't mean to look but a lipstick mark on the back of an envelope is a fairly unsubtle way of sealing it. She was one of my friends. We had dined with them the evening before." Some of the old pain had returned to her voice.

"I couldn't believe it. When I showed him the letter it was even worse." She was silent for a few minutes, remembering. "In my naivety I thought he would be as shattered as I was. That he would be terribly distressed and ashamed. I suppose I saw myself as being noble and forgiving him and carrying on with life a little older and a little wiser. Only it wasn't like that."

The room was ethereal in the light of early dawn.

"He was annoyed at being found out, and he never even suggested terminating the affair. In the end my tears gave way to bewilderment and then to anger. I remember shouting in utter incomprehension that *I* didn't sleep with other men." She smiled sadly.

"I didn't understand the look he gave me, but I do now: he said I was frigid."

She leaned close against Ramon's chest, his arm protectively around her.

"And so it went on. One affair following another. Always discreetly, of course. Jack already knew what he wanted and he was a senator by 1925."

"And what did you do?" His deep voice was compassionate.

She shrugged imperceptibly. "Very little. I did pluck up the courage to speak to my doctor but that was an utter failure."

Some humour had returned. She put her arms around his naked chest, savouring his warmth.

"He told me there was no such thing as frigidity. That it was a new-fangled idea he had no time for. He said I'd been brought up to be a lady and that I *was* a lady and he couldn't understand why I should want to be anything else." She giggled. "He said that Rudolph Valentino had a lot to answer for and that I'd nothing to worry about where Jack was concerned; that he was too discreet to allow his 'flings', as he called them, to ruin his public life. I didn't give a damn about his public life; it was his private one that was putting me through hell. After Loretta and the doctor I'd run out of sources of help. I began to spend more and more time at the Cape with Verity. Jack drove up from Washington a couple of times a month and I was always in attendance at any public functions. We were held up as a shining example of happy American family life. So much so that I almost believed it myself. After all, we never quarrelled or suffered any of the domestic dramas that so many of our friends experienced. Jack had his life and I had mine."

"Living alone with a child, like a widow or an unmarried mother?" he said, his voice betraying the anger he felt.

She laughed throatily. "You make it sound as if I was scrubbing floors. I was living in the greatest of luxury, flying to Paris twice a year for the Collections, taking Verity to Cap d'Antibes, playing hostess to President Coolidge."

"And sleeping alone."

"President Coolidge never propositioned me," she said and he laughed as he pulled her down against him.

"And in between Paris and the Riviera and Calvin Coolidge?"

"Things you've never heard of." She slid her hands down over the strong smooth curve of his spine. "Strawberry festivals and clambakes; blueberry picnics and summer theatres; swimming galas and yachting regattas; games of softball, quilting pageants . . ."

"Dear God," Ramon said, with devout fervour. "Is that what having a child entails?"

"Not for anyone else that I know," Nancy said with candour. "They have nannies, private tutors and finishing schools. By the time they make their offsprings' acquaintance, they have generally reached a civilized eighteen or nineteen."

"I'm very glad to hear it," Ramon said, and proceeded to make love to her again as the sun rose above the glittering shafts of the skyscrapers.

As the city hummed into life below them, they slept: Nancy protectively curled in Ramon's arms. Once she stirred and he kissed the pulse beating in her throat.

"I love you," she murmured, and drifted back into sleep as he cupped her breasts in his hands.

It was midday before they dressed. Ramon's manservant had left them a lunch of paté de foie gras and cold meats and a chilled bottle of Sauterne.

"Come away with me," he said. "I've a home in Acapulco and one in Tobago."

"And Portugal?"

"A family mausoleum." He grinned. "And Madeira is now Zia's province. I'm barred from it until I change my ways and marry a suitable woman. Come to the Caribbean with me, Nancy."

Unbeknown to her, it was the first time he had ever asked for anything.

She shook her head. Her ease and vulnerability had gone. The gentleness remained but was tempered with a new-found self-assurance.

"Not yet. I have things to do. Jack to see. Most of all, I want to be on my own to think."

"And you can't think with me?"

She laughed. "No. I can only think *about* you."

He kissed her and her fingertips touched his cheekbones wonderingly. Leaving him, even if only for a little while, would be the hardest thing she had ever done. "I'm going back to the Cape. Today."

"When you return it will be to me." It was a statement of fact.

She did not reply but said only, "I love you," as he slipped her fur around her shoulders.

The mid-morning air was crisp and sharp. She refused to let him drive her home and insisted that his chauffeur did so. New York was a hotbed of gossip and she had no desire for it to tarnish their relationship. They would be like lambs to the slaughter when the story did break. Until then she wanted to hug the knowledge to herself.

She had no wish to have it desecrated by innuendo and rumour.

Reluctantly he let her go. Before he did so, he gripped her shoulders tightly, his eyes sombre.

"Don't panic or go back to your role as senator's wife, Nancy. If you do I shall only take you away by force."

A smile hovered around the corners of her mouth. "Like your grandfather did the Condessa de Gama?"

"I've never understood old Leo more. From now on his photograph will have pride of place on my desk."

They laughed.

The chauffeur cleared his throat impatiently as he waited at the Daimler's door. The freezing cold was striking up into his boots and he had seen too many ladies leave at midday in evening dress to take any special interest.

"Goodbye," she said, her laughter dying.

"*Au revoir*," he corrected, taking her hand and kissing it, palm upwards. "A week on the Cape is long enough for you to think. If you're not back by next Saturday, I shall come for you."

Her spine tingled. "Yes," she said. For a wild impulsive moment she hesitated. She could stay with him. They could leave for Mexico or the Caribbean within hours. They need never be separated again. She thought of the ensuing scandal and Jack and her father. It made no difference. Then she thought of Verity.

"A week," she said, and stepped into the Daimler.

Five minutes later Ramon drove a two-seater Austin Swallow through the maelstrom of New York traffic to the Ritz-Carlton apartment occupied by Mrs. Chips O'Shaughnessy.

"How *dare* you walk in here as if nothing had happened?

You leave me waiting nearly two hours! Two bloody *hours*! And now I'm supposed to forgive you and say it doesn't matter. Well, I won't. I never want to see you again in my life! We're finished! Through! Kaput!"

All the time she had been spitting out the words she had been pacing the floor like an enraged cat, her eyes flashing, her arms, with their multitudes of bracelets, gesticulating angrily. She caught sight of herself in the mirror and tossed her golden curls. Her bosom heaved in a tight-fitting dress and on the final word she stood arrogantly before him, one hand on her hip, knowing how every line of her body showed to advantage.

There was a mocking gleam in his eyes and instead of seizing her brutally and making savage love to her as she expected, he merely blew her a kiss.

"As you say, my sweet: finished. Through. Kaput. The European in me prompted me to deliver the news in person, but you have done it for me with far more style and panache."

"Where the hell do you think you're going?" Gloria forgot her poise. She had a sudden feeling of anxiety.

He shrugged. "Who knows, my sweet. Acapulco, Tobago . . ." He laughed, white teeth gleaming. "Paradise."

She was at the door before he reached it, her eyes wary. She had seen him in many moods but never one like this. She ran her tongue nervously around carmine-painted lips.

"I'm sorry I was so angry." She pouted prettily. "Silly me, getting so cross when I'm sure you couldn't help it." She stepped towards him and raised her hands, circling his neck. "Little Gloria has missed you dreadfully. Aren't you going to let her show you how much?" She pressed herself against him and he clasped her wrists and removed them as if they were something distasteful.

"No. I hate prolonged goodbyes." He brushed her out

of the way and opened the door.

"You can't go!" It was a shriek.

Ramon noticed how ugly she looked when she was not trying to please. The painted lips were a bloody gash across her face. Her nostrils were pinched and white and her excessively plucked brows made her small eyes even smaller.

"Don't treat *me* like one of your little lap dogs, Gloria," he said, his voice deceptively soft, "*or* your gullible husband. Our affair, if such a loveless relationship can be described as such, is over. I would prefer it to be an amicable arrangement but I don't give a damn if it isn't."

"It's that Marinsky whore, isn't it?" All self-control had deserted her. She rushed at him with blood-red nails and he seized her wrists so cruelly they nearly snapped.

"Sofka Marinsky is no more of a whore than you are. And she does have one very strong advantage in her favour. She has breeding. Something that none of O'Shaughnessy's money will buy you."

"I knew it was her!"

He flung her away and she went sprawling across the floor.

"As a matter of fact it isn't. It happens to be someone to whom the word 'whore' could never apply in a million years. Which rules out any friends of yours."

"*Wop!*" Gloria screamed, all pretence to gentility deserting her as the door slammed behind him. "Dirty, half-breed *wop!*" And then she pummelled the floor in a storm of tears and drummed her feet on the lilac carpet until the banker in the suite below rang for room service to complain about the noise.

Nancy was deeply preoccupied as she bathed and changed and prepared to leave for the Cape. Only when Morris informed her that there had been a Washington telephone call for her did she emerge from her reverie.

"Did my husband leave a message as to when it would be convenient to call him back?"

Jack's Washington schedule was notoriously tight and Nancy had no intention of wasting time in trying to contact him if he was in a meeting.

"No, madame. It wasn't Mr. Cameron who phoned. It was Miss Geeson."

"I see. Did Miss Geeson leave a message?"

"Yes, madame. She wished to tell you that the senator is flying to Chicago tonight and will be out of contact until Friday."

"Thank you, Morris."

Nancy allowed Morris to settle her fur around her shoulders and drew on her gloves. There was a meeting of businessmen in Chicago to discuss the latest Federal plans for increasing employment. It was a matter of more importance than a distraught wife. She had needed him and he had failed her.

She stepped out into the dazzling light of the snow. Perhaps he had asked Syrie to telephone while they had been in bed together. She could imagine it quite easily. "By the way, Syrie. Phone Chambers about the new Appropriation Plan. Stall that idiot from Pennsylvania and tell Nancy I'll ring her when I'm back from Chicago."

No doubt Syrie kept a notepad and pen beside the bed. She was efficient enough to do so. She shivered momentarily and stepped into the Rolls. She had promised herself that she would think of nothing until she reached Hyannis. Not Jack. Not Dr. Lorrimer. Not even Ramon.

Collins tucked a sealskin-lined rug around her knees. It was almost impossible not to think of Ramon. She could feel his presence as if he were in the Rolls with her.

She closed her eyes as they sped under the Lincoln Tunnel. She was in love. Totally, utterly and irrevocably in love. In the early years she had believed herself to be in love with Jack. Now she knew she never had been. He had never sent her senses reeling or initiated her into an understanding of her own passionate nature. In her ignorance she had thought herself frigid. If she never slept with another man again, she would know it was not true. She was grateful to Ramon and she liked him as well as loved him. She liked watching him move; she liked laughing with him; listening to him; talking to him. He had asked her to go away with him and she knew that she would. She had only a few months of life left and she was not going to waste them sitting in her lonely New York mansion waiting for Jack to call. Hyannis would be no different. It was the place she instinctively fled to because it was the place she regarded as home. It was where she had spent the major part of her life bringing up Verity. But Verity was thousands of miles away now and no longer needed her. All that Hyannis could now offer was long walks on the beach and lonely rounds of golf on the Coonamesett links. She would go with Ramon wherever he asked her, but first she would set her affairs in order. She had made no will and she was a wealthy woman. From her grandfather she had inherited investments in railroads, banking, tobacco and even cotton. Patrick O'Shaughnessy may have made his money by building up a food empire, but he had distributed the profits in a whole range of other ventures. With her canny father as adviser, Nancy had never gambled on margin. The Wall Street crash had left her virtually unscathed. The first thing she would do when she reached Hyannis was to summon her financial advisers and lawyers from Boston and settle her affairs. Jack and his family had more than enough money of their own. The noughts after Mr. Cameron Senior's estimated wealth left even Nancy blinking. Verity was the one who needed the bulwark of her money. Verity and her titled husband living in an unstable Europe.

Nancy had listened to her son-in-law's effusive admiration of the German Chancellor and had not been impressed. She had heard different stories from Rosa Goldstein, her dressmaker. Rosa was Jewish and no longer visited her homeland. None of Dieter's passionate avowals that the Treaty of Versailles had treated Germans shamefully and that the Chancellor was right to adopt conscription in defiance of it, could make Nancy forget her friend's face when she had returned from Berlin only months earlier.

"It is no longer possible to be a Jew in Germany," she had said sadly. "At the last dinner party I attended one of the guests said that the heads of all leading Jews should be stuck on telegraph poles the length and breadth of the country." She had shrugged. "I hated myself because I said nothing. I did not say that I was Jewish. I tried to ease my conscience by telling myself that I had no wish to cause embarrassment to my host, but that was not the reason. I am a coward, and Germany is no place for a Jew to be a coward."

Nancy had taxed Dieter with Rosa's allegations and he had laughed and said that her friend was reacting hysterically to Jewish propaganda. The Chancellor would make Germany great again and families like his own, who had suffered defeat and humiliation in the last war, would once more regain their dignity and be strong.

For Verity's sake Nancy hoped that he was right. Jack had cupped his after-dinner Grand Marnier in his hand and said blandly that Jews were notoriously paranoid. If Hitler was feverishly rearming Germany and filling the minds of his countrymen with nationalistic nonsense, it was none of their concern. Verity could return to America at a moment's notice. Let Great Britain do the worrying. Her father had been angry and had called his son-in-law a fool. Baldwin, he had said, was short-sighted and an appeaser. Pouring oil on troubled waters was not the right action to pursue when the waters were troubled by a man as vitriolic as the German Chancellor.

Nancy had often wondered about the alliance between her father and her husband. Privately they fell out whenever they met, but publicly Jack Cameron had the Mayor of Boston's wholehearted support. She supposed her father would have given it to any member of the family who had a chance of becoming president.

They were in Connecticut and travelling at a sedate pace towards Bridgeport. She remembered the way Ramon had driven the Daimler and suppressed a smile. There was nothing cautious in Ramon's nature.

The slim gold watch on her wrist showed her it was just after two o'clock. Twenty-four hours since she had stood in Dr. Lorrimer's office and been dealt the most devastating blow of her life. Bridgeport came and went and Nancy stared musingly out of the windows at the rolling countryside. None of her initial reactions remained. They had been supplanted by quite different thoughts and feelings. On her semi-conscious trek through the snow-filled streets of downtown Manhattan there had been times when she had thought she was losing her mind. She had been faced with death without any preparation, and the prospect of falling headlong into that dark void, of the uprooting and rending apart of her body and spirit, had filled her with a fear that had been total. Hard on its heels had come the realization that she was to die without ever having really lived. That had been the harshest truth of all. Now everything was changed. She was in love and she was loved, and love had transformed her. Unbidden, the scripture saying; "Perfect love casteth out fear" came into her mind. She was no longer frightened. Death would come when it would come, as it would if she had been perfectly healthy and had stepped off a sidewalk and under the wheels of a tram.

There were people of her acquaintance who would die suddenly and tragically long before she did. Three of her friends and a cousin had died in the last year. A yachting tragedy in one case; a motor crash in another. A liver rotted by alcohol had killed off Oonagh Manning at twenty-six, and an overdose of sleeping tablets had been Lola Montgomery's last cry for help. The frenetic pace of their lives was conducive to early death. Lola and Oonagh had died unprepared.

It had never been Lola's intention to succeed at suicide. She had lain on her scented lace pillows, seductively posed in a thigh splitting negligée, confident of being found. Only she had not reckoned on the vagaries of her lover. He had promised to come for her at six o'clock and had been sidetracked at the Waldorf by friends. As Lola slipped peacefully into the eternities, he was drinking Gin-Slings and arranging a game of baccarat with Teddy Stuyvesant.

She was luckier. She had been given the chance to evaluate her life and it had been shown to be sadly lacking. She had lived out the roles she had been given—dutiful daughter, faithful wife—and they had brought no deep happiness. Openly embarking on an affair with Ramon Sanford was something she would never have had the courage to do before. Years of remembering who she was would have seen to that. They crossed into the Cape and, on the right, Wequaquet Lake shimmered beneath a coating of ice. Whoever she had been before, it was not the person she was now.

She would do nothing intentionally to hurt anybody else. Jack's horrified reaction when she told him she was leaving him would be precipitated by fear for the future of his career, nothing else. Besides, she already had a scheme in the back of her mind whereby his career would not be harmed. She had plenty of time to think it out in full. A whole week. In that time she would also speak to her father. He could hardly be critical of her. His marriage to Gloria could quite easily have severed all contact between them. Certainly, Gloria had done her best to see that it did so. Only Nancy's basic good sense had enabled her to forgive Chips for choosing as a second wife a girl twelve years her junior and forty-six years his, *and* one who couldn't possibly give a damn about him: only his money.

There were thick trees on either side of the narrow road and then the white clapboard houses of Hyannis. A few miles further on the Rolls turned down the drive that led to Ocean View, and for the first time since Verity's marriage Nancy did not feel a sense of loss as the large, rambling house came into view.

It stood high and lonely on the edge of the dunes, couch-grass reaching up to the very edge of the carefully tended lawns. It was the gardener's constant request that a wall be built, separating his province from the encroaching beach. Nancy would not hear of it. The way the house merged into the desolate landscape was the reason it had so attracted her; she loved the heaving vastness of the Atlantic; the cries of the seabirds as they wheeled above her head on her daily walks along the shoreline. She stepped out of the warmth of the Rolls and into the bitter wind blowing in off the sea.

Mrs. Ambrosil, her housekeeper, stood at the porch to meet her. "I hope you had an enjoyable stay in New York, madame."

The Ford containing Maria and Morris drew up smoothly behind the Rolls.

"I had a very enjoyable stay, thank you," Nancy said, a

secret smile curving her lips as her fur was removed and she stepped towards the glorious heat of a log fire. "And now I have some telephone calls to make."

She kicked off her shoes and reached for her telephone book. First her lawyer and accountant; then Jack and her father. The next few days were going to be busy.

Chapter Four

Chips O'Shaughnessy sat in the Georgian grandeur of his Beacon Hill dining room and surveyed the array of newspapers littering his breakfast table.

A local paper, not known for its sympathy for the mayor, had given prominence to the obituary of two septuagenarians. The next column featured an article on Mayor O'Shaughnessy's decision to run for re-election and wrongly gave his age as seventy, not sixty-nine. The allusion was clear. "O'Shaughnessy shakes them again" was the headline in a paper more favourably disposed towards him. "No retirement for Boston's ebullient mayor" it continued. The accompanying photograph was one of Chips and Gloria attending a Boston Symphony concert. Chips grinned. His jaunty figure didn't look a day over fifty and the sight of Gloria would more than dispel any attempt to depict him as an old man on the border of senility. No old man would be able to keep a woman like Gloria happy. That was obvious to the meanest intelligence.

The paragraphs in the *The Daily Globe* and *The New York Times* did not give the same pleasure. One read simply that Mrs. Gloria O'Shaughnessy had attended Mrs. Astor's fancy dress ball in the company of Mr. and Mrs. Haverstock, Commodore Stuyvesant, Nina Gradzinka and the Russian conductor Felix Zapolski. There was no inference as to who Gloria's escort had been. *The Tribune* carried a photograph of the event. Gloria was absent from the throng of partygoers entering the Astor mansion. Other faces were familiar. Chips took his black fountain pen and ringed one particular face in heavy black ink. *The Globe* carried a list of people who had attended Sybil Nawn's exclusive birthday party at the Ritz. Among the list of names was that of Gloria O'Shaughnessy. That was to be expected. Chips had not only known that she was going, but had insisted that she do so. Howard Nawn contributed heavily to Democratic Party funds. What caused his shrewd blue eyes to glimmer brilliantly was another name further down on the guest list. This time there was no accompanying photograph. Simply the statement that Ramon Sanford had escorted Princess Marinsky and that the couple were shortly expected to announce their engagement.

Chips snorted in derision. There was as little chance of a Sanford being harnessed as there was of a blooded stallion.

He pushed his empty coffee cup away bad-temperedly. Sanford's son was back in New York and doing the social rounds. Gloria was kitting herself out for the next few months and it was inevitable that they should be present at the same functions. The social world in which they moved was a small one. Theirs was a tight-knit élite; at least it was, outside Boston. In his home town Chips took great care to remain one of the boys. Instead of living in a palatial manion in some distant suburb, he chose to remain in the exclusive but parochial Beacon Hill district. He was Boston's mayor. He wanted to continue to be Boston's mayor and to do so he needed the allegiance of the people of the city. His homes in Palm Springs and Rhode Island were given little coverage by the press. They barely knew of their existence.

"I'm Irish, Catholic and a Bostonian," Chips would shout above the sea of faces crowding his election platforms. "And I'm proud of being all three!"

The crowd would roar its approval. The older inhabitants could well remember Patrick O'Shaughnessy's beginnings in the North End and Chips continued to cultivate carefully the image of being a local boy making good. Of still being a North Ender, though Patrick had been a millionaire and living in Jamaica Plain by the time Chips was ten. Chips preferred the electorate to forget these aspects of his background. He spoke of the North End as if he had emerged from it only seconds before becoming mayor. "Make the people believe what they want to believe" was his favourite maxim. It was one that had served him well.

The ringed face seemed to stare back at him from the printed page with unconcealed arrogance. The eyes were those of a predator. Ramon Sanford was every inch his father's son and the warning bells in the back of Chips' mind began to ring loud and clear. He pushed his chair abruptly away from the table and crossed to the telephone.

"The Ritz-Carlton, please. Mrs. O'Shaughnessy's suite."

There was a click of a connection to the Ritz and the sound of the receptionist trying to contact Mrs. O'Shaughnessy's room. At last the apologetic voice informed the mayor that Mrs. O'Shaughnessy was not answering and that, on inspection, her key was also absent. It was thought that Mrs. O'Shaughnessy had left the hotel early on a shopping trip.

Chips slammed the receiver down and glared at his watch. It was barely 9:30. Gloria never rose before noon. If her room was empty it was because she hadn't slept in it. He swept the newspapers off the table, and into the waste-basket and sat thoughtfully. Few knew it, but he was a man who never reacted without thinking. He thought now while his two main aides waited patiently in the dining room, anxious to speak to him before he left for City Hall.

When he married Gloria it had not been in a fit of besotted love, blind to realities. He had never been a fool and he certainly wasn't an old fool. Since his wife's death there had been many women. He was a man of immense physical energy and zest for life. Women were as necessary as eating and drinking. His capacity for the enjoyment of all three pleasures had not waned with his increasing years. Gloria was a lot luckier than many young brides with rich, elderly husbands. At least he still gave a more than creditable performance in bed. Sometimes he amazed even himself.

He had married because, at sixty-five, he had regained his life's ambition. After an interval of nearly thirty years he was once more his city's mayor. He needed a wife to provide a decorative trimming. He also needed to steer clear of scandal. Boston would not look kindly upon a mayor bedding down with floozies young enough to be his grandchildren. Chips had no intention of foregoing his favourite pastime. What could not be indulged in privately, could be indulged in openly. He would marry and enjoy himself with the church's blessing. It was a marriage solemnized by the cardinal himself. Chips had hardly been able to keep a straight face throughout the service. The cardinal had been reluctant to perform the ceremony, but as there were no valid grounds for refusing to do so, he had had to acquiesce or face unfavourable publicity.

Gloria had been a waitress in a San Francisco roadhouse when Chips had first met her. As not even his most loyal supporters would have found this fact acceptable, Chips, with his usual gusto, had created a complete mythical background for her. She was an orphan, the last child in a family with a history going back to the days when Los Angeles had been El Pueblo de Nuestra Senora Le Reina de los Angeles de Porciuncula. Her uncle, a recluse, had brought her up. The recluse was uncontactable—obsessed with his privacy. The improbable story had stood the test of time. If anyone privately wondered whether Gloria O'Shaughnessy was all that she was reputed to be, they never had the temerity to voice their suspicions.

The marriage had been nothing but an asset to him in his career. Having Gloria on his arm automatically took twenty years off his age in the eyes of the electorate. The only thing that could damage him would be if Gloria's name were to be linked romantically with that of someone else, by the gossip columnists. Then he would no longer be the virile, devil-may-care boyo from the North End, but simply an old and gullible fool.

Gloria's shopping spree in New York had gone on long enough. It was time she returned to Boston and acted out her role of adoring wife. Gloria's denials were a foregone conclusion. If he wanted to know who she had been pussyfooting around with in New York he would have to find out by more subtle means. He reached for the telephone again and called a number that was never written down, not even in his private diary.

"Hello Chips! Nice to hear from you," a male voice boomed over the line. "I see you've been hitting the headlines again."

"Merely serving my country," Chips replied drily. "Duty before pleasure and all that. Retirement would be sweet, but public service calls."

"Ass-holes," his listener said disrespectfully. "What is it you want?"

"The low-down on my dear wife's activities these last two weeks. She's been in New York supplementing her wardrobe and debilitating my bank account."

"And you want to know if she's been shopping day or night?"

"Exactly. And if she paid in cash or kind."

There was a deep chuckle. "I told you you were taking too much on, you old goat. Twenty-three-year-olds are bad for the heart. They induce palpitations."

"They induce a lot more, thank God."

There was loud laughter. "I'll check out your beloved's nocturnal activities and let you know immediately."

"Thanks."

The receiver was replaced. He would have Gloria sewn up so tight by the end of the week that she'd never travel farther than Brookline without an armed escort. He opened the door and admitted his aides, listening attentively as his valet adjusted a heavy astrakhan coat around his shoulders.

"We need to talk about the longshoremen, Mayor. Their vote is vital and we can't discuss that at City Hall with Sean Flynn listening at every keyhole."

"The longshoremen are in our pockets," Chips said complacently, donning a grey velvet fedora, more suitable for a Mafia gang boss than a mayor.

"They're campaigning hard against you and it's going to be a tough fight; a lot tougher than the last."

"I'm used to tough fights," Chips said, taking the ebony-topped cane held out for him. "I enjoy them."

He swept from the house and they hurried in his wake, still clamouring to be heard.

"Henry Mortimer, the reporter on *The Globe*, says the word 'graft' has already been used. If *The Globe* should turn . . ."

"They're putting up a candidate who is promising to dispense with all ward bosses; to revolutionize local politics . . ."

Chips entered his glossy black sedan. The two aides were relegated to their Ford. This was the part of the day Chips liked best. His chauffeur had strict instructions not to slow down for pedestrians, traffic or any other minor inconveniences. Flags flew on either side of the motor car; the horn blared almost perpetually, as Chips O'Shaughnessy rode in state to the centre of his kingdom. If he could have been preceded every morning by a brass band he would have been even happier. He was a man, he reflected, born out of his time. He should have been a Roman emperor or Mogul warrior. He was convinced the blood of Irish princes ran in his veins and he acted accordingly. Indulging all the dash and flair of which he was capable, he made his ostentatious entrance at City Hall and proceeded to conduct municipal affairs with oblivious disregard for anyone else's judgement but his own.

He had waited too long for power and had enjoyed it for too short a time. He had made history by being the youngest mayor to hold office. His future had shone before him, limitless in its possibilities, and in those heady days there had not been a man or woman who didn't believe he would be re-elected. Not all of them wanted it: there were plenty who objected to having their city run by a genial-faced, shrewd-eyed, ruthless dictator who had come to power via the ward bosses; yet all had believed that the dictatorship would last for at least another four years. His withdrawal from the election only hours before polling had stunned the city into immobility. Old Fergus Conway had died of a stroke and his widow had laid the blame fairly and squarely on the shoulders of O'Shaughnessy. No explanation had been given—or at least none that was believed.

His assertion that he was bowing out of the race because his four years in office had shown him that the city needed a mayor of more maturity, had been poo-pooed even by schoolchildren. Lack of maturity had never been apparent during his term as mayor. Besides, the speech had reeked of modesty, humility and candour. None of them were qualities that could be attributed to Chips.

No one in Boston ever knew the truth—not even his family. The only person to know why Boston's flamboyant mayor voluntarily stepped down and remained a ward boss for the next thirty years, was Duarte Sanford.

Chips was signing a paper confirming the building of a new freeway when, unexpectedly, the memory engulfed him. The hatred of years surged through his veins and his hand trembled violently.

His secretary looked at him anxiously. "Are you all right, sir?"

"Of course I'm all right," Chips snapped, signing the documents with a flourish.

What the hell had brought that on? The face he had so heavily ringed in the morning newspaper? The prospect of standing once again for re-election? "Goddamn it to hell," he said and wrote a refusal on the pile of requests before him without even bothering to read what the petitioners wanted.

Thirty years of waiting: thirty years of making politics his life and never being able to enjoy the highest office. His authority as a ward boss had been unchallenged, but what was power without its trappings? Very little for a man of his temperament. The day of Duarte Sanford's death had been the happiest day of his life. Not an hour had been wasted. He had announced his intention to run for mayor when the existing incumbent still had eight months left in office. It had been a landslide victory: a balm for his bitterness. Immediately after the inauguration he had driven alone to Boston's cemetary and had stood before the grave of his parents.

"I kept my promise," he said, and bent down, letting the earth that covered the grave and on which carefully tended flowers bloomed, run through his fingers. It was Irish earth—brought from a land Chips had never seen for the parents who had loved it with all their hearts.

He had stayed until dusk and then he had returned to the celebration of his victory.

Four short years and gossip had it that he was going to retire. He smiled grimly as he went about the work of municipal government. Boston hadn't heard the last of Chips O'Shaughnessy: or America either. If he did fail to be re-elected he would do what he had burned to do for years. He would run for governor. He laughed to himself out loud and his secretary pursed her lips. Perhaps those who thought sixty-nine was too old for a man actively to pursue a public career were right. Perhaps the mayor was cracking up after all.

The speed of his dictation did not give her time to dwell on it further. Chips O'Shaughnessy was in his element working an eighteen-hour-day and he expected all those around him to do the same.

"Mrs.O'Shaughnessy is calling you from New York," she said a little while later, grateful for a respite.

Chips had forgotten about Gloria. He kept her waiting while he lit a cigar and signalled his secretary to return to her own office. He blew a fragrant cloud of blue smoke into the air and said genially: "Gloria, how thoughtful of you to call."

He thought he detected a note of strain in Gloria's voice.

"I'm sorry I missed you. I was out shopping with Mimi Farquharson."

"Ah," Chips said, as if this explanation clarified

everything. His eyes were overly bright. Mimi Farquharson did not emerge into daylight until cocktail hours. "And how is New York? Lively as usual?"

"The Winthrops are back from the Riviera. They've bought a villa at Cap Ferrat. The Whitneys gave a nice dinner party on Wednesday for the Peruvian ambassador."

"And how was the fancy dress ball?"

Gloria injected false gaiety into her voice as she said: "Splendid fun."

For the sake of convention she had been escorted by safe old Billy Walters. The night had been spent with Ramon and there would not be another like it. Her head ached from crying.

"I need you back in Boston for the rally tonight," Chips was saying.

"Yes . . . Of course."

"Six-thirty?" Chips raised his bushy eyebrows. Gloria was being unusually amenable.

"Yes." Her voice was brittle and tightly controlled, but Chips did not notice. He was already feeling mean at having doubted her fidelity. If she had stepped beyond the limits of flirtation she would not be so willing to return to Boston.

"I've missed you," he said gruffly.

"Yes." It was a whisper.

He said "goodbye" and severed the connection. A big rally such as the Faneuil Hall one buoyed him up and set his adrenalin going. It was hard to return to an empty house after the euphoria of applauding crowds and the passionate singing of "The Star-Spangled Banner" and "The Wearing of the Green". Gloria's return would be doubly welcome. With her Gibson Girl curls and glossy lips, she would be sensational on the platform and his excess energy could later be released most satisfactorily.

An old opponent in the political stakes, Sean Flynn,

was reputed to unwind after heavy electioneering by taking tepid baths and drinking hot cocoa. It was no wonder the man had never won the mayoralty. In Chip's eyes he hadn't the blood for it.

He lit another cigar and rammed his thumb on the bell on his desk. His entourage entered and Chips said with his usual zest, "Good morning, gentlemen. I believe the longshoremen need a little encouraging to give us their votes. Ideas please."

Gloria mixed herself a Martini and stared in the mirror, dull-eyed. Her china-doll prettiness seemed to have blurred and aged. She had behaved like a fool. Ramon was not a man to tolerate feminine tantrums. Intuition had told her from the outset that his capacity for scenes was strictly limited and she had behaved accordingly: until yesterday. She drank the Martini without tasting it. Her friends had warned her she was playing with fire and she had taken no notice. She had been mesmerized by him. Power excited her: it was one of the reasons she had first been attracted to Chips. He was accustomed to power and revelled in it. It was a sensation Gloria understood. Ramon's power was of a different kind. It lay in his complete domination over her body. She had wanted to keep him more than anything else in the world and her own behaviour had been instrumental in driving him away. She had behaved like the cigarette girl she had once been, shrieking and screaming, and he had treated her accordingly.

She poured herself another drink. What she had done afterwards had been even worse. Colour burned her pale cheeks. She had been so determined to prove to herself that any other man could take Ramon's place that within minutes of his leaving she had brazenly rung Baby Santorini and intimated that she was free for the evening.

Baby was the reason Loretta had taken a drug overdose. He had three wives behind him and more mistresses than there were days in a year. If any man could drive Ramon from her mind it was surely Baby. It had been a disillusioning experience.

She had returned to her hotel suite feeling cheap and soiled. When a large bouquet of white roses had arrived half an hour later she had crushed them angrily into the waste-bin.

It was 9:45: she had had two stiff Martinis and no breakfast. Her head pounded. She wondered where Ramon had spent the night and who with. Three times she had asked the switchboard operator to connect her with his number and three times she had cancelled her instructions. She tried to recreate the short, hideous scene that had taken place between them. *She* had been the one who had angrily declared that their relationship was at an end. He had simply agreed, coolly and indifferently. He had done so because of her behaviour. Hope sparked into life. Perhaps it wasn't too late. If she said she was sorry; if she was sweet and reasonable . . . She rang for black coffee and dry toast and sat down at the dressing table, applying cream and powder with hurried, shaking hands.

Half an hour later she left the Ritz, heavily swathed in white mink. When she arrived at Ramon's apartment block she had to suffer the indignity of waiting until the doorman had ascertained whether or not Mr. Sanford wished to see her. He did, and Gloria felt momentarily faint.

Everything was going to be all right. He opened the door to her, naked apart from a towel wound loosely around his waist. His hair and chest still gleamed with droplets of water from the shower. There was no sign of his valet.

She smiled tremulously. "I'm sorry for behaving like a

fishwife, darling. Will you forgive me?"

Some yards behind the O'Shaughnessy limousine, Charlie Daubenay stubbed out his cigarette and emerged from his battered Ford. Gloria's New York chauffeur was not a permanent member of the O'Shaughnessy staff and Charlie doubted whether the man would have the sort of loyalty that withstood the attraction of dollar bills. He tapped on the window lightly and lazed on the bonnet. The chauffeur wound down his window.

"What the hell are you playing at?"

"Making friends," Charlie said pleasantly, and flicked open a packet of cigarettes.

"Then make them somewhere else."

The cigarette packet was offered to him, the dollar bills protruding invitingly.

The chauffeur's eyes narrowed. "What's your game?"

Charlie nodded in the direction of New York's most exclusive apartment block. "Does Mrs. O'Shaughnessy visit here regularly?"

The chauffeur smiled craftily and made no move towards the dollar bills. These guys made thousands out of jealous husbands and he was supposed to part with information for the price of a bottle of bourbon.

Charlie saw the expression and interpreted it correctly. He grinned.

"This is only for openers. If you tell me what I want to know the pay-off will be in the hundreds."

"Peanuts," the chauffeur said derisively.

Charlie shrugged and pocketed his cigarettes. "Perhaps so, but the gentleman in question doesn't think the situation warrants more."

He pulled the collar of his coat up around his ears as protection against the biting wind. "Nice talking to you," he said and walked briskly back to the Ford.

The chauffeur watched him through his driving mirror. Charlie slammed the car door shut behind him, revved the engine, and with a laconic wave did a three-point turn and began to motor speedily in the opposite direction.

The chauffeur glanced nervously at the glass-fronted entrance. There was no sign of Mrs. O'Shaughnessy. Decisively, he turned the key in the ignition and swung the car round after Charlie.

Charlie saw him and grinned. He would have liked to have given the greedy son-of-a-bitch a run for his money, but it was cold and the sooner he had the information he wanted, the better.

He pulled over and waited. He was damned if he was going to freeze to death again. The chauffeur had as little liking for the elements as Charlie and, uninvited, he opened the passenger door and slid in beside him.

"It's worth at least a thousand dollars."

"Then take it to someone who'll pay that price," Charlie said disinterestedly.

"The husband's a mayor, isn't he? It must be worth that price."

"Retiring," Charlie lied.

"She's giving him a real runaround. You won't get the information anywhere else. What about eight hundred dollars?"

"Five hundred. It's for curiosity only, not divorce. I've strict instructions not to pay one cent over five hundred."

"Bog Irish," the chauffeur said disgustedly, and held out his hand.

Charlie regarded him pityingly. "*After* the information, old son. I'm not paying five hundred dollars to discover Mrs. O'Shaughnessy visits her hairdresser twice a week."

"He's no bloody hairdresser."

"Who is he?"

"You don't know?"

Charlie swore silently. "If I knew, sonny boy, I wouldn't be sitting here talking to you and paying for the pleasure."

"Ramon Sanford," the chauffeur said. "He's as active as a tom cat. She isn't the only one."

"I'm not interested in the others." It was all Charlie could do to keep his voice steady. For Christ's sake, of all the men in New York the stupid little bitch had to light on a Sanford! Charlie's last assignment for Chips had concerned a Sanford. It hadn't been a pleasant one and Charlie was still trying to forget it.

"Give me some dates and times," he said mechanically. Was it possible that Sanford had made a beeline for Gloria O'Shaughnessy on purpose? Did he know? Sweat broke out on Charlie's forehead.

"He was at Mrs. O'Shaughnessy's hotel suite yesterday—midday. She stayed over here the nights of the fifteenth and sixteenth. On the seventeenth the doorman said it was a real stunner. He's too tight-lipped to give names, but some dollar bills might make him talkative."

"I'm not interested in a list a mile long," Charlie said brusquely. "Anyone else who can corroborate what you say?"

"Like I said, the doorman. Sanford has a valet up there, but I doubt if you'll get anything from him."

Charlie did as well. Sanford staff fell into the category of old family retainers. He handed the money over and the chauffeur grinned and tucked it into his breast pocket.

"Has there been anyone else apart from Sanford?" Charlie asked, almost as an afterthought. The shock of the Sanford name had robbed him of his usual efficiency.

"No all-nighters, though Mrs. O'Shaughnessy likes to enjoy herself and who can blame her, married to a man of seventy."

"Sixty-nine," Charlie amended, and lit a cigarette. It was no longer just a case of surveillance to give Chips the upper hand where his pretty young wife was concerned. There could be far more to it than that and, if there was, then he himself would be deeply involved.

He was hardly aware of the chauffeur's jaunty departure. Ramon Sanford and Gloria O'Shaughnessy. Was it coincidence or something far more sinister? Whatever it was, he was going to find out a lot more about it before he returned to Boston.

Chips left City Hall at midday and led his cavalcade down to the docks. The fishermens' vote could usually be counted on and Chips was courting it assiduously. At two o'clock he was breezing through the city's largest hospital and at four o'clock he was addressing an open-air meeting in the North End. He returned to his Beacon Hill home at six-thirty in fine fettle for the evening rally and was exuberantly pleased to find his wife waiting for him.

"I suppose Newport and Palm Beach won't be enough for you now the Winthrops have bought a villa at Cap Ferrat," he said, vigorously soaping himself down as he sat in his bath, a cigar firmly wedged between his teeth.

Gloria paused from the delicate task of plucking her eyebrows into non-existence. "I *do* like the Riviera," she said, reflecting that Ramon spent most of his time in Europe. The Riviera was within easy access of Paris and London: and Portugal and Madeira. She put down her tweezers and walked through the partitioned dressing room and into Chips' bathroom.

"I can't hear a word you're saying," Chips said, throwing water over his back like a water buffalo.

"I said I do like the Riviera and a house there would be nice."

"And how would I keep my eye on you with the Atlantic between us?" Chips asked good-humouredly. "It's bad enough wondering what you're up to in New York."

Beneath her rouge Gloria was unusually pale. Chips was too busy anticipating the evening ahead to notice. She leaned forward and kissed him on the forehead.

"Silly thing," she murmured, and was glad he could not see the expression in her eyes.

Chips tossed his cigar into a giant ashtray on the bathside and squeezed her breasts. Sean Flynn could keep his hot cocoa; he had married Gloria for expediency but it was turning out to be far more of a success than he had envisaged.

"Put your glad rags on and let's shake our tail-feathers," he said, stepping out of the bath and reaching for an outsize towel. Despite herself Gloria giggled. Chips' opponents and detractors were always pointing out that he was second generation Irish and had no breeding whatsoever. Chips had not been even slightly offended. He had worked hard at being second generation Irish and had carefully cultivated his image of outrageous flamboyance. From an early age he had been aware that political power for an Irish Catholic lay in the Catholic vote. Instead of putting his background behind him as speedily as possible, he had capitalized on it.

He was the only person she could truly relax with. He knew her background and didn't give a damn about it. She wished she could feel so at ease with Ramon.

"Did you see Nancy while you were in town?"

"No, I didn't know she was there."

"Would it have made any difference if you had?" He was zipping her into her frock and enjoying the sight of her supple spine. His first wife had always been heavily corseted and the sight of Gloria's nearly naked body slipping into silks and satins never failed to arouse him.

"Of course it would," Gloria tried to sound indignant and failed.

Chips laughed. "Why the hell you two can't like each other more, I'll never know. Come on. I can hear half the town waiting for us downstairs."

"They'd better not be," Gloria said with a spark of gutsy humour, "or Faneuil Hall will be half empty!"

Chips roared with laughter, slapped his wife lightly on the bottom and went down to meet his supporters.

Faneuil Hall was packed to capacity. The cheers were deafening as Chips and Gloria mounted the platform. Gloria blew lavish kisses and the crowd went wild. Chips was ebullient. Gloria was the best vote-puller he had ever had. Brought up without a political thought in her head, she had become a dedicated Democrat with consummate ease. There were even times when Chips thought his fluffy-haired wife was more naturally political than his daughter.

Nancy had been steeped in politics since babyhood. He had carried her around the hustings on his shoulders before she was old enough to walk. As a little girl she had handed out prizes and received bouquets. He had involved her in every political decision he had made, discussing ideas with her that she could barely understand. He had seen to it that she had met and spoken freely with all the well-known figures he had come into contact with. There had been no dismissal to the nursery for Nancy. At eight years old she had sat at dinner parties attended by men who were shaping world events. He had been preparing her to fulfil a dream he hadn't dared put into words, even to himself. He was a young man and he was mayor of one of America's greatest cities. He wanted to be more, much more. And when he arrived there he wanted Nancy to be at his side. It was a dream that Duarte Sanford had crushed with bitter finality.

Ten years later it had sparked into life again when

Nancy had married Jack Cameron. If he could never occupy the White House, there was still a possibility that his daughter could.

With that hope had come bitter dissatisfaction at his own thwarted ambitions. The dissatisfaction had lurked until he had met Charlie Daubenay and taken fate into his own hands. He hadn't regretted it. He never took any action that wasn't perfectly justifiable in his own eyes. Only occasionally did he remember the past; as when he had opened the newspapers and seen the familiar dark eyes and satanic brows of Sanford's son.

It was far from his mind now as he stepped up to the microphone and began to preach to the converted.

Gloria sat bathed in a spotlight, showing enough leg to arouse envy in the bosom of Chips' band of political guerillas who had choice front seats. She didn't hear a word her husband said, but her fixed smile parted in laughter at appropriate moments. Flashbulbs popped and she knew the morning press would carry reports on how vivacious young Mrs. O'Shaughnessy was out campaigning with her veteran husband.

She had to tell him about herself and Ramon and she had no courage to do so. There was applause and cries of "For he's a jolly good fellow"; then the band struck up and Chips, a wide beam on his face, started the singing of "The Wearing of the Green".

All the way home she tried to phrase the right words and failed. Chips hummed happily, helping himself to a large slice of cheesecake the minute they entered the house, and carrying a bottle of Irish whiskey up to the bedroom with him.

Gloria removed her diamond earclips and two broad silver bracelets that had hidden the bruises on her wrists. She undressed hurriedly and slipped on a loose-sleeved negligée as Chips strolled from his bedroom into hers.

"It was a good evening," she said, avoiding his eyes.

"Not one single catcall."

"I should hope not." Chips poured two large measures of whiskey into squat tumblers. "Tonight was a vote clincher, not a vote catcher. The Back Bay set will be a very different proposition."

"But you've no real opposition, have you?" She slipped into bed, her hands hidden beneath the rose-scented sheets.

Chips swallowed his whiskey, his eyes thoughtful. "There's old Monihan. Any man who has been mayor before is always a danger."

"And disadvantaged," Gloria said. He looked like an ageing lion, his mane of steel-grey hair springing back from his forehead in thick, dense waves.

"After all, people will remember what he *didn't* do, as well as what he *did*."

Chips grinned and slid his empty tumbler across the glass-topped surface of Gloria's dressing table. "That goes for all mayors, me included."

"*You've* carried out your election promises. Who else is there for you to worry about?"

"Not the Republicans, that's for sure."

She laughed. She was beginning to feel better already. Chips always had that effect on her.

"My old enemies are clanning together and supporting a new candidate. His face is as bland as a baby's bottom. He'll get nowhere."

He had been sitting on the edge of the bed. Now he leaned towards her, a wicked gleam in his eyes.

"Talking of bottoms," he said and to Gloria's relief he turned off the light before slipping his square, capable hands down beneath the sheets.

The next morning at six o'clock he was eating a breakfast of ham and eggs and preparing for the day ahead. He had municipal business to attend to; two luncheons, a radio broadcast and was booked as principal speaker at three banquets in the evening. It had also occurred to him that Gloria was looking a little peaky and he was toying with the remarkable thought that she might be pregnant.

His principal advisers were still in bed when Chips made his speedy way to the magnificent pile of bricks and mortar that was City Hall.

"A Mr. Daubenay for you on line 2," his secretary said shortly after nine o'clock. For the briefest of moments Chips wondered what the devil Charlie wanted, and then he remembered.

"Hello there, Charlie. Earning easy money again?"

"No." Charlie's voice was humourless.

Chips grinned. Charlie never did like wild goose chases, even when he was paid for them.

"Forget it," Chips said easily. "I'll put a cheque in the post. Did you see the Faneuil Hall reports this morning? Gloria's legs give me more press coverage than Douglas Fairbanks." He chuckled.

Charlie said, "Is this line private?"

Chips stopped smiling. "Why?"

"Because what I have to tell you isn't for anyone else's ears."

Chips' zest ebbed. "Out with it, Charlie. I don't like mysteries."

"The answer to what you wanted to know is yes, and the name is Sanford. Ramon Sanford."

There was silence.

"Did you hear me?" Charlie asked. "I said . . ."

"*I heard you!*"

Charlie flinched physically at the other end of the line.

"Are you still in New York?"

"Yes, I . . ."

"Then get the hell up here. No more telephone calls. And Charlie . . ."

"Yes?"

"Make quite, *quite* sure you've got all your facts right."

"I have, Chips. I swear . . ."

Chips didn't care whether he swore or not. He had slammed the receiver back on to its cradle, and was staring into the middle distance, his body rigid. Sanford. The very name made the hairs on the nape of his neck prickle like the rising hackles of a dog. Sanford. Of all the men in the world Gloria had chosen a Sanford: as Zia had done.

His big hands clenched and unclenched on the leather-topped surface of his desk. Or had she? Like Charlie, he was immediately suspicious. Perhaps Sanford had done the choosing and if so, why? The answers were numerous and not at all pleasant.

Very slowly he lifted the telephone receiver. "Put me through to my wife," he said in a flat, expressionless voice that his secretary barely recognized.

For forty years he had never let a woman get close enough to him to hurt him. Not his wife, nor the scores of girlfriends both before and after her death. He had regarded Gloria as a pretty toy; something to show off and enjoy. Something to add to his prestige. With bitter surprise he realized she had become something more. He felt suddenly old and painfully cheated as he waited to speak to her . . .

Chapter Five

"When will Mr. Cameron be returning to the Cape?" Henry Harding of Harding, Harding and Summers asked, after a pleasant but lengthy day at Ocean View.

"Not for some time."

A faint shadow crossed the senior Mr. Harding's face. "But I understood you were very anxious to have these formalities completed."

"I am."

The will lay on the table between them.

"Then I'll see to it that the documents are sent to Mr. Cameron by personal delivery and . . ."

"What on earth for?" Nancy was unable to keep the exasperation out of her voice. "It's *my* will. Why does Jack have to see it?"

"Well, of course he doesn't *have* to," Henry blustered. "It's just that he's always taken a great interest in your business affairs and . . ."

"My will is of no concern to anyone but myself."

"But as you haven't made your husband a beneficiary,

then there's no reason why he shouldn't be asked for his comments." Henry Harding's voice held a note of pain. In his opinion wives should be obliged to bequeath their estates to their husbands. Children were far too reckless to handle money unless it was sewn up tight in trust funds.

"I wish to sign the will now, Mr. Harding," Nancy said firmly. "My housekeeper and maid can act as witnesses."

Mr. Harding took off his rimless glasses and polished them furiously. He thought Nancy's haste extremely unladylike.

Nancy rang for Mrs. Ambrosil and when she entered, said to her, "I'd like Maria as well, please."

"Certainly, madame."

Mrs. Ambrosil's sharp eyes had seen the green-ribboned documents on the table and she was filled with anticipation. Mrs. Cameron's financial advisers had been at the house for two days and when they had left Mr. Harding had arrived. The conclusion to be drawn, especially with the tell-tale vellum documents on view, was obvious.

"I'd like you to witness the signature of my will," Nancy said as they entered.

They signed below her signature and Mr. Harding shook his head disapprovingly. Things were bad when a woman could will over two million dollars without consulting her husband. Of course, a codicil could always be added; but he disregarded the thought as soon as it entered his head. What was needed was a completely new will. There would be plenty of time to draw one up. In his professional experience women made new wills at least once a year. It formed a major part of his income. Mrs. Cameron was beginning the hobby at an unusually early age, but it only meant greater fees for Harding, Harding and Summers. The prospect cheered him considerably and he smiled with genuine warmth as he bade her goodbye.

Nancy leaned back in her chair with a great sense of relief. For two days she had been inundated with facts and figures and a great deal of unwelcome advice. Now it was over and her will, made out to her own satisfaction and no one else's, was safely on its way to the Harding vaults. Patrick O'Shaughnessy's legacy of wealth would not be incorporated into the Cameron millions.

Dusk was falling and hundreds of seabirds wheeled around Ocean View, perching on the gables and settling themselves for the night. The house was empty except for the small permanent staff who stayed there the year round, and Maria and Morris. The log fire crackled, the pleasant smell of pine filling the room. She rose to her feet and without summoning Maria, donned an English camel coat over her warm sweater and the trousers that Mr. Harding had so silently disapproved of. Her shoes were stiletto-heeled and she did not change them for her walk on the beach. She tied the coat belt tightly around her waist, turned the collar up, and with her hands deep in her pockets, slipped quietly out of the house.

At a brisk pace, she walked over the damp grass of Ocean View's immaculately kept lawns and down to the wildness of the dunes and the desolate expanse of beach.

She had been seven when her grandfather died and she remembered him clearly. Her grandmother had died a year earlier and she was a much more shadowy figure. She remembered that Maura's hair had still been dark and that her voice had been soft with a fascinating Irish lilt. Chips had been devastated when she died. It had been the only time in her life that she had seen him cry. It was Patrick who had perched her on his knee and regaled her with stories of Ireland. Nancy had listened enraptured, but they had not instilled in her the same sense of Irishness that had been her father's inheritance. The opposing element of a mother who came from the very

English class her grandfather so hated, had seen to that. She could never remember her mother and grandfather being in the same room together. When Patrick died, her mother had not even attended the funeral. As a child, she had found such behaviour strange—now she understood.

Patrick and Maura had been two of the hundreds of thousands who had fled a famine-stricken Ireland in the middle of the eighteen hundreds. Patrick had told her how the English, with a talent ages old, had ignored the devastation so near to their shores. His deep resounding voice had been bitter as he recounted how the British aristocracy had retreated from their Irish estates and waited in the comfort of their St. James's clubs for the time when their tenants no longer so inconveniently sickened and died.

Her grandparents on her mother's side had been members of that aristocracy. It was no wonder that Patrick would not have his daughter-in-law's name mentioned in his presence.

Gulls circled her head and the strong wind blowing in from the sea stung her cheeks and blew her hair wildly around her face. Some of her grandfather's stories had given her nightmares when she was a child; he had told her of the coffin ships that had ferried the starving to America. The way he had threatened the landlord's factor with violence in order to receive what was due to him to enable him to buy tickets for the three-week crossing to a land he had scarcely heard of. Then the harsh lines of his face had softened as he had ruffled her curls and said with a chuckle that God had looked after those who looked after themselves.

Nancy had always thought that God should have looked after them a little earlier and then they would never have had to leave Ireland with its green fields and blue mountains and its lakes that were called loughs, and pixies and fairies. She had a vague idea that her grandfather would not mind her voicing this opinion, but her grandmother would, so she had kept it to herself.

It was on board the ship that Patrick's fortunes had taken a turn for the better. Ramon's father had fallen overboard and it had been Patrick who saved him. Nancy threw back her head and breathed in the salt-fresh air deeply. If he had not done so, Ramon would never have been born and she would not now be walking the darkening beach and counting the hours till she would be with him again.

Her grandfather had cherished Leo Sanford's friendship deeply. Nancy could not remember his reaction when his son and Leo's had fallen out so irrevocably, but she could imagine the hurt it had caused him. He would have been pleased that Leo's grandchild and his own had found the kind of love that had bound him so devoutly to Maura.

She picked up a handful of pebbles and began to skim them across the leaden waves.

She was leaving a husband to be with Ramon, and it would be natural to assume that Patrick's Catholicism would have been outraged at such an act. Strangely enough, she felt he would have sympathized. There had been a strong streak of unconventionality in Patrick O'Shaughnessy. Her father had inherited this in a richer and more eccentric form, and she had thought herself to be free of it. Now she wondered. She was not going to indulge in a clandestine *affaire*: she was not going to be cautious or discreet or level-headed. She was going to abandon everything that made up the fabric of her life—her home, family, friends, reputation—all for a man she had spent only eighteen hours of her life with. Already, the previous thirty-five years seemed inconsequential and unreal. Ramon was reality.

It was dark now and in the distance the lights of Hyannis glimmered like a string of fairylights.

She turned for home. Tomorrow she would write to Verity: it would be a difficult letter, but she no longer shrank from the task. Verity had made her own life and had not been deterred by the knowledge that it had caused Nancy much anxiety and heartache. It would doubtless come as a shock to her to realize that her mother had a life of her own, but it was one she would have to bear. She would write a second letter to her daughter: one to be opened after her death.

Like an animal that instinctively knows its way, she climbed the pitch-black dunes. Ocean View stood white and welcoming against its background of trees. Nancy paused to look at it before entering. When she left at the end of the week she knew she would never return. Seagulls clustered beneath the roof, and the blinds at what had been Verity's room were drawn, with no light to indicate a little girl reading in bed. She dug her hands deeper into her pockets. Home was where the heart was and hers was no longer at Ocean View: it was with Ramon and wherever Ramon chose to take her.

The next morning Dr. Lorrimer telephoned. Nancy was curled up in a window seat, a writing case resting on her knees, a blank piece of paper in front of her. It was almost a relief to turn her attention elsewhere.

"Perhaps five days in the clinic? No longer, unless you wish it."

"But why?" Nancy asked for the third time in ten minutes. "You said that nothing had changed. Why should I enter the clinic?"

"We must keep an eye on you," Dr. Lorrimer said, with what he thought was comforting joviality. "Monitor the disease and take some fresh blood samples."

"Will they show anything different?"

"Different? In what way different?"

"Different in that I may be perfectly healthy," Nancy snapped.

"No, no. The diagnosis was conclusive."

Nancy said exasperatedly, "I'm sorry, Dr. Lorrimer, but I can see no point in spending five days having useless blood tests taken."

"But the disease must be . . ."

". . . monitored," Nancy finished for him. "I can see no point in it, Dr. Lorrimer. I want to be reminded of my illness as little as possible and having frequent blood tests would make that impossible. I'm also leaving the country in a few days' time, so it would be highly inconvenient and impractical."

"A cruise?" Dr. Lorrimer asked happily, and wondered why he hadn't prescribed it himself. Most of his clients sought solace in a world cruise, though sadly only a few completed the trip. "A very sensible decision, Mrs. Cameron. I feel sure, however, that Mr. Cameron will want to take the extra precaution of having a doctor as well as a nurse in attendance."

Nancy resisted the urge to tell the good doctor that her husband had still not telephoned her from Chicago and was in blissful ignorance of her condition. Instead, she said sweetly:

"I believe my husband has made all the necessary arrangements, Dr. Lorrimer."

"But is he a blood man?" Dr. Lorrimer began.

"Extremely bloody," Nancy said and ruthlessly replaced the receiver.

Dr. Lorrimer hesitated and wondered whether he should call her back. He decided against it. Terminal patients were apt to be extremely temperamental. Mrs. Cameron had adjusted beautifully and he could congratulate himself on the handling of the affair. "Next, please," he said to Nurse Duggan, and wondered if he could get the next marlin he hooked, stuffed and displayed for the benefit of his patients.

Nancy returned to her window seat and wrote boldly. *Dearest Verity*: then she sucked the top of her pen and studied a flock of terns winging their way out to sea, before continuing.

I know this letter will come as something of a shock to you, darling, but I've thought long and hard about the decision I've taken.

She stopped again and watched as a lone walker threw a ball to his yapping terrier. She *had* thought long and hard about it. For three days she had thought of nothing else and she had never wavered in her decision. She knew what she was going to do, and why. But how could she make Verity understand when she could not tell her of the medical report lying in Henry Lorrimer's office?

It was an impossible task. In the end she wrote simply: *I have fallen in love with Ramon Sanford. We are going away together in a few days' time. Where to, I still don't know. I will write to you as soon as I have an address for you to reply to: that is, if you want to. I hope that you do, Verity. You will understand one day. Until then, all I can say is that I love you.* She signed it simply, *Mummy*, and then began the longer yet easier task of writing a letter that would not be read until after her death.

She made no excuses. She did not refer to Jack's long line of mistresses. Jack had always been too preoccupied with first the bank and then politics to be an involved father, but perhaps after her death he would draw closer to his daughter. She hoped so and wrote nothing that would hinder such a relationship.

When the letters were sealed she telephoned her father in Boston.

"I shall be coming to Boston tomorrow. I need to talk to you."

"Not tomorrow," Chips said hastily. The next

twenty-four hours in the O'Shaughnessy home were not going to be pleasant ones, and he didn't want his daughter involved. "I'm up to my eyes, sweetheart," he said, by way of explanation. "Can you make it later in the week?"

He sounded tired and Nancy could well understand it. The months and weeks preceding an election were exhausting ones.

"Will Friday be all right?" It would give her time to see Jack; it would be better that way. Her father would not treat the matter seriously if he knew she still hadn't told her husband. He would have to listen and believe her once Jack had been told.

Telling her father would be the hardest task. She had always been his blue-eyed girl, the apple of his eye. She had never disappointed him. When her mother had made her dislike of electioneering clear, Nancy had replaced her at his side. She had been bright and pretty and she had been his girl. He had never shown the slightest disappointment at not having a son because he had never felt any. Nancy was enough for him, and she had known it. Now he was in the middle of a drive to be re-elected mayor of the city that he had served all his life. Adverse publicity would kill that ambition stone dead. Nancy thought she had found a way of avoiding public scandal. Her alliance with Ramon would be for months only. Perhaps less. For that length of time they could live quietly. It had been Ramon himself who had suggested retreating to Acapulco or Tobago.

"Fine, sweetheart. It's the firemen's dinner. I've a speech prepared that will rock old Flynn to his roots."

Nancy laughed. "I'll be there," she said, and rang off.

Jack was uncontactable. His Washington secretary gave her the number of the Chicago convention hall and they gave her his hotel number. It was only after she had spent twenty minutes trying to determine her husband's whereabouts that she realized how truly apart they had drifted.

The convention was in full swing. The senator could not be disturbed. Nancy left a message asking him to ring her at their Cape Cod home. At three-thirty she rang again, only to be told that the senator had been given her message.

At six-thirty Nancy rang again. The convention had wound up for the day. "Perhaps," a kindly voice suggested, "the senator could be contacted at his hotel suite?"

Nancy curbed her temper and waited patiently to be reconnected to Chicago. The senator was at dinner. Nancy asked to speak to his personal assistant. Miss Geeson was accompanying the senator.

Nancy replaced the receiver and poured herself a Courvoisier. Her anger was not for herself. Jack's behaviour no longer had the power to hurt her. It was the knowledge that if Verity had had an accident Jack would have been oblivious to it for days. She had never in her life tried to contact him when he was in the middle of important discussions. The fact that she had persistently tried to do so over the last few days was surely indicative that the situation was serious. She denied herself her usual walk and sat in front of the log fire, waiting for him to return from his evening out and finally turn his attention homewards. The slim volume of poetry on her lap was open at Emerson's "Give all to love". She was going to do just that.

The telephone rang and she laid the book down.

"What did Lorrimer have to say?" Jack asked across the crackling line.

"He said I was suffering from anaemia," she had to shout, the line was so bad.

"What's the answer? Dr. Pinkerton's little pink pills?"

It was unlike Jack to be humorous. She wondered if he

had been drinking.

"I'll be home be the end of the month. If you're worried we'll get a second opinion."

Nancy didn't bother to point out that Dr. Lorrimer was the world's leading expert on blood diseases and that any second opinion would only corroborate what she already knew—or would be valueless. Her illness was not what she wished to discuss with him.

She said, "It's not Dr. Lorrimer's diagonisis that I want to talk to you about."

"Fine, Nancy. I'm glad you're keeping well. I'll see you very soon."

"I won't be here, Jack."

"What do you mean? Are you going to Boston?"

"No. I don't know where I'm going."

"You'd better tell me in case I need to get in touch with you." He didn't sound as if it would be likely.

"Please come home so that we can talk. We never have, not for years. I don't want to finish this conversation off over the telephone."

"You'll have to, Nancy, and you'll have to be quick. I have reports to dictate."

She had wanted to sit down with him and try to establish some form of genuine contact. She wanted him to understand why she was behaving like this. It wasn't her fault if it had been made impossible.

She said helplessly, "I'm leaving you."

"It would be more convenient if you took a vacation in March. I'll need you to accompany me on the Texas trip. After that there's only the usual round and Syrie can stand in."

"Yes," Nancy said swiftly, "she's very good at that, isn't she?"

There was a stunned silence at the other end of the line. "I don't think I heard you correctly, Nancy."

"You did, and I'm not going to apologize. Neither am I

going to talk about it. Syrie Geeson has nothing to do with my going away. Nor, any more, do you."

"You're talking in riddles, Nancy," her husband said coldly. "It's late and I'm tired. I'll see you soon at the Cape."

"I'm leaving the Cape this weekend," Nancy said steadily. "I'm packing my bags and I'm leaving the country with Ramon Sanford. I've already written to Verity. I'm sorry, Jack."

She meant it. She was sorry and she was sad, but not for her actions. Her sadness was for the wasted years and the final death of the major part of her life.

"With *who*?" He sounded incredulous.

"Ramon Sanford," Nancy said tightly. "I'm in love with him."

There was a sharp intake of breath, and then a long pause. When at last he spoke there was a cruel edge to his voice. "He's way out of your league, Nancy. Only yesterday Ria Doltrice ran a full column on his impending engagement to Princess Marinsky. The princess is a fledgling of twenty-five and still seven years older than most of his companions. I'll phone Lorrimer in the morning. Perhaps there's more to it than anaemia. Perhaps you're suffering from an early menopause . . ."

"Friday" she said between her teeth. "I shall be here until Friday. Goodbye, Jack."

She replaced the receiver and stood for a few minutes hugging herself, as if for warmth. Then she turned out the lights and went to bed. She tossed restlessly, trying to still the doubts that Jack had raised. She was not experienced in extra-marital affairs. What if she had read more into Ramon's words than had been intended? Perhaps he had told Princess Marinsky and Lady Linderdowne and a hundred others that nothing would ever be the same: that he loved them. Certainly he had made love *to* them. He had never made any secret of that.

She closed her eyes against unwelcome images. Tomorrow she would pack. It would not take long. There was very little she wanted to take with her. On Friday she would go to Boston and see her father. On Saturday she would join Ramon in New York. Three days. Sixty hours. She closed her eyes and began to count the minutes.

Maria showed no surprise at being asked to repack after only a five day stay. When Mrs. Cameron ordered Morris to bring her two extra calfskin suitcases, she dutifully filled them with the mementos and bric-à-brac that Mrs. Cameron had collected and placed on the bed. There was a photograph album of Verity; half a dozen slim volumes of poetry; a cheap beaded rosary that had belonged to Mrs. Cameron's grandmother and was worthless apart from its sentimental value. Her mother's waist-length double rope of priceless pearls lay incongruously next to it. Maria quickly averted her eyes as Mrs. Cameron took off her emerald and diamond engagement ring and placed it inside the jewellery box that usually accompanied her. This time it was to be left behind.

Maria and Morris went about their tasks quietly and efficiently and wondered if they were to accompany their mistress and where to. Twice the telephone rang and Mrs. Cameron answered it eagerly. Twice she replaced the receiver with ill-concealed disappointment after making excuses for not being able to accept the given invitations.

Her restlessness grew more acute as the morning merged into afternoon. The cases were packed and Collins was informed that they would be leaving for Boston at nine o'clock the following morning. Maria and Morris eyed each other with raised brows. Boston? They had packed enough for a trip to the Bahamas.

"I'm going for a walk," Nancy said at last. "If Mr. Cameron arrives, please tell him I'm down on the beach."

The camel coat was belted tightly, the collar turned up against the biting wind as she headed down towards the heaving desolation of the Atlantic.

If Jack had wanted to, he could have been with her by now. Her high heels sank deeply into the loose sand of the dunes. She brushed a clump of clinging furze away from her trousered legs and walked straight out to the firm sand of the beach. The spray from the sea stung her cheeks and flecked her hair. Head down against the wind, she walked unseeingly.

Jack's non-arrival was ample proof of his conviction that Ramon had not meant a single word he had said to her. A wave ran high up the shingle, creaming around her feet. It receded, leaving the scarlet leather of her peep-toed shoes watermarked and coated with salt. She trudged on, oblivious. Perhaps he was right. Perhaps she had been gullible and naive. Perhaps even now Ramon was seducing another foolish and love-starved woman, and perhaps the name of Nancy Leigh Cameron was only another on a very long list.

Boats bobbed emptily in the distance, their masts stark against a mackerel sky. If so, she would have to continue to live with the knowledge, at least for a few weeks or months.

She clenched her fists tightly in her pockets. "*Please* God, let Jack be wrong," she said aloud. "Let Ramon love me. Just for a little while." Shearwaters flying out to sea, flapped noisily over her head.

"Nancy!"

She didn't hear him. The letter to Verity had been taken to Hyannis by Collins hours ago. She didn't regret it. Whatever happened she had told the truth. She had fallen in love with a man other than Jack and she was leaving Ocean View and the Cape. Nothing would change that.

"*Nancy!*"

She stumbled in her haste to turn around. He was a barely discernible figure, running and leaping down the high bank of the dunes. She stared in disbelief. He had come after all. He had placed her higher than the importance of his conference.

"Nancy!"

Her heart twisted and leapt. She began to laugh and cry as she broke into a heedless run. It wasn't Jack: it was Ramon.

He raced towards her, catching her breathlessly, swinging her off her feet and round and round.

"I love you!" she gasped, and the wind tore the words away as he crushed her to him and brought his mouth down hard on hers.

"A week was too long to wait," he said at last, grinning wickedly as he picked her up in his arms and began to walk back towards the house.

"I thought you were Jack." Her hands were clasped around his neck, her cheeks pressed close to his thick black curls.

He stopped abruptly. "If that's how you would have greeted him, I'll drop you in the sea."

She screamed in protest as he carried her threateningly towards the shoreline. "No! Please! I wouldn't have . . . !"

"I'm a very jealous man." He was laughing but his eyes were deadly serious.

"I know," she whispered, clinging to him with all of her strength. "And I'm glad."

"Give me your mouth," he said huskily. "I want to make love to you and this beach is too damn cold."

"What about in front of a log fire?"

"A log fire would be admirable," he said, continuing to carry her in his arms as he strode back to Ocean View.

There were no preliminaries. They undressed hastily and he made love to her with a savagery that left her on the edge of unconsciousness. As his climax came shatteringly and explosively, she cried out beneath him; oblivious of their surroundings, of Maria and Morris only rooms away; of Mrs. Ambrosil in the kitchen; of Jack perhaps entering the house. The world rocked on its axis and spiralled into the eternities.

Afterwards he leaned on his elbow and stroked the perfect line of her jaw with his forefinger.

"I thought New York had been a mirage," he said, a crooked smile on his lips. "I didn't dare believe it could happen again."

"It just did."

"Yes." He kissed her with infinite tenderness. "I know."

She pulled on her sweater and reached for her slacks. "Would you like some tea?"

He grinned. "Now I know you're half English, and yes, I would."

He was fully dressed by the time Mrs. Ambrosil entered with the tea trolley.

"Thank you," Nancy said to her and the housekeeper's eyes widened at the sight of her mistress with bare feet and an unmistakable expression on her face.

She withdrew hastily. Unlike Maria, her loyalty was to the senator as well as to his wife. Entertaining a man-friend at four o'clock in the afternoon was not the sort of behaviour Mrs. Ambrosil could condone. Nor did she understand it. She had recognized the dark face, swarthy as a pirate's, immediately. Ramon Sanford, Panther of the Playboys, and the man her favourite movie star had nearly married last year. He was not at all the sort of man she would have expected Mrs. Cameron to be friendly with—if "friendly" was the right word to use.

"Come back with me tonight."

"No. I'm seeing my father tomorrow. I have to tell him myself."

Ramon froze. It had not occurred to him that she would tell her father before leaving. He said carefully, "Your father will do everything he can to make you change your mind."

"I know, but he won't succeed."

"You don't know yet what he will say."

"I don't care. Whatever it is, it will make no difference."

She crossed the room to where he stood. Without her shoes her head only reached the middle of his chest. His arms encircled her but when he stared down at her he was grim-faced.

"Come away with me now, Nancy. Write to your father, or telephone him. Don't see him."

"I have to. I wouldn't be able to live with myself if I didn't." She pressed herself close to him. "I know that he'll be like a raging bull. I'm not expecting him to understand. I know he's going to throw that old feud he had with your father in my face. It won't make any difference. Why or how they fell out has no bearing whatsoever on what you and I do."

"Don't put it to the test," he said urgently.

She laughed and stood on her toes to kiss him. "I've burned all my boats. I've written to Verity and I've told Jack. Nothing my father can say or do will make any difference."

She closed her eyes and kissed him and did not see the frightening expression on his face.

It was a gamble. Possibly the biggest he had ever taken. He knew the relationship between father and daughter, and he knew that if he insisted she did not see her father it would awaken doubts that would never be stilled. Yet if she did . . .

He could feel the heavy slam of her heart against his chest.

"I love you," he said fiercely. "Never forget it."

"I couldn't." Her love for him was so intense that her bones ached with it.

The tea stood forgotten. He kissed her gently, caressing her with infinite tenderness. When they made love it was as if they did so in slow motion. Every moment lengthened in time: to be treasured and savoured, remembered at will. He thought: This is what it must be like when making a child, and then remembered that she could have no more children. It didn't matter. She fulfilled his every need. She was the only person he had ever found who could make him feel; make him give as well receive; make him hurt with longing. He thought of the small, barrel-bodied man in Boston's City Hall; of his loudness and insensitivity; of his capacity for love and hate, and he experienced a sensation totally alien to him. One of fear.

His face was hard and uncompromising as he looked down at her. Her cloud of dark, feathery curls shone in the firelight. Her lashes lay like soft dark wings on the smooth whiteness of her cheek. He had meant what he said in New York. He would take her away by force if necessary. Even against her own will. He would allow nothing to separate them; certainly not Boston's sturdy-legged and swaggering mayor.

"Have you packed for an island-hopping trip to Tobago or a long haul to Acapulco?" he asked, not wanting to dwell on thoughts of Mayor Chips O'Shaughnessy.

"I've just packed. I don't care where we go."

"Or how?" His eyes were teasing.

"By train to Acapulco, by yacht to Tobago."

The smile that transformed his face widened. "What about by plane?"

"There are no planes to Tobago."

"When you're the pilot you can go where you choose."

She began to laugh. "So we really are going to take off

into the sunset?"

"Like two birds," he said, and kissed the delicate curve of her jaw and the fullness of her mouth. Then her lips sought his and it was a long time before they spoke again.

"No pressmen, no photographers?" she asked, her face pressed close against his chest.

"None."

She sighed and ran her fingertips lightly over the strong muscles of his arm.

"What will we do?"

"Make love," he said. "Be happy."

"Won't you miss New York and Paris and . . ."

". . . the life that late I led?" he finished for her in amusement.

"Yes." Her eyes held his, anxious for reassurance.

He said quietly, "No. I've had enough of the playboy circuit. It was fun in my teens, routine in my twenties. Now I'm bored with it and have been for years."

The logs crackled and spat and the flames lit the room with a golden glow.

"Boredom was the reason I spent four months climbing in the Himalayas and another six months on a very uncomfortable expedition to the upper reaches of the Amazon. It was boredom that made me vie for the world water-speed record; fly my Gipsy Moth as fast and as high as possible. Ria Doltrice wrote that I had a death wish. I hadn't. I was bored. Sated by too many mindless, adoring debutantes, exiled princesses and American daughters of railroad barons and steel kings. Bored with ephemera and platitudes. Making love physically and never emotionally."

He drew her close, her breasts pushing against him.

"I won't miss any of it," he said. "I would only miss you."

"You'll always have me." Her soft, deep voice was utterly assured. "Always."

"Come back with me to New York," he said for the last time.

She shook her head. "No. Tomorrow I'm seeing my father in Boston. Saturday I'll be in New York and we'll have the rest of our lives together."

"It won't be long enough," he said, and he was smiling.

A knife turned in Nancy's heart. "No," she said. "It won't."

Half an hour later she stood in the tree-flanked drive and watched until the lights of his Daimler vanished into the night. Thirty-six hours, perhaps forty, and then they would be together again. She walked back into the house knowing that when next she left it, it would be for good.

"Good morning, Mrs. Cameron!"

"Welcome back, Mrs. Cameron!"

Nancy's progress along City Hall's warren of corridors was almost royal. As news of her presence spread, heads poked out of musty office doors. Everyone was eager to catch a glimpse of her, to wish her good-day. Many of the older inhabitants of City Hall remembered her being carried there, shoulder-high, by her triumphant father, when she was no more than a toddler. For them, the intervening years when Chips had stubbornly refused to run for office, had been years of exile. Now they were back in the centre of things and enjoying themselves with relish.

"It'll be a grand night, tonight," Seamus Flannery called to her.

She smiled and waved. Seamus Flannery was her father's shadow. The man who had told her bedtime stories about Ireland with such conviction that she still had a sneaking belief in fairies and leprechauns. In Chips' outer office scurrying aides halted to wish her good-day. Young Billy Williamson, who had never seen her before, watched her retreat into the mayor's inner sanctum with a glazed expression on his face. The wide smile she gave everyone, the way she happily answered to her first name from menials like Walter Elliot, was a revelation to him. Now at last he understood the magic she exercised over those who had met her. It wasn't just that she was beautiful. He struggled for a word and his tedious years of schooling at last stood him in good stead. She had charisma. The way her eyes tilted at the corners gave her the mischievous look of a kitten. There was nothing remote or glacial about her. He watched the tail of her fox fur disappear behind the mayor's door and knew that he was in love.

Nancy's first impression was that her father was ill. The blue eyes that usually twinkled so brilliantly were curiously flat and lifeless. His shoulders were hunched and the thrusting chin had merged into a heavy jowl. Within seconds he was beaming, hugging her, and enthusiastically jabbing his forefinger at the plan for a new freeway.

She kissed him, brushed the cigar ash from the front of his chest, sat down and said, ignoring his raptures over the freeway, "What's the matter?"

"Nothing." His denial was emphatic.

She remained silent and waited.

He grinned suddenly like a schoolboy. "Nothing you need bother your pretty little head about."

"Then it's not you or the city?"

"I'm fine and the city's even better. It's going to rush into the 1940s, not creep in like a sick dog." He snipped the end off a cigar. "Leastways, it will with me as mayor."

She laughed, glad to see him recovering his zest so quickly. He wasn't ill, merely tired.

"It will be just like old times tonight," he said, clouds of cigar smoke wreathing his head. "It's the firemen's dinner. You always were a favourite with them.

Tomorrow I'm speaking at the Nahant Club and a few words from you would be worth more than gold. In the afternoon it's old Monaghan's funeral. All the North End will be there so I must put in an appearance. After that you can play hostess to the Ladies' Club."

"Is Gloria still in New York?" Nancy asked, stalling for time before telling him she would not be staying long enough to charm the ladies.

Chips' teeth clenched tightly on his cigar. "No," he said shortly. "She's in Jamaica Plain."

Nancy's eyes widened. For the first few months of her father's marriage she had expected Gloria to flee, or be sent away. Just when she had bewilderedly accepted that the strange marriage was one that worked, her initial instincts were proved to be right.

"Oh," she said, and understood now why he had looked so unlike himself when she had entered. "I see."

"You don't, but it doesn't matter."

He had turned his back to her, his short sturdy legs braced apart, his hands clasped behind him, the fingers clenching and unclenching. When he swung round his face was free of all traces of hurt or bitterness.

He grinned again. "It's good to see you, Nancy. You spend too much time on the Cape. Now that Verity is in Europe, why don't you come back to Boston? It would make life pleasanter for me and easier for Jack."

Nancy wasn't fooled by his reassumed grin and joviality. Gloria had hurt him. It would make what she was going to say twice as difficult.

She said carefully, "Where I am makes very little difference to Jack."

Her father's eyes sharpened. "Not thinking of going to Europe, are you? Leave Verity alone for a while, Nancy. She's chosen her life. Let her get on with it." He chuckled. "Countess Mezriczky. What would your grandparents have said to that, I wonder?"

"I should think their comments would have been sharp and very terse," Nancy said drily.

Chips threw back his head and roared with laughter. "My God, and I think you're right! Still, I bet when they left Ireland with only the rags they stood up in they would have been well pleased if they'd seen the future. My father would never speak to your mother, but I always felt he took a perverse sort of pride in the fact that his son had married into a class that had always been as far removed from him as the sky."

"Your father lived his life exactly as he wanted."

"He did, and he was an amazing man. When I was five I was running the streets of the North End with patched trousers and bare feet. When I was ten I was leaving Beacon Hill and a house full of servants for the Boston Latin School. That's what my father did in only a few short years. He seized his chances and he worked twenty hours out of twenty-four."

"And you've always lived life exactly as you pleased," Nancy continued.

Chips was about to finish his often-told story of his father's meteoric rise when he detected the undercurrent in his daughter's voice.

"And?" he asked suspiciously.

"And I want to," Nancy said simply.

Chips shrugged. "Of course you do. You're an O'Shaughnessy. Haven't you always done what you wanted?"

"No," Nancy said calmly. "I haven't. I've done what you wanted and then what Jack wanted."

Chips' bulldog face creased in perplexity. He hadn't thought about it when he had assumed they were the same things. She leaned towards him and took his hand.

"I'm going to do something for myself. It's going to hurt you and I would give anything to avoid that, but I can't."

"What are you talking about, Nancy?" His eyes were watchful and wary.

"I'm going to leave Jack."

"*Sainted Mary*!" The cigar was spat from his mouth; his eyes bulged; his cheeks mottled with angry colour. "You'll do no such damn fool thing!"

"I will," Nancy said quietly. "I already have."

He kicked his chair out of the way and charged round his desk, gripping her shoulders and shaking her as if she were a rag doll.

"*You*—will—*not*!" he shouted.

She remained perfectly still. So did the people in the outer office.

Breathing heavily, Chips released her and yanked open the door. "*Out*!" he yelled, the veins on his forehead protruding.

His chief secretary and two principal advisers fell over themselves in their rush.

Chips fought for control. He had never before shouted at Nancy. When the outer room was clear he closed his door and said with unnerving calm:

"Tell me what this is all about, Nancy. If Jack's upset you I'll speak to him."

She refused to be sidetracked. The time for anyone speaking to Jack was long past.

"I'm sorry, Daddy." It was a diminutive she hadn't used for years. In the ensuing stillness she could hear the faint wail of a steamship whistle and the distant clang of the East Boston ferry bell. "I've fallen in love with another man and I'm leaving Jack to live with him. I've already written to Verity telling her what I'm going to do and I've told Jack."

"And who *is* this other man you think yourself in love with?" The venom in his voice was like a whiplash. "Please be so good as to tell me who it is that's about to ruin your chances of becoming the First Lady of the greatest country on earth? Who is it that's going to destroy my hope of becoming mayor of this city again? Who is it that's going to drag the name of O'Shaughnessy down to gutter level?"

"Ramon Sanford."

Whatever reaction she had expected, it was not this. He opened and closed his mouth silently, like a beached fish, struggling for words that would not come. The angry red staining his face and neck fled, leaving behind an ashen colour. His eyes bulged in their sockets as he clutched at his chest and fell sideways over his desk.

Nancy screamed and rushed to catch him as a brass lamp rolled heavily on to the floor and papers and pens scattered the room.

"*Daddy*!" She clutched at his shoulders as he slid to the floor. She was sobbing, calling out for help, undoing his collar and tie, pleading with him to speak to her.

He tried and could not. His eyes reflected her own panic and fear.

"The hospital," she gasped, as Seamus Flannery hesitantly put his head around the door.

"The mayor's ill!" Seamus' cry summoned all those who had been wary of intruding.

Strong hands lifted her father from her. She sat in the chair, trembling and crying, as he was wrapped in a blanket.

"I'm sorry," she said incoherently, time and time again, as the mayor's official limousine sped through the streets towards the City Hospital, followed by a stream of Fords and Cadillacs. "I'm sorry! Truly I am. Please don't die!"

At the hospital she could no longer hold his hand. He was wheeled swiftly away and she was surrounded by strange faces in masks and white coats. When her eyes focused on the familiar figure of Seamus Flannery she went over to him and collapsed in his arms.

"I've killed him," she sobbed. "I've killed him, Seamus!"

"There, there," Seamus said shakily. "He'll be all right, you just see if he isn't. It will take more than a little heart attack to put Chips O'Shaughnessy down."

They wanted her to go home, but she wouldn't. They promised to telephone her the minute he was well enough to see her, but she wouldn't move. She sat on a straight-backed wooden chair with Seamus at her side, and waited through the long hours of the morning and afternoon. At last a doctor approached and her knees buckled with relief as she rose to meet him and saw the expression on his face.

"Is he going to be all right?"

"If the way he's ordering me and the nurses about is any indication, he certainly is."

"Oh, thank God."

"He wants to see you."

"Yes. Yes, of course." She was still clutching Seamus' ridiculously large handkerchief in her hand as she entered the private room occupied by her father and an army of nurses.

"Out!" Chips said, motioning to the nurses. It was a much weaker command than the one given to his henchmen only hours before.

"I'm sorry, Mayor O'Shaughnessy, but . . ."

"Out!" Chips repeated, and his eyes glared angrily in his whitened face.

"Just for a minute," Nancy said to the sister. "I'll call you if necessary."

"It's most irregular. I'm not sure . . ."

"Out!" Chips repeated, raising himself on the pillows.

The sister had no wish to be responsible for a relapse in the mayor's condition. "Ten minutes," she said, tight-lipped. "The bell's there, Mrs. Cameron. Please ring immediately if there is any sign of the mayor tiring or deteriorating."

"I'd have a long way to deteriorate before I was in her condition," Chips said darkly. "Old maids, every last one of them. What she needs is a man and what I need is a cigar."

Nancy's relief was complete. "It would be more than my life is worth to give you a cigar." She sat down at his bedside and took his hand.

"You had me frightened for a minute."

Chips grinned, some of the old sparkle returning. "I wasn't too happy myself."

They laughed and then Chips said soberly, "We have to finish our conversation, Nancy."

"Later, when you're better."

"Now."

If she didn't comply with his wishes she knew she would arouse his anger and, like the sister, she was fearful of the consequences. Her inward struggle was silent and prolonged. He was expecting her to renounce her decision, to give up Ramon. He would pat her hand, beaming broadly. Life would continue as if nothing had happened. Or it would as far as he was concerned. She loved him more than anything else in the world—apart from Ramon. It was the most bitter test of that love when she said gently, "I'm deeply in love with Ramon Sanford. We were leaving New York together tomorrow. Obviously, now that you're in hospital, I shall wait until you're well again."

"And you will still go?"

"Yes."

There was nothing to be heard but the harsh breathing as his eyes held those of his daughter and he was faced with a replica of his own immovable will.

"Before you go," he said, "let me tell you something about the Sanfords."

Chapter Six

"Your grandfather saved Duarte Sanford's life."

"I know. Ramon has told me how it happened."

"Has he, indeed? Well, there's nothing but the truth to be told there. Your grandparents were paupers and Leo Sanford was a rich man. He was only on the immigrant ship because he had not dared to wait for a more suitable vessel. A little question of an aggrieved husband."

"I know," she repeated.

Chips' eyebrows rose imperceptibly. "He left no skeletons in the family cupboard, then?"

"No."

Chips was no longer looking at her. His eyes were fixed on the distant wall, seeing nothing but the past.

"The grateful Leo rewarded your grandfather by purchasing for him a small farm on the outskirts of Boston. It was a drop in the ocean of his finances. A year or two later the Sanfords, having consolidated their wealth in more than half a dozen American cities, returned to Portugal. I believe the obstruction to their earlier return had conveniently died. By that time a lifelong friendship had sprung up between the two men. I have a shrewd idea that Leo Sanford recognized in your grandfather a kindred spirit, despite the disparity in their backgrounds. By the time Leo left the New World for the Old your grandfather had bought a small grocery store in Hanover Street. He had been selling the farm produce in the city's markets. Now he sold it from his own premises. A big jump for a boy from a thatched-roof, one-roomed cottage in County Cork."

Chips fell silent for a long time. So far he had told her nothing she did not know already.

"Eventually your grandparents moved from the farm and lived above the shop in Hanover Street. That was where I was born. Your grandfather had a nice little business going; enough to have satisfied most men. It didn't satisfy him. He began buying other farms and opening other shops. It wasn't long before his profits were being channelled into real estate. Your grandfather bought land in Manhattan, regarded as worthless then. The income from it will survive for Verity's grandchildren and their grandchildren after them."

Nancy waited patiently.

"I was born with only one passion in life—politics. I was the youngest-ever member to be elected to Boston's Common Council. There were seventy-four other members, but it was a start. I knew where I was going. I knew every voter in my district by name. I assisted at every parish function. I attended every wake. I had a card index file on every man needing a job and one on all employers. When a man wanted work he came to Chips O'Shaughnessy and he didn't forget the favour." There was pride in his voice. "I was in my element in those days, Nancy. It was then that the Irish community in Boston began to emerge as a political force. We finally shook the complacency of the Protestant Yankee oligarchy and it's never been the same since.

"As a boy I formed my own gang in the spirit of the old Irish Whiteboys. As we grew older we controlled the politics of our own streets. Bar-room politics, it was then. We worked street by street, block by block, precinct by precinct, ward by ward. Until, in the end, we captured the city."

The colour was back in his cheeks.

"They were grand days, Nancy. I had a fine woman by my side. She was a Boston girl and second generation Irish, but like no other girl in the whole of the city—or the state."

To Nancy's horror she saw that he was on the verge of tears.

"We were to be married in the fall of 1890. I loved her with all my heart and I never laid a hand on her except to kiss her goodnight. I worked every hour God sent. I saved every dime I earned, because I wanted our house to be *our* house: not a gift from your grandfather. It was a three bedroomed wooden-framed house with clapboard siding, only twenty minutes from the city centre. There were chestnut trees in the street outside and a small garden for the children to play in."

His voice trailed off. This time the silence seemed to last forever. When he spoke again, the bitterness in his voice sent a chill down Nancy's spine. "And then *he* came."

"Who?" asked Nancy, hanging on to every word. It had never occurred to her that her father had loved anyone before her mother, much less been on the verge of marrying.

"Duarte Sanford." The pupils of his eyes were opaque. Nancy wondered if she should ring for the nurse but couldn't tear herself away from his side to do so.

"He was ten years older than me: sophisticated and with all the charm of a European. Your grandfather was a rich man by that time but I'd never lived on his wealth. I'd wanted to make my own way, be my own man. Sanford rode the streets of Boston in a carriage drawn by perfectly matched greys. Gold gleamed at his cuffs and diamonds in his tiepins. He wore rings that would have been ostentatious on a woman. One of them was a ruby the size of a nut."

Nancy sat rigid, her body still feeling the heat from a hand wearing that ring.

"He was as handsome as Satan with his heavy black moustache and glossily slick hair."

The next silence was so long that Nancy thought he would never break it.

"What happened?" she asked at last.

The pain in his voice chilled her. "He took her and he seduced her. He took Zia."

Nancy felt the world lurch and steady again.

"She didn't love him. She never loved him. She cried and she cried and I told her we could still be married: that I loved her more than life itself."

"And then?" Nancy could hardly form the words.

Her father looked suddenly old, shrunken in the whiteness of the bed and the room.

"And then she discovered she was carrying his child. I told her it made no difference. I told her I would accept the child as my own. I told her everything, except that I was going to kill Duarte Sanford." The minutes ticked away. "It was his child and he wanted it: and her. They were married at St. Stephen's Church on 1 May 1890. She wouldn't wear the dress that hung in her wardrobe: the dress her mother had worn: the dress that she was to have worn when she became *my* wife. She wore the dress *he* bought—an ostentatious creation of diamonds and pearls shipped in from Paris. I spent the whole of the ceremony at the docks, a shotgun in my hands as I gazed at the ship that was to take her away. I was going to kill him and it's only thanks to Seamus Flannery and the boys that he lived for another forty years. The church bells were still ringing when they knocked me unconscious. They locked me in Murphy's Bar and by the time I had battered the door down the ship had sailed."

"But she came back," Nancy said. "I remember her visiting us at Beacon Hill."

"She came back and I was mayor and married to your mother. The crossing had taken her three weeks and when she had landed the weals on her back were still festering."

"Oh God!" Nancy thought she was going to be sick.

"She had come to me for help. She had spent the last of her money on the fare. Her multi-millionaire husband never gave her so much as a cent. I told your mother what you told Jack. That I was sorry but that I loved someone else. She'd come back to me and I wasn't going to let anyone or anything take her away again—not my marriage, not my mayoralty, not even you." His voice took on a curious quality, almost detached. "I should have known he wouldn't let her go. He came here, to Boston. To Beacon Hill. He stood in my parlour in a dove-grey velvet suit and tossed an ebony-tipped cane lightly from hand to hand. He told me that unless Zia returned with him, he would break me."

"But you've already said you were prepared to lose the mayoralty," Nancy protested.

Chips gave her a strange smile. "So I was, but I wasn't prepared to destroy Patrick and Maura."

She stared at him with utter incomprehension.

"Leo Sanford knew my father better than any other man. He met him within hours of Patrick leaving Ireland; before there was any need for Patrick and Maura to pretend."

Nancy's mind was spinning. She wondered if her father was delirious. She said stupidly. "To pretend what?"

"To pretend that they were married."

"You mean they weren't married when they left Ireland?"

"No. They never married."

She struggled to take in what he was saying, and to understand its implications. If her grandparents were never married, then her father was illegitimate. A cardinal sin in a Roman Catholic community. "But why?" she asked, bewildered. "I don't understand."

"They couldn't marry," Chips said, his face as dead as if it was carved out of stone. "They were brother and sister-in-law."

Nancy dropped her head between her knees. If she hadn't she would have fainted. The blood pounded in her ears and, through swirling blackness, she heard her father continue relentlessly.

"Patrick O'Shaughnessy was married to Mary Sullivan. Maura was a mere child when her sister married. It was she who decorated the church with flowers for them. She told me so herself when I confronted her with what I thought were preposterous lies. Killaree Church, it was, in the shadow of White Mountain and the flowers were marigolds. When famine struck Ireland, your grandfather was scratching out a living on a smallholding on the Clanmar Estates. First Mary died and then the baby. It was their only child. Patrick had waited ten years for its birth and it died before it was ten days old. There was no one to bury his wife and child. Without benefit of coffin or clergy, he placed the baby in Mary's arms and committed them both to the waiting earth. Maura was sixteen then. She brought marigolds to lay on the grave, the same flowers with which she had decorated the church ten years before.

"Patrick had two sailing tickets in his pocket; one for him and one for his dead wife. Maura pleaded with him to take her with him and Patrick agreed. How long she had loved him—or if she even knew she loved him—I don't know. According to your grandmother it happened on the boat. Patrick dived overboard to save Sanford's stepson, and when he was hauled from the Atlantic, choking on sea water and more dead than alive, she threw herself into his arms and for both of them the future was determined.

"When they landed in Boston they landed as man and wife. It must have caused her endless torment to live without the church's blessing. I doubt if it caused Patrick any. They were as devoted a couple as I've ever seen.

"Duarte Sanford threatened that unless I relinquished Zia he would publicize the truth the length and breadth of Boston." The irises of his eyes resembled pinpricks. "I didn't give a damn about myself, but I did for them. They'd lived fifty years with that secret and the only people who knew it were the Sanfords. Patrick was the most respected man in Boston's Irish Catholic community. He and Maura took pride in what they had built together. They had never harmed anyone and they didn't deserve to be harmed. It was the only thing my father ever asked of me. He knew Maura could never have lived with the shame Sanford would have exposed them to. I promised him I would not subject her to it." He leaned back against the pillows, exhausted. "When Sanford returned home, Zia accompanied him."

Tears were coursing unrestrainedly down Nancy's cheeks.

"He had his revenge, though. He told me if I ever stood for mayor again he would let the city know the truth about my birth. He had gone to the trouble of obtaining copies of Killaree parish records. He had the proof of my father's marriage to Maura's sister. There was nothing I could do."

"Not even when they were dead?" Nancy whispered.

There was none of the usual bluff and bluster that was so much a part of his personality. Instead, he had a quiet dignity. "No," he said. "Their memory was alive. It still is."

She rose unsteadily to her feet and crossed to the window. After a while she returned to the bed and said, "It's a horrible story. I wish I hadn't forced you to tell me. But it doesn't make any difference to the way Ramon and I feel about each other. Ramon isn't his father. If you met him, you would realize that."

"It's my turn to be sorry, Nancy. I don't believe I've ever hurt you in my life, but I'm going to now."

He struggled to reach his personal possessions, scattered on the locker top. There was very little there: only the contents of his pockets.

"Let me get it," she said as he knocked his watch on to the floor. "What is it you want?"

"The envelope," he said with a gasp, falling back against the pillows. "Read that and then tell me that you're still going away with Ramon Sanford."

It was a cheap envelope. Charlie didn't go in for fancy stationery. The paper inside bore no letter-heading and no address. The date was scrawled large. *January 18th.* The day after she had left New York. There was no usual "Dear Sir" or "Dear Chips", simply a bald statement reading:

Mrs. O'Shaughnessy spent the night of the 15th and 16th at the apartment. Prior to that she stayed on unspecified dates in November. Your New York chauffeur [and I'd get rid of him if I were you] says the affair began some time in the summer.

"I don't think I should read any more," Nancy said. She had never liked Gloria but it was distasteful being privy to her private life.

"Read it," her father commanded, his eyes like gimlets.

Uncomfortably Nancy read on.

Mrs. O'Shaughnessy arrived at the apartment at 11 am this morning. They left together five hours later and it was then that the photograph was taken. Considering the identity of the gentleman in question, I'm not coming straight back to Boston, but will stay around for a couple of days. There was no signature.

She handed the letter back to him. He made no move to take it. "The photograph," he said, implacably.

It lay shiny and stiff in the envelope. Reluctantly, she drew it out. It had been taken at dusk and was grainy and slightly out of focus.

His hand was cupping Gloria's fur-coated arm and she was looking up at him, her lips slightly parted as if she was speaking. Behind them the glass façade of the apartment block glittered like a Christmas toy. Even the doorman could be seen clearly, his hand raised deferentially to his peaked cap. She gazed at the print stupidly, not understanding.

"They make a nice couple, don't they?" Chips' voice was distorted by pain.

"But I was with him," she said, not understanding, staring blankly from the letter to the photograph.

"I doubt if he's a once-a-day man," her father said cruelly.

"No!" She shook her head, backing away from the bed. "No! It isn't possible. There's some mistake . . ."

"There's no mistake. Ask Gloria. I did." He blanched at the memory.

"No!" Her hands groped blindly behind her, seeking something solid to hold on to. Feeling was returning: a cold flood of ice; ice and snow; snow and death. She was shaking. She felt as if she had been hit by a cyclone, yet the room around her remained unchanged. The clinically-white walls and pristine coverlet on the bed, the oxygen mask and cylinders were all in the same place they had been moments ago. Her father remained propped up against the pillows as if nothing had happened.

"Nancy!"

There was a clatter as she backed into a metal trolley, instruments flying.

"Nancy!" He was half out of the bed as the door was flung open and a regiment of nurses rushed in.

"No!" She was at the door, clinging to it for support.

"Call Dr. Trevors."

"I really must ask you to get back into bed, Mayor."

"Nurse Smith, help sister with the mayor. Is Dr. Trevors here yet?"

"Disgraceful behaviour."

"Your father is a very sick man."

The bubble of voices rose and swelled.

"Are you all right, Mrs. Cameron?"

"Fetch Mrs. Cameron a chair."

"Thank goodness you're here, Doctor."

"*Nancy*!"

"A new needle, Sister. Thank you."

"*Nancy*!" Her father's voice was a bellow over the cacophony around her.

"Please sit down, Mrs. Cameron. You look most unwell."

Her face was immobile. Her lips were white. She was frozen and she knew she would never be warm again.

"NANCY!" His roar was curtained sharply as Dr. Trevors pushed the needle home.

"Goddamn it to hell! NANCY!" His voice followed her as she stumbled down the corridor. January 18th. Gloria had been at his apartment only hours after she had left. He had been laughing at her: laughing at her father. Playing a sick, crazy game that was beyond her understanding.

"Where to, Mrs. Cameron?" her father's chauffeur asked.

"Home." Home, where she could lick her wounds in private.

The chauffeur was about to ask after the mayor and decided not to. By the expression on Mrs. Cameron's face, the mayor was dead. He sped down Tremont Street. The news-stands already had headlines of the mayor's collapse. The domed roof of the State House glowed a dull bronze as they accelerated towards it. On his left-hand side the common was bleak, the branches of the trees stark against the winter sky. The cobbles of Beacon Street slowed him down as he climbed towards Louisberg Square.

She went straight to the room that had been hers when a child and which was always kept ready for her. She locked the door, pulled the heavy velvet drapes and, still wrapped in her furs, lay down on the bed. She was shivering uncontrollably.

Gloria and Ramon: Ramon and Gloria. Not Lady Linderdowne or Princess Marinsky, but her father's wife. Her stepmother. She wanted to cry but could not. Her pain was too deep to be assuaged by tears. She wanted to think but could think no further than that she was utterly alone. No husband: no Verity: no Ramon. When she slept it was her body's sub-conscious self-defence mechanism going into action. The only way she could survive was by rendering herself unconscious. Hours later, when she awoke and pulled back the drapes, the square was in darkness. For the next three days she remained in the room, deaf to pleas to open the door and allow food to be brought in. Her father's doctor was summoned and left unseen by Nancy. Seamus stood outside the door and told her that her father was recovering and only remained in hospital under brute force. Everyone thought that her behaviour was due to guilt. It had been the row between father and daughter that had brought on the heart attack, and it was to be expected that a lady as sensitive as Mrs. Cameron would feel the responsibility heavily. Even so, her reaction was thought to be decidedly extreme and gave cause for concern.

She emerged only hours before the mayor returned with a bevy of private nurses from the hospital. His swagger was a little lacking, but his chin jutted determinedly and his manner was as snappy and brusque as when he was in the best of health. It was Mrs. Cameron who looked as if she had just had a brush with death. There were hollows beneath her cheeks and the thick sweep of her lashes emphasized her unnatural pallor. Her eyes were wide and tragic and hauntingly beautiful.

"Garbo," the cook said to the rest of the interested staff, "she looks just like Garbo."

Her father felt strangely ill-at-ease with her. She was no longer his Nancy. She had become detached and there was an inner stillness about her that unnerved him.

"I'm sorry," he said awkwardly, when they were alone together.

"There's no need to be." She ignored the Martini he had mixed and picked sparingly at the food on her plate.

"What are you going to do? Go back to the Cape?"

She looked surprised. "No. I've left there for good."

Chips wasn't accustomed to feeling out of his depth. "What about Jack? He's on his way here."

She gave a small smile. "He hardly dropped everything in the rush, did he? His wife tells him she is leaving him, his father-in-law has a heart attack, and three days later when his convention has drawn to a satisfactory close, he graces us with his presence."

"Chicago was important."

"Of course," Nancy said dispassionately. "It was politics."

Chips downed his Martini and poured himself a sensible brandy. "Where will you go then?"

"To Zia."

Chips spluttered into his glass.

"I shall never see Ramon again, but I want to feel close to him. For a little while. I'm going to Madeira and Sanfords."

Chips wondered if the shock of Charlie Daubenay's letter had unhinged his daughter's mind.

"Goddamn it to hell! If you go there you're bound to meet him!"

"No I'm not," she replied calmly. "Zia has barred him until he marries a nice girl. Madeira is the last place on earth that I am likely to meet Ramon."

"But Sanfords! After all they've done to us."

"Zia," Nancy corrected.

He stared at her helplessly and she could see the longing creep into his eyes. For a second she thought he was going to abandon Boston and join her.

"It's a long time since you saw her," he said.

"Not since my honeymoon."

Chips had forgotten that Nancy and Jack had honeymooned at Sanfords. He felt as if he were walking in a swamp.

"Then why of all places . . . ?"

"Zia has always been kind to me," Nancy said, rising to her feet. "Ever since I was a little girl. Right now I could do with a little of Zia's kindness."

She put on her coat. "I can't stay here. Gloria may return at any moment and even if she doesn't, she's only in Jamaica Plain. I can hardly forget her existence. I've no desire to see Jack and become involved in endless arguments. I simply haven't the strength. My bags are packed and the *Mauretania* sails at midnight. Your secretary managed to get me a state room. It was a last minute cancellation by Teddy Stuyvesant. It seems he's going to marry Consuelo at last." She gave a tiny smile. The world that held Teddy Stuyvesant and Consuelo seemed light years away. "I'm taking Maria with me. Morris and Collins will return to the Cape."

She slipped her arms around his neck and he hugged her tightly.

"It won't be for long," he said gruffly.

"No," she said, knowing it would be forever. "Goodbye, Daddy." She fought back her tears, kissed his cheek and left the room.

Five minutes later she was travelling south, her Rolls suffused in garish light as the setting sun sank bloodily behind the city's skyline.

Chapter Seven

"Only another day's sailing and we'll be there."

Nancy raised her eyes from the letter she was writing and smiled across at her cousin, Vere Winterton.

"And then what will you do? Continue on to the Canaries?"

He grinned. "The Canaries, dear Nancy, were nothing but a ruse to get you on board."

"You mean you never intended sailing there at all?"

He grinned again, his short blond hair ruffled by the Atlantic breeze.

"No."

"You never intended sailing anywhere?"

"No."

Nancy tried to look indignant and failed. Vere laughed and crossed the deck to where she sat. "Dearest Nancy, would you have come if I had said I was putting the *Rosslyn* under sail just for you?"

"Of course I wouldn't. I've never heard of anything so ridiculous."

He took her hand and kissed it, and the smile on his face was tender.

"Exactly. So subterfuge was necessary if I wanted your company for a little longer."

"There was a time when you couldn't bear my company," Nancy said with an answering smile. "The last time I was at Molesworth you avoided me like the plague."

"The last time you were at Molesworth you had an insufferable American husband in tow," Vere replied drily.

"My grandmother liked him. She said we could stay at Molesworth whenever we wanted."

"Grandmother was simply vastly relieved that her American grandson-in-law was an improvement on her American son-in-law."

"My mother's side of the family are snobs," Nancy said, sliding the unfinished letter into her writing case.

"Of course we are," Vere replied affably. "We're English."

Nancy laughed. "It was a pity grandmother died so soon after my marriage. Jack was very impressed with Molesworth. He would have liked to visit again."

"But not with the new incumbent as host?"

"Not when the new incumbent never invited him."

"I never invite anybody. I'm a recluse."

"You're a tease," Nancy said, laughing again. "I wish I understood you better."

"Dear Nancy, I'm an open book."

"You're not and you know it. Why did you attempt to renounce your peerage?"

He leaned back in his wicker chair, one leg across his knee, his face upturned to the sun, his eyes closed. "Because I wanted to sit in the Commons, not the Lords. I wanted to stand for Parliament, be elected and be a force to be reckoned with."

"And isn't Vere Winterton, Seventh Duke of Meldon, a force to be reckoned with?"

"No, merely a cipher."

Nancy looked across at him, a slight frown furrowing her brow. She didn't know her cousin well. The last few days was the longest she had ever spent in his company. When she and Jack had honeymooned in Europe and visited her mother's ancestral home, Vere had been openly hostile. With her grandmother's death there had been no further reason to visit Molesworth. On her subsequent trips to England she had always stayed at the Ritz and had never journeyed further than Cliveden. Vere had remained a mystery to her, which was a pity as she was finding him exceedingly likeable.

Sentimentality had seen to it that after her liner had berthed at Southampton and she had installed herself in her usual suite at the Ritz, she had made what almost felt like a pilgrimage, to Molesworth. Vere had asked her to stay, but Nancy had refused, explaining that she was only in England for a few days en route to Madeira. Vere had been delighted. It fell in perfectly with his plans. He was due to leave, at the end of the week, with a party aboard his sea-going yacht *Rosslyn*. Their destination was the Canaries. Madeira was literally on their way. In the short space of time between Nancy's acceptance and the *Rosslyn* sailing, the large party which was to have contained the Falconers, the Cassells, Lord and Lady Dunledin, and Lord Clathmar diminished almost daily in size. The Cassells were indisposed; the Falconers detained by an impending lawsuit; the press lord had business elsewhere and Lord and Lady Dunledin simply failed to arrive. Vere had been unconcerned. The *Rosslyn* was crewed and the *Rosslyn* sailed.

Looking across to where he sat, face upturned to the sun, a slight smile on his lips, Nancy felt sure that the *Rosslyn*'s intended party had been nothing but a figment of Vere's imagination. If she hadn't been journeying on to Madeira, Vere would never have sailed anywhere. If she was correct in her assumptions, then he had moved with remarkable speed. The *Rosslyn*'s food equalled that of the Ritz; and there was nothing to indicate that she had sailed in a hurry.

The sun was warm after the snows of New York and the cold and damp of London. Nancy adjusted her cardigan and wondered whether she should finish her letter to Verity. It wasn't a pleasurable task and she was quite relieved when Vere continued the conversation, saying idly:

"What is it you're running away from, Nancy?"

It was the first personal question he had asked her.

She said without any hesitation, "Nothing. I've spent the last few weeks facing up to things, not running away from them."

His eyes were a warm grey as he looked across at her. "Sure?"

"Positive."

"A pity. I was hoping for an exchange of confidences."

She couldn't tell if he was joking or not. "What sort of confidences?" she asked cautiously.

He shrugged. "Why you're travelling alone. Why your eyes are sad when you think no one is looking at you. Why I have never mentioned Clarissa's name."

"And why is that?"

"Because I can't remember the last time I saw her."

"I'm sorry."

"Don't be. She's in India at the moment. Before that it was Morocco."

Despite the lightness of his voice, the lines around his mouth had hardened slightly. He was a year older than her; three years older than Ramon. He was tall and elegant, his sleek blond hair and immaculate moustache reminiscent of an aristocratic Douglas Fairbanks. He had the inbuilt confidence of a man who came from a certain social class. His self-assurance held none of the sensuality that Ramon's did. At the thought of Ramon a knife turned in Nancy's heart. She hadn't looked at a newspaper since she had left Boston, in case it carried a picture of him. Imagining what he was doing, whom he was escorting, was torture enough: knowing for certain would be unendurable. She wondered for the hundredth time if going to Madeira was the right thing to do, and came up with the same answer. There was nowhere else for her to go: not Boston or Washington. Molesworth had never been a home to her and even Vere's welcoming presence couldn't turn it into one. The prospects of the Riviera chilled her. There would be too much false gaiety in the little enclaves at Cap Ferrat and at Cap d'Antibes. Too much Washington and New York gossip. She would not fit in. Her loneliness was too great.

Vere saw the stricken expression in her eyes and his well-shaped mouth tightened. She was suffering and she was not yet prepared to make a confidant of him. He wondered if her distress was caused by Verity's marriage. He said casually:

"A friend of mine in the Foreign Office has asked me to accompany him on a trip to Germany in May. He wants to visit the Saar. A plebiscite to decide its future is to take place later this year. We thought we'd like to have a look around generally: see what things are like for ourselves. Why don't you come with us?"

"No." Involuntarily she shivered and pulled her cardigan closer around her shoulders. If she visited Germany she might find it hard to hang on to her optimism for Verity's happiness in her adopted home.

Vere watched her closely and realized that though her daughter's German marriage was causing her disquiet, it was not the source of the pain that had clouded her eyes only moments previously. Which meant that it was a man. He had been a fool to have imagined that it could be anything else.

His hands clenched the arms of his chair and he forcibly relaxed and kept his voice light and amused as he recounted past stories of stays in Germany.

She had been the first woman he had suffered over. He had been eighteen and unbelievably gauche. She had been seventeen and had lit Molesworth with her radiance and gaiety. Even now he could remember the hatred he had felt for the smug, self-satisfied American who had been her husband. She had rendered him tongue-tied. Only in his imagination could he say the things to her that he wanted to say, and only in his imagination would she respond. He faltered in his anecdote about the Hotel Adlon in Berlin. The memory of his early imaginings were still vivid enough to send desire licking through him like a flame. He had been a fool then; inept and inarticulate. He was neither now.

He continued to recount stories of the Berlin of the '20s and marvelled at how little she had changed. Her soft, velvet-deep voice still had the same effect on his spinal cord. The fullness of her wide, mobile mouth still drew his eyes like a magnet. Her hair was no longer long; it was fashionably short, curling around her face and emphasizing the beauty of her eyes and cheekbones.

Clouds were beginning to scud across the sky and he rose to his feet. "It's getting too chilly out here. Let's go inside for a brandy."

As they descended the companionway his hand brushed hers. "Nancy . . ." His voice caught in the back of his throat.

Not understanding, she turned towards him, giving him a swift, half-smiling glance, her light elusive perfume filling the air between them.

He circled her waist with his hand restrainingly, and moved towards her, gathering her into his arms. Her smile faded and bewilderment and then panic chased through her eyes.

"No," she whispered, and then his mouth was on hers and he was kissing her with such tenderness that her initial protest died. His mouth was soft and warm and comforting. His body was solid and reassuring and the solace of being held was almost unbelievable.

As he raised his head from hers she said reluctantly, "I'm sorry, Vere. It's no good."

His arms remained around her. "Why not?" he asked gently. "Because of Jack?"

She shook her head.

"Because of someone else?"

She nodded.

He was silent for a minute, his finger tracing the line of her cheek and the sensuous curve of her mouth.

"Does he love you?"

She gave a crooked smile. "No. I don't think he knows what the word love means."

The *Rosslyn* rocked gently beneath them.

"Then forget him and learn to love someone who does."

Her smile was tremulous. "I wish I could, Vere. But I can't."

"We'll see," he said, and taking her arm he led her into the *Rosslyn*'s gold and Lalique glass bar.

Later that evening, as they ate lobster cardinale in a dining room large enough for a passenger liner, Vere said musingly:

"Why Madeira?"

"Because it's far enough away from America and England. Because it's familiar and because Zia Sanford is there."

It was nearly the whole truth.

He poured another glass of Veuve Cliquot and said, "I was there nearly a year ago. Last April. It's my favourite press lord's favourite place."

Nancy giggled. "Are you quite sure he shouldn't be aboard the *Rosslyn* now and on his way to the Canaries?"

"Not a chance. He's too busy bullying the government. Coalitions are pesky things."

Nancy had no desire to discuss politics. It always led back to Verity. "How long will you stay in Madeira?" she asked.

His hair shone silver in the lamplight. The grey eyes were sincere; the well-shaped mouth and chin were those of a man who could be trusted. They shared the same family background; the same grandmother. He was remarkably good-looking, a peer of the realm, and if her mother had been financially impoverished and obliged to marry an American, Vere Winterton had not been similarly embarrassed. There were very few men in the world who ran an ocean-going yacht of the size and luxury of the *Rosslyn*. He was perfectly cast for the role of a lover and Nancy felt a slow-burning rage at her inability to respond to him. Ramon, faithless and feckless, had bound her to him with bands of steel.

"Until you leave," he said quietly.

She felt a sweeping desolation. Would it be Vere's task to bring her body back to England? She had made no stipulation as to where she was to be buried. She hadn't cared. When she had made her will it hadn't seemed to affect anybody but herself. Now Vere was threatening to stay with her until the end and she had an obscene image of her coffin lying in state in the dining room in which they were eating.

"What's the matter?" he asked, as she shivered. "Is someone walking on your grave?"

"That's a silly expression," she said sharply and then forced a smile as he rose to his feet and fetched her evening stole.

As he draped it around her shoulders he kissed the

nape of her neck. She raised her hand to his, covering it, filled with an almost inexpressible sadness.

"I'm sorry," she said, and when she turned to kiss him goodnight it was a fraternal kiss on the cheek. "Goodnight, Vere."

For a second she thought that he was going to seize hold of her and kiss her mouth against her will, and knew that if he had a small part of her would have been glad. But Vere was not Ramon. Instead he brushed the back of her hand with his mouth and Nancy, remembering the hot imprint of Ramon's lips on her palm, blinked back tears as she closed the door of her cabin behind her and faced the darkness alone.

When Maria woke her with fresh fruit juice, the sun was streaming through the portholes.

"We're nearly there, madame," Maria said happily. "You can see the island already."

Half an hour later Nancy stood on the bridge with the *Rosslyn*'s captain and Vere and watched as they drew nearer and nearer to Madeira. First came the blue of the mountains as they rose sheer from the sea, and then the green of tropical vegetation and trees and the brilliance of bougainvillaea and mimosa and hibiscus. Even before the honeygold buildings of Funchal had taken shape, Nancy glimpsed the rose-red roofs of Sanfords standing high on the cliffs above the harbour.

"Lord Clanmar says it's the garden of Eden," Vere said, smiling down at her, "which proves newspapermen do have some romance in their hearts."

As the *Rosslyn* drew into the harbour the breeze was heavy with the scent of tamarisk, the hillsides above the town almost buried in African daisies and strelitzia.

"The Michaeljohns are here," Vere said, nodding in the direction of a gleaming seventy-foot sloop. "And the Carringtons. Are you sure you wouldn't prefer the Canaries? It would be quieter. Half of London spends

February here."

Nancy did not reply. From the moment Madeira had taken shape on the horizon her spirits had lifted. She knew now beyond any doubt that she had been right to follow her instincts. The docks were a bustle of colourfully dressed local men, immaculately uniformed crewmen and flower girls with giant baskets of blossom. Bullock carts piled high with fruit and vegetables creaked ponderously over the cobbles of the quayside. A crowd had collected as the *Rosslyn* berthed impressively, and petals were thrown as Nancy and Vere stepped ashore and into a gleaming open-topped Hispania-Suiza.

Maria, Vere's valet and the more personal items of luggage were deposited in a carriage drawn by a team of oxen, while straw-hatted men supervised the loading of Vere's innumerable calfskin suitcases into a fleet of bullock carts that had all too recently carried a load of bananas.

"You look happier already," Vere said, as they cruised up the steep hill to where Sanfords stood in imposing grandeur amidst a vast garden of flowers and palms.

"I am."

Ramon's name greeted her everywhere. It surmounted the bank; the shipping offices; the wine cellars. Only on the hotel was it absent and unnecessary. Sanfords was Sanfords. It had no need and was too exclusive to publish the fact.

"Welcome to Sanfords, Your Grace," the head porter said deferentially as a bevy of bellboys ran from the entrance to await the bullock carts and the baggage.

Nancy stepped into the chandeliered foyer and experienced an odd, almost ethereal sensation of having finally reached her spiritual home. Strange that it had never called to her before. When she had stayed with Jack it had simply been a beautiful and inimitable hotel. She had loved every minute she had spent in it but she had never craved to return. It was only since her meeting with Ramon and the complete destruction of her settled existence that she had yearned increasingly to be back.

"Sanfords" was emblazoned in gold on the bellboys' maroon uniforms, on the embossed stationery that graced marble-topped tables, and even engraved on the silver knobs of the doors. She wondered if she was the first person to have it engraved on her heart. Perhaps Zia did—for different reasons.

"Our suites of rooms are adjoining," Vere said, as they were escorted by a posse of staff into a caged lift. "We can wave to each other as we breakfast on our respective terraces. It will be more pleasant than my last stay. Lord Clanmar looks decidedly disagreeable before lunch."

"You don't," Nancy said, and meant it. In his superbly cut white silk suit with white fedora at a rakish angle over one eye, he looked exceedingly dashing. The grey of his eyes warmed and Nancy felt the colour rise in her cheeks. She had been unintentionally provocative and should have known better. Yet he did look handsome and she knew that the senses Ramon had stirred would never lie dormant again.

Her room was a vision that could only have been decorated by Oliver Messel. The bedroom was tented in white muslin and from the open windows she could see the whole sweep of the bay and the *Rosslyn* lying sleekly at anchor.

Maria, grateful to set foot on dry land again, ran a deeply-scented bath for her and was silently impressed at the solid gold taps and fittings. Her own room, instead of being secreted miles away along a draughty corridor, was adjoining Mrs. Cameron's and nearly as luxurious, with its personal rose-tinted bathroom en suite. Maria was more than happy with Mrs. Cameron's choice of destination. It made the travelling by sea almost worthwhile.

While Nancy bathed there was a discreet knock at the door and Maria answered it to a bellboy with an envelope resting on a silver salver. She thanked him politely and widened her eyes as he gave her a cheeky grin. The Duke of Meldon's valet had been even more forward and the exact position of his room from hers was very much in Maria's mind. She didn't want to have to complain to Mrs. Cameron, but neither did she want to continue the games of hide-and-seek that had taken place aboard the *Rosslyn.*

Nancy opened the envelope while still in her bath. It was from Zia and said simply: *Darling, meet me in my suite for before-lunch cocktails.* There was no mention of Vere. She rather hoped that he had not received a similar invitation. She wanted her reunion with Zia to be private.

She dressed in a pale pink dress by Vionnet, the neck gently cowled, the back plunging. She slipped on matching dyed sling-back shoes, rang for a bellboy and, as Maria sprayed her with perfume, mentally prepared herself to meet the woman who was both the love of her father's life and the mother of the man she loved.

Zia's mirrored rooms opened wide on to a lawn massed with fluttering white doves. It was not yet noon but the gown she wore was long and flowing; a cloud of silver-grey chiffon embroidered with an enormous sequinned butterfly. Her glorious hair was still a deep, burnished red and she wore it as she had always done, swept thickly upwards and dressed in a simple knot on top of her head. A choker of pearls centred with an enormous emerald clasped a still-lovely throat, and as she rose to greet Nancy she moved like a young girl, her head held high, her spine still supple. A light breeze caught her gown and the butterfly shimmered and danced as she opened her arms wide and said in a soft, warm voice:

"Nancy, how lovely to see you again."

She still smelt the same; heady and exotic like some jungle flower. They sat in a corner of the garden, beneath a jacaranda tree, on wicker chairs with enormous fanning backs that emphasized Zia's regality. There was champagne and orange juice and petits-fours for the birds.

"It's taken you a long time to come back," Zia said, holding out a narrow slender hand for a bird to perch upon. "Most people come back every year, like the handsome Duke of Meldon."

"Jack was never very European. He preferred Bar Harbor to the Riviera."

"And you?"

"I preferred my home at the Cape."

"And I prefer Madeira," Zia said with a smile. "I never leave. Dressmakers, designers, they all have to visit me here. Friends too, if they want to see me."

The birds fluttered away. "How is your father?" she asked, and in the thickly-lashed green eyes Nancy saw a reflection of her own longing.

"He wasn't very well when I left. He had a mild heart attack."

Zia sat very still.

"He returned home the day I sailed. I'm not worried about him. He has the constitution of an ox."

A smile hovered around Zia's mouth. "Yes. He is a very strong man."

"He asked me to give you his love."

"Thank you."

It was said with gratitude. In the light of the sun the web of tiny lines around her eyes and mouth were clear. She was no longer young, no longer even middle-aged, but her superb carriage had preserved the lines of her neck and throat and the bones of her face would be just as beautiful when she was ninety. Nancy suddenly felt sorry for her father—chasing after youth by marrying Gloria, when the love of his life retained a bloom and magic that Gloria could never hope to emulate.

She said, "You love him very much, don't you?"

"Yes." It was said simply. "And what of you, Nancy? Do you love?"

Coming from Zia it was a perfectly natural question.

"I have loved."

"But not the ambitious senator?"

"No. Not for a long time."

Zia did not waste words on sympathy. She had met many men like Jack Cameron. Smooth-talking, charming, ambitious men who loved easily and never deeply. Jack Cameron had never been worthy of the kind of love Zia instinctively knew Nancy capable of. A long time ago she had recognized in Nancy something of herself. Now, looking across at her, she felt a twinge of foreboding. If Nancy was capable of great love, she was also capable of great recklessness. Her Bostonian upbringing had disguised this facet of her personality, perhaps even to Nancy herself. Even Zia had wondered if her usually unerring instinct had been wrong as, from a distance, she had followed Nancy's marriage, the birth of Verity, the well-ordered trips to Paris and London, the flowering of a political hostess, always tactful, always discreet. The recklessness, if it existed, had been well-hidden. She hoped that when it showed itself it would not bring the same tragic consequences that her own behaviour had brought.

She said gently, "Is that why you have come to Madeira? To forget?"

Nancy shook her head of close-cropped glossy curls. "No. Forgetting isn't possible. But what I can do is learn to live for myself a little. He showed me that much at least."

Zia took a deep drink of her champagne. "Will living for yourself affect your position as a senator's wife?"

Nancy grinned impishly, her sloe-black eyes tilting at the corners. "I should imagine it will affect it quite a lot. I don't care. I've done everything I can for Jack for the last seventeen years. This year is for myself."

"Reliable sources tell me Jack has a very good chance of being nominated in the 1936 elections."

"Only if Roosevelt's New Deal policy collapses in ashes, and I don't think it's going to. I'm sure he will be elected for another term."

"But will that make any difference? Jack's ambitions will remain the same."

"Then he can pursue them, but I'm not going to sacrifice my life in order to help him." She rested her chin on her hand thoughtfully. "If I really felt that Jack would make a good president, then I might. But I'm his wife. I know him even better than his colleagues and advisors. I don't think Jack *will* make a good president. He isn't an original thinker like Roosevelt. He uses other people: their brains, their ideas. He's very competent and gives the impression of being brilliant. But he isn't. He's merely clever and I don't think that cleverness is enough of a qualification for the White House. So I don't feel any guilt if my leaving him destroys his chances. In fact, I feel quite patriotic."

"What about Chips?" Zia asked with amusement. "He's hardly likely to share your opinion."

"He doesn't." Nancy's eyes clouded at the memory of their hideous interview in the hospital room. She gave herself a physical shake. "But much as I love him, I can't live my life simply to please him. I've done that for too long."

"I would like to meet the man who has changed you from docility to such spirited rebellion. He must be quite remarkable."

"He is. He's also faithless, unscrupulous and unprincipled," and then she had the grace to blush as she remembered to whom she was speaking.

Zia's eyes sparkled. "My darling Nancy. With every word you make him even more irresistible." She twirled her crystal glass thoughtfully in her hands. "I hope your good intentions are firm. I have some news which might not be entirely welcome."

For an insane moment Nancy thought she was speaking of Ramon and that her secret was a secret no longer.

"Among yesterday's cables for reservations was one from Washington," Zia said.

Nancy stared at her. "Jack?" she asked incredulously.

Zia nodded.

"Is he coming alone?"

"I think so. I believe the reservation was only for him. And his secretary."

Nancy's face closed. "I take back what I said a minute ago," she said angrily. "He isn't even clever: just monumentally stupid and incredibly selfish," and to Zia's dismay she rose to her feet, kissed her hastily on the cheek, and walked quickly away, her eyes full of furious tears.

"Among our fellow guests," Vere said, leaning elegantly against the flower-decked rails of the balcony, "are Prince Nicholas Vasileyev, Count Szapary and his countess who can't be a day over seventeen, an exiled king who is theatrically insisting on being referred to as Mr. Blenheim, and the usual Park Lane set. It's really no different to being at Molesworth or Cliveden. The same people, the same gossip . . ."

"But not the same climate," Nancy said, stretching luxuriously on her lounger.

He grinned, water from his swim glinting his hair a pale gold.

"You're really quite a child of nature, aren't you? I bet you even swam at Hyannis."

"Every day, though the water is so cold it turns you blue, even in August."

"The Russians don't swim," Vere said, nodding over the balcony in the direction of the exiles who reclined at the side of the pool, draped with rugs and a hundred other conveniences, while their manservants stood at attention three yards behind them, resplendent in livery and white cotton gloves. "There must be fifty years' difference in the Szaparys' ages. She's still a mere child."

"Then she'll have a lifespan of at least five years as countess. Old Szapary tires of his wives once they've reached their twenties. The last one was discarded at twenty-one."

"What happened to her?"

"She went to London and seduced Lord Studley, which was rather unfair of her as he was still on his honeymoon. Then she dropped him, which she must have thought redressed the balance, and married a crooner in Los Angeles."

Vere wore a midnight-blue towelling robe over his swimming trunks. His legs were strong, his feet well-shaped. He lit a Dunhill and continued to survey the pool and gardens and the glittering expanse of jade and amethyst water that stretched to apparent infinity.

"Costos is here. His companion is Madeleine Mancini, the beauty who was to have married King Zog. Sir Maxwell Meade and his wife are here. Ever since he was attached to the Belgian court he's been hopelessly in love with the queen." He grinned. "A passion that is not reciprocated. Bobo is here, though not with her bandleader, thank God. Her new lover looks very Egyptian and very unsuitable."

"Bobo's lovers always are."

He laughed and sat down beside her, taking her hand

and trapping it between his. "So, apparently, are yours."

"My lover was singular, not plural."

His eyes held hers, the laughter dying, to be replaced by an emotion that quickened her pulse. She was wearing a swimming costume and for the first time was acutely aware of her near-nakedness. His eyes travelled to her lips, and then slowly downwards over her breasts and legs.

Despite herself, Nancy felt her body respond. He leaned towards her. "Then it's about time you took another," he said, and his hands were warm and strong on her shoulders as he drew her to him. "Life's short, Nancy."

She uttered a little cry and he stifled it with a long, deep kiss. She clung to him and he mistook her need, his hands moving downwards, cupping her breasts, his breath coming hot and hard.

She buried her hands in his hair, tugging his head away from hers, her violet-dark eyes helpless and despairing.

"I'm not in love with you, Vere."

His face was hardly recognizable. It was a mask of longing.

"I'm in love with you, Nancy. I've loved you since I was seventeen. I want you more than I've ever wanted anything in my life. Let me love you, Nancy. Please." He was kissing her neck, her throat.

Her voice was trembling. "I can't, Vere. Not without loving you."

His fingers dug deep into her shoulders. "I'll *make* you love me," he said fiercely.

"Oh Vere, I wish you could." It was a cry of such pain that it halted him.

"What did he do to you?" he asked wonderingly. She looked as young and vulnerable as the Russian countess.

"I thought he'd freed me," she said with a shaky smile. "But for what I'm no longer sure."

He kissed her forehead and rose to his feet. "Perhaps we can find out, given time."

She felt an overwhelming rush of tenderness for him. "Perhaps. You're very kind to me, Vere."

"I love you. I'm always kind to people I love." He was smiling again. "As there are so many old cronies here I'm holding a dinner party on the *Rosslyn* tonight. Prince Nicholas is gracing us with his presence. I'm not happy about the seating arrangements, though. Will our ex-monarch want to be seated as such, or as plain Mr. Blenheim? And if I invite Bobo, I'll be obliged to invite her Egyptian."

"It could get even more complicated in future. Jack is on his way here."

He paused, a glass in one hand and a bottle in the other. "For a reconciliation?"

"I doubt it. He's bringing his mistress with him."

Vere relaxed slightly. The Egyptian paled into insignificance. "Perhaps we'll have to seek sanctuary in the Canaries after all."

"I'm not going to be chased away by Jack. Or intimidated into going home," Nancy said spiritedly. "If he'd talked to me when I wanted him to, he could have saved himself a long trip."

"Perhaps he likes the sun," Vere said, handing her an iced Punt-es-Mes.

Her soft lips curved in a smile as she banished her ghosts and fears to a far recess of her mind.

"I think it's more likely that he wants a wife beside him on his official trips. I hadn't realized just how indispensable I was to Jack's career. There are evidently some things a mistress can't stand in for."

The telephone rang in the room behind them. There was a short pause and then Vere's valet coughed discreetly and stepped out on to the balcony. "Her Royal Highness, the Princess Louise, requests the pleasure of your company in Suite 206 for afternoon tea."

"Earl Grey and cucumber sandwiches," Vere said disrespectfully. "She's been a teetotaller ever since the prince fell into a vat of wine and drowned."

Nancy giggled, her dark shadows vanquished. "Which explains why her entourage carry hip flasks as though there was still prohibition." She swung her legs on to the ground and rose to her feet in one easy movement. "I think I'm going to follow Zia's example and relegate my fashionable clothes to the back of my wardrobe. I'm tired of looking sleek and streamlined. No more squared shoulders and skirts flapping inches above the ankle. I'm going to dress how I feel from now on."

"And how is that?" he asked, his grey eyes crinkling at the corners as he smiled across at her.

"Dreamy and romantic." To her surprise and his, she kissed him full on the lips before walking swiftly away into the privacy of her oyster-silk-lined bedroom.

"You realize you are crossing the point of no return by openly hostessing for Vere tonight?" Zia said as her Hispania-Suzia swept them down the curving coast road towards the harbour.

"Why? We're not lovers." Nancy wore a dress that would have prematurely aged Jack; a lilac-sequined, seductively clinging halter-neck that skimmed her breasts and plunged nearly to the base of her spine. Her skin was already taking on a soft honey tone from the sun, perfectly complementing her violet-dark eyes and the feathery cap of her hair.

"There were no other guests aboard the *Rosslyn*. Your suites are adjoining."

"We're cousins."

Zia shrugged and re-adjusted the inch-deep diamond bracelet on her wrist. "Half of Vere's guests are married to cousins. It's the only way they can continue to marry within their class. The Americans are just as bad. Lady Astor's famous four hundred hasn't changed that much. Poor Breda Farning was ostracized after she married her nice Scotsman. I'm very grateful for my North End upbringing. It gives me a sense of proportion so many of my friends lack."

Nancy smiled and leant back against the soft leather of her seat. She felt almost happy as they rounded the last of the bends and the *Rosslyn* came into view, glittering from stem to stern with gaily coloured fairylights. Far out in the darkness a sleek, ocean-going yacht was fast approaching Funchal Bay. Nancy barely noticed it.

She was dancing with Vere when the *Kezia* slid into harbour and Ramon strode angrily down the hastily-lowered gangplank.

Chapter Eight

Headlights flaring, Ramon recklessly drove his waiting Daimler up the dark and twisting road that led to the clifftops and the brilliant splendour of his hotel. The scurrying sense of excitement he generated in his impeccably-mannered staff was electric.

Guests strolling from the ballroom to the Palm Court caught a fleeting glimpse of him as he strode, iron-faced, towards the gilded lift that served his suite of rooms alone. The over-eager smiles of the ladies were quickly quashed as Ramon ignored their existence.

"Send Villiers to me immediately," he ordered as hurrying minions opened doors, silver-salvered trollies appeared instantaneously with a vast range of cold meats and exotic salads and fruits. A bath was run, towels warmed, champagne chilled. Anything and everything that he could possibly request was prepared with lightning speed.

Villiers, the secretary permanently based at Sanfords, entered the suite only seconds behind Ramon, pinstriped suit immaculate, silk handkerchief falling from his breast pocket, a carnation in his lapel. Four minutes previously he had been in bed, reading an Edgar Wallace novel. The liveried underlings disappeared silently and swiftly. Ramon threw his jacket onto a chair, loosened his tie, ignored the champagne and poured himself a Courvoisier.

"What suite is Mrs. Cameron occupying?" he shot at Villiers, as the Courvoisier was swallowed in a gulp and another quickly poured.

"The Garden Suite, sir."

"And adjoining?" His voice was like the crack of a whip.

"The Duke of Meldon. Prince Vasileyev is in Suite 204 and the Earl and Countess of Montcalm are in the Lilac Suite."

Ramon was not remotely interested in the prince or the earl.

"Did Mrs. Cameron arrive with the duke?"

"Yes, sir," Villiers said, concealing his alarm. Mr. Sanford's face was ashy-white, his eyes black hollows above gaunt cheekbones. He looked pale and haggard and most unwell.

"The Duke of Meldon arrived without his usual party, sir," Villiers offered. "There was only Mrs. Cameron, Mrs. Cameron's maid and the Duke's usual staff."

Ramon strode across to the heavy velvet drapes and pulled them back. Far below, the lights of Funchal glittered and the myriad coloured lights of the *Rosslyn* shimmered against the backdrop of the inky water.

"The duke is entertaining aboard his yacht, this evening," Villiers continued uncomfortably. "Prince Vasileyev is in attendance and Count and Countess Szapary and . . ."

Ramon cut him short. "And Mrs. Cameron?"

"Mrs. Cameron is also in attendance."

Villiers had known his employer for over twenty years. That his unusual behaviour was somehow caused by the Duke of Meldon and Mrs. Cameron was obvious. He said hesitantly:

"I believe Mrs. Cameron is the Duke of Meldon's cousin. I was told it was a family party, sir."

Ramon's eyes narrowed as he stared broodingly down at the distant harbour.

"Will that be all, sir?"

"Yes. Thank you, Villiers."

As the secretary departed, Ramon's hand was already reaching for the bottle of Courvoisier again. A family party. It was possible. Vere Winterton did not have the reputation of a womanizer. He was too passionately enthralled with his cool and self-contained duchess. Ramon wished him well of her. His tastes ran to women of flesh and blood; not marble statues. He picked up one of the telephones on his desk.

"Villiers?"

Villiers, who was once more esconsed under the sheets and about to discover the identity of the murderer, stifled a groan and said passionlessly, "Yes, sir?"

"The Duchess of Meldon. Whereabouts is she?"

Villiers was not secretary *extraordinaire* at Sanfords for nothing. The rich and the famous, the titled and the royal, all were, if they cared to know it, meticulously filed and indexed in Villiers' balding head: their likes and dislikes, foibles and eccentricities were as well known to him as they were to their loved ones. Their whereabouts too were of paramount importance to Villiers. If a regular client should suddenly abandon his yearly retreat to Sanfords for pastures new, Villiers had to be aware of it—and rectify it.

"Rajasathan," he said, with only a moment's hesitation. "A tiger-shoot with the Maharajah of Jathshur. I believe it is to be an extended trip. The polo in that country is excellent and I think the duchess is a keen horsewoman."

Ramon replaced the telephone and pondered darkly. Villiers allowed himself a sigh and returned to Edgar Wallace. The duchess' long absences from England had caused some speculation in the press. Discreet speculation, but speculation all the same. If all was not well with the Winterton marriage it was possible that Vere was at last beginning to look elsewhere for feminine comforts. On the other hand, what was more natural than that his cousin should be his guest? A muscle throbbed in his cheek. The bedding of cousins was hardly incestuous. It had been the norm in England for generations. It was a prime means of consolidating family wealth and land. His head pounded. He stripped off his clothes and showered, turning the cold jet on for a full minute after he had soaped his body. Why in God's name had she left as she had? Even more unfathomable, why was she here? Was she mad or was he?

The shower had revived him. It was nearly two in the morning but he dressed again. He had travelled thousands of miles to see her; it was not a meeting that would wait until morning.

He stepped out on to the verandah and stared down at the *Rosslyn*. Over the water the sound of music and laughter carried faintly: a band was playing Cole Porter's "Miss Otis Regrets". It changed to the dreamy, romantic "Night and Day" and he wondered whose arms she was in and resisted the urge to charge down and board the *Rosslyn* like an avenging fury. He was leaping to conclusions. She had been emotionally disturbed in New York and, despite the fierceness of their lovemaking, he had never succeeded in discovering the reason for her paralyzing distress on the day they had met. Something had happened between his leaving Hyannis and the day they were to have met in New York. He paced the room, unable to settle; the personification of his nickname. A panther without a leash.

Had Jack Cameron flown suddenly to Hyannis? Had there been a scene between husband and wife that he knew nothing about? He dismissed the idea immediately. The talkative Morris would have told him that when he had told him of Mrs. Cameron's destination. What else could have happened in the short interval between their passionate goodbyes and her mysterious flight?

Boston's mayor had suffered a heart attack. Ramon swore audibly. That might well have caused her to postpone her plans, but could not possibly be an explanation for her abrupt departure. The mere fact that she had left when Chips was only hours out of hospital was a further deepening of the mystery. It was out of character. He lit a black Sobraine, inhaled twice and crushed it out in an onyx ashtray. What did he know of her character? He barely knew her. A night in New York and an afternoon in Hyannis; was that enough to build a world on? He groaned and ran his fingers through his shock of dark hair. It had been enough to fall in love; they hadn't needed any more time—it had been instinctive, primeval. She was his and he was hers. The one without the other was incomplete. He wasn't a boy to be besotted by a pretty face; to be seduced by feminine wiles. He had seen her, he had wanted her and he had taken her . . . she was his.

Why then had she fled from him? For the whole day of their arranged reunion he had waited for her. First in joyous anticipation, then growing anxiety, then bewilderment. In the early hours of the following morning he had driven to Hyannis like a bat out of hell. The housekeeper had been terrified when he had thundered on the door, pushing past her, mounting the stairs two at a time, calling Nancy's name. The house, apart from its permanent staff, had been empty. Shakily Morris had informed him of the mayor's collapse and then, as Ramon had sprinted to his car, had called after him that Madame was not in Boston but had left for Europe—for Madeira.

He had felt as if he was in a bizarre dream from which he could not wake. The hospital authorities had informed him that the mayor was under nursing supervision at his Beacon Hill home. Seamus Flannery had mercifully deflected him from confronting Chips in person. The mayor's daughter had sailed aboard the *Mauretania.* The *Boston Courier* carried the same information; the shipping line confirmed it.

He had ignored the massive pile of correspondence in his New York apartment; Gloria's desperately scrawled letters were left unread. He had sailed on the *Bremen* for Southampton, shunning his fellow passengers and standing hour upon hour on the deck, smoking endlessly, his face an inscrutable mask that deterred any approaches. At Southampton the *Kezia* had been undergoing her annual overhaul and he had ordered her to sail immediately.

On the four day voyage south he had been consumed with the longing to see her again. She was at Sanfords and was waiting for him. A letter had gone astray, a message. God alone knew what had happened, but whatever it had been it had been a human error. Then he had arrived and she had been absent; wining and dining aboard Vere Winterton's yacht . . . aboard the yacht that she had arrived on. And Winterton's and her suite were adjoining. His restless dark eyes narrowed as he strode yet again on to the verandah and gazed down to where the *Rosslyn*'s party showed no signs of ending.

She had told him she had never had another lover. He had known that she had spoken the truth. Was it possible that once the barrier had been crossed she had rushed headlong from his arms into those of Winterton? Everything inside him cried out that it was impossible.

She was not another Gloria; another Princess Marinsky; another bored society beauty seeking fun and titillation when her husband's back was turned.

She was nakedly honest and she had brought him purity as well as passion. He breathed in the fragrant night air, and felt himself steady. He had been a fool, torturing himself unnecessarily. Travelling with Winterton had ensured that she reached Madeira in the fastest time possible and with the minimum of publicity. *The New York Times* had mentioned that Mrs. Cameron was a passenger aboard the *Mauretania*. There had been nothing more; none of the London papers had picked up the story. In Madeira both of them would be safe from the sort of gossip Nancy so disliked. Zia autocratically barred any society columnist or photographer from Sanfords, no matter how illustrious their name. It was one of the few havens in the world where the rich and royal could disport themselves without forever looking over their shoulders. If they chose to be indiscreet, only their equals would know. Sanfords' wild parties never made public headlines. Prime ministers could swim in the nude with impunity. Grand duchesses could drink till they tottered. No word would leak to the outside world.

He picked up a dripping bottle of Dom Perignon, wrapped it in a towel and, with a champagne glass in his other hand, walked out of his suite and along the deeply carpeted corridor and down the gilded staircase to the Garden Suite. A bellboy hurried in his wake and was speedily sent for the required key.

Ramon closed the door behind him, poured a glass of champagne and gazed around, a slight smile on his lips. Nancy's occupancy had lasted only hours, yet already the room bore the imprint of her presence. Verity's photograph smiled from an oval silver frame. Beside it, Chips O'Shaughnessy beamed broadly, a cigar wedged firmly between his teeth. There was no sign of a photograph of Jack Cameron or any other man. Ramon felt his certainty solidify. She was waiting for him. There could be no other reason for her presence. A slim volume of Eliabeth Barrett Browning's *Sonnets from the Portuguese* lay on her bedside table. He picked it up, holding it reverently because she had so recently held it. A silk, lavishly lace-trimmed nightdress lay in a pretty swirl on the bed. The delicately scented sheets were turned down and ready for occupancy. On the dressing table a simple beaded rosary lay entwined with beautifully matched pearls. The faint odour of her perfume clung around him and as he sat in a pearl-pink velvet giltwood armchair, he dimmed the lights. In the moonlight a Matisse on the far wall shimmered and danced. He was burning as he poured another glass of champagne and settled down to wait for her. The fire that hadn't been quenched since he had first taken her in his arms, began to rise and rage, consuming him until it was a physical pain. Soon, very soon, he would hold her again. He fastened his eyes on to the door and counted the minutes away.

"I have often wanted to make your acquaintance, but you hide away like a butterfly in a chrysalis," Prince Nicholas said, as he waltzed Nancy around the edge of the *Rosslyn*'s pool, the stars brilliant above them.

Nancy laughed. "I haven't hidden myself away at the Copley Plaza or the Waldorf."

The prince pulled a face. "The new world. I have no time for it. It has no grace; no elegance, like the city of my youth."

"St. Petersburg?" Nancy asked.

He nodded, his arm holding her lightly and securely as the music changed smoothly from a waltz to a tango.

"There have never been balls since to compete with the grandeur of those given by the dowager empress at the

Anitchkov Palace: no parties as scintillating as those of the Grand Duchess Marie Pavlovna: no magnificence like that of the Winter Palace: no thrill akin to that of riding down the Nevsky Prospect with a troop of Cossacks at your heels."

His eyes glinted. "Some day we will return and that world will live again. The Russia of our fathers and our grandfathers will be restored to us."

"Do you really believe that?"

Beneath his carefully trimmed beard and moustache, his grin was almost elated. "I *know* it," he said, and spun her round so breathlessly and with such panache that Bobo and Costas applauded loudly.

Vere smiled in their direction but the smile did not reach his eyes. Nicky was extremely attractive to women and ever since dinner he had given Nancy the full benefit of his charm. His American girlfriend had seemed unperturbed and had danced and flirted with all the men present, with the exception of Sir Maxwell. Sir Maxwell would have been quite game for a flirtation but Lavinia Meade gave him no opportunity. Vere turned his attention back to Nicky's girlfriend, who was leaning against the deck rail, a glass in one hand and her head thrown slightly back, pearly teeth gleaming as she laughed at one of Sonny's more outrageous remarks.

She was a descendant of Elizabeth Winthrop, one of the first women to settle in New England. Elizabeth Winthrop had been a rebel, shunning the Puritan code that ruled the lives of the early settlers—and suffering dearly for it in the process. Samantha Hedley had the same steel to her beauty that must have enabled her ancestor to endure the privations and hardships of seventeenth century American life. As he watched Nicky escort Nancy to the buffet where Lady Michaeljohn was still holding forth on the Prince of Wales' latest affair, he had the uncomfortable feeling that Nancy had made herself an enemy.

He moved across to them, hooking a proprietorial arm around Nancy's shoulders and feeling gratified at her easy acceptance of his gesture.

"How is dear Clarissa?" Lady Michaeljohn asked as he approached, and then hiccoughed loudly. Vere's champagne was always excellent and the stewards had topped her glass up regularly. Her husband's attempts to freeze her with a look from below his bushy eyebrows were wasted.

"She's keeping very well," Vere said smoothly. "She's in India, shooting."

"Tigers or elephants?" Lord Michaeljohn asked. "I was on a damned good tiger shoot last year. Got five of the beggars."

"Tigers," Vere said pleasantly, and taking Nancy in his arms he danced her to the far side of the deck, his hand caressing the satin-softness of her back as he drew her so close that his lips brushed her cheek.

Nancy had felt his tenseness at Lady Michaeljohn's questions. She would have liked to ask him more about Clarissa, but now was not the time or place. His lips were on her mouth and she did not pull away. She felt warm and relaxed: loving and alive. She wound her arms tightly around his neck and felt the spasm of his body as he pressed her to him. She needed to feel alive; to feel her blood running warmly through her veins. She had so much love in her and no one to give it to. Unless she gave it to Vere. Jack had no need of it. Ramon, leaving her bed within hours for that of her father's wife, even less. There was no passion in her for Vere, but there was tenderness and affection and liking.

"Let's go," he said huskily, and she mutely agreed.

The stewards continued to ply the guests with champagne and caviar, lobster and quail. The band continued to play and the host and his hostess slipped away. Vere's arm was around her shoulders, his mouth murmuring soft endearments in her ear as his chauffeur whisked them up the darkened roads to the softly-lit edifice of Sanfords.

As the night wind blew against her face, ruffling her hair, Nancy blinked back hot tears. She was with a man who loved her; who esteemed and respected her. A knife twisted in her heart with longing for a man who had felt none of those things. She had never understood what the words "sexual power" meant, but she did now. It was the power Ramon exercised over her, and always would. The power that made her forget pride and dignity. That would make her plead for just one touch, one kiss.

"I love you," Vere said, as he clasped her hand and led her down the rose-pink carpeted corridors to the splendour of the Garden Suite. Nancy, unable to speak for the tears that choked her throat, squeezed his hand silently and fought for control.

At the doorway he swept her up in his arms, carrying her across the threshhold as if she were his bride. She smiled and he was too intoxicated with his victory to see that it wavered tremulously at the corners of her mouth.

"I dreamed of this, when I was a boy at Molesworth. When you were a bride and scarcely aware of my existence."

"I'm aware now," she said softly.

At the edge of the bed he set her gently on her feet. She stood passively, her face upturned and he showered it with kisses and then slipped the slender sequined straps off her shoulders and allowed the clinging, shimmering material to slide into a glittering pool on the floor.

"God in heaven, but you're beautiful," Vere Winterton said reverently as she stood in the full glory of her nakedness before him.

"And virtually untouched by human hand," a throbbing voice said from the corner of the room.

Nancy screamed. Vere shouted and dived for the light switch. The room flooded with cruel light and Ramon remained seated in the deeply winged chair, a champagne glass in one hand, a Sobraine in the other. His voice was studiedly insolent. Only his eyes were out of control, glazed with an almost maniacal anger.

"Or that is what she told me and what I so gullibly believed," he continued, leisurely stubbing out his cigarette and draining the contents of his glass. He rose to his feet and smiled across to where Nancy stood, rooted to the spot and spinning into regions of nightmare, her nakedness exposed so that she felt like a whore of Babylon; a weight on her chest so crushing that she could not move, could not speak.

"It convinced me and I'm not a man to easily believe a woman's lies, however practised the liar."

"No!" It was a strangled sob. She had to move, had to reach him.

Indolently his dark eyes travelled from her face, moving slowly, almost lazily, over her rose-red nipples to the tight curly mass of her pubic hair. His mouth was a tight line of pain; his eyes those of a man who has seen an inner hell.

"Have fun," he said carelessly and slammed the door shut behind him.

Vere yanked at the handle, cursing incoherently. Nancy threw herself at him, dragging on his arms.

"No! Please! Oh God, no!"

"I'll kill him!" Vere was trying to fend off Nancy's restraining hold as she flung herself against the door, pressing her back against it, her eyes those of a madwoman.

"No! No! Let him go! Oh please God, let him go!"

She was shaking convulsively, her face drained of blood, her eyes two dark pits in her whitened face. He was here. He had come to her room. He had been waiting for her and she had entered with another man. She had stood naked in front of him, her arms around his neck, her face receptive to his kisses.

"Oh Jesus God," she moaned, sliding on to her knees. "Let me die. Now. Before morning. Before I have to face him again."

Vere abandoned his intention of going after Sanford. He covered her with a negligée and stumbled into the bathroom for aspirin, sleeping tablets, anything. The shock to his system had robbed him of his usual *savoir faire.* Nancy's distress was so extreme that it frightened him. He wished fervently that he had stayed aboard his yacht with his guests. He came back into the room with a glass of water and two sleeping tablets.

"Take these," he said, physically raising her to her feet and putting her to bed.

Obediently she swallowed them. He had the unnerving sensation that she was completely unaware of him. Her reputation: he'd been a fool not to realize what it meant to her. Despite her flippant remarks, she was destined one day to be the First Lady of America. Even at this moment her husband was on his way here.

She lay still and quiet. She no longer needed him.

Much later, his nerves restored by several whiskies, it occurred to him to wonder what Ramon Sanford had been doing in Nancy's room at three o'clock in the morning. It was a thought that robbed him of sleep for the rest of the night.

Shame and humiliation swept over Nancy in drowning waves. Till the day she died she would remember the way he had looked at her—the contempt in his eyes. Eventually the sleeping tablets induced a kind of stupor and she lay staring at the ceiling as the room began to pale eerily with the first light of dawn. As morning broke anger began to take the place of shame.

Her behaviour was none of his affair. He had had no right to be in her room; no right to judge her morals. She wondered bitterly whose bed he had just left before making his night-time visit; whose bed he had returned to. As her father had pointed out, Ramon Sanford was no once-a-day man.

He had visited Sanfords and found her there and no doubt assumed he could entertain himself with her as he had done previously. Her head pounded and she wondered if aspirin on top of sleeping tablets would be harmful. She decided she didn't care and went into the bathroom to find the pills.

His presence here was perfectly natural. After all, it was his hotel. He had told her that Madeira was out of limits until he married. She had been a fool to have believed anything he said. Unless a Mrs. Sanford or prospective Mrs. Sanford was accompanying him. Bile rose in her throat and she shuddered, gulping down iced water. Leaving a bride for a sortie into an ex-lover's room would be normal behaviour for a man who thought nothing of making love to a woman and her stepmother in the same twenty-four hours. If Verity hadn't been in Germany he would probably have made love to her as well. A sexual hat-trick to enliven his jaded palate.

Her anger gave her back her self-respect. She was thirty-five years old. If she wished to take a lover it was none of Ramon Sanford's business. The only drawback to this sensible thinking was that she had no real desire to take Vere as a lover at all. Or anyone else: only Ramon.

"Damn him," she said to her reflection in the mirror. "Damn him. Damn him. Damn him."

She had breakfast in bed and when Maria entered to dress her there were blue, weary hollows beneath her eyes. Maria's pretty little face tightened. Mrs. Cameron's world had turned upside down this last month and she would have given a lot to know the reason why. She was having her own troubles as well. The English valet who attended the duke seemed to think she was there for his convenience. He had trapped her outside the ironing room when she had been pressing one of Mrs. Cameron's cocktail dresses and this time sharp words and a box on his ears hadn't been enough to deter him. He had pinned her against the wall, forcing greedy, hungry kisses on her, oblivious of Maria's struggles and the precious dress crushed between them. He had been removed by a strong brown hand gripping his collar and nearly choking him. Then, as he struggled for air, a hefty kick in the seat of his pants had sent him stumbling ignominiously down the corridor.

"Thank you." Maria scrambled on the floor for the dress, overcome with confusion. Her rescuer was tall and lithe and his dark good looks reminded Maria of Mr. Sanford.

Luis Chavez shrugged and smiled. As swimming coach he usually exerted his not-inconsiderable charms on the female guests. Especially the older ones. They were so much more appreciative. He regarded maids as social inferiors. However, this one was remarkably pretty and there was a fire lurking in the depths of her honey-gold eyes that stimulated him.

"Any time," he said easily, and smiled the devastating smile that had rendered duchesses helpless. "I'm Luis Chavez, the swimming coach." His manner inferred that the title should automatically impress.

"Maria Saldhana," Maria said, recovering her composure and deciding that her rescuer had rather a high opinion of himself. "Mrs. Cameron's personal maid."

Luis' dark eyebrows rose slightly in recognition. News of the dusky beauty accompanying Mrs. Cameron had spread quickly along the hotel grapevine. He wondered if he had five minutes to spare in the pursuit of pleasure, and decided he had not. Viscountess Lothermere was waiting for him, and though she had so far shown not the slightest interest in flirting with her coach, Luis was impressed by her figure as well as her fortune and was determined to exert himself to the utmost.

Maria, well aware of some, though not all of Luis' thoughts, smoothed down Mrs. Cameron's dress and, with another polite "thank you", walked away. He frowned as he watched her neat bottom sway towards the service stairs. *He* was supposed to have left *her* hoping the conversation would be continued. She had successfully given the impression that the reverse was true and that he, Luis Chavez, had been hanging around in the hope of deepening the acquaintance. He determined to treat her with cool indifference in the future until she had learned her lesson.

Maria, busying herself with Mrs. Cameron's toilette, found herself thinking more and more of the handsome Portuguese. He had far too high an opinion of himself. He was blatantly conceited. The gold chains around his neck, the carefully slicked hair, showed a vanity equal to that of a woman. Yet he was undeniably handsome. Portuguese men, Maria decided as she buffed Nancy's nails to a pearly sheen, were decidedly sexy. Backstairs gossip had already informed her that Mr. Sanford had arrived the previous evening and she wondered if that accounted for the lines of strain on Mrs. Cameron's face and if so, why? *She* was not going to be hurt by a man. Luis Chavez had the air of a man who found conquests easy. He would not find her so. But she would enjoy watching him try.

Nancy had breakfasted in bed. Thanks to a deep, hot bath and Maria's careful ministrations, when she emerged in public she looked as glossily chic and poised as normal. Vere was breakfasting on his terrace, clad in a silk dressing-gown, when Nancy strolled out to join him.

She had decided that the sooner she faced him again, the better.

He rose hastily to his feet, dropping his napkin on the table as Nancy sat down opposite him, a smile on her face, dark glasses shielding her eyes from the morning sun and hiding the ravages of the previous night.

"My God, wasn't last night a fiasco?" Her laugh was brittle but her manner was perfectly composed. She let her hands hang elegantly over the arms of her chair and turned her face to the sun as if she hadn't a care in the world. "That fool Sanford took me completely by surprise. No wonder I had hysterics. I thought he was a member of Jack's rather extensive spy network."

Vere's waiter poured coffee and Nancy sipped it, crossing her legs seductively, one sandalled foot tapping lightly on the mosaic-tiled floor.

"It really isn't worth saying anything to him, Vere. He must have been drunk to have entered my room like that and spoken as he did. Or mad. I believe his father was mentally unstable."

Vere felt an overpowering sense of relief. Nancy was right. Sanford had been drunk. He was a man who could drink a whole room under the table and still seem no worse for wear. Though he had been outwardly sober the previous night, he must have been smashed out of his mind.

"I wonder whose room he thought he was in," Nancy said idly. "No doubt the lady will have some explaining to do this morning."

Vere laughed. Ramon Sanford's amorous exploits were legion and the room had been lit only by shafts of moonlight. The wrong room; the wrong lady. The embarrassment was Sanford's, not his. "Good Lord, yes," he said, buttering his toast with zest. "Bobo's near you, isn't she? They were on more than friendly terms at one time."

"Then if she appears this morning with a black eye, we'll know the reason," Nancy said lightly. "I'm going down for a swim. I'll see you later."

Vere watched her go with a return of his usual sense of well-being. She hadn't demanded that he satisfy her honour. There was no need even to mention the incident to Sanford unless he mentioned it first. And he wouldn't do that unless it was to apologize. When Sir Maxwell cornered him for an early morning chat on the decreasing number of game on his Scottish estates, Vere for once listened to him attentively.

Nancy had no desire for a swim. She had faced Vere, placed the ideas she wanted in his head, and was now intent only on escape. Bobo and Ramon. She hadn't known about it but it came as no surprise. She wondered if Ramon had also enjoyed passing *affaires* with Madeleine Mancini and Venetia Bessbrook. It was probably harder to find a woman he hadn't had a liaison with than one he had. And he had had the nerve to call *her* immoral!

A white-suited boy hurried to place a lounger in the exact position she required. Another lay thick, inch-soft towels upon it, placing a cushion at exactly the right angle for her head, bringing a portable table complete with miniature bar and bucket, chilling the ubiquitous bottle of champagne.

Georgina Montcalm strolled past, her long legs attracting every eye. As she approached Nancy she paused and smiled in recognition.

"Nancy! How divine. I had no idea you were here."

Nancy viewed her with relief. She had no desire for Bobo's company—or that of anybody else who had been present at the previous night's party.

"Who are you with, darling?"

"Vere."

Georgina Montcalm sat on the edge of Nancy's

lounger. "How super. One of my favourite men. Charles told me the *Rosslyn* was in harbour." She laughed prettily. "I'm so short-sighted I wouldn't be able to tell if the *Queen Mary* was in dock. It never occurred to me that you would be with him. I didn't think the American and the British sides of your family were very close."

Nancy managed a genuine grin. "They're not. If my father arrived I'm pretty sure Vere would have an urgent need to set sail. He's rather more than Vere can take."

"He's a darling," Georgina said. "I absolutely adore him. I'm surprised that Jack is taking time off at the moment. I thought he was playing the indispensable aide to your fascinating president."

Nancy was beginning to feel that the world had righted on its axis. Georgina Montcalm had a natural spontaneity lacking in many of her class. In anyone else it would have caused criticism. Georgina Montcalm was above criticism. Earl Montcalm was within feasible distance of the throne and it said much for Georgina's background that she had been judged an entirely worthy match for him. Her grandfather on her mother's side was the millionaire financier, Sir Albert Loessel, who had been a friend of King Edward VII and who had been privileged to give much sensible advice to both his monarch and government. Her father was a much-respected minister and through him Georgina was descended from the Seventh Earl of Narnesbury, the famous nineteenth century eccentric. Georgina had inherited beauty, brains, wealth and a healthy dash of her ancestor's disregard for convention.

"Jack's not with me, though I'm expecting him any time."

"Enjoy yourself while you may, then," Georgina said, shaking her pale golden hair over her shoulders. "Once he comes it will be nothing but FDR, the New Deal and fighting recession. Charles is just as bad. He talks about nothing but the navy. He's commanding the HMS *Defiant* now and I think he's more in love with that damned ship than he is with me. He's also becoming a boring prophet of gloom where Europe is concerned. He hates Lansbury's pacifist policies."

"Hardly surprising when he's the captain of a destroyer," Nancy said drily. A pool boy had efficiently rolled a lounger alongside Nancy's and Georgina reclined luxuriously, raising her hand the merest fraction to indicate that she wanted her champagne opened. It fizzed and frothed and she sipped it.

"I don't eat now, or drink spirits. Only champagne. It's Zia's latest recommended diet and it works wonders, darling. I've lost simply pounds."

They laughed and talked and Nancy refused to allow her eyes to roam the surrounding gardens in the fearful dread of seeing Ramon. Instead she watched as Luis helped perfect Viscountess Lothermere's already excellent front crawl and then, with a great deal of unnecessary bodily contact, attempted to show a middle-aged steel magnate's wife the intricacies of the breast stroke.

"A subject he's an expert on, darling," Georgina said, shaking her beautiful head at the follies of her sex. "Cora van de Gale was here two weeks ago and she absolutely monopolized him. She didn't learn to swim but she learnt plenty of other things that old van de Gale had never taught her. At fifty you'd think she would have lost interest. The day I have to shower gifts on my lovers in order to ensure their attention is the day I shall take a vow of celibacy."

"I didn't know you had lovers," Nancy said, teasingly.

"I don't," Georgina replied with equanimity. "It would shock HM terribly. I do believe our much-loved king has never strayed from the straight and narrow in his life." A smile curved her lips. "I doubt if his successor will be so strong-willed. No doubt that Michaeljohn woman has already told you that Wallis Simpson is keeping the prince company while Thelma is in New York."

"She has mentioned it," Nancy said. Georgina never gossiped about the royals. She would affectionately refer to King George V as "HM", but though she was in the very best position to know exactly who was enjoying the Prince of Wales' attentions, she kept the knowledge to herself. "She couldn't have done a more thorough job if she had a megaphone. That woman missed her vocation in life; she should have been a town crier."

"You sound as if it bothers you."

"It bothers Charles. HM is not in very good health and the Prince of Wales will soon be king. It's natural to hope he will marry and cease his pointless entanglements with married American women. No offence meant, Nancy, but an American on the throne of England? What would Queen Victoria have said?"

They swam a leisurely few lengths in the Olympic-size pool and then Nancy returned to her suite through gardens ablaze with Abyssinia red-hot pokers and riotous bougainvillaea. As she emerged from the shade of a tamarisk tree into the secluded entrance that led to her Garden Suite, Ramon stepped forward, his eyes as hard as flints.

She cried out, instinctively stepping backwards. His hand shot out, seizing her wrist so hard she thought it would snap.

"What game are you playing, Nancy?" The harshness in his voice made her wince.

"No game," she said, her breath coming in panting gasps. "At least not the sort of games that you play." She could feel her pulse pounding beneath the cruel imprint of his thumb. Her nerves were throbbing. In one move she could be in his arms, pressed close against the strong body that tormented her, waking and sleeping. She thought of Gloria with her bleached hair and carmine-painted lips; of her father propped against the hospital pillows, his pride shattered at his wife's adultery. She wanted to hurt him as she had never wanted to hurt another human being in her life.

"My game is to enjoy myself with my lover. Preferably *à deux* and not *à trois*."

If she had stabbed him in the chest, his shock could not have been more palpable.

"Goddamn you to hell!" he said, and the weight of his hand caught her full across the face.

She screamed, tasting blood and blinded by pain.

There was no sound. His furious footsteps echoed distantly on the tiled floors. In the tamarisk tree a small bird fluttered, the sun glinting on brilliant wings. She lay huddled against the wall, her hands to her mouth, blood seeping from her cut lip through her fingers. In the tree the bird sang mockingly; from the poolside came the sound of distant laughter. Scarlet drops of blood spattered on to the ground. Like father, like son: blood, violence, destruction. After an endless age she forced herself to move, and with stumbling foosteps sought the sanctuary of her room.

Chapter Nine

Ramon was like a man possessed. Never before had he struck a woman. He wanted to kill her; to crush the life out of her. For a brief while he had believed he had discovered the simple, natural joy of giving complete love to another human being . . . and having that love returned. Now he saw it had all been a mirage. She was no different from the hundreds of women who had gone before her: shallow, soft-tongued and lying. Strumpets who would be called such if it wasn't for the accident of their birth. He had thought he had found his twin soul. The person who would make him complete. The other half of himself that he had been restlessly questing after for lonely years. He laughed harshly. He had found nothing. Only a bored wife with a disposition for play-acting and hysterics.

His fury could find no release. He marched through the glittering lobbies like a demonic arch-angel, guests and staff alike scattering before him. The screech of his car tires as he sped at breakneck speed down the curving driveway could be heard in Zia's secluded garden. She paused in her conversation with Earl Montcalm, a slight frown puckering her brow.

Ramon's eyes were glazed, his face contorted as he screamed suicidally down the narrow, cobbled streets. Flower sellers grabbed their baskets out of his way; pedestrians scurried for their lives. At the harbour he sprang out of the car and, without a word of civility to the *Kezia*'s crew, jumped into his speedboat. He raced out of the harbour, a danger to every piece of shipping at dock, entering or leaving.

From the terraces at Sanfords guests halted in their afternoon strolls to stare seawards where the white foaming line knifed the bay.

Zia excused herself from the tea table spread beneath the jacaranda tree and walked quickly across to the point where her garden fell in steep escarpments to the sea. The speedboat was being pushed to the utmost, flying across the water towards the mountainous cliffs at the far side of the bay. Zia's hands clutched her heart as Ramon, to all intents and purposes, attempted to kill himself. All around Funchal shopkeepers, housewives, fishermen, halted in their daily tasks and stared seawards. The *Kezia*'s crew lined the deck. The hotel guests crowded the balconies with binoculars. As the point of no return was reached, there was a concerted intake of breath. Zia faltered, and the earl ran to her, supporting her with his arm. The foaming line of spray veered, so close to the rust-red cliffs that for a moment several of the men thought it had merely bounced off. Bobo and Lady Michaeljohn turned away; Madeleine Mancini watched with overly bright eyes, a small pink tongue licking her lips.

The gasp of relief was audible as the speedboat headed towards the open sea, faster and faster so that it hurt the eye to follow the flashing line of spray. "Young fool," the earl said savagely. "He'll blow himself up. He should be arrested. Who the devil is he?"

"My son," Zia said faintly. "Send the maid for a brandy, Charles. I feel most awfully ill."

The speedboat streaked to the far horizon and then, as the spectators began to turn away, there were fresh cries of "He's coming back!" "Just look at him go!"

The boat swooped and leapt over the water, heading straight for the harbour at the same maniacal speed it had the cliffside. There was a scramble to shore from the anchored boats. Like a meteor, Ramon careered towards the other shipping. Captains closed their eyes and thought of insurance. Madeirans prayed for their fishing boats and their livelihoods.

Zia grasped the earl's arm tightly, her lips moving soundlessly.

When a collision seemed unavoidable he swerved in a cloud of spray, the boat scarcely touching the water, his dark, distinctive figure unmistakable. The veer was too great, the strain unsupportable. There was the blast of an engine, the rifle crack of splitting wood, great jets of foam and then nothing; only a lathering surf, floating wood and ominous silence. Zia cried out his name and fainted, old and shrunken in the earl's arms. The officers in the *Kezia* were already in a launch speeding to the wreckage at breakneck speed. Crowds had gathered at the harbour; the abandoned fishing boats were quickly manned, scudding in the wake of the launch. On the hotel terraces pandemonium had broken out. Several guests forgot their dignity and raced for their Daimlers and Lagondas, dispensing with their chauffeurs in their haste to reach the harbour. Others gave hysterical reports as they fixed their binoculars on the racing rescue ships and the swirling wreckage. Countess Szapary was sobbing uncontrollably. Bobo was semi-conscious. Lavinia Meade beat her massive chest with her hands and told all and sundry she had known he would come to a bad end. Venetia Bessbrook watched from her balcony, her face white and her hands clasped tightly together. Sonny Zakar was wishing he'd had his camera at the ready and disliking himself intensely for the thought. Georgina Montcalm was hurrying towards Zia's apartments to be of practical help. Nancy was oblivious, locked in a darkened room, an ice-pack on her cheek: desolation in her heart.

From the *Kezia*'s crew came a whoop of joy as a tousled head swam strongly towards them. First officer Henderson swallowed the lump in his throat, forced himself not to cry out with relief and said with the nonchalance he knew his employer would approve of, "A tidy smash, sir."

"Not bad," Ramon admitted, grinning as they pulled him aboard, his silk shirt ripped at the shoulder, blood oozing from a cut, the flimsy material clinging transparently to his skin. His knuckles were raw and bleeding and there was a deep gash slicing his cheekbone. He was superbly unconcerned about the wreckage that floated around them and the hundreds of bystanders standing on the shoreline, the sun glinting on the lenses of their binoculars.

"Malcolm Campbell wouldn't have thought much of it, would he?" he said, and with a careless grin accepted a handkerchief to staunch the blood spurting from his cheek and allowed Second Lieutenant Fitzsimmons to hold a rapidly staining scarlet pad against his shoulder.

"Bloody suicidal," Lord Michaeljohn said, reviving himself with a whisky and soda. Lady Michaeljohn fanned her face and sent her maid for aspirin and a bottle of the dark mysterious liquid that accompanied her everywhere and was resorted to in times of stress.

"Ria Doltrice says he has a death wish. I never usually take any notice of that silly woman—she so often gets her facts wrong. She said John Jacob Astor was going to marry Carol Lombard on the sixth of the month and he married that pretty little Eileen Gillespie. Besides, Carol Lombard has two husbands already, doesn't she? Or is that impossible? Really, the shock has made me quite confused."

Sonny lit a cigar and returned to his sun lounger and the Michaeljohns. "Ria may be right," he said. "There was that Himalayan trip. I wanted to film *Mountain of Death* there, but the unions wouldn't allow it. Believe me, those mountains aren't toys. They're for real."

"Isn't that where Clarissa is, Vere?"

Vere had viewed the whole proceedings passive-faced. He turned now from watching Ramon being hauled aboard the *Kezia* and said, "No. Clarissa is only interested in hunting and riding. Mountaineering isn't yet one of her enthusiasms."

"She'd make an awfully good mountaineer," Lady Michaeljohn said loyally. Such courage and physical fitness."

"And beauty," Sonny added. "You're a lucky man, Vere."

Vere smiled thinly.

Lady Michaeljohn's maid returned with the preparation that the Knightsbridge chemist made especially and after helping herself liberally she returned to the topic that was so intriguing her. "Do you remember his Amazon expedition? When was that? Last year or the year before? I know it upset dear Zia terribly. *Why* can't he settle down and marry some nice girl. Princess Marinsky is really very sweet. Foreign, of course, but then so is he. One tends to forget with him being Eton and Oxford. Poor, poor Zia. What a trial he must be." She turned confidingly to Sonny. "My son married last April. Such a darling girl. One of the Clarendons, you know. The *Wiltshire* Clarendons."

Sonny puffed on his cigar, unimpressed. He had met

the faggot in question and felt tolerably sorry for the horse-faced bride.

"Thank the Lord the Doltrice woman wasn't here to view this afternoon's exhibition," Lord Michaeljohn said with a shudder. "She'd have made a bigger meal of it than she did the Rudy Vallee divorce."

Lady Michaeljohn's attention was caught. She grasped hold of the escaping Sonny and said pleadingly, "Now, you're a man of the film world, Mr. Zakar. *You* will know the truth of the Vallee divorce. Were the things the columnists said really true?"

Sonny had no intention of providing titillation for Sophronia Michaeljohn. What the woman needed were the services of a swimming coach. He decided he'd drop a word in the guy's ear and do both him and Lady Michaeljohn a favour. Sonny had watched Luis with admiration. His style had rivetted the American. He had the old girls simply panting for his favours. Sonny wondered how he'd shape up in a screen test. It was just possible that he had found a rival to Clark Gable. "Madeleine is waiting," he said, escaping from the clawing hand. "I think the accident has distressed her." It was a blatant lie as Sonny knew all too well. The sight of blood never distressed Madeleine. Not as long as it wasn't her own.

When Ramon had surfaced, whole and relatively unhurt, she had lost interest in the drama and her sultry eyes had fastened on Bobo's Egyptian. Eastern men knew tricks that Europeans didn't: or so she had been told. The exception being Ramon Sanford who, it was rumoured, had been sent to Cairo by his father to learn the love techniques and philosophy of Imsàk, with that other legendary lover, Prince Aly Khan.

Ramon Sanford was definitely a dish to be savoured. Unfortunately, he had proved unobtainable in the past, preferring to do the chasing rather than be chased.

Madeleine had a plan of campaign for the seduction of Mr. Ramon Sanford. It was one that would take time. Meanwhile Bobo's lover would make an interesting diversion.

Vere turned abruptly from Lady Michaeljohn's inane chatter and walked quickly towards Nancy's suite. All around him guests buzzed with the foolhardiness of Ramon's exploit. He had been disturbed by his own lack of emotion. He had watched at first with mild interest, not knowing who was behind the wheel of the zooming speedboat. When he had seen Ramon's tall, swarthy figure, he had felt a terrible stillness take control of him. He had watched Sanford speed like a tornado towards the cliffs and he had felt no emotion. If contact had been made, if Sanford's body had floated in disjointed smithereens, he would simply have felt a measure of relief. An awkward social situation would have been resolved. A man would have died and he, Vere Winterton, would have been unmoved. He shrugged. Why should he have been? The man was no friend of his: barely an acquaintance. Any doubts he had entertained concerning Ramon's stability after the previous evening were now confirmed. His only anxiety was for Nancy. She had suffered enough shocks in the past twenty-fours without suffering more.

At Vere's knock Maria answered the door, her face strained.

"Mrs. Cameron is not well, sir. She has suffered a fall . . ." Maria was about to tell him that Mrs. Cameron had requested no visitors for at least twenty-four hours but Vere had marched swiftly past her, leaving Maria to run anxiously in his wake, uttering protests that were ignored.

"My poor darling, are you all right? Why didn't the maid tell me? Has the doctor been?" The last thing Nancy wanted was Vere's ministrations. She shook her head.

"There's no need for the doctor. I slipped, that's all. My mouth is cut a little but it looks far worse than it is." She managed a reassuring laugh. "Please, Vere. There's no need to look so concerned. I simply wanted to rest, that's all."

Relieved, Vere sat on the small gilt chair at her bedside and took her hand in his. "It's perhaps a good thing you did. You must be the only person in Funchal to have avoided witnessing the debacle this afternoon."

"What debacle?" Nancy forced an element of interest into her voice. Had Madeleine lost the top or bottom half of her swimming costume? Had Lavinia Meade become publicly drunk? Had Bobo's Egyptian committed an unforgivable indiscretion?

"Sanford," Vere said with grim satisfaction. "A more blatant piece of exhibitionism I've never seen. The man's obviously unhinged. He could have mown down scores of small boats and killed countless people."

"What did he do?" Nancy forced the words through stiff lips, her heart pounding.

Vere laughed mirthlessly. "Acted like an overgrown schoolboy. Knowing he had an audience, he raced his speedboat at breakneck speed towards the cliffs. His reputation as a speed merchant has gone to his head. There was no sense or responsibility in his action at all. He missed by a hair's breadth and headed out to sea, then rocketed shorewards like a maniac."

"And?" Nancy thought she had tasted fear on her long walk through the Manhattan streets. She had, but she had not plumbed its depth. The seconds between her question and Vere's indifferent answer seemed agonizing light years.

"The whole boat went up like a miniature bomb."

Nancy cried out, springing from the bed, prepared to run to him as she was, barefoot and in her slip, her face still swollen from his brutal blow.

Vere leaped after her. "Steady on, sweetheart. I'm

sorry I shocked you like that. There was no damage done—except to the boat. Sanford came up smelling like roses and no doubt well pleased at having scared half the population out of their wits."

"He isn't hurt?" She was shaking uncontrollably.

"Not significantly." Vere wasn't certain of the truth of this last statement, but did not greatly care. As far as he was concerned, Sanford deserved all he got. "The Montcalms are having a small party this evening. It should be fun. No Michaeljohn or Meades."

She had herself under iron control. She smiled. "I couldn't, Vere. Not with my face all puffed up. I'm going to have an early night for once."

Vere was disappointed but did not argue. Her reason for not going was valid. No woman liked to put in an appearance unless she was looking her best. He kissed her forehead.

"Look after yourself. I'll see you tomorrow." Maria ushered him out and Nancy crawled gratefully back into bed. Vere's passion had waned noticeably since the shock of the previous evening. He would be calling her "old girl" soon. She lay quietly and thought of Ramon.

Higher, faster, more dangerous. That was the creed he had said he lived by. In that heart-stopping moment when Vere had told her of the accident but not of his fate, Nancy had faced a truth she had known all along. She would keep her pride and he would never know it, but he would always have her heart. She hated him as intensely as she had ever hated anyone. And she loved him. A destroyer, her father had called him. A destroyer, as his father had been before him. Sanfords and O'Shaughnessys: Patrick and Leo: Chips and Duarte: Ramon and herself. At least the saga had come to an end, no matter how ignominiously. Wearily she closed her eyes and slept.

* * *

Georgina flew into Zia's apartment just as her husband lay Zia on a chaise longue. "He's all right," she said abruptly to her husband, pushing Zia's maid away and kneeling beside her. "At least that's what I heard called out as I ran here. They've taken him aboard the *Kezia.*"

"Conscious or unconscious?"

"Conscious, I think. Dear God in heaven, Charles do you think he was drunk?"

"I think he deserves horse-whipping."

Zia's eyelids fluttered open.

"He's all right," Georgina said briskly. "They've taken him aboard the *Kezia.*"

Zia's hand clutched hold of Georgina's. Her skin had taken on a translucent texture. Her lustrous eyes under their sea-green tinted lids were terrified. "I must go to him. Now."

"Darling, you're not strong enough . . ."

Zia's eyes flashed with some of their old fire. "Of course I'm strong enough! Mario! Philippe!" The bevy of servants surrounding her was claustrophobic. The earl suppressed a sigh of irritation.

"We'd better go down with her. This lot look on the verge of hysterics."

The Portuguese maids had tears streaming down their faces and were crossing themselves as though Ramon was already dead and buried.

"Your motor car is still garaged, my lord," an anxious page said as they emerged into daylight. "Mrs. Sanford's chauffeur is available."

"Anyone or anything except one of those damned ox carts," the earl said testily. As commander of one of the biggest destroyers in His Majesty's fleet, he didn't suffer fools gladly and he seemed to be surrounded by them.

The journey down to the harbour was a silent one. The earl could say nothing about Zia's son that was complimentary. Georgina was too unsure as to Ramon's physical well-being to raise hopes that might be immediately dashed. Zia was too anxious. She sat like a statue, the earl on one side of her, Georgina gripping her hand on the other.

The throng on the jetty parted as the impressive trio walked with hurrying steps towards the *Kezia*'s gangplank. Zia's afternoon tea dress of swirling pastels floated around her, and in the paling afternoon light she looked like a fairy queen from another world. She didn't feel like one. She felt old and she had never before felt like that.

"Mr. Sanford is perfectly all right, madame."

The steady reassurances sent floods of relief through the earl and countess but none at all through Zia. She would not feel relieved until she saw him with her own eyes.

He sat at the head of the *Kezia*'s giant mahogany dining table, designed to hold twenty-four with ease and thirty in friendly comfort. His shirt had been abandoned, his shoulder neatly bandaged and his cheekbone strapped with elastoplast and bruising magnificently. There was a bottle of brandy in front of him and a chicken leg in his hand. As they entered he grinned broadly, looking for all the world like a Corsican pirate.

"Ramon!" Zia said with a sob, and flew towards him. Chicken bone and drink were discarded as he held her in his arms.

"Bloody fool," the earl said bad-temperedly.

"Idiot," Georgina said affectionately, and sank wearily on to one of the chairs.

Ramon released his mother gently. He had vented his rage and jealousy in the only way he knew and in doing so he had aged her ten years. Never before had he knowingly hurt her. It had taken Nancy to make him capable of such an action.

"The Salt Flats of America are best for speed records," Zia said unsteadily, forcing a smile.

"The Salt Flats of America are boring," Ramon said gently.

"So are some people," Charles Montcalm snapped, draining a glass of brandy. "There are times and places for foolhardy bravery and late afternoon in Funchal Harbour is neither."

Ramon, who well knew Charles Montcalm's own track record of bravery, rose to his feet and flung his arm around his shoulders in a conciliatory gesture. "Sorry, Charles. I was letting off steam."

"Let it off where it will do some good. At the Fascists," the earl said darkly as they left the ship.

"Charles is obsessed with what's happening in Germany and Austria," Georgina explained as the earl strode ahead of them.

Zia had disassociated herself from politics long since and said vaguely, "I thought Great Britain, Italy and France had warned Germany to adopt a 'hands off' policy towards Austria?"

"So they have and a fat lot of good a warning will do," the earl said with more than accustomed rudeness as they entered Zia's Daimler and began to ascend more sedately to Sanfords than they had descended.

"The most unlikely people are becoming concerned," Georgina said as the road twisted and turned and Sanfords glittered with a thousand lights high above them. "The Astors held a large political weekend party at Cliveden just a few weeks ago. Vere was there, of course. I always feel there's rather more to Vere than meets the eye, but I'm not sure what it is."

"And I," Ramon said with disarming charm as the motor car swept towards Sanfords' imposing entrance, "am not remotely interested."

The Montcalms took their leave of them, Georgina thoughtfully, the earl with relief. As Ramon accompanied his mother to her suite she asked tentatively:

"Is there a woman involved, darling?"

He had never lied to her. They paused at the bronze-studded door that led to Zia's private world and he held her hands, staring down at her with a mixture of tenderness and concern.

"There was. She's out of my system now, I promise."

Zia's eyes were unhappy. "I wish you would marry, darling. There are so many nice girls about. The Rossmans are at their Camara de Lobos villa. Tessa Rossman is eighteen now and sweet-natured as well as beautiful. It would be a perfect match." Her voice was wistful.

He looked down at her, none of his inward battle showing in his eyes. At last he said, "You're quite right. I'll invite Tessa over this evening. Will that make you happy?"

Zia looked up at her fine, strong, handsome son. "Very happy, darling. Thank you."

He saw her into her rooms and handed her over to the ministrations of her maids and then returned to his own rooms.

Tessa Rossman was an obvious choice. Like the Sandemans, the Cockburns, the Sanfords, the Rossmans had been entrenched in Portuguese life for generations. Their family home was in Oporto, as were the family homes of all the great wine shipping families. Her parents were English, her grandparents English, her great-grandparents English. No Rossman had ever intermarried. However, Ramon had a shrewd suspicion that tradition would be no barrier if he chose to ask for Tessa's hand in marriage. He was half-American; English public school educated; a millionaire several times over and the marriage would amalgamate two of the greatest wine houses in the world. An admirable marriage by any count. Tessa Rossman had been an extremely pretty child: flaxen hair, blue eyes, smiling lips. He hadn't seen her for years. The Rossmans had carefully guarded their blooming beauty from the eyes of fortune hunters. Nightclubs were taboo. Since leaving her Swiss finishing school six months ago, Tessa had endured a cultural trip with her mother to Florence and Venice and had since been immured at the family's luxurious villa in the isolated but beautiful village of Camara de Lobos, some nine kilometres from Funchal. The Rossmans were becoming increasingly worried. There was a limit to the length of time they could keep Tessa away from the riff-raff who haunted every heiress. Ramon Sanford would be more than welcome—he would be a gift from heaven.

That evening Ramon drove out to Camara de Lobos and escorted a delighted Tessa back for an evening of wining and dining at Sanfords. Later they visited the casino and Tessa, with beginner's luck, won handsomely on the *chemin de fer* table. She was refreshingly unsophisticated. When he kissed her goodnight he was gentle and her mouth fluttered inexpertly beneath his. With sudden tenderness he realized that it was the first kiss she had ever experienced.

"It's been a beautiful, wonderful evening," she said, her eys glowing as she stepped from the car and the Rossmans' butler opened the door of her prison.

Ramon twined his fingers in hers. She was little more than a child, but a sweet and beautiful child. His mouth brushed her hand, but not with the hot impassioned imprint of lips with which he had kissed Nancy's.

"Tomorrow," he said. "Sanfords' evening ball."

She gasped, her mind racing over her wardrobe, her mother's jewels.

Ramon, reading her thoughts, smiled. "No jewels," he said. "I'll bring you a rose. It's all the ornamention you need."

He blew her a kiss as he drove himself away and Tessa was left to the inquisition of her parents. The night wind ruffled his hair as he took the corners at dangerous speeds. She was young, she was pretty, she was pure. What the devil else did he want? Brakes screeched and there was a horrific glimpse of moonlit water thousands of feet below. His car swerved the corner widely and continued on its precarious way.

He wanted Nancy. He wanted a woman, not a child bride. He wanted wit and warmth and sophistication. His mouth was a hard line. He wanted a whore: a woman who blatantly conducted her lastest *affaire* beneath the roofs of his home. A woman who promised eternal love and left without explanation. A woman with whom he had shared a dream and who had trampled on it, laughing.

He slammed the brakes on hard, pebbles bouncing down the cliffside as he missed the perilous drop by inches, scorching the grass as he picked up speed, ramming his way through the gears. He would marry Tessa Rossman. He would care for her, protect her, love her. Passion was for fools. There was no such thing as twin souls: human beings destined for each other and each other alone. That was for dreamers. He would be practical and level-headed. He would combine the Rossman and Sanford fortunes. He would have sons that he could never have had with the woman who fired his loins and tormented his mind. He would make Zia happy. That at least was some comfort.

He left his Daimler for his chauffeur to garage and strode to his room, issuing only the tersest of courtesies to his world-famous guests. He dismissed his valet and, as the darkness paled to dawn and sleep eluded him, struggled with an iron will to focus on the face of his bride-to-be. But blue eyes paled before seductive, thick-lashed violet ones: fair hair would not predominate over dark glossy curls. The bloom of youth was poor contrast to high, perfect cheekbones and flawless, creamy skin. If he had been born in the Middle Ages he would have believed himself bewitched.

"Goddamn her to hell" he said, pummeling his pillows savagely and determining to propose to Tessa Rossman before the week was out.

* * *

"I've cut my lip, Vere. Not broken my leg," Nancy said in laughing protest as her room was filled with so many baskets of flowers that it looked like a tropical garden.

"There are no marks now, I promise you." He kissed her as if to prove it. "I want you to look absolutely ravishing this evening and be the envy of every male in the room."

"I will. I promise." It would be the first time she had left her room for several days and Vere had been in constant attendance. His concern had touched her.

Zia had sent her own personal beautician to apply cooling face packs and had spent a whole afternoon sipping at her permanent glass of champagne and reminiscing about her youth in Boston's North End.

"In those days masts and spars were a permanent part of the horizon. I've always loved the sea. I love to sit in my garden now and see the yachts leave and enter harbour. The Cunarders especially. The *Aquitania* is due here within the week. She is the most beautiful ship imaginable." She did not mention that it was the vessel Jack Cameron would be arriving on.

"I always remember the summer in Boston: hot humid summers without a vestige of air. The winters are completely erased from my memory. I remember the squirrels on the common and the linden trees and the elms and walking past the pond, hand in hand."

Nancy had no need to ask whose hand she had been holding in those far off years of her youth.

"I was born in Hanover Street, only yards from your grandparents' home. To me it was the most exciting place in the world. There were oyster bars and fish stalls, barber shops and the nickelodeon when we had enough money." She laughed. "We used to creep into St. Leonard's Church just to be on our own and hold hands." Her smile faded. Nancy remembered that St. Stephen's Church was also in Hanover Street.

"Sometimes we went to the music hall in Tremont Street. Once, we went to the Central Square Theatre." She sat at the open window of Nancy's room, her chin resting in her hands, her eyes seeing another world.

"We used to swim in the Charles River and on Sunday afternoons we strolled through Franklin Park and Chips would tell me of his dreams and how he was going to be mayor or governor." She laughed again. "President, though even he never dared to put that into words. My mother used to make us griddle cakes and quahog chowder. Chips loved it. By then, of course, he was monied and the cooks in the O'Shaughnessy home did not present quahog chowder or grapenut custard and ice cream. I used to bake them." She looked down at her lily-white, beautifully manicured hands with something like surprise. "I haven't prepared so much as a sandwich for myself for decades. In those days I used to make Indian pudding and blueberry pie and muffins." A deep, long-drawn-out sigh escaped. "So long ago. I thought my life would be baking pies and griddle cakes for hungry children. I was always determined never to hand them over to governesses or nannies or desert my kitchen. My mother used to tell me that the kitchen was the heart of the home." Her laugh was hollow.

"I never saw a kitchen after I married Duarte. I hardly saw my son."

There was a long silence that Nancy did not break. Zia had never before mentioned her husband's name. It was as if doing so had clouded all her happy reflections.

She rose to her feet. "I'm planning a fancy dress ball for the tenth. The theme will be Eastern royalty. I know you haven't brought your own dressmaker with you, darling, but there's no need to worry. I have a first-rate team of seamstresses for such occasions. I myself am going as Catherine the Great of Russia. Not a particularly pleasant lady but at least she was in command." She kissed Nancy warmly on her cheek. "What about Queen Christina of Sweden for yourself? I know she wasn't Eastern, but I'll allow a little poetic licence and since Garbo's film has only just been released, it would be very topical. Anyhow, I'll leave it up to you. I just insist you appear and desert this shaded room. Life is for living and enjoying."

Vere gasped that evening when he saw her. Her evening gown was by Chanel. A diaphanous creation of pale orange, yellow and pink flowers carelessly scattered on a white background. The neck was high in front, low at the back. The skirt fitted sleekly over her hips and then foamed in a dozen lavish flounces from her knees to the floor.

"You look magnificent," he said and reverently placed a gold-embossed box into her hands.

The chandelier earrings were of diamonds. As he clasped them on to her ears, so many hung in the sparkling, breathtaking fall that they were beyond counting.

"A family heirloom," he lied. "A gift you can't refuse." He kissed her and with her hand resting lightly on his arm led her towards the glittering ballroom.

Nancy's expert eye for fashion told her the tall and stately Lady Michaeljohn had rightly chosen to be gowned by Vionnet. Samantha Hedley's golden beauty was set off to perfection in a superb black dress by Lanvin, a flame chiffon scarf draped carelessly across her neck and shoulders. Bobo was entrancing in a dress of crushed raspberry crèpe and Venetia Bessbrook was breathtaking. Her dress was of silver lamé, clinging over every sensual curve. Her fur was silver fox, her nails silver lacquered. Her hair and her eyelids were silvered, as were her unseen nipples. Venetia never did anything by halves.

Madeleine Mancini, in a black Bagota crèpe dress designed by Adrian who dressed such stars as Dietrich and Garbo, fumed. The dramatic accents of ermine and the exquisite drapery of the material paled into insignificance beside Venetia's glory.

Lavinia Meade looked like a magnificent Rubens. Her massive arms and shoulders were bare, the heavy expanse of her bosom exposed daringly to the public gaze. Her gown was of red velvet, a colour that seared the eye when seen in such close contrast to her hair.

"Do you think that she's colour blind?" Georgina asked Nancy interestedly. She herself was wearing an evening dress of coffee-coloured faille, the stiff material ideally suited to the ruffles at the bottom of the arrow-like sheathed skirt.

Zia, in her wide-sleeved, floating gown of emerald shot silk, weaved among her guests, her cloud of shining, waving hair a vibrant burnished auburn that looked as though it belonged to a girl of seventeen.

Countess Szapary, still favouring the white chiffon that made her look like a shy debutante, said gently, "I think perhaps Lady Meade is not very interested in clothes. Her interests are elsewhere."

"Are they indeed?" Georgina asked with a quirk of her brow. "I'd never have guessed it."

Nancy, on her second glass of champagne, smiled. Countess Szapary, not understanding, said, "Yes, she is helping me enormously with my French. When Leopold was in Russia, of course, French was spoken in his home all the time." She smiled apologetically. "I was born an exile and did not have all the advantages that a wife of Leopold should have, so Lady Meade helps me by coaching me every afternoon."

Georgina Montcalm's eyes softened. She had an overwhelming urge to put her arm around the child.

"Then I shall make no more unkind remarks about Lavinia. She can dress like a Turk and I'll silence the least word of criticism."

Countess Szapary's smile was grateful. Her husband, excusing himself from Prince Vasileyev, was approaching them. The little countess saw him and stiffened, her smile fading. When the punctilious count had borne her away Nancy and Georgina's eyes met silently. The little countess was not happy, which was a great pity.

"My dear, of course it's a Chanel," Lady Carrington was heard to whisper, *sotto voce* behind a potted plant. "Do you know, she's dressing Ina Clare, Lady Henrietta Davis and the Marquise de Paris now? If Nancy Cameron is going to her as well, perhaps we should alter our allegiance . . ."

The voice of the elderly Princess Louise carried clearly. "I couldn't possibly, Beatrice. She mixes with such extraordinary people. Picasso and Stravinsky and Cocteau."

"Who? Nancy Cameron?" Beatrice Carrington asked in perplexity.

"No dear. The dressmaker woman. It wouldn't surprise me if she didn't take lovers as well."

Nancy and Georgina giggled. Vere was dancing with Bobo, his eyes continuously on Nancy. Bobo's eyes were continuously on her Egyptian. Madeleine Mancini had him firmly ensconced behind a Grecian pillar, and though Bobo could only see the back of Hassan's head, she could quite well see the predatory look in Madeleine Mancini's cat-like eyes.

Sonny Zakar's girlfriend, Hildegarde Gaynor, was informing the unimpressed Costas that she had unfortunately had to turn down an invitation aboard the Vanderbilts' yacht *Alva* due to the scheduling of her last film. It would place her on box-office par with Jean Harlow and Norman Shearer when it was released.

Costas listened and looked down the revealing cleavage of her dress. Whatever her acting ability was like—and it was a matter of complete indifference to Costas—she would probably be a good lay. Sonny didn't waste his time on amateurs.

"I see my interpretation of the part as an in-depth study . . . Hildegarde was saying.

"Let's fuck," Costas said, not bothering to remove his cigar from his mouth.

Hildegarde remembered the Costas millions, decided simulated shock was out of place, and disappeared speedily with him before he could change his mind.

Prince Nicholas Vasileyev escorted Venetia Bessbrook back to her literary lion after a foxtrot rendered virtually impossible by the limitations of Venetia's dress.

Vere was already walking quickly in Nancy's direction. The prince bowed low over her hand, and clicked his heels together.

"My pleasure," he murmured.

There was more in his words than a request for a dance. His eyes were suggestive, his admiration for her blatant. He had a strong face, high Slavic cheekbones and, beneath the dark moustache and meticulously trimmed beard, a mouth both sensuous and determined. He aroused a response in her that Vere, with all his kindness and consideration, failed to do.

"Thank you," she said and slid into his arms as the music changed to the slow rhythm of a waltz.

"Better luck next time," Georgina Montcalm said as Vere glared after them. "You'll have to make do with me, Vere darling. Or Clarissa." Their eyes met. Vere's face was impassive. He should have known that if anyone knew, or guessed, it would be the perceptive Georgina Montcalm.

"Let's not talk about Clarissa," he said as he spun her round and passed the pillar concealing Madeleine and Hassan.

"You'll have to sometime, darling. For Nancy's sake."

The prince was holding her very close. She could feel the whole length of his body against hers. "I find you a very desirable woman, Nancy Leigh Cameron," he said and his voice was deep, the voice of a man used to being obeyed.

She thought of her lonely room and the long empty hours of the night. She thought of her fury at how little she had lived. She thought of how little time she had left.

"I know," she said, a tantalizing smile on her lips—and knew something else: that the lover she took would be Nicky, not Vere.

His arms tightened around her and above the music Zia's voice could be heard saying delightedly, "Tessa, how lovely to see you."

Above Nicky's shoulder Nancy saw Ramon, tall and straight, brashly handsome. With indolent self-assurance his eyes swept the room carelessly until they fastened on her. There was a sardonic twist to his lean mouth as he held her long in the grasp of his eyes, and then dropped her and let his glance move away to the girl at his side.

She was radiant, looking up at him with worshipping adoration. She was dressed simply, her only jewellery a rose pinned in her hair. She was unutterably lovely and she was no older than Verity.

"I think I'd like a drink," Nancy said, the room swimming round her in a dizzying vortex.

"Perhaps in my suite?" the prince suggested, his voice low, desire flaming through him.

As blackness receded, Nancy could see Ramon take his pretty escort into his strong arms, holding her close, whispering intimately into her ear. She saw the girl's response, the blush on her cheeks, the glow in her eyes.

"Yes," she said bleakly. "Why not?"

Chapter Ten

The prince's lovemaking was a revelation to Nancy. She had participated out of a sense of defiance; a need not to be alone and unloved while Ramon flaunted his latest conquest. She had not expected pleasure. She had believed that could only come with love: that it was instantaneous all-consuming passion for Ramon that had led her to physical bliss. She had been wrong. Ramon had broken an emotional barrier and it was one that was broken for all time. Nicky was a skilled lover and Nancy, in Ramon's arms, had proved a willing pupil. Together they reached a physical joy that was a delight to the prince and an overwhelming relief to Nancy. There could be other men. As well as giving pleasure, she could receive it. She would not think of Ramon: she could not bear to.

There had been a moment, a hairsbreadth of time when, in the final throes of their lovemaking, she had been so out of control that the name she had cried out had been his. Nicky, reaching his own unbearable summit, had heard only her cry and drowned it with his own.

Afterwards he stroked her body in rapturous conquest. Samantha had been a pretty girl, nothing more. Nancy Leigh Cameron had been a challenge and one well worth laying siege to.

"Do you think it's time we returned?"

Nancy stared at him. "You can't mean it? What will everybody think?"

He laughed, his gold wristwatch gleaming on his naked arm as he sat up in the bed and reached for his shirt. "What will they think if we do *not* return? Your attentive English duke will be hammering on the door and demanding an explanation if we are absent for much longer. As it is, we appear in the ballroom cool and unperturbed. A little walk in the garden for some air . . . A waltz beside the pool. A quiet corner in which to enjoy Zia's glorious food. I believe she enticed her cook from the Paris Ritz. Whatever explanation we give, it will be one that will be accepted. Your Englishman does not have a devious mind."

Nancy hadn't either. As Nicky zipped her into her evening gown, she wondered how she was going to handle a situation so alien and bizarre. It proved remarkably easy.

The band was playing a tango and the prince swung her out on to the floor, murmuring appreciation of her sexual talents that brought high colour to her cheeks. With a new awareness Nancy realized that several couples were also absent. There was no sign of Costas, though Madeleine was laughing gaily in the arms of Sonny Zakar. Venetia Bessbrook was looking most unhappy and Luke Golding was absent; as was Hildegarde. Vere was dancing with Countess Szapary and the little countess was smiling again. His eyes, when they met hers, were anguished and querying. She smiled at him and danced on.

Georgina and Charles were steadfastly together. HM's influence was obviously far-reaching. Viscount Lothermere was in deep conversation with Sir Maxwell and Nancy failed to see any sign of his lovely viscountess. Samantha Hedley was laughing too loudly, picking up glass after glass of champagne from the trays the waiters neverendingly circulated. Her companion was Lord Michaeljohn, who had an expression in his eyes that had never been there when in the company of his stately wife.

The Carringtons, Princess Louise and the unsmiling Mr. Blenheim held a royal court of their own and it was obvious from the expressions on their faces that criticism was the main stream of their conversation.

There were other familiar faces from cocktail parties, embassy balls and first nights at the opera. Madame Molière was as resplendent as always: the French wife of a Detroit car manufacturer, she clung desperately to her maiden name rather than be known by the name of a world-famous motor car. She crossed the Atlantic twice a year and enjoyed the kind of social life that Detroit did not provide. Her American husband did not accompany her. As Madame Molière so charmingly explained: "Someone had to earn the money." Her audience laughed at such Gallic frankness, dazzled by her chic and knowing, long-lashed eyes.

She was accompanied everywhere not only by her hairdresser, beautician endlessly-changing streams of lovers, but also by a violinist. It was Madame Molière's whim that she be woken every morning by the sweet tone of her favourite instrument. Fellow guests, remembering a Scottish lord who had insisted on being woken at 6 am by a rousing blast on the bagpipes, indulged her.

Villiers appeared discreetly at Zia's elbow and Nancy saw her leave the room. Nicky laughed.

"The arrival of a fellow emigre, the Grand Duchess Livada. She never travels with fewer than a hundred trunks, valises or jewel cases and her arrival always necessitates Zia's personal supervision. Her suite is the Royal Suite, a pretty affectation of Zia's. It used to be simply the Rose Suite, but Nadejda has never reconciled herself to exile. To occupy the Royal Suite is more in keeping for a Russian grand duchess than a mere rose one."

"Who is the dignified-looking gentleman talking to Bobo?" Nancy asked, surveying the vast range of her fellow guests with interest.

"The Sultan of Mohore. He was engaged to Venetia Bessbrook in the late twenties. I wonder if we will witness a reconciliation?"

"She's too much in love with her literary lion."

"Venetia has never been in love in her life," Nicky replied smoothly. "Did you know Reggie Minter is here? He's over there, dancing with Lavinia. He's a bit difficult to see, clutched so tightly against that magnificent chest. I wonder if she lets him come up for air or if he's just suffocating soundlessly? He's the son of the American tin-plate magnate and all last season at Cap d'Antibes Venetia was swearing undying love to him and announcing their engagement at every lunch, dinner and supper. It never came to anything of course. Venetia's intended engagements never do."

The dance ended and Nicky escorted her back to Vere and the Montcalms. "I shall have to leave you, *ma petite*, otherwise your Englishman will grow aggressive. Tomorrow will be soon enough to let him know that he is the loser in this particular game of love." His fingertips slid against the nakedness of her arm and then he was exchanging civilities with the Montcalms and excusing himself to renew his friendship with the sultan.

"I missed you," Vere said, half turning his head so that the Montcalms should not hear. "Where were you?"

Nancy was not a liar and did not want to become one.

"With Nicky," she said.

Vere was about to say more but was stalled by Zia sweeping down on them, her arms outstretched, her hair like a flame in the light of the hundreds of chandeliers.

"Darlings. Do let me introduce Tessa Rossman. She only left finishing school in September and since then her mother has been keeping her hidden, which is a sin and a shame. Tessa, the Earl and Countess of Montcalm."

"Georgina and Charles," Georgina said, taking Tessa's hand and immediately sensing her shyness.

Nancy could feel the blood pounding in her temples. A happy Zia was introducing her to Tessa. They were shaking hands. Ramon was beside her. Tessa's eyes were shining as Nancy forced herself to smile and speak. Nancy was a heroine of hers. The kind of sophisticated beauty she so desperately wanted to emulate. Nancy was barely aware of her. Ramon's hawk-like face was sardonic, the sparkling eyes as hard as agates. It seemed impossible that they had looked at her with laughter and desire and burning love.

"Of course, you two haven't met since childhood, have you?" Zia was saying.

Tessa was laughing as Georgina put her at ease.

"We have," Ramon said, his eyes never flinching from hers. "Briefly."

The physical impact of his words was even worse than the physical blow he had inflicted earlier. If she could have killed him she would have done so.

"I barely remember," she said coolly and was rewarded by a flash of unconcealed fury.

Vere and Ramon had exchanged only the briefest of nods, and now, to Nancy's intense gratitude, Vere excused himself and firmly walked her back on to the dance floor.

"Insolent devil," he said beneath his breath. Ramon Sanford was the only man he had ever met who could make him feel as if he was walking a tightrope.

Nancy said nothing. She couldn't trust herself to speak.

Lord Michaeljohn was back with his lady. Costas had reappeared and was exerting his charm on Samantha Hedly. Madeleine Mancini was dancing with Hassan. Bobo was sparkling overmuch and in the arms of Lord Carrington. Venetia and Luke Golding were once again gazing deep into each other's eyes. Sonny had his arm proprietorially around Hildegarde. Viscountess Lothermere had re-merged with a stray curl descending in the nape of her neck and a secretive smile on her face. Her viscount had been coerced into dancing and was performing very badly. Beatrice Carrington was held tightly to the chest of the royal Mr. Blenheim. Madame Molière was flirting delicately with Charles Montcalm. Reggie Minter was whirling a sparkling-eyed Countess Szapary around the ballroom, while her husband glowered from beside a six-foot statue of a naked Venus. The Sultan of Mohore and Nicky were talking, heads close together. As she circled past them in Vere's arms, Nicky raised his head. His eyes lit up at the sight of her. He had not been seen with Samantha for the whole of the evening. Tomorrow she knew he would intimate to Vere that they were more than close friends and that he was *de trop*. She had to decide whether to allow him to do so or whether to ask him to remain silent. Decisions, decisions. Her head ached.

Ramon passed within inches, Tessa held lovingly and protectively in his arms.

"My sweet love," he was saying to her in an amused voice, the expression on his face one of tender indulgence.

She felt cold and sick and involuntarily stumbled.

"I'm tired, Vere," she said apologetically as his grasp tightened.

"Of course, your silly fall." He was concerned and at that moment she wanted to respond to him more than anything else in the world.

They weaved their way through the dancers and off the dance floor. As they made their exit Nicky's eyes met hers, his brows raised slightly. No expression flitted across her face. She had no need to make any gestures. Nicky would be with her within the hour. Lovemaking would replace lonely sleeplessness.

Afterwards they lay in the vast bed amidst its tent of white chiffon looped with golden braid, and drank vermouth and Nicky told her something of his life as a prince of Mother Russia.

"On my father's side the Vasileyevs can trace their origins back to AD 850."

"On my mother's side to AD 700," Nancy said, not to be outdone.

Nicky laughed, "Unfortunately my mother's pedigree is not quite so unimpeachable. Her *seize quartiers* were non-existent. It was rumoured that she was born on the wrong side of one of the royal blankets and given to a Russian nobleman to rear. The rumour was strong enough to allow my father to marry her without social stigma. As a child I spent most of my time in Paris; my mother far preferred the French way of life to that of her own country. I did not share her preference. I lived only for the times we were in St. Petersburg or on our family estate in the Crimea."

His hand ruffled her hair, his voice was inexpressively sad. Not the vibrant, confident voice she was used to. She did not ask, but sensed that he rarely, if ever, spoke of his life before the Revolution or his exile. She lay in the crook of his arm, her bruised heart solaced by the intimacies he was revealing to her, bringing to the surface memories too painful to be spoken of lightly: memories of a way of life erased for ever.

"The Vasileyev palace at Kuchersko was set in wooded foothills high above the sea. As a child I could stand at the highest window and as far as I could see the land was Vasileyev land: my land. The Tartars had their villages high in the hills. It was there that I learned to ride and infuriate my father by escaping my tutor and running wild. Lesser nobility had their summer *dachas* nearer the coast, so there was always congenial company. 1917 was the last summer we all spent there. Incredibly it was a gay and carefree one, for we expected the rebellion in the north to be dispersed within months. It wasn't. Things grew worse. I was fourteen . . . too young to fight. My father was with the White Army defending Yalta. He died there. My lush, rose-clouded Crimea was transformed first by the Soviets and then, later by the Germans. When the British sent cruisers and destroyers in to rescue their own countrymen and the dowager empress, we went along with them. We and a hundred others. I did not want to go. I fought and struggled and tried to run away but a British officer despatched me aboard the HMS *Marlborough* as though I were no more than an inconvenient parcel—much to my mother's weeping gratitude."

He stared up at the ceiling where the first light of dawn was beginning to cast vague shadows. "I have never set foot on my native land again. But I will. We all will."

"Poor Nicky." Her arms encircled him. "Will nowhere else ever be home?"

"No. Only Russia is home."

They remained in each other's arms, silent and finally sleeping.

Ramon had known she would be there. He was practised

in the art of meeting old and cast-off lovers. He did so smoothly and impertubedly and with a coolness that immediately quelled any vain hopes that the *affaire* might once more flare into life. When a woman went out of Ramon's life she did so forever.

His eyes had flickered across the plumes and feathers, jewels and decorations of the dancers with careless nonchalance. She was with her Englishman. He was gazing at her like a devoted puppy dog and she was smiling. He could feel every nerve, every muscle in his body tighten. Her smile was dazzling, generous, effortlessly sensuous, her mouth soft, ready to be kissed.

Their eyes met and held: velvet dark eyes that a man could drown in. He turned away and smiled down at Tessa who was gazing around with the disarming enjoyment of a child. His mother was talking animatedly and Charles was reflecting that if he hadn't more sense, girls like Tessa Rossman could seriously disturb his peace of mind. Ramon was conscious only of Nancy.

She was dancing with Nicky now and Nicky had a familiar expression on his too handsome face. He took Tessa in his arms and danced nearer to them. Nearer and nearer. He could not see her but he could smell her perfume, hear the unmistakable tone of Nicky's caressing voice.

"My sweet love," he said to Tessa and waltzed her away, not having heard a word that she had been saying to him.

Zia did not see Nicky and Nancy's discreet exit. Nor did the Montcalms or the Szaparys or anyone else with whom they had been laughing and talking. Ramon saw. He felt a blaze of anger rush through him, a blaze he had thought he had quenched. There was a word for women like her: an ugly word. He should feel sorry for her. He could feel nothing but the kind of fury that causes a man to kill.

They were with the sultan now. His mother was introducing Tessa. From somewhere in the background Costas was laughing loudly. He would marry Tessa. He would speak to the Rossman's tomorrow: his mother tonight. It never occurred to him to speak to Tessa first. Her consent was taken for granted. Every woman he had ever wanted had been his for the asking: remaining his until he had tired of them. Apart from one.

The effort of continued courtesy was too much. It was well after midnight, Tessa was still barely out of the schoolroom. It was reason enough to curtail the evening. He did so with smooth politeness and when he kissed her goodnight Tessa's response was warm and loving and totally unfulfilling. When he returned to the still blazing lights of Sanfords, he strode into the ballroom and danced with the first woman he saw. It was Samantha Hedley. He also went to bed with her. It was physically satisfying and emotionally chilling. He was only glad the woman nearest the Grand Entrance had not been Lavinia Meade. In that case, satisfaction at any level would have been an impossibility.

"Darling, it would be perfect, but are you sure?" It was early morning and they were breakfasting on Zia's terrace. "Are you only doing it because it was my suggestion?"

Ramon's smile was fleeting. "Have I ever done anything at anyone else's suggestion?"

"No, darling, which is what makes this most strange. You hardly know her. You've only escorted her twice."

"Twice can be long enough to fall in love," his voice was bitter. Zia's sea-green eyes darkened with anxiety.

"The other day, after the escapade in the bay, you said it was caused by anger over a woman. Don't marry Tessa Rossman in order to put the memory of another woman behind you. To do so would bring nothing but unhappiness for both of you. It would be cruelty of an unimaginable degree."

Her face paled. Her husband had been capable of great cruelty and in the harsh light of the morning sun Ramon's mouth wore the same relentless lines that his father's so often had.

He didn't reply. Far below them thickly wooded terraces shelved to the sea. Lord and Lady Michaeljohn were strolling arm in arm. Out of their sight and down on another level, half hidden behind hibiscus and strelitza, Countess Szapary sat alone, her head bowed as she listlessly shredded a rose's petals. Sea bathing was not as popular as the safer waters of the pool. Costas and Sonny Zakar were frolicking in the treacherously deep water like a couple of ageing sea lions. Bobo's Egyptian was smoking a cigarette and watching them from the shade of a dragon tree. A woman stepped up behind him and slid caressing hands around his neck. It was Madeleine Mancini.

On the lowest level, as the last of the garden walks ended and the rocks began, Ramon could see a figure deep in concentration, painting. Giovanni Ferranzi, Picasso's contemporary, worked feverishly. In front of him was the surging sea, the mountains at the far side of the bay and great expanses of cloudless sky. Ramon wondered what would show on Giovanni's canvas. Certainly nothing that any other eye regarding the same scene would see.

His eyes sharpened as she emerged from the deep cover of the trees. Her dress was white and simple, a silver rouleau belt circling her waist. Her sandals were high-heeled and thin strapped. Giovanni detested an audience. Sanfords' vast grounds and the tiny villages strung along the coastline gave him the privacy he needed. He never participated in the evenings' frivolities or joined the pleasure-seekers at the side of the pool. He came to paint. Single-mindedly and uninterruptedly. For a long time she did not speak: simply stood, perfectly still, watching.

Ramon waited for the Italian to signal her away brusquely. He could tell by the inclination of her head that she was speaking to him. The master paused, brush in hand, the conversation lengthened. Then to his complete stupefaction, the Italian motioned for her to sit and laid his brush down.

Nicky had been gone when she had awoken. She hadn't wanted Vere's company or anyone else's. She avoided the pool and lounger-filled terraces and walked unhurriedly and without purpose down one of the winding paths overhung with heavy blossom. The day was not yet hot, a cool breeze blew refreshingly against her face as she neared the crags that jutted out into the surging sea. She had not known Giovanni Ferranzi was staying at the hotel. In the past his paintings had intrigued, confused and often astounded her. Now she watched with rapt attention as the brush worked ceaselessly, filling the canvas with light and colour and shape and form.

She opened her mouth to say "hello" and found herself saying instead:

"Might I paint with you?"

Immediately the words were out of her mouth the audacity of her request stunned her. "I'm sorry," she said in confusion as he turned and stared at her. "I didn't mean . . . I was thinking aloud . . . I'm most dreadfully sorry."

His bright black eyes held hers and then dropped to the long narrow hands with the beautiful, almond-shaped nails.

"Yes," he said, "if you do exactly as I say."

He rose to his feet and from the array of canvasses and

paint behind him he extracted a stool, an easel and a canvas. Glorious colour was squeezed from tubes into thick whirls on to the palette.

"What do I do?" she asked weakly as he positioned her at the easel, handing her the palette and brush, knife and cloth.

"What you want," he said simply. He had placed her opposite to himself. When he returned to his seat she could no longer see him. Only the awesome black canvas in front of her and above it the riotous tropical gardens climbing up to the hotel.

"What you do not do is watch me . . . Or copy."

She did not know how to mix colours; she knew nothing. She took a deep breath and stroked a brushful of searing red across the canvas. They worked opposite each other for four hours and did not speak. A waiter came down with the master's lunch: bread, cheese and a rough red wine served to no one else but the Italian who demanded it. They ate and drank and continued to paint. At last, when the light began to fade he put down his brush and rose to his feet, standing silently behind her.

There were no flowers; no trees; no depiction of the scene in front of her. It was rough and crude and full of frightening force. A Dante's inferno of dark and light: a chasm of blood reds and blacks seared by brilliant white and a dove rising as if from a bottomless pit.

He nodded slowly. He had been right. His instinct was infallible. "Tell me," he said.

"I'm dying," she said simply, "of a wretched disease I'm barely aware of."

"And so you abandon your former life and come to Madeira to take lovers like the English duke and the Russian prince?"

"I abandoned my former life because it was a sham. I'd lived it for thirty-five years and decided that if I was dying I was going to die being me and no one else."

He looked at the painting. It was a tangible creation of the rending apart of body and spirit.

"We will paint tomorrow," he said and drank his wine from the neck of the bottle and wiped his mouth with the back of his hand.

She walked dazedly back to the hotel. Something new had been born within her. Something new and wonderful. Something akin to the revelation she had first experienced in Ramon's arms. Only this wonder was within her control. The days stretching ahead suddenly had a purpose. She would paint, create. She was so totally engrossed in her own thoughts that she was unaware of the *Aquitania* pulling smoothly into Funchal harbour.

Senator Jack Cameron disembarked tight-lipped and ashen-faced. He had not enjoyed his enforced voyage across the Atlantic. Behind him Syrie Geeson descended, bright-eyed and alert. Europe was a new experience and Syrie valued new experiences. Only smooth-talking and tenacity had secured her a place on the trip. Jack had intended travelling to see his wife alone. Syrie knew Nancy Leigh Cameron as well as any woman knows her boss's wife and perhaps a little better. She had made it her business to do so. It was, after all, in her own interests to know exactly what made Nancy Leigh Cameron tick. What her strengths and weaknesses were. Syrie Geeson had long since determined to become the second Mrs. Cameron but Nancy had proved impossible to usurp. Until now. Syrie had the definite feeling that, handled correctly, her moment of glory had come.

The path was steep and crooked, winding up through thick foliage. It skirted the rocks and the sea for a little way and then meandered up and round thickets of myrtle and pastel-petalled fransciscea. Occasionally there was a rose-red glint of one of Sanfords' shelving roofs high above, and then nothing. Only greenery and sweet fragrance and the sound of the birds singing in the trees. She rounded the huge glossy leaves of a giant shrub and halted abruptly. The peace and tranquility fled.

He stood full square in the path before her, his legs astride. He showed not the least intention of moving. Her heart began to pound painfully. There was barely five yards of dust-blown track between them. Their eyes locked, their bodies as tense as those of two wild animals in sudden confrontation.

She felt herself colouring beneath his gaze, painfully aware of his closeness, of the hardness of his muscles, of the restlessness that so aroused her.

"Please let me pass," she said through parched lips, her nerves throbbing.

He stared down at her, grim-faced.

"I came to apologize." His black eyes would not let her go.

"I . . ." The words would not come. How did one accept an apology from a man who had struck you across the face so hard that he had drawn blood? A man who loved and lied with equal expertise, leaving one bed for another with the ease of an indolent tom cat. There were no words. She could only say again, stiffly and foolishly.

"Please let me pass."

The expression in his eyes changed. He, Ramon Sanford, had come to her, drawn by God knows what force. Had actually apologized and she stood before him, cool and collected, totally disregarding his apology.

This time there was studied carelessness in his voice as he said:

"Believe it or not, I've never struck a woman before."

She wanted to cry out "why me then? Why me?" but she could not. His sun-bronzed face had taken on a look of frightening indifference. She could not expose her feelings to him—her hurt and her pain. To do so would be to feed his ego and male vanity. Her nails dug deep into the palms of her hands.

"Please let me pass," she said for the third time, and summoning up all her strength she moved, one foot before the other, nearer and nearer to him, praying that he would give way. He did not. She side-stepped, trampling small yellow flowers. His hand shot out, lean and strong, encircling her wrist, holding her fast.

"Nancy!"

"Let me go!" Her voice was choked with unshed tears and fear. They were far from the cultivated gardens and grounds. Far from the revellers at the poolside. He had slapped her semi-conscious within yards of scores of people. What might he do to her here, out of sight and out of earshot?

"What happened, for Christ's sake? Why did you leave?" And then, with naked ferociousness, "Why *him*?"

"Why not?" she shouted back. "Is promiscuity a male prerogative?"

He blasphemed, whirling her around, slamming her hard against the trunk of a tree, the weight of his body forcing her to be still.

His mouth came down hard on hers, his hands brutal. From the depth of her being came an anguished sob and instead of struggling, instead of fighting, she wound her fingers desperately in the coarseness of his hair and slipped her tongue willingly past his as he took her fiercely where she stood.

"Mrs. Cameron booked her suite privately, sir. I'm afraid I would have to have her permission before allowing you to share occupancy."

"Mrs. Cameron is my wife!" Jack said icily, aware of the interest being shown by a couple of guests passing by.

"I'm sorry, sir, we have you booked in Suite 17 and your secretary in Room 25."

Jack leaned threateningly over the mahogany polished surface of the desk. "I wish to be in the same suite as my wife," he repeated, his fingers itching to grab the collar of the desk clerk and throttle him to death for the embarrassment he was causing. Unless he shared a suite with Nancy, rumours would be rife.

"My dear senator, how delightful to see you after so many years." Zia swept forward, heavy ropes of grey and white baroque pearls hanging waist-length against a flowing dress of pale lilac chiffon. "Is there a problem?"

Jack took a deep, steadying breath, smiled his practised, charming smile and said with a tightly controlled composure, "I naturally wish to occupy the same suite as my wife. I appear to have been booked in on a different floor."

"Ah," Zia laughed, a graceful wave of her hand dismissing such a trifling inconvenience. "Mrs. Cameron's suite is exceptionally small."

Guido lowered his eyes. A bedroom fit for a Tsarina, two drawing rooms furnished with a Matisse and a Picasso, a palatial bathroom with gold fittings, and an extensive terrace hardly amounted to a small suite.

"Suite 17 is much larger and no doubt it will be of very little inconvenience to move Mrs. Cameron if she so wishes."

There was something under the lightness of Zia's voice that brooked no opposition.

With extreme bad grace Senator Cameron allowed his trunks and valises to be ferried to Suite 25. Syrie, in her role as dutiful secretary and personal assistant, disappeared unobtrusively behind them.

"A drink and a rest while the maids unpack for you," Zia was saying disarmingly, leading him firmly away from the foyer and towards her own private apartments. She had no idea where Nancy was, but the senator's mood indicated that it would be better if they did not meet publicly. Jack Cameron had the sense to be flattered by the personal welcome he was receiving from Zia Sanford. Very few people were entertained in Zia's private garden: only the closest of friends and reigning royalty, and not even all royalty, gained entrance.

His temper soothed by being singled out as a person of importance, his impatience curbed by excellent wine, Jack sat beneath Zia's jacaranda tree and with the air of a man of world affairs brought Zia up to date with the happenings in America.

Zia listened to him with half an ear. Where was Ramon? He would have sized the situation up at a glance and speedily captured the Montcalms or the Michaeljohns to join them and spare her the tedium of Jack Cameron's ceaseless monologue.

"The President is continuing to widen his powers. The depression was bad and hit hard but it's now well in hand. There'll be a free gold market, tariff control . . ."

Zia fixed an interested look on her delicately boned face. Where was Nancy? She hadn't seen her all day and it was now late afternoon.

"Of course Henry Morgenthau Junior wouldn't have been my choice for the Treasury Secretaryship but he'll do a good job. He's a disciple of Professor George F. Warren of Cornell and I go along all the way with Warren's commodity dollar theories."

Zia wondered if she wasn't carrying charity too far and should simply unleash Senator Cameron on her unsuspecting guests.

"That's what has launched the Administration on its current dollar devaluation experiment . . ."

Politics had never been boring with Chips. She wondered what he thought of his son-in-law. La Guardia was mayor of New York now. She would have liked to ask

Jack Cameron what his father-in-law thought of that particular changeover in local government but shrank from the hour-long lecture that would ensue.

"Roosevelt has lifted the curb on Agency finance . . ."

Zia had always thought she would have liked the Roosevelts. Eleanor was so serious and devoted: FDR so blue-eyed and charming, sexually attractive despite his wheelchair. What would the White House be like with Jack Cameron in it? She suppressed a smile. Nancy had been right. In spoiling his chances of nomination she was doing her country a favour.

She laid a hand lightly on his arm. "I'm so sorry, Senator, I'm keeping you and you will want to bathe and change for dinner. I was so rivetted by your explanation of the President's policies, that I simply forgot the time."

Jack smiled indulgently. He liked to be addressed as "Senator" and he liked Zia Sanford.

Zia's staff ushered him from her presence and Zia rose to her feet and wandered over to the far edge of the velvety lawn. The pools, the tennis courts, the gardens were all hidden from view. No one could see into Zia's domain from the public terraces or grounds. Down below her the seldom used pathways that wound to the rocks were empty. It would soon be cocktail hour. The ladies would be changing: the gentlemen resting. A rustle of leaves and a sudden flutter of birds caught her attention. Two figures emerged momentarily, heads close together, arms around each other's waists. Zia stiffened, straining her eyes into the rapidly approaching twilight. The path curved, the trees gave way. They were walking slowly, arms wrapped tightly around each other's bodies. This was no casual embrace but a fierce clinging and a desperate holding that could be seen in every line of their bodies. She had known it was her son the instant she had caught sight of them. It was the woman she had been unsure of. That dark head of hair could have belonged to

Madeleine Mancini or Viscountess Lothermere or a score of other females ensconsed under Sanfords' roofs. It did not. The dark curls resting on her son's shoulder, the slender arms holding on to him so steadfastly, were those of Nancy Leigh Cameron.

Zia walked unsteadily back to her seat beneath the jacaranda tree and did the unimaginable. She poured herself a drink without ringing for someone to do it for her.

Ramon and Nancy. She closed her eyes. Ramon nearly killing himself in pent up anger over an unnamed woman. Nancy grieving and abandoning her marriage for an unnamed man. Nancy flirting recklessly and uncharacteristically with Prince Vasileyev; Ramon proposing marriage to a child he had known scarcely a week.

Ramon and Nancy. Nancy and Ramon.

It was the fitting end to a three-act Greek tragedy. Her hand trembled as it reached for her glass. Tragedy. There could be no happiness for them: if Chips did not tell them, she would have to. It would have been better if Patrick O'Shaughnessy had never saved Duarte Sanford from the icy seas of the Atlantic. Then she and Chips would have grown up poor but happy, in Boston's North End. There would have been no Duarte: no long nightmare years, and no son either. She opened her eyes wearily: no dashing, handsome, unbelievably magnificent son. Impossible to wish that life had been otherwise if it would have robbed her of Ramon. She felt cold and unutterably tired. The trees and sea and sky darkened and merged and the glass fell from her hand.

She was sobbing, clinging to him, self-control gone and sanity rapidly following. The smell of sex hung between them: sex and love. Love and longing. He had meant to hurl her away in contempt. He had raped her and she had given to him freely, willingly. He held on to her, trembling, an inner war raging and burning. At last he could stand it no longer. He slammed his fist into the tree.

"Why?" he yelled. "Why leave me? Why take Vasileyev for a lover? Winterton? In God's name, Nancy, *why*?"

Her eyes were two black hollows in her whitened face. Without the support of the tree she would have fallen.

"I trusted you." Her voice was a mere whisper. "I thought you loved me. I *knew* I loved you. I told my daughter so; my husband . . ." Her tongue clung to the roof of her mouth, ". . . my father."

Ramon drew in an agonized breath. Something terrible flamed through his dark eyes.

"He told me about Gloria. He had dates, photographs."

His hands grasped her shoulders savagely. "Gloria was a cheap, transient *affaire*. As meaningless as the hundreds that had gone before her." He raised his face to the heavens as if seeking for a strength suddenly denied him. She waited, her pulses pounding. He lowered his head, her eyes meeting hers.

"It's true that the fact she was the wife of my father's enemy added amusement. But I never loved her. I never loved any woman but you."

"You went to her after me." Her voice sounded alien, a racking sob of accusation that could not possibly have come from her. "You went to her the day after I left New York."

His voice was barely controlled, his fingers imprisonign her. "*She* came to *me*! She came because I finished the *affaire*."

She could see only his face, his eyes, his mouth. "You weren't lovers?" Her voice was barely audible.

"*Mae de Deus*! What kind of a man do you think I am? I loved you! I told you I loved you!" The intensity of his emotions sublimated English upbringing and American genes. He was totally Latin.

Her relief was absolute. She was laughing and crying at the same time, clinging to him, kissing him. "How could you put me through so much hell—so much agony?"

"*Me*? Put *you* through agony?" A nerve throbbed at his temple. "What about Winterton? What about Vasileyev?"

She seized his face in her hands, pulling it down to hers. Explanations could wait. They didn't matter any more. All that mattered was that he loved her and she loved him. His mouth was on hers, on her throat, on her breast, and when he lowered her willingly beneath him on the trampled flowers and entered her, it was with the tenderness of absolute love.

Chapter Eleven

Dusk was beginning to filter through the thick foliage when he at last drew her to her feet and into the circle of his arms.

"And now," he said for the third time, "what about Winterton and Vasileyev?"

Despite the tenderness with which he was holding her, there was a dangerous glint of green in his near-black eyes.

Her arms were around his waist, her head against the strength of his chest. "Vere was never my lover," she said softly.

"Then my arrival was timely." There was dry humour in his voice.

She smiled. She had thought she would never forget the horror of that dreadful scene. Now it was already blurring.

"Yes." He tilted her face up to his.

"I never wanted to take Vere as a lover. I was lonely and he cared for me and I thought perhaps it would help the hurt and the pain that losing you created."

"And Nicky?"

She held his eyes steadily. "Nicky was my lover. For one night."

"I see." His voice told her that he did not.

She twisted her fingers through his and now it was she who held him, her eyes wide and dark and full of honesty.

"When I came here it was to escape you, not to find you. You had told me once that Madeira was out of bounds to you, and I believed you. I thought it was the one place in the world where I would not accidentally see or meet you. I could have packed my bags and fled, but I had nowhere to flee to." Her voice thickened. "Besides, once faced with your nearness again, I no longer had the strength to move away from it. You were like a magnet to me. No matter how indifferent you were, how cruel, I had to have the solace of at least seeing you.

"When I saw you with Tessa, when I saw how young and pretty she was, how adoring, when I saw the way you looked at her and held her, I could bear it no longer. It was then that Nicky and I became lovers. I needed physical comfort. I needed to be loved, however transiently." She smiled: a small crooked smile, willing him to understand. "Nicky is a man who takes many lovers—as you did. They mean nothing to him as they meant nothing to you. He is not in love with me, nor I with him. For a brief moment in time we needed each other and gave to each other. That is all."

"Can you forgive me?" His eyes were brilliant with pain.

Her kiss was his answer. Long and deep and full of love.

Slowly, arms entwined, they began to climb the path to the hotel.

"Jack is on his way here," she said. "But then you'll know that already."

"I didn't, but it makes no difference."

"No."

They continued in silence. She could feel the heat of his body against the filmy silk of her dress, the strength of his thigh against hers. Some of the old mockery was back in his voice as he said:

"I'll have some explaining to do to Zia. I told her only hours ago that I was going to marry Tessa Rossman."

She halted, her eyes huge. "And were you?"

He laughed. "Yes, so help me. But only because I couldn't have you and if I didn't have you it didn't matter who I had."

"But that poor child . . ."

He silenced her with a kiss. "That poor child is none the wiser."

She shivered suddenly. "If you hadn't come . . . If you'd stayed in New York . . . If you'd gone to Paris or Rome or . . ."

He halted, his hands on her shoulders, staring down at her with impatient amusement. "Don't you still understand? My coming here wasn't an accident. I came here because I knew you were here. What do you think I did in New York when you didn't arrive? Shrugged my shoulders?"

"No. I don't know . . ."

"I'll tell you what I did." His voice was grim again. "I drove to Hyannis to fetch you by force. But you weren't there." His rage and pain were transparent. She trembled at the realization of his desire and love for her.

"Your butler told me that the mayor had had a heart attack and that you had left for Madeira."

She held on to him, her legs suddenly weak. He felt her response and suddenly grinned.

"Don't worry. I didn't barge in on him, but I would have done if the shipping line hadn't confirmed you had sailed aboard the *Mauretania*. I followed on the *Bremen* and picked up the *Kezia* at Southampton."

"What did you think?"

The harsh lines that had gathered around his mouth softened. "That I was mad. That you were mad. That you had run away from me. That you were waiting for me. By the time I reached Madeira I was sure it was the latter. You had to be waiting for me. I couldn't come to terms with any other alternative."

"And so you came to my room?"

"Yes."

They were silent, mimosa blossom drifting above them, catching in their hair.

After a little while she said gently, "I'm sorry, Ramon. I should have stayed in New York and faced you with my father's accusations."

"No more apologies. No more 'might have been'."

Sanfords' honey-gold walls and rose-red roofs could be seen between the last of the trees.

"I love you, lady. That's all that matters."

They kissed for a long time, then walked through the flowers and trees and across the lawn, hand in hand.

Bobo, in a pair of glorious cerise velvet lounging pants and very little else, halted in her conversation with Luke Golding and stared. Costas chuckled and dived into the pool for a last swim. When Nancy kicked over the traces, she did so all the way. First Winterton, then Vasileyev, now Sanford. He surfaced with a wide grin and shook the water from his eyes. Jack oh-so-careful Cameron had a rebellion on his hands. Costas wondered how he would handle it.

Lady Michaeljohn's lips closed in a grim line of disapproval. She blamed it on the mother. She should never have married an American. They were unstable and immoral, and this was the result: a married daughter flaunting an intimacy with a single gentleman. Not, she thought as she snapped her spectacle case shut, that

Ramon Sanford had ever come under the heading of gentleman.

Georgina saw them from her balcony and frowned. What was Nancy doing? Didn't she know Jack had arrived? Besides, she had been sure that last night Nicky and Nancy had slipped away away from the ballroom. Nicky had been looking very pleased with himself all day, and it was obvious that the Hedley girl had been crying. Thoughtfully she sat at her dressing table whilst her maid brushed her hair. It was time she talked to Nancy. Indiscretions were one thing. Scandals another.

Zia's aides saw Ramon's approach and were oblivious of his companion. Villiers hurried towards them, his narrow, ascetic face an unpleasant shade of grey.

"Madame has been taken ill . . ."

Ramon broke into a run and Nancy followed, hampered by her high heels. When she breathlessly reached the door of Zia's room Ramon was already at his mother's side, her hand in his. Nancy stood awkwardly, not wanting to intrude. The staff surrounded her, instinctively giving mother and son an element of privacy.

"Darling, what is it? What's the matter?"

Her eyelids fluttered open at the sound of the beloved voice. The corners of her mouth tilted in the effort to smile. She was too tired to move. Too tired to speak.

"Dr. Serrado is here, sir."

The servants and Nancy left the room quietly. Only Ramon and Zia's maid remained. It seemed an eternity before the doctor re-emerged with Ramon at his side. Again, unasked, she followed in his wake as he escorted the doctor to the corridor leading away from Zia's private rooms. He had forgotten her existence. She remembered Boston and her father, and understood.

The doctor departed and Ramon turned in search of

her. She was there, only yards away, and his thankfulness was apparent. He took her in his arms and for the first time she had the sensation of giving solace instead of receiving it.

"Dr. Serrado says there's nothing seriously wrong. It isn't a heart attack or a stroke. She's simply exhausted: physically and emotionally. She needs a long rest."

With his arm still around her, they began to walk back to Zia's suite. "She's been working sixteen hours out of twenty-four and at her age it's too much. People don't see it as work, but it is. Receiving people, hostessing, doing all the paperwork, seeing the hotel runs smoothly. Not going to bed till dawn. That staff and guests are happy. The only directrice Sanfords has is Zia."

"What will happen now?"

"Villiers will take over the paperwork and our autocratic guests will have to adapt to a new hostess."

"But who? You've just said that Zia did everything herself. That she had no deputy and no one to replace her."

The familiar wicked gleam was back in his eyes as he paused at Zia's bronze-studded door. "True, and even if such a person existed, she would be a poor replacement for my mother. To hostess Sanfords a woman needs brains, beauty, wit and charm. She needs to be at ease with royalty and government ministers, film idols and artists, millionaires and megalomaniacs. She needs to be able to scintillate and sparkle in a roomful of the richest and most beautiful women in the world."

He smiled his devastating smile. "She needs to be you," he said, and led her through the doorway.

"Under the circumstances . . ." Viller was saying as they entered.

Ramon's smile vanished. "My mother is ill! If you have anything to say, say it to me in my office, later."

Villiers retreated with as much dignity as he could

muster. The blazing anger in Ramon's voice indicated that he was within an inch of being evicted manually.

"Stupid fool," Ramon said under his breath, as he struggled to regain his temper for his mother's sake. Villiers was usually superhumanly efficient and tactful. His mother's collapse had obviously affected him. There could be no other explanation for his uncharacteristic behaviour.

He neared the bed, leading Nancy by the hand. Zia lay sunken against her embroidered crèpe de chine pillow cases and, despite herself, smiled faintly. They were both so magnificent; both so beautiful; both so blatantly happy. They saw only the smile and not the pain behind it.

"Nancy will hostess for you."

They stood together, already a team. Tessa would have been in his shadow. Nancy shone with a flame of her own.

"Jack Cameron arrived this afternoon," she said weakly.

Her son's strong face was impassive. "Don't worry about Jack Cameron. Don't worry about anything." He had not told her he loved the woman at his side: he had no need to.

Zia closed her eyes momentarily to summon extra strength. She had to tell them. It was her duty to do so. They could not continue to live in their Garden of Eden unaware of the serpent about to destroy their happiness with its evil and malignancy.

She was too weak and besides, Villiers had shown her the cable. Boston's mayor was on his way. He would deal with the situation. He would tell them.

"Old sins," she murmured as she slipped into sleep. "Old sins . . ."

They waited a few minutes and then, leaving Zia's maid sitting at her bedside and a nurse sitting beside the door, quietly left.

"If Jack has arrived I must see him immediately."

"We'll see him together."

"No. I owe it to him to see him alone. Later, perhaps, we can all talk together though I doubt if Jack will want to. Besides, there's nothing to talk about any more."

"I don't want to let you go. I don't want to let you out of my sight."

She could feel the heat throbbing beneath her skin as his fingers touched her naked arm.

"I must," she said, and turned from him before she could weaken.

The man desired by countless women desired her. He loved her. It was a heady, intoxicating thought that filled her with wonder. She was no longer Nancy Leigh Cameron, or even Nancy Leigh O'Shaughnessy. She was simply Nancy: the woman Ramon Sanford loved. She knocked on the door of Suite 17 and at Jack's brusque command, entered. He had been a stranger to her for years. Now he, too, faced a stranger. She had always been beautiful and poised: now she was radiant. A glowing goddess in a simple white dress, exuding sex appeal from every pore.

"Hello Jack," she said, and closed the door behind her.

He stared. He had expected to find her pale and showing signs of stress. From the moment of their Chicago-Hyannis telephone call, he had attributed her behaviour to a temporary derangement caused by the onset of an early menopause. Jack Cameron knew nothing about menopause, except how to spell it, but it was the only explanation his unimaginative mind could think of. He had lived with Nancy for eighteen years. He *knew* her. She was level-headed, sensible, as beautiful as a marble sculpture and as responsive. The idea of her acting recklessly was ludicrous. The idea of such recklessness being caused by sexual passion, an absurdity. Sexual passion was not part of Nancy's make-up.

He ought to know: he was married to her. He had half expected that she would be relieved at the sight of him, would welcome being rescued from her folly. He had already checked out two gynaecologists—one in New York and one in Washington. What he had not expected was to be confronted by a woman totally self-assured, showing not the least sign of stress or remorse and very little similarity to the woman he had last seen. The *wife* he had last seen, he mentally corrected himself.

For one insane moment he had reacted to her as if she was a stranger and his reaction had been entirely sexual. It wasn't a feeling he associated with his wife. Nancy's cool, orchid-like beauty had been lost somewhere between the New World and the Old, to be replaced by a glowing lushness, like that of a full-blown rose.

He said stiffly, "I've come to take you home. The inconvenience has been considerable. I've spoken to Dr. Claire at the Haversham Clinic and he thinks it best that he treat you for a little while."

She had been going to move forward and take his hand. Instead she sat on one of the gilt chairs and crossed slim, sun-tanned legs. Naked legs. Her husband averted his eyes and smoothed down his hair and adjusted his cuff links.

"Dr. Claire is a gynaecologist, not a blood specialist."

Jack had forgotten all about blood specialists. He said testily, "I'm perfectly aware of Dr. Claire's qualifications, Nancy. I've spoken to him about your condition . . ."

"What condition? I only have one and Dr. Lorrimer is treating it."

He adjusted his cuff links again and toyed with the silver-backed brush and comb on his dressing table.

"I've no desire to hurt your feelings, Nancy, but you are thirty-five years old and I'm assured by Dr. Claire that such things do occur."

Nancy stared at him in utter fascination. "Do you mean that you really believe I'm suffering adversely from an early menopause?"

He was glad that she'd said it. He found the word distasteful. "Of course. What else?"

She began to laugh and a slow red flush stained his neck and face. He slammed the hairbrush down.

"I fail to see anything amusing in this situation. You've made an utter fool of yourself and you're going to do so no longer. I've already ordered that your bags be packed."

Her laughter ended as she looked across at the man who was her husband. He was so rigidly formal. Even now he wore a dark suit, more suited to the Senate than a sub-tropical island. His hair was beginning to thin slightly and was immaculately slicked down with brilliantine. The regular, all-American boy features were blurring and losing their attraction. He was beginning to develop a jowl and his body was softening. Another five years and he would no longer have a waistline.

She said without anger, "I don't need the services of Dr. Claire. I'm sorry you have come so far on a wasted journey. I did ask to speak to you before I left America. It was you who couldn't find the time."

"I hardly imagined you'd go haring off, making a public exhibition of yourself!"

"I told you exactly what I was going to do. I told you I was in love with Ramon Sanford and that I was leaving you for him. I also tried to tell you that I would do so in a way that would not jeopardize your career . . ."

"For Christ's sake!" His face was mottled. "I'm a family man! I want to be president. I *have* to be a family man! A beautiful and faithful wife is essential! Why else do you think I married you?"

The words hung in the air for a long time. At last she said quietly, "I thought it was because you loved me."

He was struggling, one emotion after another chasing across his face: regret, rage, bewilderment.

"I *did* love you, Nancy. I do love you. Now let's pack your bags and leave."

She shook her head sadly. "No. You've never loved me, Jack. You married me because I was suitable and I imagine that you have been grateful for the fact that until now I have remained suitable. But gratitude isn't love."

"Gratitude?" he said exasperatedly. "You make it sound as if it's a retiring speech. 'We have been grateful for the services of . . .'."

"It is in a way. I'm not going back with you. I'm not going to be the public prop that will turn you into a family man for the nation to admire. You've never been a family man and you never will be. Family men spend time with their wives. They enjoy the company of their children. They care."

"*I* care, but I'm a very busy man!"

"If you cared, you wouldn't have needed a long line of mistresses. I'd have been enough for you. If you cared you would have had more sensitivity than to bring your current mistress with you when trying to recover a recalcitrant wife."

"Syrie isn't . . ."

"Of course she is." She rose to her feet. "I'm tired of lies, Jack. I'm tired of pretending and I'm not going to do it any longer; nor do I want you to either."

"Then why lie about Sanford?" Confusion had given way to anger. He was the one accustomed to being in control and Nancy, who always did as she was told, had somehow taken over. "You didn't leave New York with Sanford. He didn't sail on the *Mauretania*. You came here to make your stay more credible, but it's a fantasy. A fantasy of a sick, frigid mind."

She halted, staring at him, her blood chilling.

He laughed mirthlessly. "You've always been a cripple

in bed, Nancy. I know it and you know it. A man like Sanford wouldn't look at you twice."

She said regretfully. "No. I'm not the sexual cripple Jack, you are."

He laughed again and poured a tumberful of whisky, drinking it as if it were medicine. "Not me, Nancy. Not me. Let me tell you I've screwed more women than your pea brain can count. Sure I've had *affaires*. Sure I'm having an *affaire* with Syrie. I was having an *affaire* when I married you. I can make love anytime, anywhere, anyhow."

"You've never made love," she said quietly. "You've coupled, but you've never made love in your life." And she walked away from him, out of the room and out of the hotel. She needed fresh air. She had expected a scene and some unpleasantness, but she had not expected to feel contempt for him, or pity. When he had said he had a mistress when they were married, he had been telling the truth. Her marriage had been a sham from the beginning. So many wasted years. She looked down to where the sea gleamed silkily in the moonlight. If it hadn't been for Dr. Lorrimer's frankness, it would have been a wasted life.

She turned in search of Ramon. Time was precious. There was a dinner party to hostess in place of Zia; a painting to finish and another one to start; a man to love and be loved by.

Jack loosened his tie, swore and poured himself another tumbler of whisky. He felt as he had once done playing baseball when he had been smashed in the groin and left half senseless. His well-ordered, carefully structured world was falling to bits around him. She had always been amenable, always done what he had asked. The whole conversation had teetered from its planned course into chaos. Why the hell had he lost his temper? Why had he told her about Carline? No. He gulped the whisky. He hadn't told her about Carline. He had only said he had had a mistress when he had married her. Hell! If she found it was one of her bridesmaids there would be no chance of her returning to America with him. The whisky seemed to be having no effect at all. The conversation was not at an end, of course. She would return with him in the *Aquitania.* They would finish the cruise. It could be quite pleasant. There had been something about her, as she stood before him, something he hadn't been aware of for a long time, if ever. His sex throbbed. Had she seen? Had she been aware? Hell, she was his wife. Did it matter if she had? A reconciliation. He hadn't thought of his coming for her as that, but now it seemed a good idea. He had booked a double suite on the *Aquitania* and a single one for Syrie. Of course, on the journey here, the double suite had been occupied by himself and Syrie. Hell. He drained the glass. There could be no reconciliation with Syrie in attendance: not now Nancy knew. Syrie would have to return to America direct.

He was beginning to feel cooler now. Logic was taking over. She had discovered his *affaire* with Syrie and reacted by telling him she loved another man and was leaving him. It had been a bluff, of course, and he hadn't risen to it. He should have done. He should have raced to Hyannis like Rhet Butler on his way to Tara. That was all it needed. Now, thanks to his temper, it would need much more. She now knew that Syrie wasn't the first. He'd tell her he'd been lying; that his pride had been hurt. What else had he said? His head was beginning to buzz. He sat down on the bed, the whisky bottle grasped tightly by its neck. He'd called her a sexual cripple. He groaned. That would take more than a few words to remedy. As for what she'd said to him . . . He stood up and the room swayed around him. She hadn't meant it, of course. It had only been a form of self-defence. Nancy had always been clever with words. He would tell her he loved her. Why the hell hadn't he said it before? He hadn't said it, because it wasn't true and he'd wanted to teach her a lesson. Make her feel ashamed at the trouble she had caused, cut her down to size. Christ! If ever he'd misjudged a situation, he'd misjudged this one. He'd always known there was more to Nancy than met the eye. He remembered the nakedness of her golden legs and the outline of her breasts and reached between his legs to ease the tightness of his pants. He never remembered seeing her like that before. She was always silk stockinged for the Washington parties and balls, or trousered for her long walks at Hyannis. It occurred to him that he hadn't seen her undressed for years, and that he had been missing something. Separate bedrooms had been his idea. He needed a dressing room of his own, privacy. Besides, sharing the same bedroom was a middle-class convention, and whatever else he was, he certainly wasn't middle class.

He began to strip off his clothes. He needed a shower. He would go to her suite and apologize: be charming and loving. The *Aquitania* sailed in two days' time. They could enjoy the delights of the Mediterranean and return to America without one rumoured word of a split being uttered.

He turned on the shower and swore again. Shit. If one word of this leaked out he would not only have lost any chance of a future presidency, he'd have lost any chance of further government responsibility. Eleanor Roosevelt's code of morals was notoriously tight. Nancy *had* to return with him. He towelled himself dry. He'd handled the affair badly, but it was nothing that couldn't be put right. He should never have mentioned her age or Dr. Claire. She had been jealous and he had done nothing to relieve her jealousy. He had been a fool. Well, he wasn't going to be a fool again. Too much was at stake. He needed a stylish wife with class and breeding. He'd got one and he damned well wasn't going to lose her.

"How did it go, darling? Was she weeping and contrite or just completely deranged?" Syrie asked, entering the room and slipping her arms around his waist.

He shook her off irritably. "My wife's sanity has never been called into question."

Syrie raised her eyebrows. "My, my, we are defensive, aren't we? What's the matter, darling? Was Miss Frigidaire more unreasonable than usual?"

"I wish you'd stop referring to my wife by such stupid nicknames."

Syrie's ice-green eyes narrowed. She lit a cigarette before saying, "*You* were the one who christened her 'Frigidaire'. What happened?"

Syrie was privy to his most intimate secrets—professional and personal. For once he had no wish to confide in her.

"I blew it, thanks to you."

"Me?" She stared, fine auburn hair parted decorously in the centre and rolled up and over in the nape of her neck. Her suit was pale grey, her shirt pristine white. She was the epitome of the perfect secretary. Only the exquisite cut of the Dior suit and the sheer silk of the blouse indicated that she was also something more.

"You and your idiotic statement that Nancy was suffering from an early menopause."

Syrie suppressed a smile. She would have liked to have seen Nancy Leigh Cameron's reaction to *that* remark.

"You shouldn't have told her," she said indifferently. "The truth can be harmful. No woman likes to feel she is growing old and sexless."

Jack struggled into his trousers and glared at his twenty-three year old mistress. "My wife is *not* growing old, and she's far from sexless."

Syrie stared at him in amazement. "What's been

happening here? For the last three years all you've done is tell me how frigid and passionless she is. How you wished you could divorce her without damaging your future. Now all of a sudden you're leaping to her defence and making her out to be an upper class Jean Harlow."

Jack was breathing hard as he buttoned his shirt. "Are you quite sure that Sanford did not accompany her when she left New York?"

"Positive. Anyway, the idea of him and your wife as lovers is ridiculous. He's as handsome as the devil and twice as dangerous. His women are all fast livers."

Jack adjusted his bow tie and slicked his hair, his face grim. He was beginning to think that Nancy would fit quite well into that last category. He said tersely, "It would be better for you to eat in your room tonight."

"What the . . ." she began amazed, but the door had already slammed behind him.

She crushed out her cigarette and lit another with a trembling hand. For three years she had managed and manipulated Jack Cameron. She had foreseen all events and she had the future carefully planned out. She had no real desire for Jack and Nancy to divorce. If they did so, Jack would no longer have a future of power to look forward to. She wanted to share that future. Already, she was indispensable. She had brains and ambition and her ruthlessness was absolute. Many women in history had been the true power behind royal thrones; she intended to be the power behind the desk in the Oval Office. Behind the American throne.

She inhaled deeply. If Jack and Nancy divorced there would be no such future. If Jack no longer depended on her sexually, but was reconciled with his wife, there would be no such future. Nancy Leigh Cameron had to be made to come to heel. Syrie smoothed her skirt and walked through Sanfords' sumptuous drawing rooms on to the balcony where several couples and groups lingered over drinks before going in to dinner. She sat unobtrusively in a corner, ordered a dry Martini and listened. Nancy Leigh Cameron had been at Sanfords for over a week. Syrie needed to know what she had been doing in that time: she needed a hold over her lover's wife.

"I'm faced with an impossible choice," Ramon said, a meaningful gleam in his eyes. Her hands circled his neck, her lips bruised from his kisses.

"What is that?" she asked in the soft, whispery, honey-filled voice that melted his spine.

"Make love to you now and have you hostess in what you stand up in or deny myself the pleasure and allow you to change."

"My initiation as Sanfords' hostess would be a catastrophe if I were to wear this. You'll simply have to deny yourself the pleasure. Until later."

They kissed again and he said, "The list for Zia's private dinner party is on the desk. The Grand-Duchess Nadejda Livada is guest of honour. The other guests are Count and Countess Szapary, Mr. Blenheim, Princess Louise, the Earl and Countess of Montcalm, the Sultan of Mohore and his rather incredible-looking companion, and the Lothermeres."

Reluctantly he let her go. She rang for Maria and glanced through the list. Against every name were biographical details. The bottom names had been crossed through entirely. They were those of Prince Nicholas Vasileyev and Samantha Hedley.

Her dress was a Grecian swathe of tobacco-coloured silk, her only adornment her pearls. Her skin had a satin soft gleam, her eyes sparkled, her hair shone. Maria adjusted a fold in the softly falling skirt, sprayed her with perfume and stepped back to survey her.

The hotel was full of rich and royal women but not one

of them had a shadow of her mistress's effortless beauty. Her pride in Nancy temporarily took her mind off Luis.

Since their encounter in the laundry room he had not spoken to her, though he had seen her many times. Maria knew he was as aware of her as she was of him. She could sense it. She could sense too that he was waiting for her to make the first move, because she was a maid and Luis Chavez did not associate with maids. He would associate with her though, she knew it. But only if she gave to him what he received all too easily elsewhere and from the most surprising sources. Maria had no intention of behaving in a like manner. She was a good Catholic girl and her virginity was for her husband and her wedding night. All the same, his eyes when they met hers were bold and black and frankly appraising, and it was hard to remain indifferent and turn away coolly as if he did not exist.

Viscountess Lothermere was still continuing her daily lessons and Maria's quick eyes had noticed that when the viscountess took her afternoon nap, Luis was never to be seen. The viscountess also relieved her maid of her duties from one to three every afternoon. In the pool the viscountess seemed hardly aware of her coach's presence, but Maria had her suspicions. There was another one too. An elderly Czech countess who summoned him to her side time and time again when sunbathing in a ridiculous dress that exposed grossly fat legs and arms.

There was a knock on the door. Maria answered it to a bellboy carrying an envelope embossed with a coat of arms on a silver salver. She took it and handed it to her mistress. It read: *I must see you. Vere.*

Before Nancy had refolded the letter there was another knock. This time a giant basket of orchids and birds of paradise and a note reading: *I love you. Nicky.*

A husband, an ex-lover, an ex-would-be lover. Life was getting very complicated. Nancy put the letter and card to one side and as she did so there came a third knock.

"Mr. Cameron wishes to see you," Maria said apprehensively.

Nancy glanced at the small, ebony-cased clock on her desk. She had ten minutes before she was due to receive Zia's guests.

"Please show him in."

Jack was already in. He glared at Maria and, at a nod from her mistress, Maria left the room.

"I hope you haven't come to continue our previous conversation," Nancy said quietly. "I don't want to hear any more about your mistresses, past or present, and I don't want any more personal abuse."

"It was anger, sweetheart. I didn't mean it."

Nancy knew the new tone of voice very well. She had listened and believed in it for years. It was Jack being conciliatory.

"There haven't been other women. It's true about Syrie . . ." He had decided there was no point in denying his *affaire* with Syrie. Nancy knew of it. She didn't just suspect. To deny it would make everything else he said less credible.

"And the judge's wife in New York in 1919? And Fiona Rice in Washington in 1929, and Helen Jefferson in New York in 1931?"

He could feel the sweat break out on his forehead.

"If you knew, why didn't you say?"

Despite her intention to be cool and controlled her temper flared.

"Because I thought it was *my* fault you went to other women! I thought it was something lacking in me!" Her flare of anger and emotion released his.

"And so it bloody well was! What did you ever do in bed?"

"I *tried*!" She had thought it was all in the past, all forgotten. Insanely, tears were streaming down her face.

"I tried. I'd never been made love to when I married you. On our wedding night I was shy and apprehensive. I didn't know what to do or what to expect. What I didn't expect was that you would come to our room, disgustingly drunk, and order me to take off my clothes as if I were at a school medical!" The tears had turned to sobs. "I didn't expect to be hurt. To undergo some loveless form of examination that left me injured and bleeding! You never once, in the whole of our married life, tried to make sex pleasurable for me. You never kissed me, touched me for my pleasure, loved me with words. All you ever did was take. As if I was a whore in a brothel that you'd paid for!"

"You're out of your mind. You don't know a thing about sex and bed and you never will. If I was such a lousy lover, how come I had the long line of mistresses that you don't dispute? How come Syrie is mad for me?"

Her anger fled to be replaced by pity. "They used you, Jack. They used you for your money, for prestige, or to make someone else jealous." She was about to tell him why Syrie was his mistress, but stopped herself in time. He didn't deserve that. Without her, he would need Syrie Geeson.

"No way, Nancy. No woman has ever used me. You're living in a fantasy world. Sure, you're beautiful, but you've as much sex appeal as a cube of ice. The only knowledge of bed that you have comes from books. You're frigid and passionless and no man worthy of the name would waste his time with you!"

"I've always regarded myself as worthy of the name," a dangerously quiet voice said lazily from the doorway. Nancy gasped and Jack whirled around, the colour draining from his voice.

Dark eyes studied Jack's face, then moved slowly and insolently downwards. "I don't, however, see one before me now."

"What . . . ? How . . . ?" Jack was blustering incoherently, turning from Ramon to Nancy and back again as if he couldn't believe his eyes. "It's true then?" he spluttered at last. "You and Sanford? You and my wife?" He lunged at Ramon and he was caught by the wrists, his arm twisted behind his back so high that Jack cried out in protest.

"Yes, it's true." There was no laziness in his voice now. Even Nancy felt herself chilled at the tone. "I'm in love with your wife. After hearing your opinion of her I feel not the slightest trace of conscience: only incredible amazement that any member of my sex could be so blind and stupid." He let go of Jack so suddenly that Jack stumbled, clutching his bruised wrists.

"She has to come back with me," Jack repeated stubbornly. "I'm going to be president. I have to have a wife and no scandal."

Ramon laughed, this time with genuine amusement. "You'll never be president. You couldn't even govern a flock of sheep." He held out his hand to Nancy. "Our guests are waiting."

"In a few minutes. I'll catch you up."

His face was impassive. He didn't bother to look at Jack Cameron as he left the room.

Jack groaned, holding his arm. "Sonofabitch! The motherfucking sonofabitch!"

"I'm sorry." She stood a few yards away from him. She wanted to go to him: to offer assistance, but knew that if she did so it would be utterly rejected.

"I told you when you were in Washington," she said again, feeling an overwhelming helplessness. "I told you I loved him but you didn't believe me. You didn't believe me because you found it incredible that any man would find me desirable. I don't believe you've ever truly seen me, Jack. You've certainly never known me. I don't want any bitterness. Despite what Ramon says, there's no need for your career to be jeopardized. I can't explain now because it would take too long and Ramon and the grand duchess are waiting for me. We'll speak together tomorrow."

"Sonofabitch," Jack Cameron repeated, and turned away from her and towards the whisky decanter.

Chapter Twelve

Nancy had never felt less like playing the part of a scintillating hostess in her life. She knew the reason for Jack's uncharacteristic lack of composure and she knew it was not grief at losing her, herself. Only what she represented to him. Nevertheless, it was hard to turn her back on him and join Ramon in Zia's private dining room. Silver gleamed on white napery. The name "Sanford" was not embroidered on the intricately folded napkins or exquisite tablecloth, but woven into their centres, and surrounding the name was the crest of the de Gamas. Ramon's father had taken the name of Sanford for financial expediency but he had never forgotten that he had been born the son of the Visconde de Gama, a minister in Queen Maria's government and scion of one of the most prestigious families in Portugal.

Afterwards she could hardly remember what had been said or taken place during the whole of the evening. She had felt like an actress, word perfect in her part, her mind elsewhere. For the first time since her collapse at the

Metropolitan Opera House, she felt unutterably tired; completely drained of energy. It was the first recurrence of her illness since she had left New York.

Countess Szapary, too, looked strained, but for different reasons. Georgina's eyes met hers often as the meal progressed and there was sympathy in them. The little countess would have liked to make a *confidante* of Georgina Montcalm but her husband's eyes were so watchful . . . She felt them on her again and began to peck dutifully at the salmon mousse.

The grand duchess was as heavily perfumed as the Queen of Sheba, her short fingers hidden by vast rings, a Fabergé brooch emblazoning her vast bosom. Her personal footman stood behind her chair, white-gloved and gloriously liveried in scarlet and gold. She scarcely spoke. There was no one of equal rank to speak to. Szapary was a mere count. The Lothermeres, the Montcalms and Princess Louise foreigners. Mr. Blenheim was unforthcoming and besides, exiled kings were below her contempt. They should stay and die in their countries as hers had done.

The conversation was saved by Marisa, the Sultan of Mohore's companion, smoothly blonde and soignée and dressed in clinging black crèpe that gave way to revealing net, from a position fractionally south of her breasts to a perilous line skimming her hips.

Viscount Lothermere's breeding deserted him. He gazed in rapt attention at every sinuous movement. His viscountess smiled distantly, her mind elsewhere.

Mr. Blenheim seemed not to hear most of the grand duchess' remarks. Marisa's navel showed clearly beneath the black net. It occurred to the ex-royal that a ruby or emerald would look very well placed in such a strategic position. He decided he would no longer play the part of a recluse. Europe would soon be shaken up like a giant jigsaw and, when the pieces were reassembled, it was quite possible that he would regain his throne. A potential reigning monarch had far more pull than an obscure Eastern sultan, however rich.

"But how tragic to play the starring part in a film of the magnitude of *Golden Dreams* and not to see it screened," Georgina was saying, after Marisa had given them a racy account of her time spent in Hollywood the previous summer.

Ramon grinned. He had heard about Marisa's performance in *Golden Dreams* from Sonny. Sonny had said that the American public, or indeed any public, were not yet ready for the kind of love scenes that Marisa seemed unable to tone down. The film had been a joy to director, cameramen and male lead, but had ended up on the cutting-room floor, or would have done so if the director had not been foresighted enough to have retrieved it for his own personal viewing and pleasure. As an artist, when Marisa gave she gave her all. Sonny had not yet made her acquaintance but was looking forward to doing so. It would put Hildegarde back on her toes and that particular little lady was getting all too complacent these days.

"A tragedy," Marisa agreed, a small pink tongue circling a peach slowly and lingeringly, before biting delicately into it.

The viscount experienced an erection that nearly lifted the table, and blew his nose furiously.

"But then," she shrugged slender shoulders and the lower half of pink nipples were momentarily visible as her dress shifted direction. "My life has been a series of tragedies. I lost my parents aboard the *Titanic* and was only saved by clinging to a crate of champagne."

Ramon's grin deepened. Marisa's parents were alive and well and living in Minnesota. "My poor first husband died, shot through the head in a duel with a French count who was madly in love with me. When I vowed to leave my second husband, he was so demented that he threw himself from the Eiffel Tower."

"He showed an abysmal lack of taste," the grand duchess said icily. "Only the working class commits suicide by throwing themselves from the Eiffel Tower. He should have chosen the Paris Ritz or Notre Dame."

"But he was deranged with love," Marisa said imperturbedly.

"He was certainly deranged," the grand duchess agreed tartly.

"What did you do after you left Hollywood?" Nancy asked.

"Oh . . ." Marisa was vague. "I went to England but the only eligible man was the Prince of Wales and the weather was so cold and damp that I did not think it worth my while to stay."

"How fortunate for the prince," Earl Montcalm said *sotto voce* to Viscount Lothermere.

The Viscount was not listening: the net moved and shifted. Another inch . . . another fraction . . . If she raised her arm, reached for a grape . . .

"To seek the sun I travelled to Madrid and it was there I found my true vocation."

The Princess Louise laid down her knife and fork. Surely the woman could not be talking about Holy orders. If so, she would write to the Pope.

"And what was that?" Ramon asked, aware that Marisa had found her true vocation at a much earlier stage of her life.

Marisa's eyes smouldered suggestively at the man rightly nicknamed The Panther. She had been alight with sexual tension ever since sitting at the same table as him. He was magnificent: his hair a curling black pelt, the lines of his mouth sensual—almost brutal. She shivered, seeing in imagination his nakedness: his granite-hard body, his broad shoulders and chest, his lean hips. She had heard about Ramon Sanford's capabilities as a lover, but though there was a mocking gleam in his eyes when he addressed her, she sensed there was no desire there. It was strange: her eyes had told him of her willingness.

"To be a matador."

"A *bull-fighter*?" Even Charles Montcalm lost his British indifference.

"In Spain I am known as one of the greatest of matadors."

"But isn't it frightfully dangerous?" Serena Lothermere asked with mild interest.

"It is a matter of life and death. Every time I step into the ring and face the bull, it is a battle to the death. His death or mine."

"I etch," the grand duchess said reprovingly. "It is a much more suitable pastime. The Tsarina herself was remarkably talented in that direction and Queen Mary is also extremely accomplished."

"Aren't you afraid?" Serena asked, a strange light in the back of her eyes.

"Of course I'm afraid. Fear is the excitement. It is the edge which gives life meaning. Unless you are afraid of losing your life, how can you appreciate it?"

"Quite easily, I should think," Georgina said with a laugh. "Don't you agree, Nancy?"

"No. I don't," Nancy said unexpectedly. "I agree with Marisa. Only when you are faced with death do you appreciate life."

"Well, I've been faced with death for the last ten years and it hasn't sent me into the realms of excitement," the grand duchess said acidly.

"You used to fight bulls, didn't you?" Georgina asked Ramon as the grand duchess and Marisa glared at each other with open antagonism.

"But of course. I'm Portuguese."

Nancy's eyes met his and she felt something deep melt within her. There was so much she did not know about him. So much to find out.

"My father urged me to manly deeds, even bullfighting and trying to throw cows by their horns, from a very early age. I was only nine years old when I faced my first bull and very, very frightened."

Duarte de Gama. Duarte Sanford. A man who had mistreated his wife and had faced his young son with a bull. Yet the son had never indicated anything but love and respect for a man who must have been extremely unlovable. He had never spoken of his father, except in the context of the Sanford-O'Shaughnessy saga. She would like to hear him speak of his father: to know what his true feelings were.

"Do you attend Cowes?" Princess Louise was asking her.

Nancy smiled. "Not for a long time." Not since as a little girl she had met the boy who was to become the love of her life.

Again their eyes met. Georgina pursed her lips. Though very little had been said directly between Nancy and Ramon during dinner, there was an atmosphere that no one, not even the grand duchess, could fail to be aware of. The taut excitement between them sent its reverberations around the whole table. Nancy glowed with an inner luminosity of pure happiness. Ramon's restlessness seemed to have suddenly stilled, as if he had found peace he had long been searching for. And though the guests seated with them did not know it, Senator Jack Cameron was installed only rooms away from them, uninvited to the select dinner party presided over by his wife.

"Regatta week," the sultan said knowledgeably. "I am always in England for regatta week."

"Will you be there with the *Kezia* this year, Ramon?" Georgina asked.

"My plans for the coming year are extremely fluid."

Again his eyes met Nancy's. This time the entire table glanced from one to the other with undisguised interest. Even Charles. If Charles had cottoned on to the fact that there was a rip-roaring love affair taking place between the "Panther" of the international pack of playboys and the normally circumspect wife of the man destined to be the President of the United States of America, then they would be like lambs to the slaughter.

Nancy's reputation would be ruined. Jack would divorce her—he would have to if he were to salvage his career. Georgina wondered if Ramon was aware of the havoc he was about to cause. His *affaires* were legion, but always before the ladies had been well able to take care of themselves. Nancy was different. Like herself, she could not afford the luxury of a casual lover. Georgina could barely control the exasperation she felt at Ramon's reckless behaviour. In a few weeks he would be in Paris or Rome or London, another society beauty clinging adoringly to his arm. His life would go on as it always had and Nancy's life would be shattered. All because of a heady infatuation. She wondered who was the bigger fool, Ramon or Nancy, and decided that it was Nancy. Ramon had nothing to lose: Nancy everything.

"The Royal Yacht Squadron is the most exclusive club in the world," Charles was saying in answer to a query from the sultan. Viscountess Lothermere was telling Maria of Schiaparelli's intention of visiting Moscow later in the year, and speculating on what that would mean in the change of future fashion.

Mr. Blenheim was strenuously denying any family connection to King Zog of Albania, and agreeing with the grand duchess that the gentleman in question had been most wise in marrying his impoverished Hungarian countess instead of another lady who should remain nameless.

Princess Louise was asking Ramon why he had not

been in St. Moritz as usual for the winter sports, and if Zia would be attending the Paris fashion shows in February. Nancy was soothing the count's displeasure by informing him of the prestigeousness of the other guests invited aboard the Montcalms' yacht, and bringing a sparkle of hapiness into the countess's eyes by telling her of the impromptu dances and cocktail parties aboard the many yachts, and of how splendid they looked riding at anchor, be-flagged and lit from stem to stern.

Nancy drew on an inner strength she did not know she possessed, to laugh and talk and be gay. Inside she was tired to the point of collapse. It came upon her like this; suddenly and for no reason, a fatigue that was crippling.

At last Ramon rose to escort her from the table. The room seemed suddenly hot. Airless and suffocating. The footman drew back her chair. The grand duchess was saying something to her but Nancy could not hear for the thundering in her ears. The shrivelled, crimson-painted lips continued ceaselessly and Nancy felt the sweat break out on her hands and on her forehead. With supreme willpower she struggled to her feet. The footman caught hold of her elbow, steadying her and then Ramon was at her side, saying anxiously:

"Do you feel ill, darling?"

She could not see him. She could see nothing but a kaleidoscope of lights. With a small cry she reached out for him and the dazzling white of the tablecloth rose up and met her as she pitched forward.

The guests leapt to their feet, chairs overturning in their haste. Glasses fell and rolled, wine and brandy staining the handwoven linen.

"*Nancy*!" Ramon sprang towards her, lifting her from the wreck of glass and china.

"My God, Sanford. Is she all right?" Charles brushed a scattering of gardenia petals from his evening suit as he disentangled himself from the overturned table decoration and strode towards them.

Ramon swung her up into his arms. She lay limp, her skin chalk-white, her eyes closed.

"Send for Serrado," he said grimly to a footman, and then he strode towards the door, his horrified guests hastily making way for him. Nancy's high-heeled, backless sandals fell onto the floor and Countess Szapary bent and picked them up, ignoring her husband's furious glare.

"I didn't think she looked well," Viscountess Lothermere said to Georgina.

"Her mother was a Winterton. They've never been a robust family," Princess Louise said knowledgeably.

Marisa said nothing. She was too busy exchanging meaningful glances with the viscount, leaving him in no doubt as to the delights the future held for him.

Georgina stared after Ramon. For the first time it occurred to her that his affair with Nancy might be more than the usual week or month of fun and games. His eyes had been tortured as he lifted Nancy from the wrecked dinner table. She frowned. If Ramon had fallen in love with Nancy it would solve no problems. If anything, it would increase them. She sighed and slipped her arm through her husband's, grateful for the stable state of her own marriage and the unflamboyant rock upon which it was built.

By the time Ramon had swept into the Garden Suite Nancy's dark eyes had fluttered open and the colour was returning to her cheeks. She felt safe and secure. Protected by the depth of his love. It had been years since anyone cared whether she felt ill or well. Jack had no time for illness and always removed himself as speedily as possible if it threatened either his wife or daughter. Verity had always been too much of a child to understand on the rare occasions when Nancy had been laid low with a violent headache or flu. Ramon would have been tucking her up in bed with hot water bottles and warm brandy. Though they had never had those years together and though they never would have years together, it gave her intense happiness to know instinctively and beyond a shadow of a doubt what those years would have been like.

"You should have told me you didn't feel well," he said tightly, his handsome features as concerned as they had been earlier for his mother.

"I'm tired, my love. It was a silly faint, that's all. There's nothing for you to look so worried about."

"I should never have asked you to hostess tonight, not after the scene you endured with Cameron."

His face was anguished as he slipped off her dress and slid a filmy silk nightdress over her head. Unresisting, she allowed him to lift her and lay her with unspeakable gentleness on the vast bed.

Dr. Serrado entered breathlessly and Ramon remained at her side as he examined her. The doctor's liquid brown eyes were worried as he prescribed iron tablets, red wine and rest. Nancy agreed to pills and wine but refused adamantly to travel to Lisbon for a second opinion. She had fainted. She often fainted. She had done so since she was a child. It was a lie, but it was one Dr. Serrado believed. American women were not as strong as Portuguese women. They had no peasant vigour in their blood.

Dr. Serrado returned to his rich, elderly and insomniac patients and Ramon pulled the lavishly embroidered sheets high over her shoulders. He dimmed the lights and then sat on the edge of the bed, her slim-boned hand in his strong one. Her eyes had closed, she felt his kiss on her brow and his touch as he tenderly stroked a stray curl away from her cheek and behind her ear, and then she was asleep, a smile on her lips. Beloved at last.

* * *

When she awoke the sun was streaming through the wooden slats of the shutters at her window. There was the familiar sound of perfumed water running into her bath. Maria was moving noiselessly, laying out silk lingerie, spreading a selection of dresses she thought Nancy might like to wear along the brass rail that fronted the wall-length wardrobe.

Nancy lay for a few moments, cocooned in the warmth of her bed, remembering the previous evening. Musingly she touched her forehead where he had kissed her as tenderly as if she had been a child. No one had ever shown such concern for her before. Not Jack. Not Verity. Not even her father. No one had ever sat by her side before, holding her hand until she slept.

She stretched cautiously. No limbs ached; no effort was required. She opened her eyes wide. She felt perfectly rested; perfectly fit. She sat up in bed and Maria adjusted the pillows, bringing in her breakfast tray. She ignored the chilled champagne and orange juice that Zia seemed to think the perfect early morning drink, and drank instead two cups of hot, strong, black coffee. She ignored the scrambled eggs and ate only a piece of toast. Then she sang as she swung her feet to the thickly carpeted floor and padded into the bathroom. She sang as she bathed and hummed as Maria did her hair and nails. The dress she chose to wear had a halter-neck and was deceptively simple. "Did you say Mr. Sanford said he would be in conference with his secretary until noon, Maria?"

"Yes, madame. He said that you were not to be disturbed; that you had to rest."

Nancy gave a small laugh. "I don't need to rest, Maria. I've never felt better in my life. Where did Mr. Sanford say he would meet me for lunch?"

"He said you were to meet him in his suite, madame."

She had the whole morning to live through until she

saw him again. She knew the reason for his working morning. He was instructing Villiers on the extra work necessary now that Zia was unwell. No doubt, if she could convince him that she was strong enough, he would tell her the less obvious duties normally executed by Zia.

Out on the terrace only one sun-lounger was occupied. It was still only nine o'clock and Sanfords' guests had not long been in bed.

"Well, am I glad to see you," Georgina said lazily, shifting her position as Nancy approached.

A white-shorted, attentive pool-boy was already trundling another sun-lounger in close proximity to Georgina's, providing cushions and the ubiquitous drinks trolley. Nancy thanked him and lay down beside Georgina. It was very quiet. There was no raucous laughter or high-pitched giggles. Nancy determined to sunbathe at an early hour every day. It was far more pleasant than when the terraces were alive with Meades and Carringtons, Michaeljohns and Lothermeres.

"I thought you were going to die on us last night. You looked ghastly."

"It had been a long day."

Georgina rolled over on to her stomach, her fall of golden hair spilling down so that it trailed in the dew-wet grass.

"Vere, Nicky, Ramon and husband would make any day pretty tiring," she said drily.

Nancy felt the colour heighten in her cheeks. "Is everything so obvious?"

"Until last night, only to me. Even now I think your name will only be linked with Ramon's. That is, if you continue to gaze at each other with such unconcealed lust."

"I don't lust after Ramon," Nancy said quietly. "I love him."

"So have a hundred others."

"It's different this time."

Georgina laughed kindly. "I wish I had a guinea for every time I've heard that."

Despite herself, Nancy grinned. "It does all sound trite, doesn't it? But it's true. I do love him and he loves me."

Georgina sighed. This was going to be harder than she had anticipated.

"What about Princess Marinsky? Are you quite sure she isn't waiting for him in Paris? I know rumours about Ramon's future bride have been bandied about for years, but this time it did seem as if there might be some truth in them."

Nancy shook her head. "No. If Ramon were to marry, he would marry Tessa Rossman."

Georgina sat bolt upright and stared at her. "That child? Have you gone completely mad?"

Nancy giggled. It wasn't often that Georgina lost her composure. "No, I have what is known in the trade as inside information."

"I bet you have," Georgina said darkly, laying down once again. "So you love Ramon and Ramon loves you? Taking this slowly and step by step, what about Vere? I had the distinct impression that he loves you too."

"Did you?" Nancy frowned. Georgina's perception was acute and she was intimately acquainted with Vere. He was part of the Montcalm set and Georgina was not a person to reach rash conclusions.

"Yes," Georgina continued mercilessly, "I did. He looked happier than I have seen him look for years when he arrived here with you and then within days he had the eyes of a man being publicly tortured."

This time it was Nancy who sat up, hugging her knees. Her thoughts had been so full of Ramon she could scarcely remember when she had last seen Vere.

"Well?" Georgina waited expectantly.

Nancy continued to hug her knees, staring out over the still waters of the Olympic-size pool. "I never meant to hurt Vere. I never told him I loved him or led him to expect anything from me. We are family and though we hadn't met for years simply being related created its own bond."

"But he did fall in love with you?"

"He said he had."

"Then I should believe him. He isn't notorious for being a womanizer despite his undoubted charms and blond good-looks."

"We were never lovers," Nancy said defensively.

"Neither are he and Clarissa."

"He never spoke about Clarissa. I knew he was unhappy but that was all."

"Vere never has, and I doubt he ever will, speak of Clarissa with truth. It would be too painful." She shaded her eyes against the rising glare of the morning sun. "Clarissa Chase is a very English beauty: fair-haired and blue-eyed. Rather too tall and athletically built for the tastes of many men. She rides to hounds, prefers the country to the city." Georgina fell silent. Nancy waited.

". . . and women to men."

"You mean as companions?" Nancy asked, grasping at straws.

"I mean as lovers," Georgina said bluntly, "which is why she is abroad so often. India, Morocco, Turkey. London society regards her as a modern-day Lady Stanhope, nothing more. I doubt if more than three people know. Vere, myself and now you."

"Why did you tell me?" Nancy's voice was low.

"Because I'm extremely fond of Vere. He's suffered enough hurt and humiliation in the past without suffering more. Now that you know the truth about his private life perhaps you will be kinder to him when you tell him you are in love with Ramon Sanford. Also, as you appear to have got closer to him than anyone else has, perhaps you can help him. He should divorce her and remarry. He's terrified that if he does, Clarissa's personal tastes will become public knowledge. Naturally they wouldn't. It could be arranged that he appear the guilty party and she divorce him."

"Then why doesn't he?"

"Presumably because Clarissa enjoys the title of duchess and the Meldon millions. If he threatened her with exposure she would soon come to heel, but the trouble with Vere is that he belongs to that rare breed of men who are truly nice. He wouldn't dream of taking such an attitude with her, which is a tragedy because his life is being ruined. Perhaps, at a suitable moment, you could make him see that. Give him the strength to endure some temporary unpleasantness and publicity for the sake of his future happiness, though not, apparently, with you."

"No."

There was silence for a little while. Serena Lothermere emerged in a two-piece swimming costume and dived cleanly into the pool, swimming with strong, confident strokes.

"Now for number two," Georgina said, and raised her hand, summoning an unseen but seeing waiter. "A daiquiri please."

He turned to Nancy.

"An iced coffee, please." He disappeared.

"Number two?"

"Stop playing dumb and stalling for time. Prince Nicholas Vasileyev. Am I right or am I wrong?"

"You're right."

"I thought I was. Does Ramon know about your little escapade with our dashing Russian?"

"Yes."

Georgina raised her eyebrows. She hadn't expected

that. Ramon might not be faithful but he expected his mistresses to be. Unless the *affaire* had only flowered in the last twenty-four hours. She dismissed the idea. The intensity of feeling that was apparent whenever they were in the same room together made a mockery of that theory. There seemed little more to be said about "number two". She could hardly ask Nancy if she was conducting two *affaires* simultaneously.

"Number three," she said as she took her daiquiri from a silver tray. "Is he aware of one, two and four?"

"Being questioned by you is like being questioned by Torquemada."

"Being questioned by me is child's play compared to the press," Georgina returned complacently. "Now, how much does Jack know? More important, what is he going to do about it?"

"He knows that I'm in love with Ramon and he knows that I'm leaving him."

"Good God! You must be joking!" For the first time Georgina was genuinely shocked. "You've been married for seventeen or eighteen years, Nancy. You can't divorce him for a man like Sanford!"

"I never used the word divorce. I said 'leave'."

"You mean you intend to leave Jack to live with Ramon and when the *affaire* loses its attraction, return home as a dutiful wife? With no one the wiser? You must be out of your mind. In the kind of world that you and I and Ramon live in every move we make is noted and commented upon."

There was no way that Nancy could explain that time itself would solve the problem. She remained silent.

Georgina asked, awe-struck, "Has Sanford asked you to marry him?"

"No. As a matter of fact, he hasn't."

Georgina slammed a clenched fist against her smooth brow in complete mystification. "You've taken leave of your senses! What will you have when Ramon leaves you? What will happen to you? What will your future be?"

Nancy could have told her, but she didn't. She was beginning to feel the old fear rising; the fear of the dark and the unknown. Only with Ramon did she feel truly safe.

"Is Nicky aware that you are openly associating with Ramon and acting as hostess for him?"

"No. Not yet."

"Is Vere?"

"No."

"Is Jack aware that you have had a fleeting *affaire* with Nicky or that Vere is in love with you?"

"No."

"My God." Georgina leaned back exhausted against her cushions. "I don't envy you your explanations. Thank goodness I had the sense to marry a nice, uncomplicated man."

"Then all this faithful bit isn't just for old HM's benefit?"

"Good heavens no!" Georgina was affronted. "If I'd wanted to bolt, all the tea in China wouldn't have stopped me. I'll have you know that between the sheets Charles is a mixture of Clark Gable and Valentino. But don't ever tell him I told you so. He'd think it frightfully un-British."

Nancy grinned. She had seen Giovanni descending down the deeply wooded path at the far side of the pool. Behind him a bellboy carried easel, paints and canvas.

She rose to her feet. "Try not to worry too much about me, Georgina. I know what I'm doing."

"I hope you do. I'm damn sure I don't," and she raised her hand to summon a waiter to refill her glass. At this rate she would be tight before lunch. If she was, it would all be Nancy Cameron's fault.

Chapter Thirteen

Four satisfying hours later Nancy walked up the dusty path beneath the shade of the trees. Even for Ramon she had felt a reluctance to leave her painting. Like yesterday, they had worked together silently. Again he had risen when the bellboy brought his simple lunch and surveyed her work. He had still said nothing—merely nodded. The painting held primitive strength and passion. It was the work of a natural artist. It moved him and it would move others. Nancy Leigh Cameron had put her soul into oil and it showed in every brush stroke.

As the wilderness of tangled flowers and shrubbery gave way to the immaculate, carefully-tended gardens Nancy changed course, taking the longer way back to the entrance of Ramon's suite, avoiding the pool and its laughing cliques. She was deep in thought, remembering the few words Giovanni had spoken when they had put down their brushes and he had broken the still-warm crusty bread and bitten deep into the hunk of cheese.

He was her Father Confessor. The only man who knew

the truth about her. Today, life, not death, was what they had talked about: her life with Jack; her love for Ramon; the feeling of guilt and pity that tore at her now that Jack had arrived. Giovanni had listened, making no comments, finishing his peasant lunch and drinking his wine. When she had risen to leave he had said simply:

"Never insult the person you have loved by offering duty or pity."

She began to cross the velvet-smooth lawns that were barred to the public. She had been pitying Jack and Giovanni was right. In doing so, she had been insulting him. No more pity and no more loveless duty.

As to her painting, her mentor had said only, "Continue as you have begun. Always paint your interior world; the world of the mind, of dreams and nightmares, of unbridled imagination. That is where your talent lies, not in the world we see, copying landscapes or figures or jugs and fruit. Leave that to others. Your talent is of a different kind."

"Am I invisible?" He was laughing down at her, only yards away.

She blinked and smiled. "I was miles away—thinking."

"You should have been in bed, resting and not painting."

Her arm slid around the now-familiar leanness of his waist as his arm circled hers. "How do you know I've been painting?"

"It was a difficult deduction, but the scarlet streak on your cheek and the smudge of blue on the tip of your nose gave me a clue."

Her hands shot to her face, horrified. "Is it as bad as all that? I must look like a clown."

"You look delightful," and to prove that she did, he kissed her long and lingeringly.

When they parted the blue had transferred itself to his

darkly handsome face. She laughed and rubbed it away with her fingers.

"I must wash and change."

"You will do no such thing." His voice was firm. "I haven't seen you for sixteen hours and I'm not letting you out of my sight. Besides, I like your feudal warpaint. It makes me feel as if we are in our own private villa and not surrounded by hundreds of irritating guests; as if you have just come in from a morning's painting and I have been pottering in the garden and preparing lunch."

She giggled. "I can't imagine you either pottering in a garden or preparing lunch."

His face was mockingly chastising. "You have a lot to learn about me, Nancy Leigh O'Shaughnessy."

She felt his grip on her waist tighten and was aware that he never called her by her married name of Cameron. "There is a side to me that no one, not even I, have seen." There was a note of deadly seriousness in his previously laughing voice. "But it's there, sweet love, and about to emerge. Will it bore you? A white-stoned villa in the sun, miles from anywhere and anyone? Groves of oranges and lemons; figs and olives and goats' bells tinkling in the distance?"

"I'm not too sure about the goats," she said gravely.

"Perhaps not," he conceded. "A picturesque touch, but a trifle unsavoury. The peace and quiet and only each other for company from morning to night, and night until morning."

"It sounds like heaven," she said truthfully. There was a sudden trace of sadness in her voice. "Can two people be so happy, Ramon? Is it humanly possible?"

"It would appear to be," he said and at the expression in his eyes, her heart turned within her breast.

She had no idea whether heaven existed in the hereafter, and for a woman so close to death, a strange indifference. Her heaven was here. Whatever came after would be either eternal unconsciousness or a very pale copy of what she was now experiencing. There could be no heaven without Ramon.

They ate on Ramon's terrace. Vichysoisse and lobster and fat stuffed quails and chaud-froid with truffle designs on them. As they ate they talked, this time not about themselves, but about Sanfords.

"After lunch and after I reluctantly allow you to remove the traces of your morning's work from your face, we will meet with Senora Henriques. She is housekeeper and will be able to tell you a hundred and one things that I can't. Also we will go on a Grand Tour of the hotel. There is a maze of kitchens and pantries and staff quarters. You will need to be familiar with them and know where they are, even if you never visit them personally again."

"Did Zia?"

"Daily."

"Than I shall too."

He grinned, white teeth flashing in his dark face, his silk shirt casually open at the neck, exposing his strong chest and thickly curling hair. She felt herself colouring at her thoughts, aching with desire for him.

"Sanfords emerged as the grandest of grand hotels back in the early 1870s when the New World discovered the Old and began to do the Grand European Tour. There was the Hotel d'Italie and Bauer on the Grand Canal and in Monte Carlo there was the Grand Hotel Victoria. At Menton there was the Grand Hotel de Venise and in Zurich the Baur au Lac. In Paris there was simply the Grand Hotel, one of the first to introduce music while the guests ate. For the English and Americans who summered at St. Moritz, there was the Beau Rivage near Lausanne, where they rested for a few weeks before returning home. And for the truly rich there was Sanfords in Madeira." He paused and smiled his devastating smile. "There is still Sanfords. Only the clientèle has changed."

"In what way?"

Strawberries, ices and fresh-picked peaches were placed on the table. "It is now not enough to be simply rich to stay at Sanfords. Zia has turned it into a very prestigious and exclusive club. Every application for a reservation is vetted by her. To gain entry the applicants need to be either a personal friend—in which case blood and money are immaterial—royal or near royal, talented or eccentric. Members of the elegant wolfpack who ski in St. Moritz. Sanfords has become the epitome of the world of the Cole Porters, the Astors, the Barbara Huttons and Pola Negris, the glamorous and the beautiful. In the last twenty years Zia has turned Sanfords into a cult. Its fame rests on the virtual impossibility of admittance. Zia chooses the guests as she would for a dinner party. A tight-knit élite of people who will rub sparks off each other, antagonize and entertain. Hence such diverse personalities as the grand duchess and Marisa, the Lothermeres and Costas and Sonny Zakar. It is no accident that the guests are so different, it is careful management.

"And you expect me to do that?" Nancy asked, aghast.

"Yes. Why not?"

"Because I don't *know* these people. I'm American. I've only spent a few weeks of each year in Europe and then only in Paris for the Collections."

He slipped a piece of Sanford-embossed paper on to the table. On it was a neatly typed list.

Request for rooms at the moment:
Mr. & Mrs. Merriman, Michigan.

Ramon looked at the notes Villiers had made opposite the names.

Mr. Merriman has made his millions on the fame of his corned beef.
Nina Correlli; the mezzo soprano, who has taken the operatic world by storm with her interpretation of Salome.
Prince Felix Zaronski of the House of Romanov.

"Villiers' notes say the prince travels everywhere with a snow-white stallion and its berth aboard ship is even more luxurious than its master's."

Lady Claire McLean: no sense of humour and even less style.
Polly Watertight.

"*Who?*" Nancy nearly choked on her ice cream.

"It's her real name and she won't change it. She's eighty if she's a day. She comes from Boston North End and is given to doing high kicks after her second glass of champagne."

The Duke and Duchess of Corrington: ardent Christian Scientists.
Mr. Percy Harvard-Jones.

"How Villiers comes by such knowledge, I have no idea, but the word 'celibate' is written large."

Kate Murphy.

"She's the ex-wife of an English duke whose name she long ago abandoned, also ex-wife of an American steel magnate whose alimony she still clings to, ex-wife of a Russian with the dubious title of 'Prince', but neither the Vasileyevs nor Szaparys have ever heard of him and the only time I ever met him I detected a decidedly Western twang to his accent: ex-wife of a twenty-year-old Californian lifeguard.

"I should mention that Kate is a decade older than Zia, and ex-wife of Desmond Murphy, described simply as an Irish entrepreneur. She is addicted to wigs of startling and various colours and these are apt to come adrift when she swims in the pool. This does not disconcert her. She simply finishes the length and retrieves her headgear on her return journey."

The prime minister of a country that I would have thought needed his presence.
A Papal legate.
Mrs. Honey-Smith of Wyoming (who has been applying for entrance for over a decade).

"Villiers does not trouble me with the hordes of wealthy businessmen and their wives who also apply. Now, who of those mentioned would you admit?"

"Nina Correlli," Nancy said, without hesitation. "She might even sing if asked nicely. I think Prince Felix's white stallion would look quite pretty pawing the ground, surrounded by doves and peacocks. Definitely Polly Watertight and Kate Murphy and I do feel for Mrs. Honey-Smith. Such persistence should be allowed to pay off."

"Ten out of ten," Ramon said complacently. "They are exactly the names that Zia marked."

"Then if you knew who was to be admitted, why ask me?" Nancy said indignantly as the table was deftly cleared, only the chilled wine and half-full glasses remaining.

"Just testing you," he said wickedly, and was rewarded by a sharp kick on his ankle.

His retaliation was to move so fast that Nancy had no time to even push her chair away from the table. His arms were around her, crushingly tight.

"For that you will pay a forfeit."

The waiter emerged with the liqueur trolly and quietly withdrew.

Some while later a braver Villiers coughed discreetly and announced that Senora Henriques was ready and waiting for her appointment with Mrs. Cameron.

"Damn," Ramon said, and released her. "You'll have to go. She's a busy lady and I don't want to disrupt her timetable."

"Aren't you coming with me?"

He shook his head. "Linen cupboards and still-rooms hold no charms for me, my love. I'll see you later, for pre-dinner cocktails with the privileged few."

Senora Henriques was a pleasant-faced, elegantly-dressed woman of indeterminate years. Her gleaming black hair was brushed smoothly into a glossy chignon at the nape of her neck. Her pale grey dress bore traces of Paris; her hands bore merely a simple gold band and her nails were perfectly manicured. She wore pearl earrings and silk stockings, and escorted Nancy without displaying anything as vulgar as curiosity.

In the next two hours Nancy learned so much about the organization behind the scenes at Sanfords that her head reeled.

The crèpe de chine sheets and pillow cases were changed twice a day. Sanfords' guests were accustomed to taking afternoon naps. They could not be expected to return to sheets already slept in. Personal initials were embroidered on *all* linen, even if the guest was staying for only a few days. For royals and ex-royals a crown was also lavishly embroidered above the monogram.

The personal maids of several guests had their own maids. Nancy was shown the quarters for guests' staff and for hotel staff. She met the man whose only job was to polish and re-polish the vast acres of the ballroom floor and she noticed, now that the ballroom was temporarily empty, that the glittering crystal chandeliers gave a slight tinkling sound as the air moved them.

She met numerous chefs, pantry boys, butlers and underbutlers. House maids, laundry maids, footmen, bellboys and gardeners. In the still-room she watched as bread and cakes were adeptly prepared by the hundred. She gazed in wonder at the amount of laundry done daily on the premises. She was informed that all soaps were specially imported from France; that there was a different table decoration every night for a month; that red carpet was always rolled from Sanfords' marble-floored hall to the doors of arriving motor cars, so that no feet should be sullied on the short journey from car to hotel. Savonnerie carpets graced the unlikeliest rooms. The tea caddies were solid silver and George III. Beds ranged from vast modern creations tented in chiffon like her own, to Hepplewhite mahogany four-posters with fluted posts and lavish carvings of flowers and lilies.

In the writing room the bureaux ranged from a French *bureau de dame* of Louis XV to an eighteenth century Dutch marquetry bookcase. The ink stands were silver and George IV. The minutest details of guests' whims and foibles were carefully indexed, the files resting in Senora Henriques' spacious private room with a rosewood desk inlaid with satinwood and dull gold leather surface. A duplicate file was in Villiers' possession.

Sanfords, she learned, employed its own hair stylists, beauticians and masseurs. There was a team of seamstresses under the guidance of a tiny, bird-like woman who created all Zia's personal clothes. For fancy dress balls and masques they worked day and night preparing lavish costumes that would be worn only once.

She was informed that the grand duchess was accompanied by an equerry with the rank of baron; that European nobility habitually travelled with a "man of affairs"; that several rooms, whose beds were changed twice a day were never occupied; that these were the rooms that Senora Henrique termed delicately as those of "travelling companions". For example, Lady Bessbrook's Venetian-style suit of rooms was adjoining those of Mr. Luke Golding—a more austere single suite. Mr. Golding's rooms were never used and his clothes hung in Lady Bessbrook's wardrobes. Nevertheless, the ritual of behaving as if Mr. Golding did occupy his suite was scrupulously adhered to. It occurred to Nancy that this quiet, efficient woman at her side probably knew more about the sexual indiscretions of the International Set than anyone else alive. That none of that set were even aware of her existence only made the supposition more fascinating.

Charmingly, Senora Henriques put herself at Nancy's disposal. Sanfords' wheels ran smoothly and would continue to do so. However, if Mrs. Cameron wanted anything changed . . .

Nancy assured her that she would not wish anything to be changed. Certainly not for the moment. They drank a glass of Malvasia together and Nancy was relieved to find not the least trace of coolness in Senora Henriques' manner. If she was to have a new mistress, temporarily or permanently, she was going to work as amicably for her as she had for her former mistress.

As Nancy put down her glass and was about to take her leave, the first hint of faint unease crossed her cultured features.

"May I be so bold, madame, as to suggest the seating arrangements at dinner of yourself, Mr. Cameron and Mr. Sanford, are resolved as soon as possible?"

"Yes." Nancy paused. Senora Henrique had far more experience of such "arrangements" than she herself. "May I ask what you would suggest, Senora Henriques?"

There was no hint of embarrassment on the housekeeper's face as she said circumspectly, "The easiest solution would be for Senator Cameron to leave aboard the ship he arrived on. I believe the *Aquitania* sails on Wednesday. Failing that, it is usual for the wife to be seated with her husband and her gentleman friend as their guest. In this case, of course, Senator Cameron and yourself would be Mr. Sanford's guests. Not that this situation has ever arisen at Sanfords before with Mr. Sanford," she added hastily.

"No. Thank you."

Senora Henriques knew and understood. It seemed to Nancy that everyone knew and understood except those to whom it should have been obvious: Vere and Nicky and Jack. Jack knew, but she doubted if he would understand and she doubted if he would sail aboard the *Aquitania* on Wednesday.

They parted with the cordial warmth proper to their respective stations, and the unspoken knowledge that if Nancy needed an ally and friend, Senora Henriques would prove herself to be one.

When she opened the door of her suite she gasped and stood rooted to the ground. Baskets of ornately arranged flowers filled every foot of floor-space, cascaded from the bed, the dressing table, the wardrobes. Gingerly she picked her way between them. In her bathroom the bath was lost under a welter of orchids and roses, birds of paradise, jasmines, lilies and mimosa.

Maria was nearly in tears as she tried to negotiate a path towards her mistress.

"I can't get to your dresses, madame, or your toilet things . . ."

"Who?"

"The prince."

In the centre of Nancy's dressing table a giant bouquet of white orchids, freesias and lilies stood out against a cascade of red roses like snowflakes on blood. Between the flowers something gleamed. With great difficulty Nancy edged her way through the baskets. The something gleaming was a rope of perfectly-matched pearls, circling the flowers with careless magnificence. She looked around her. In a huge bouquet of strelitza a jewel sparkled and shone. She crossed to it, petals scattering in her wake.

It was a slim gold chain with a ruby pendant. In another bouquet a lily held a diamond ring in its fluted heart.

"What are we going to do, madame? We must get rid of them. We can't move and they're making me sneeze."

Nancy lifted the ring from its petal-soft bed. "We can't simply ask for them to be removed, Maria. See, there's a ring here and over there, in the strelitza, a necklace and in the bouquet of all-white flowers, pearls."

Maria's eyes widened. "You mean there are jewels hidden in *all* the baskets?"

"Not all." Nancy was frantically searching between leaves, stems and petals. "But some. We must find them and return them to the prince. Of all the crazy, idiotic . . ."

"That's not all." Maria's pretty face was strained with anxiety. "His Grace, the Duke of Meldon is sitting on the terrace. He's been there since before lunch. He's been there for *hours*!"

If there had been room to sit down in weak exhaustion, Nancy would have done so. There was no room. She said despairingly, "Search every basket of flowers minutely, Maria. Any jewels you find put to one side and then place the basket outside the door. Ring for a bellboy to remove them when you are quite certain there is nothing of value hidden in the foliage. I will be out on the terrace with the duke."

"Yes, madame."

Dutifully she began her search for treasure, and just as

dutifully, deposited all she found on a silver tray. It would no more have occurred to her to slip a pendant or bracelet into her pocket, than it would have occurred to Nancy that she might do so. The pile grew: rubies, emeralds, diamonds, gold clasps and necklaces, pearls. Maria sighed. She had never met with madness but felt she was meeting it now.

He was smoking, his face impassive. He looked very English. His blond hair was short and parted neatly, brushed to a healthy shine. His white flannels were impeccably creased, his shirt immaculate. He sat, one leg crossed idly over the other, waiting.

"Hello, Vere," she said inadequately.

"Hello." He looked at her and felt only pain. Her dress was a filmy silk and the fabric seemed to float as she walked towards him and sat down.

How naive he had been to think the dream of childhood could be retrieved twenty years later. She was as far beyond his grasp now as she had ever been. Her kindness had blinded him to the truth. He had not known of her whereabouts since the night of the ball. The tasteless, extravagant exhibition in her rooms told him why.

She moved towards him as he rose to his feet, and took his hands. He said stiffly, "I misjudged the situation badly, didn't I? You must think me a complete fool."

"Dearest Vere." She held his hand against her cheek and then released it, sitting down on one of the gaily painted wicker chairs. He sat opposite, crushing out his cigarette. Below them were the carefully tended gardens and a triangle of brilliant blue that was the corner of the pool. A few voices could be heard faintly, there was some soft laughter but not much. Twilight was approaching and cocktail hour. Maids were filling perfumed baths, valets brushing recently pressed evening suits. Venetia Bessbrook was having a secret shot of bourbon. Despite

Senora Henriques' conclusions, Luke Golding had not occupied her room for two nights. Countess Szapary was crying. Madeleine Mancini was raking deep scratchmarks down Hassan's back and Viscountess Lothermere was daydreaming of men far darker than the handsome Luis. Mr. Blenheim was waiting to see how his gift of a large, uncut emerald had been received by Marisa and Madame Molière was having gold powder brushed lavishly through her hair to highlight it.

"Of course I don't think you're a fool," Nancy said gently. "And you didn't misjudge the situation. I was frightfully lonely when I met you in England and very grateful for your company."

"If I did not misjudge the situation, I misjudged you." His eyes turned towards the exotic profusion of flowers spilling out on to the terrace. "I would never have imagined you falling for such obvious flattery." His voice was tight and controlled, but the throb of anguish was obvious.

Nancy said quietly, "Prince Vasileyev is not the reason our relationship has changed, Vere. Indeed, our relationship hasn't changed. We are family and we were friends. We are still family, nothing can alter that—and I want us still to be friends."

"We were on the verge of becoming something more."

"I know, and it would have been wrong."

"It wasn't wrong with him!"

"No, because despite the flamboyant display in there, Nicky does not love me and he is not going to be hurt. I don't believe you really love me, Vere, but nevertheless you would have been hurt if we had become lovers and I had told you afterwards that I loved someone else."

"Who?" The aristocratic, fine-boned face was pinched and white.

"Ramon Sanford," she said simply.

The mask fell. His eyes showed pure astonishment. "*Sanford*?"

"Yes, we met in New York. There was a . . . misunderstanding. He followed me here."

Another man would have blasphemed. Vere's lips closed in a tight line. At least the scene in her bedroom now made sense. Even gave him a measure of satisfaction. He had nearly stolen the Panther's latest plaything from beneath his nose and the world-renowned lover was well aware of it.

"I see."

It seemed to Nancy that the more she heard people say that, the less they meant it. She said gently. "You're not in love with me, Vere. And you weren't. You were as lonely and unhappy as I was. You remembered the last time we met and the infatuation you had felt for me and suddenly, romantically, there I was. A storybook love story with a storybook ending." She smiled sadly. "Not even the most perfect love stories have storybook endings, Vere."

"You mean he doesn't want to marry you."

"I don't know. We haven't discussed it. It hasn't been . . . necessary."

There was bitterness in his voice. "I would have divorced Clarissa, forced you to divorce Cameron. I wouldn't have cared about the publicity and scandal. That was how much I loved you. He doesn't love you like that. He never will. If he did he would want to marry you."

"I know just how much Ramon loves me," Nancy said with quiet conviction. "It is totally and utterly, as I love him."

He rose abruptly to his feet, digging his hands deep in the pockets of his trousers, turning his back to her, staring steadfastly out to where the dusk was rapidly creeping down the distant mountainside, enveloping the yacht-dotted harbour. Compassionately she rose and laid her hand lightly on his shoulder.

"You are carrying your own unhappiness with you, Vere, wherever you go. I couldn't have relieved you of the burden. Only you can do that."

"What do you mean?" He was refusing to look at her. His jaw was clenched and she could feel the tenseness of his body. He was like a little boy longing for love and steadfastly refusing to show his need.

"I mean that if you are so bitterly unhappy with Clarissa, you should part from her permanently and seek happiness elsewhere."

"I told you I was prepared to do that but the elsewhere proved to be nothing but a mirage."

"No. Not a mirage. A mistake. At least now you know that you *could* find the strength to divorce her. Isn't that what you had always doubted?"

"Wintertons don't divorce."

"They do if their marriage is non-existent and they find love elsewhere. You said only seconds ago that you would have done so. Vere, dearest," she turned him towards her, forcing him to meet her eyes. "If your marriage is truly nothing but a sham, make the break and marry again. You have no children and Molesworth needs children to fill its empty rooms. It needs an heir and you need love. You will find it easily enough when you are single again. You're too moral and honourable for *affaires*. Besides, the girl who is worthy of a love like you are capable of giving is not going to be the kind of girl that indulges in illicit liaisons."

"It isn't that easy." He had turned away again, gazing sightlessly out to sea.

"Do you still love Clarissa?"

"No, but I *care* about her. I don't want her feelings to be hurt or for her to be ridiculed."

She had to choose her words carefully. She had no desire for him to know that Georgina had told her the truth about Clarissa and the reason for the barrenness of their relationship.

"Would Clarissa mind awfully if the marriage came to an end?"

He shrugged, his lips tightly compressed.

"If you asked her to divorce you, citing someone no one knew about, would she care very greatly? You could leave her financially secure and she might even be," Nancy strugged for the right words, "she might even be *relieved.*"

"What about the woman whose name is dragged through the mud of the courts?"

Nancy suppressed a sudden smile, tactfully not pointing out that if he had had his way, it would have been *her* name that would have suffered thus. Instead she said, "That's no problem. It doesn't have to be anyone you are actually having an *affaire* with. Your lawyer would arrange everything. I believe all you have to do is meet with a lady supplied by the lawyer and go and register in the same hotel room. You don't actually have to *commit* adultery to be divorced for it. One of the idiocies of the law. The lady in question gets paid accordingly, and as no one knows her name socially, suffers not a whit. It wouldn't surprise me if some enterprising young ladies weren't making quite a profession of adultery and keeping their virtue intact at the same time." She giggled and even Vere allowed himself a smile.

"Do you think that it could really be so easy?"

"Yes. If you want it to be."

"I do. I just don't want to *hurt* anyone."

"Darling, Vere. I don't think you're capable of hurting anyone, but inadvertently it would seem to me that you and Clarissa are hurting each other continually."

"Yes." He moved away towards the open doors leading into the room where Maria still worked, sitting on her heels on the floor, only her dark head showing above the mass of flowers as she prodded and searched. He gave a crooked smile. "I'm glad to know Sanford isn't the crazy coot I thought he was. However, if things go wrong I shall be here. I'm not leaving yet."

"I'm glad. I need all the strength and support I can get this next few days. Jack isn't making things easy for me."

"Have you told him you are divorcing him?"

"No, because I'm not."

He stared at her uncomprehendingly. "I don't understand you, Nancy," he said at last. "Your character and the way you are behaving just don't add up."

"Only because I'm behaving as *I* want to behave and not as society dictates. I'm very happy, Vere. It's taken me a long time to discover happiness and now I'm full up and brimming over with it. I want you to be happy too."

"I envy you," he said simply, and was gone, Nicky's orchids and roses crushed heedlessly beneath his hand-sewn shoes.

Nancy sat alone on the terrace as the twilight deepened and when she eventually returned indoors Maria had succeeded in clearing some floor space and removing the baskets that had been blocking the wardrobe and cramming the dressing table. The treasure-trove of jewels was piled in a shimmering pyramid on a silver dressing tray. Nancy laughed and ran her fingers through them wonderingly.

"There must be a king's ransom here, and I thought emigrés were always bordering on the penniless."

"This one isn't," Maria said tartly, pushing her curls away from her sweat-dampened forehead.

"Apparently not. We must return them but how?" She gazed at them musingly. She couldn't just thrust them back at him as if they were an unwelcome box of chocolates. "Any ideas, Maria?"

"No, madame. Did you know that Miss Hedley left today?"

"No." She continued to stare at the glittering and glowing stones. With Samantha gone there could be no question of a reconciliation between Nicky and his former mistress. She was not a meddler by nature, especially when it came to other peoples' lives, all the same . . .

"Continue with the flowers, Maria. I'll run my own bath. Would you also ring reception and ask them to give a message to Madame Molière. I don't know her suite number—to say that I would like to see her."

"Now, madame?" Maria asked, astonished.

"No. In about thirty minutes' time. Before cocktails," and enigmatically she disappeared into the bathroom.

Maria began to think with fond remembrance of the sanity of Boston and Washington and did as she was bid.

The evening dress Nancy chose to wear was of white silk, long and clinging, almost skin-tight, backless and strapless. Her perfectly shaped shoulders and the rising crescents of her breasts were satin-soft and honey-gold. She looked blatantly erotic and revelled in it. It was a dress that could never have been worn in New York or Washington; a dress the Nancy Leigh Cameron of a month before would have shrunk from wearing. Originally it had been halter-necked and always worn with a black silk, mandarin-collared jacket. Zia's dressmaker had dispensed with the halter, reshaped the bodice and skillfully tightened the lines from breasts to hips. The mandarin jacket was discarded. Since meeting Ramon she had been discovering new things about herself daily. One of the most startling was that she enjoyed being not only beautiful but sexily beautiful. She was at the peak of her loveliness and she knew it. After years of dressing suitably as behoved her position as the Mayor of Boston's daughter and Senator Jack Cameron's wife, she was dressing for herself. She slid two diamond bracelets slave-like high up her arm, above the elbow. When Maria began to brush her hair, she took the silver-backed hairbrush from her and began to brush her hair forward at the sides, smoothing it into two scimitar-like curls over her high cheekbones. The effect, combined with her heavy-lashed, kitten-slanted eyes, was devastating.

"Madame Molière," Maria announced, unable to take her eyes off her mistress.

Fleur Molière entered and at the sight of Nancy clapped her soft, scarlet-tipped hands delightedly.

"*C'est magnifique*," she said generously. "You will create a sensation and a whole new fashion craze. I feel quite provincial."

She said it complacently, knowing that in her Lucien Lelong creation of shimmering silk she could never look provincial. Provincials did not have gold dust in their hair and a tiny diamond stuck provocatively at the corner of one eye.

"I wonder if you would do me a great favour, Madame Molière."

"Yes, of course." Fleur Molière was always ready to be a party of an intrigue and this favour must surely denote one.

Nancy rose and crossed to the silver dish with its priceless contents. Fleur gasped and sank weakly on to the bed when she saw what Nancy held in her hands. "*Mon Dieu*! You are mad, *ma petite*. It should be in the vaults! In the bank!" She stared at them, transfixed.

"They are not mine, Madame Molière. They belong to a friend and I wish to return them."

"Fleur," she corrected, not lifting her eyes from the

careless pile of rubies and sapphires, emeralds and diamonds, pearls and coral, jade and lapis-lazuli.

"I would like you to do it for me."

"Me?" She looked at Nancy with a dazed expression. That the Americans were a strange breed of people she already knew. She was married to one and was no nearer to understanding him now than she had been ten years ago.

"Yes. I want you to put on every single piece of jewellery and return them to Prince Nicholas Vasileyev. There is a message. It is here."

A small envelope lay on the corner of the dressing table. On the card inside she had written: *Thank you for the time we shared together and today's ridiculous peep into fairyland. As I'm deeply in love elsewhere I must return your jewels with a jewel. Nancy.*

"Oh, but I couldn't," the pretty Frenchwoman was saying, picking up a necklace with shaking hands and fastening it around her throat as she spoke. "I couldn't possibly . . ." A broad gold bracelet studded with sapphires slipped over her wrist. "Not under any circumstances . . ." A ruby-centered gold pin was fastened on her shoulderstrap. She was threading the pearls through her hair.

Nancy and Maria began to laugh, diving into the pile of necklaces and bracelets like children, adorning the intoxicated Madame Molière until she resembled a petite, dazzling Christmas tree. She glittered from the top of her head to her gold-sandalled feet where two diamond earrings had been clipped on to the ankle straps of her shoes.

"I think I am dreaming. At this moment I must be wearing more jewellery than any other woman in the world! What should I say to him? What should I do?"

"You say nothing. You knock on his door and then enter. You hand him my card and you look demure. As to what you should do . . . The prince will no doubt inform you if he wants you to do anything."

"I still don't understand," Fleur Molière said, allowing Maria to lead her towards the door. "Am I awake or am I asleep? Perhaps I have been smoking Luke Golding's marijuana . . ."

Maria did not know what the message was in the envelope that Nancy was placing in Fleure Molière's dainty hand, but she had a very good idea. Eyes alight with mischief, she led the glittering Madame Molière down the thickly carpeted, mirrored corridors toward the suite occupied by the prince.

Lavinia Meade stepped from her suite en route to the Bridge Room and her husband and fell backwards, unable to believe her eyes. When she summoned the strength to take another look and see if her eyes had been deceiving her or not, the corridor was empty.

"The Malmsy," Lavinia said to herself weakly. "I've been drinking too much Malmsy."

Glittering and sparkling, Madame Molière stood at Maria's side as Maria informed the prince's valet that Mrs. Cameron had a message for him. Then, as the astounded valet escorted Madame Molière over the threshhold, she scurried laughingly back to the Garden Suite. How she would have loved to see the prince's face. She paused. What if he were angry? No. He couldn't possibly be angry. The jewels had to be returned. As to whether Madame Molière proved compensation for the loss of Nancy Cameron, only the prince would know. If she did not, she would be none the wiser and no feelings would be hurt. She hoped most fervently that the prince was enchanted by the delightful Frenchwoman. She knew that Madame Molière would be more than enchanted with the prince.

Luis was walking towards her, walking in a part of the hotel he had no business to be in. All thoughts of the prince and Madame Molière vanished.

Nicky wheeled around, expecting to see Nancy. It took him less than a second to take in the situation. He knew what was in Nancy's note even before he read it. His disappointment was acute but well hidden. One could not always win, but if one lost it was best to lose with style.

"Allow me, madame," he said with a click of his heels and a sweeping bow, and began to remove his family heirlooms slowly, one by one. As the last of the jewels was deposited in the jewel case, his hands did not stop their slow, unhurried movement and Madame Molière did not protest as shimmering silk and exquisite French lingerie skillfully followed jewels.

Chapter Fourteen

As Nancy approached the sumptuous dining room in which cocktails were to be served, she could hear the rise and fall of voices, laughter and coquettish giggles. She entered and there was a momentary hush. Not many women were beautiful enough to silence a room in which kings and princes rubbed shoulders with the world's most famous film stars. Nancy succeeded effortlessly. Ramon was talking to Charles and Georgina Montcalm, introducing them to an Indian lady, her silken sky-blue sari embroidered with complementing sapphires. His eyes met hers and he excused himself from the Montcalms and moved across to her, taking her openly by the arm.

"Have you any idea what you do to my blood pressure, dressed like that?"

"Have you any idea what you do to mine, touching me like that?"

For one precious moment they were in their own private world. They laughed and turned, host and hostess, conscious of a score of curious eyes and whispered speculations.

"Countess Zmitsky," Ramon was saying, and Nancy's fingers touched the white-gloved hand of a massively built lady with several chins. Pleasantries were exchanged and as they moved away Ramon whispered to Nancy:

"She's Czech and extremely active for her age."

"She doesn't look as if she would be active with all that weight on her. I've never seen her down at the pool."

Ramon was laughing, but at what Nancy did not understand. "Countess Zmitsky's sports are of the indoor variety."

"No, I went to Wellesly," Bobo was saying as a sultry-eyed Italian in a heavily beaded dress asked if she had attended the Sacred Heart Convent in Rome.

Nancy thought Bobo was beginning to look strained and determined to seek her out later on and see if anything was wrong. She had already forgotten any jealousy she had momentarily experienced by the knowledge that Bobo had been one of Ramon's ex-escorts. If she went through the remainder of her life conscious of who all the females were who had once clung to his arm, then she would never be able to attend any function without torturing herself needlessly. The past was past. Only the present mattered.

Princess Louise clung to her glass of tonic and lemon amid a sea of champagne and asked Mr. Blenheim for news of King Carol of Romania.

An ex-world-heavyweight champion was surprisingly tête à tête with Countess Szapary, who had forgone her virginal white for coffee-coloured chiffon which clung to her bosom, black velvet ribbon circling her hand-span waist and hanging in streamers to the ground. A black silk rose was pinned at her throat. She no longer looked a child, but Nancy noticed that her hands fluttered nervously as she talked and that her eyes were in constant search of her husband.

Mrs. Minnie Peckwin-Peake wore a million dollars of diamonds on her fingers, neck and wrists. She had more money than all the royals and ex-royals put together and was flaunting it. Mr. Peckwin-Peake had left strict instructions in his will that she was to enjoy herself and she was doing just that. She gazed across at Countess Zmitsky with distaste. She had the uncomfortable feeling that the white mound of ugly flesh was also enjoying herself and in the same manner and at the same hands. If so, it would have to stop. Minnie had long experience of keeping her young men in line. With the kind of money she had, there was always another willing young gentleman to be found if the present one proved inadequate or unsuitable. Luis Chavez was more than adequate but might, just might, be unsuitable, which would be a pity.

Viscountess Lothermere was standing at the side of her husband, her exquisitely boned face devoid of expression as he discussed the reversing American financial tide with the president of the Chetwynd Cork Company.

"Don't you find Serena's mysterious detachment intriguing?" asked Ramon, as they moved deftly from one group to another.

"I don't know," Nancy answered. "I've never thought about it. Would you prefer if I withdrew into a private world and had to be coaxed into conversation?"

"I would prefer it if we hadn't to go into dinner, and I could take you straight to bed."

Lavinia Meade turned on them, her heavy eyebrows rising. Surely she had not heard aright? But then, she had not seen aright earlier in the evening. She needed a complete medical check up. Sir Guthro Moone in Harley Street would be the best man to see. She would speak to Maxwell about it when they retired later that night.

Madeleine Mancini wore a dress of palest gold lamé and

viewed Bobo's strained face with female satisfaction. Hassan was proving a welcome diversion from Costas and it was pleasurable to know that his attention had been temporarily withdrawn from his official companion.

Dinner was announced and the *crème de la crème* made their way into the mirrored dining room reserved for Ramon's and Zia's hand-picked dinner guests. As on the previous evening, Ramon sat at one end of the table and Nancy at the other. Georgina wondered how much longer Jack Cameron would remain out of sight and relatively silent and thought it might be better to leave and journey south to the Canaries before Sanfords erupted like a volcano.

Down the vast length of the table, Ramon's eyes sought her face and travelled suggestively to her lips. He was the only man she had ever met who could make love with his eyes. She felt the familiar rise of pleasure and turned to Venetia Bessbrook who was seated on her right.

"What were you saying, Venetia? I'm sorry, my mind was elsewhere."

"I was saying that Jennifer Alleynian's broken engagement and her subsequent marriage to Freddie Bingham was remarkably sudden. Between Tatler and Tatler, so to speak."

Nancy giggled and Venetia found it infectious. Luke could go to damnation for all she cared. She was going to spend no more time pining over him. Or paying for him . . . which would curtail his activities considerably.

She slid her eyes across to Reggie and wondered if he remembered their heady romance of the previous year in Amalfi. By the gleam in his eyes he did. An old lover was less work than a new one, and for once in her life Venetia was tired. She wished Henry hadn't died. He hadn't been the most exciting of lovers, but as a husband he had been dependable and kind—qualities she had so far failed to find elsewhere.

It was a successful dinner party. Minnie Peckwin-Peake's risqué comments were entertaining. Costas had loaded Princess Louise's innocuous drink with vodka and the princess found herself recounting stories of her youth that she had almost forgotten herself. Why, she had been quite the toast of Vienna and Paris. A renowned beauty who had received sixty proposals of marriage before the age of thirteen.

Hassan, whose back was more than a trifle sore from Madeleine's passionate scratchmarks, was once more giving his undivided attention to the less tigerish Bobo, and Bobo was glowing with her old radiance.

Margot Alleynian's intelligent remarks about the present political situation in Europe lifted the conversation above the usual trivia and Charles Montcalm and the viscount joined in the talk with more than usual zest.

The only cloud on Nancy's horizon was the knowledge that when the party broke up and ventured into the ballroom to mix with the other guests, she would have to return to Jack's suite and another painful discussion.

Ramon had not been pleased. He had insisted that she have nothing more to do with her husband and that she allow him to deal with the situation. Nancy had not dared. She knew Ramon's idea of dealing tactfully with such a situation. With his total lack of regard for what others might say or think, he would have ejected Jack forcibly from the hotel and had him loaded aboard the *Aquitania* bound and gagged, if necessary.

Luke Golding had been unable to tear his eyes away from her all through dinner. The president of the Chetwynd Cork Company had been so mesmerized by her that he had eaten his fish course with his meat knife and been none the wiser. Even Charles Montcalm had regarded her with a new light in his deep grey eyes. Ramon had watched them and pitied them. She was his. No other man would ever possess her. She knew of his thoughts and she ached for his touch. The orange blaze of his shirt brought out the golden lights that lay hidden deep in his eyes. His black hair tumbled low over straight brows, curling decadently in the nape of his neck. It was impossible to see him and not want to reach out and feel the heat of his flesh against hers.

Far too soon the footmen pulled away the chairs, doors were opened and the distant sound of Sanfords' resident crooner could be heard singing a Rudi Vallee song, "Life is just a bowl of cherries."

It wouldn't be for the next few minutes.

"One hour," Ramon said grimly. "I'll give you just one hour with him and that's all. If you're not back by my side by then I shall come for you." It was no idle threat.

"One hour." She promised and hoped that Jack would prove reasonable. She had so not wanted him to be hurt by her behaviour. When she had decided to leave him for Ramon, it had been with the conviction that she could do so without harming his career. It was still possible, but only just. She had resolved long ago not to tell him the truth about her condition and so explain things the easy way. They had lived together for seventeen years and no confidences had been shared. Now was not the time to begin. Besides, if she told Jack he would tell Ramon . . . She pushed the thought from her mind and made her way towards her husband's suite.

"I simply don't understand," Syrie said, crushing out one cigarette and lighting another. "What on earth is Nancy doing with a man like Ramon Sanford?"

"Sleeping with him," Jack said, with the coarseness he never showed in public.

"And before? In New York and Boston and Washington? Who was she sleeping with then?"

"For Christ's sake, Syrie. No one. Sanford swept her

off her feet. Turned her head . . ."

Syrie sat down and crossed her silk-stockinged legs, smoothing her tailored skirt as she said, "Are you quite sure of that, darling?"

"Of course I'm sure of it! Nancy's reputation was spotless. Christ! She didn't even sleep with me!"

"Forgive me for saying so, but that makes it all the more likely she's been sleeping elsewhere."

"Not Nancy," Jack said firmly, pacing the room as he tried to form a plan of action. "She hated being touched. She couldn't bear it."

"I hope you're not suggesting that she and Sanford are doing an Abelard and Heloise routine because I just don't believe it. I doubt if Sanford knows what the word celibate means."

"Never mind the witticisms. What do we do? She's adamantly refusing to board the *Aquitania* on Wednesday, and with Sanford here I can hardly force her."

Syrie had already formed a plan that would ensure Mrs. Nancy Leigh Cameron boarded the *Aquitania*, but she had no intention of informing Jack of it yet. It would do him good to sweat a little. He would be all the more grateful when she solved his problem. Her eavesdropping had paid off. It had also taught her a lesson she would always remember. Never make assumptions: about anything or anyone. She had assumed about Nancy Leigh Cameron and she had been wrong. It was only human nature that she give herself the pleasure of informing Jack of the true nature of his so virtuous, so spotless wife. She ignored his questions and said:

"Nancy may have been discreet in America but she's thrown caution to the winds here."

"I *know* that. That is why she has to be removed from Sanford's presence as quickly as possible."

"I'm not talking just about Sanford."

Jack stopped his pacing. When Syrie used that tone of

voice it was sensible to listen.

"Sanford is only one of many."

Jack's agile mind let him down for once. "One what of many?"

"One lover," Syrie answered complacently, taking care not to let her pleasure at what she was saying show. "She came here with the Duke of Meldon. No aged dodderer, but a rather dishy Nordic type in his early thirties."

"They're cousins," Jack snapped.

"Kissing cousins," Syrie agreed. "I overheard the Countess of Montcalm telling her husband that Vere was deeply in love with Nancy. Vere being an unusual name, and the duke's name, I put two and two together and decided to confirm it. A small financial outlay induced the bellboy to tell me that not only are their suites adjoining, but that the duke has been seen entering and leaving Nancy's room at somewhat irregular hours."

"It isn't possible. She's as cold as the Arctic."

"Russia doesn't think so."

"What the devil are you talking about, Syrie? Come to the point, for Christ's sake."

"Prince Nicholas Vasileyev. He's Nancy's lover, too."

"Rubbish," Jack said, and sat down wearily. He was accustomed to sense from Syrie and she was letting him down badly.

"Bellboys are a useful breed of people when handled correctly," Syrie said, withdrawing two pieces of card from her pocket and handing them to him. He didn't even have to fit them together to read what they said.

I burn with the memory of our night together and kiss you a thousand times. Your adoring Nicky.

"It wasn't heartburn he was suffering from," Syrie said drily. "It was lust."

Jack flipped the cards angrily against his fingers. He couldn't speak. A red mist was building up behind his eyes. What had men like Sanford and Vasileyev found in his wife that he had not? She was reserved, inhibited, self-conscious. Her lack of bedroom expertize had driven him back into his mistress' arms the first night they had returned from their honeymoon. Yet Sanford could have his pick of women. Any women. He thought of the photographs he had seen of Princess Marinsky and Lady Linderdowne. What the devil was he doing wasting his time on Nancy? Vasileyev was almost as predatory. A man who bed-hopped international beauties with effortless ease. And Meldon as well? He wondered if nymphomania was a disease that could be caught like pneumonia, and dismissed the idea as absurd. If his wife was a nymphomaniac now, she had always been one and she hadn't been. She *couldn't* have been. Hc would have known. He hadn't known about Vasileyev and Meldon. It was Syrie he had to thank for that information.

"Any others?" he asked harshly. "Any footmen or butlers you haven't accounted for?"

Syrie suppressed a smile. "Luke Golding, the author, is here with Lady Bessbrook. Apparently Lady Bessbrook has been looking very unhappy lately and from a remark of Mr. Golding's that I overheard when he was talking to Sonny Zakar, the film producer, he finds Nancy hypnotically alluring."

"If all this is true . . ." The two pieces of card clicked savagely against his nails. ". . . maybe we should act differently."

Her clear green eyes sharpened. "In what way?"

"A divorce. On this sort of evidence I couldn't possibly emerge the loser."

"No." Now it was Syrie who rose to her feet and began to pace the floor. "A divorced man would never be acceptable as president. No matter what the circumstances."

"What if *she* wanted a divorce? She says she's in love

with Sanford, and she knows about my *affaire* with you. If she wants to marry this half-breed playboy then she'll need a divorce first."

"And have her name splashed over the world's press with details not only of her *affaire* with Sanford, but also of those with Vasileyev and Meldon and innuendos as to scores of others? No. Nancy isn't such a fool. Besides, if she'd wanted a divorce she would have asked for one before now."

"Then what do I do?" Jack's face was contorted with frustration and helpless rage. "I *have* to have a wife beyond reproach. One hint of this and everything I've worked for is finished."

"You separate her from Sanford. A week, two at the most, will do it. I looked up all his old press cuttings before we left. His *affaires* are always torrid and short-lived. As one lady moves out, another moves in."

"That I can well believe," Jack said bitterly. "But how do I separate them? Ask nicely? He's not a beach boy, Syrie. I can't pay him off. He has more millions than he knows what to do with."

"We dope her," Syrie said calmly. "We dope her and remove her from the hotel under sedation. We make her believe that she's ill and we separate them neatly and easily and without fuss."

"What do we dope her with?" Jack's acquiescence was immediate.

"Morphine-sulphate. It's odourless and can be put in her drink. Once she's semi-conscious we can inject her with an even stronger dose and that will induce a twilight sleep that will keep her unconscious until we reach Washington. And we can keep on giving it for as long as is necessary."

"What about Sanford?"

"Sanford will have forgotten her in a week. Skilfully done, we can convince Nancy that she is genuinely ill.

Her being ill, even if it's for a long period, will have no effect on your chances of becoming president. Rather the reverse. It will get you a certain amount of sympathy. Roosevelt will serve another term after this. We've reconciled ourselves to that. But your turn will come eventually, Jack. You have very powerful men behind you. Men who want you to be president. The ultimate goal is one well worth waiting for. We must continue to plan and then, when the time is right, seize our chance."

He crossed the room and took her in his arms, kissing her fiercely.

"Why the hell couldn't you have been born the daughter of Boston's mayor instead of Nancy?"

"Because I was born the daughter of a miner," Syrie retorted, and he was too relieved at seeing a solution to his problem to notice the bitterness in her voice.

She knew Jack Cameron better than he knew himself. She would have made a far better wife for him than Nancy. Nancy endured public life but did not enjoy it. Given the chance, Syrie would have revelled in it. She was naturally political. Nancy, for all her upbringing, remained aloof from the hurly-burly of the hustings. The intrigue and ruthlessness necessary for survival in the political arena left Nancy cold. She found such things distasteful. If she had known half the things her husband had done to further his career she would have been physically ill. Syrie had no such qualms. For the first twelve years of her life she wished she had been born a boy, and then she had come to terms with the cruelty of fate and used her sex to her advantage.

She knew Jack's flaws and weaknesses as well as his strengths. That he had lived with Nancy for seventeen years with so little knowledge of her was a frightening revelation. Usually his perception, if not his sensitivity, was acute. It was a good job that she had been the only witness to the debacle of the last few days. Syrie had been in Washington long enough to have gleaned the fact that a good president did not have to be superhuman or even perfect. He simply had to have the innate ability to choose sound advisers. Often the truly influential men were nondescript and without charisma. The president was the figurehead. He needed to look and act like a great leader. Jack had presence and charm and a wilyness that often took her by surprise; which is why his reaction to Nancy's defection had been so out of character. Perhaps no man truly knew his wife, or wife her husband. Syrie had no idea. Marriage had never formed part of her plans for the future.

Jack, his problem resolved, had disappeared into the bathroom. She sat at the dressing table and gazed at herself in the triple mirrors.

They had been at Sanfords for forty-eight hours. In that time not once had she been able to emerge as Jack's equal. Empty-headed socialties without the ability to pen a grammatical letter, had avoided her like the plague. She was neither fish nor fowl. She fell into no easy category. She was not a servant, a maid or a chauffeur. She was not even simply a secretary. She was Senator Jack Cameron's personal assistant—whatever that meant. Whatever it was, it was simply a position: a post. Syrie Geeson was an employee and was to be treated as such. Syrie sat alone and watched and listened and built up a store of hatred against several members of her sex and nationality that would not soon be forgotten. Her day would come and then how they would crawl. Without her say-so there would be no admittance to the White House balls, to the lavish dinners and the grand receptions. She stared glittering-eyed into the mirror, no longer seeing her own reflection. Instead, she saw herself standing on the inaugural platform a few feet from Jack. She was chic and poised and there was no other woman at Jack's side. Nancy was long dead. How, when or where, Syrie did not know. But she knew that when Jack placed his hand on his family Bible and took the presidential oath, she would be the wife at his side. In her imagination she heard the crowd's adulation and it was not wholly for Jack. It was for her, Syrie Geeson, the daughter of a coal miner from Pittsburgh. Syrie had discovered long ago that everything could be put to good use. That handicaps could be turned to advantages. The world was changing though the cossetted and pampered inmates of Sanfords seemed blissfully unaware of it. The old order would be gone for ever in the upheaval that was about to overtake them. The world of the rich and royal was about to disappear, and when it did Syrie believed it would disappear for ever. There would be a new order and the American public would be more than ready to accept a woman from their own ranks as First Lady. A woman they could identify with. The cheers and clapping grew louder and she closed her eyes, her orgasm coming deeply and satisfyingly where she sat.

There was a knock at the door and Nancy entered. Seeing her through the mirror Syrie at first thought it was her ghost, her imagination had taken her so vividly and clearly into the future. She rose to her feet, disconcerted.

Nancy smiled, moving with the ease and self-assurance that, it seemed to Syrie, only wealth from birth could ever bring.

"I hope you are enjoying your trip, Syrie. Where is it after Madeira? Gibraltar? Or did you call there on your way here?"

"Athens, I think," Syrie said, recovering her composure and hating herself for having lost it.

"Then do me a favour and make sure Jack travels with you. His continued presence here is making things very difficult. For him, not for me." The soft, throaty voice held only sincerity.

"Jack isn't the one whose reputation will suffer," Syrie said boldly. If Nancy Leigh Cameron wanted plain speaking she would be only too happy to oblige.

"No," Nancy said, "but his career will suffer if my reputation is tarnished."

"What difference would his going away make? You haven't been keeping your affairs secret."

"Nor you," Nancy said pointedly. "At least not any longer."

"Whatever Jack has told you, I can assure you there is no truth in it."

"Then you're not his mistress?"

"No." Syrie's ice-green eyes met Nancy's with ease.

"The lady in Cohasset will be relieved to hear it," Nancy said drily.

"What lady in Cohasset?"

"The one he visits when he tells you he's visiting me."

Syrie laughed. "I'm not so easily caught as that, Mrs. Cameron."

"No, I dare say you're not. Neither are you quite as clever as you think. I may not love Jack, but I'm extremely fond of him. I'd like to see him being loved for himself and not for his position in life."

"I don't think anything further can be gained from this conversation," Syrie said and marched rather than walked from the room. The door closed loudly behind her.

"What the hell . . . ?" Jack said, emerging from the steaming bathroom with a towel around his waist.

"Syrie," Nancy said smoothly. "She's wisely terminated our rather fruitless conversation."

The thought of any conversation between Syrie and Nancy made Jack feel ill.

"I didn't expect you for another fifteen minutes."

"No. I gathered that." Her voice was so pleasant and soft that he wasn't sure whether there was a hidden barb in her words or not. With only a towel for covering he felt at a psychological disadvantage.

"Pour yourself a drink while I dress," he said, trying to sound master of the situation.

"Where's Shelby? Did you lose him between New York and Funchal?"

"He's aboard the *Aquitania.* I didn't want him knowing what was going on. No employee is ever trustworthy."

"Maria is."

"You're naive, Nancy. You always have been."

"No." She poured herself a fresh orange juice. When it came to retrieving precious stones from the hearts of flowers, she trusted Maria a darn sight more than she would have trusted Jack. His fingers would have been yellow with pollen dust.

When he re-emerged, struggling with his own bow tie, she went across and helped him. He was buoyant and confident again, full of boyish charm.

"I'm glad you've reconsidered, Nancy. It's time we took a trip together. When was the last one?"

"Our honeymoon," Nancy said with a faint trace of amusement. "And I haven't reconsidered."

"Sure you have." He was cajoling. "Think of your name. Think of my future. Think of your father's health. Think of Verity."

"You really are pulling out all the stops, aren't you?" Nancy said, her amusement fading to be replaced by a wave of deep depression. "Why won't you simply listen to me Jack, and believe what I say?"

"Because it's crazy. You're behaving like Marisa what's-her-name who fights the bulls. You're Nancy Leigh Cameron and before that you were Nancy Leigh O'Shaughnessy. You come from strong religious Bostonian stock."

"My grandparents were lace-curtain Irish," Nancy

said, her amusement returning. Jack always chose to forget what he had no wish to remember. He was making her sound like a Winthrop or a Whitney.

"New England doesn't breed nymphomaniacs," Jack said authoritatively.

Her mouth twitched and she raised her eyebrows. "Am I to understand that I now fall into that category?"

"No, of course you don't. Though to listen to what some people are saying . . ."

"What are they saying?"

Jack squirted soda into a generous measure of scotch. "That it isn't only Sanford that you have been screwing around with, but Meldon and Vasileyev as well."

"Why do you have to use such coarse expressions, Jack? Screwing is a horrible word. Why not simply say 'making love'?"

"Hell, Nancy," Jack said with rising irritation. "Stop splitting hairs. They're both the same thing."

"They're not. There's a world of difference between them."

"If there is, I don't see it."

"No. I know you don't." Her voice was sad.

"Well the least you can do is be angry and deny it."

"No I can't, because it's true. At least, where Nicky is concerned."

Jack stared at her incredulously. "You've only been here a God-damned week!"

"I was lonely."

"*Lonely*? There are a hundred people here! How on earth can you be lonely in a crowd of people?"

"Easily."

He shook his head uncomprehendingly. "I don't understand you, Nancy. I don't feel I even *know* you."

"You never did know me, Jack. You never took the time or the trouble to get to know me." Exasperation and helplessness crept into her voice. "We're going round in circles, Jack. This is the same ground we covered yesterday."

"And we're going to cover it again tonight. I want you aboard the *Aquitania* with me. I'm . . ." He searched for the right words. He had a professional speech-writer in Washington. He could have done with him now. ". . . I'm *concerned* about you."

She laughed weakly. "For goodness sake, Jack. When have you ever been concerned with anyone else? With their sins, their griefs, their happiness? Your only concern is yourself and the future you envisage."

"That's not true."

"It is. That future may never materialize, Jack. There's a thousand obstacles between even the most favoured candidate for the presidency, and the deciding election. I wish you weren't so *sure* of it. There's no humility in you, no room for self-doubt."

"No weakness," he added for good measure.

She was about to tell him that there was a lot of weakness but stopped herself in time.

"I just don't want to see you at sixty, your life's ambition unfulfilled, and nothing, not even a family, for comfort."

As soon as she had said it she realized the idiocy of it. According to Henry Lorrimer, she would not be around in six months' time, let alone when Jack was sixty.

"The only obstacle between me and my lifetime's ambition is you." His voice was no longer cajoling. He was on the verge of anger. He checked himself in time. "What can Sanford give you that I can't?"

"Love."

"If Ria Doltrice is to be believed, he's given that to half the women in Europe already!" There was a limit to human patience and he had reached it. The fact that Nancy remained perfectly calm only incensed him further. He took three deep breaths and tried again. "You didn't *like* it when I made love to you!"

"You made love to me only with your body."

"How else does anyone make love?" he shouted exasperatedly.

"With their hearts."

There was no reciprocal anger in her voice—not even any irritation; only the profound sadness he had caught traces of before.

"What the devil do you think *I* was doing?"

She didn't want to answer him. It was a long time before she replied.

"Masturbating, Jack," she said quietly. "When you were making love to me you were making love to no one. You don't know how."

His face paled and he was shaking. "Don't you ever, *ever* use such filthy language to me!"

Jack, who blasphemed at every other word when not in public! If it wasn't so tragic it would have been laughable.

She put down her empty glass of orange on the drinks trolley and moved towards the door. "You're right, Jack, I shouldn't use any language to you. We don't speak the same one and we never have done."

"Where are you going?" He caught her wrist.

"To Ramon."

"A million dollars," he said.

She blinked.

"A million dollars if you return to Washington as if nothing had happened and behave as you always did."

She stared at him and fought down rising nausea. It seemed impossible that she could ever have believed herself in love with him. Her head throbbed and her limbs ached. It was as if Jack's very presence was enough to trigger off all the symptoms of her illness.

"No," she said, and her voice seemed to come from a long distance away. There was pressure behind her eyes and a curious buzzing noise in her ears.

"Nancy . . ."

"No, Jack. I'm sorry." Unsteadily she moved past him towards the door.

"Nancy!" He caught hold of her arm and swung her round and as he did so the blood began to pour.

"*Nancy*!" He fumbled urgently for his handkerchief but it was too late. By the time she had clutched it to her nose, her silk white dress was spattered with ugly, spreading stains.

"Nancy, for the love of God . . ."

She was choking on blood. It ran through her fingers, trickling down her bare arms. As Jack stood horror-struck, she pushed past him rushing into the bathroom, her face a bloody, unrecognizable mask.

When Ramon hammered on the door and flung it open Jack almost felt relieved to see him.

"Nancy," he said inarticulately, a shower of red seeping into the pristine whiteness of his shirt.

Ramon took in his shock, the sight and smell of blood, the table lamp that had fallen in Nancy's panic-stricken dash, and wasted no words.

He hurtled into the bathroom, calling out as he did so, "Ring for the doctor, for Christ's sake!"

Dazed, Jack obeyed. "A nosebleed," he heard himself saying. "A nosebleed . . ." Then he gazed in disbelief through the open bathroom door to where Nancy hung over the washbasin. There was so much blood it looked like a world war battlefield. Ramon had turned the cold tap on full and plunged Nancy's wrists into the icy water. The blood continued to flow and the water foamed a ghastly red as he soaked a towel in its depths and pressed it against her forehead.

"It's all right, darling. It's all right." His voice was low and calm and even to Jack, reassuring.

Sanford would sort it out. Sickness and accidents were

not in his line. The sight of blood turned his stomach. His face registered distaste as he slipped off his jacket and began to remove his marked shirt. She had given him her answer and he had made his decision. The morphine-sulphate it would have to be.

He had not asked Syrie if she had had the forethought to bring it with her. Syrie always prepared for every contingency. He would hire private nurses at Athens to make it look better. No damned arrogant Portuguese or senseless wife was going to stand between him and the White House.

There was a discreet knock at the door and Sanfords' resident doctor entered.

"In there," Jack said unnecessarily, and pulled on a clean shirt.

It was half an hour before Nancy left the bathroom. Her face was white; her eyes haggard. She leant heavily on Ramon and seemed oblivious to Jack's presence. He watched them go, took another shuddering look into his bathroom and rang room service to demand removal to another suite.

"Rest," Dr. Serrado said impassively, as Ramon swept Nancy into his arms and carried her over the threshhold of the Garden Suite.

Nancy gave him a shaky smile. "I'm all right now, Doctor. It was only a nosebleed."

The doctor looked at her queryingly and Nancy's eyes slid uncomfortably away from his.

"Thank you, Serrado. I'll see to Mrs. Cameron," said Ramon.

The doctor shrugged, his face grim as he returned to his duties elsewhere.

Ramon laid her tenderly on the bed and sat beside her, his strong hands imprisoning hers. For a few seconds he didn't speak and a deep frown drew his eyebrows together so that they met. At last he said:

"Are you ill, Nancy?"

Her mouth felt dry and her breath came short and hard. She could tell him: share the burden. She closed her eyes and ran her tongue nervously along her lower lip. If she told him, she would destroy his happiness. Whatever his reaction, he would not be able to be natural with her. Their whole relationship would be strained by the knowledge that it was so soon to be curtailed. He would pity her, feel obliged to stay with her even if he no longer wished to do so. It was better as it was. She had learned to live with the truth, but the process had been agonizing. She could not submit Ramon to the same pain.

Her smile was tender as she opened her eyes. "I'm a little tired, that's all. A nosebleed isn't the end of the world."

She saw the tense lines of his jaw relax, the worry in his eyes subside.

"I want, very much, to return to the ballroom. Will you ring Maria for me so that I can bathe and change."

He drew her hands to his mouth and kissed them, then he slipped his arms around her with infinite care and held her close.

"I love you, lady," he said, his mouth warm on her cheek.

She turned her face so that her lips met his. "I love you, my darling. More than you'll ever know," and in the bliss of his kiss she forgot all about her illness; about Jack; even about Maria and her need to bathe and change her dress.

It was Ramon who said at last, reluctantly, "If we are to put in an appearance again this evening, we will have to hurry. On the other hand, if you've changed your mind . . ."

She pushed him away, laughing, as he lowered his head to her breasts and kissed her.

"I haven't changed my mind. I'll join you in the

ballroom in twenty minutes."

With a deep sigh he relinquished his hold on her and said threateningly, "If you're not there on the exact minute I shall come back and lock us both in here until morning."

She laughed and picked up the telephone receiver to speak to Maria.

•

"You're late," he said grimly as he met her halfway down the corridor. "Five minutes and thirty seconds."

Her eyes danced and the colour had returned to her cheeks. "Darling, you look like an avenging angel," she said, and slipped into his arms, her body fitting as nearly in his as if it had been constructed for no other purpose.

When his lips finally released hers he said, "I've just been in to see Zia and she's feeling stronger. She also has some news. Your father is on his way here."

"Because of Jack?" Her gaiety vanished to be replaced by horror.

"No. Apparently his request for a booking was sent before Cameron arrived."

She relaxed. Her father had wanted to come to Madeira with her and had fought the impulse. Apparently he had now given in to it. She frowned. When he had been tempted into accompanying her, it had been because of Zia. He could have no inkling that Ramon was here. She had told him quite categorically that it was the last place in the world Ramon would be found. She smiled and held on to him.

"Quite the gathering of the clans," she said drily.

"An interesting assortment, certainly," Ramon agreed. They laughed, entering the crowded ballroom as the band began to play "I get a kick out of you".

"Ramon, darling!" A handsome matron in dove-grey

silk with a white plume in her hair, bore down on them. "I'd heard you were here, but simply refused to believe it."

"Let me introduce Lady Penelope Lovesy," Ramon said, "Penelope, Nancy Leigh O'Shaughnessy."

Lady Lovesy took Nancy's hand. The face was familiar but the name didn't fit. She tapped Ramon's cheek chastisingly with her closed fan.

"You really are too bad. You told me implicitly that you were not returning here until you returned with the girl you intended to marry!"

"I did, and I meant it."

Lady Penelope looked startled.

"I have met her and she's with me now."

Lady Penelope's eyes went unhesitatingly to the third finger of Nancy's hand and the thin gold ring encircling it.

"Excuse me," Ramon was saying, and Lady Penelope was left behind as they approached the Indian lady and Sonny Zakar. Nancy felt as if there was a band of steel around her chest.

"Ramon . . ."

"Glorious music," the Indian lady was saying in unaccented English.

"Ramon . . ."

"He's producing *Catherine the Great* with Garbo . . ."

"Ramon . . ."

At last he heard her, and turned, his eyes smiling down into hers.

"Yes, sweetheart."

"Ramon, I never said I'd marry you. I can't . . ."

There was a dreadful silence. The smile faded from his eyes. "Why not?" he asked, and it was the voice of a stranger.

"I can't, because of Jack. It would ruin his career."

People were beginning to look in their direction. He grasped her wrist so tight that she cried out in pain.

"Who's been labouring under an illusion?" he asked through clenched teeth. "Me or Cameron?" and to the amazement of his guests he strode from the ballroom, a captive Nancy struggling to keep pace with him in her tight-fitting satin dress.

Chapter Fifteen

"Ramon, please . . ."

The pianist faltered in his rendering of "Blue Moon". Potted palms swayed perilously as Ramon strode past them, the bejewelled, bemedalled throng parted hurriedly to let them through.

"Ramon . . ."

The gold-embossed doors of the ballroom closed behind them.

"Well!" the grand duchess' voice could be heard saying with loud disapproval, and then the pianist gathered his scattered wits and, backed by his startled drummer, began to play a tango that drowned the flood of excited speculation.

Her wrist felt as if it were broken. "Ramon . . ."

He swung her round to face him, frowning fiercely, his handsome features satanic in anger.

"When I said we were going away together, I didn't mean a mild diversion. A month's frolic in the sun and then back into the well-worn international trap for a change of bed companion. I thought I made it quite clear. I've had enough of that particular kind of musical chairs."

"Yes, but . . ."

"Of course, I was only speaking for myself. It hadn't occurred to me that *your* ideas on the subject might be different. That once making the traumatic break from that pompous, hypocritical, monumental bore that you married, you might find your sights set on a very different kind of fortune. One that contained not only me but Vasileyev and Minter and Golding and anybody else in pants that moves as well."

Hot, angry tears stung the back of her eyelids. She blinked them away fiercely. "You're being unfair, Ramon. The only future I ever envisaged was with you."

"Then why?" he repeated through clenched teeth, ". . . the reluctance to set yourself free from Cameron?"

"Oh my darling, it isn't necessary. Please believe me, we can be together, be happy . . ."

"I want a wife," he hissed, his eyes flashing sparks that would have set wet wood alight. "Not a mistress. God knows, there's been enough of them. End to end they'd probably circle the globe!"

The tears in her eyes were brilliant. She began to giggle, hysteria only a hair's breadth away.

"What's so damned funny?" His face was frightening, his hold on her merciless.

She was laughing and crying at the same time. "Nothing. Nothing at all. I love you with all my might, mind and body and strength. I'd give anything in the world to be your wife. I'd give my life if I could have only a few years of being Mrs. Ramon Sanford, bearing your children, loving you, living with you." She was half incoherent. "But you can't barter with your life. It gets taken from you and you can't make bargains with it! And I can't bear your children because I'm barren!"

"For Christ's sake." At the agony in her eyes his volcanic rage fled. "I don't *care* about children, Nancy. It's *you* I want. You, with your feline eyes and laughing mouth; with your ridiculous changes of style—looking as unapproachable as a goddess one moment in diaphanous chiffon, and like the latest sex screen symbol the next, in clinging satin that makes every man that looks at you break out in a sweat. I want you. I want you to make me laugh and make me cry; to understand what I feel without my having to put it into words. I want to love you, be angry with you. I want to have you within my sight and within my gaze every minute of every day. Don't you understand that? I want utter commitment. I want what I have always scorned. I want marriage, Nancy. Marriage with you. I want my ring on your finger—my name on your signature. I won't settle for anything less. Not if it means changing the whole damned constitution of the United States of America and getting a dispensation from the Pope!"

"Oh, Ramon!" She twisted violently from his grasp and flung her arms around his neck. "I want you as well. I need you. I love you." Her face was wet with tears as he brought his mouth down savagely on hers.

Later he said huskily, "Then you'll divorce Cameron?"

She nodded, hating herself for her duplicity yet knowing it was the only way to spare him unbearable pain.

"Yes. It will take a while: six months or a year. I won't know until I speak to my lawyer."

"I can wait six months," he said, and the harsh line of his mouth had softened. "Six months is only a heartbeat away."

"Oh Ramon!" Her voice broke and she clung to him with the ferocity of a lonely child.

"It's time the sex screen symbol reverted to naked reality. How the devil do I get you out of this? It fits like a second skin."

With enormous self-control she steadied her voice. "I'll show you," she said, "but not in Sanfords' Bridge Room."

"Good God," he looked around him for the first time. "Is that where we are?" and with a sudden grin he swept her up in his arms as if she weighed no more than a feather, and carried her to her room.

There was no need for Nancy to dismiss Maria, who would usually have been in attendance to help her undress and prepare her for bed. Maria knew that Sanfords' balls did not end until three or four in the morning. Nancy had told her repeatedly that she had no need of her services at such an hour, but Maria stubbornly refused to allow her beloved mistress so much as to hang up a dress on her own account. Nancy had long since given up the battle. If she returned to her room accompanied, Maria melted away diplomatically. Tonight, no diplomacy was needed. It was not yet midnight and Maria had thought herself free of her self-imposed duties for at least another three hours.

She was with Luis, not walking the fragrant subtropical gardens as other, more privileged lovers were doing, but strolling hand in hand up the darkened rough and narrow road that led eventually to Camara de Lobos. Hand-holding was the furthest intimacy Maria allowed. Luis, unused to such chastity, was finding his desire for the little Puerto Rican maid increasing daily.

"A swim?" he coaxed. If she swam she would have to remove the demure high-necked dress under which her breasts pushed so tantalizingly. Maria, reading his mind, laughed.

"No swimming. The cliffs are too steep. I'm not a mountain goat."

"You're a damned nuisance," Luis said, reverting to frankness for the first time in years.

Maria laughed again, pleased at her ability to tease and torment him. "If I am such a nuisance, why do you spend so much time with me?"

"I don't!" His male vanity was stunned. "I had nothing else to do. It was a nice night and I fancied a walk."

"It makes a change from your usual occupations," Maria said lightly.

"I've no idea what you mean."

"Oh." Maria's voice was studiedly careless as their clasped hands swung to the rhythm of their steps. "Countess Zmitsky, Viscountess Lothermere, that ridiculous Mrs. Peckwyn-Peake and I think, though I'm not sure, the greedy Miss Mancini as well."

Their handclasp was broken abruptly.

"Have you been spying on me?"

"No." Maria's voice was indignant. "I wouldn't waste my time."

Luis' sun-bronzed face was troubled. If Madame Sanford or Mr. Sanford found out he was in the habit of offering small services for rather large rewards, then he might very well lose his job. If Maria had guessed, why had not other members of Sanfords' staff? Perhaps she had already spoken of it to them. Perhaps even now his comfortable life style was in jeopardy.

"My position at Sanfords is that of swimming coach," he said icily. "That entails not only coaching the guests in the pool, but also discussing technique with my pupils at other times."

Maria could barely keep the amusement out of her voice. "Is your . . . technique . . . very interesting for the ladies? I would have thought some of them might be too old to learn new skills."

"*Mae de Deus*! Is that what this is all about. Why you keep me at arm's length: do not even permit me, Luis Chavez, to kiss you goodnight? Because you are jealous of the time I have to spend with these old ladies? Jealous of my job?"

"Not all your pupils are old," she said as they stood high on the cliff path, Luis bad-temperedly scuffing pebbles with the toe of his tennis shoe. "The English viscountess is very beautiful and Miss Mancini . . ."

Miss Mancini was rapacious and had not even offered him a glass of wine, let alone a gift.

"Miss Mancini is the girlfriend of the Greek. She has also discontinued her lessons."

"I'm pleased to hear it," Maria replied complacently. "She is also the girlfriend of the Egyptian, the Englishman who writes the books, and the American president of the Chetwynd Cork Company. It would not give her much time for swimming," she added considerately.

Luis cursed again. In the moonlight Maria's kitten face and large eyes looked infinitely more desirable than the blonde and soignée sophistication of Viscountess Lothermere. As for the Czech countess, Luis shuddered. Once, when coaching a young Englishman who was carrying on a conversation with his friend on the poolside, he had heard the Englishman use the expression "whitened sepulchres". Ever eager to enlarge his education and his English he had liked the strange expression and stored it away at the back of his mind. Whenever he thought of the countess and her waxen body, the expression came forcefully to mind.

His visits to the countess' red velvet and brocade bedroom were only made bearable by the largesse of her gifts: a gold chain bracelet that he would sell on his next visit to Oporto; several bottles of the very best English whisky. And, for a service that daunted even the hardened Luis, a blood-red stone that could only be a ruby.

With an expertise that had never before failed him, he

pulled Maria into his arms and lowered his head. Maria moved as deftly as an eel, running away from him down the darkened track.

"Nice girls do not come second to ladies of great age and ladies with husbands," she called back over her shoulder, and at the amusement in her voice Luis ground his teeth and gave chase.

"If I promise to stop seeing them?" he asked as he caught her arm and halted her flight.

She raised her slim fingers to his chest, pushing him away. "Ah," she said and her eyes were dark and searching. "But would you? For me? For Maria Saldhana: a maid?"

"Yes," he said rashly. "I would, Maria." And this time when he kissed her she did not resist.

It was like kissing a fresh spring day. His first thought had been that he would have to be more discreet, more careful. His second, as Maria's soft lips parted beneath his, was that he was twenty-five and that a man had to have sons. In Portuguese eyes he was already old to be starting a family. With another girl it would have been different. She would have remained in his parents' house in Oporto and he would have visited two, three, perhaps four times a year. Maria would not be content to live in Oporto under the stringent gaze of his mother whilst he continued his career and intrigues at Sanfords. Perhaps a home in Funchal? He could afford it. He had been prudent with the gifts showered on him. All had been turned into hard cash. The bracelet and ruby alone were worth twenty years' pay.

"Maria," he said, but she was already moving away from him.

"I must go. Mrs. Cameron wil be needing me."

"Maria!" She was off, running with the agility of a peasant down the velvet black track.

"*Mae de Deus*!" he repeated, under his breath. No girl

had ever received a kiss from Luis Chavez and sped away as if it were no more than a handshake. They waited, trembling, willing and hopeful.

One blasphemy followed another. If he married a firebrand like Maria there would be no more Czech countesses and their boundless wealth. That, with sons instead to compensate, he could accept. There would also be no more adventures with the likes of the blonde and titled Englishwoman. That would be a little harder to forgo. He swore again. Viscountesses would not give him sons. Maria's sons would be dark and strong and full of spirit. If they were girls they would grow up like their mother, and his life would not be worth living. He wandered despondently back to the hotel and ignored his promise to visit Mrs. Peckwyn-Peake from one-thirty to two. Mrs. Peckwyn-Peake could go to sleep alone. For a woman of fifty she was very agile but wearing. For once Luis wanted to be the one to call the tune. He was beginning to feel like an organ-grinder's monkey. "Do this, Luis. Do that, Luis". A carelessly tossed trinket as a reward. After Maria's kiss he could not bring himself to run through his usual faultless performance. He returned to his own room and his own bed and slept in monastic celibacy.

This season would be his last. He would marry Maria, but they would need all the money possible if they were to start married life with none of the handsome perks he had grown accustomed to. In the next few weeks he would take all that he could from Countess Zmitsky and Mrs. Peckwyn-Peake.

With a ring on her finger and a promise of marriage, Maria would be more tractable. He would cease to attempt her seduction. It was unthinkable that any bride of Luis Chavez should be anything but a virgin when she stood at the foot of the altar.

Satisfied with his plans for the future, Luis pummelled

his pillow and slept.

Maria did not sleep. She returned to her own room and lay awake until the dawn broke. She felt no laughter now: that had all been for Luis' benefit—to show him that she did not care. To refuse to give him the pleasure of knowing the intensity of jealousy she felt when she thought of the foolish women who gazed on his sun-gold body with lusting eyes.

The Czech was the worst; old and fat and unutterably obscene. Maria stared steadfastly at the ceiling. She would put an end to Luis Chavez' escapades and she would start with the Czech. A slow smile turned her mouth. Countess Zmitsky would not be at Sanfords long enough to tempt Luis, even if she offered him the jewels of the crown of England. Instead of closing her eyes and sleeping, Maria dressed and prepared to put her plan into action.

The sky was lightening to a pale grey, the garden deserted except for a lone figure that sat on one of the garden seats with bowed shoulders, tears falling silently down her cheeks. Madeira's dawns were cold and the little Countess Szapary was wearing only a thin dressing robe over her silk nightdress. She cried and cried and the cold that she felt was nothing to the ice that lay in her heart and refused to thaw.

Vere had left the ball early and slept badly, his mind full of Clarissa and the future that stretched so barrenly ahead of him. He had tried reading books, but tossed Mr. Hemingway away in despair. He couldn't concentrate on the pages of print. All he could think of were Nancy's words and the commonsense behind them. He rose restlessly and lit a cigarette, opening the shuttered doors of his balcony.

The *Kezia* and the *Aquitania* gleamed white in the

darkness as they rode at anchor. The *Aquitania*'s sleek lines looked even lovelier in the stillness of the receding night. The gardens were dew wet; birds were beginning, cautiously, to sing. Another ten minutes and the pearl would change to a dull gold as the sun edged over the horizon. He halted in the process of raising his cigarette to his lips.

She was alone and the coffee-coloured chiffon with the black velvet ribbons had been replaced by a pale lemon wrap that was surely insufficient for such cold morning air.

He hesitated. Obviously, if she had sought the sanctuary of the garden at such an hour, it was because she wanted solitude. Dejection was in every line of her slim body. He felt like a voyeur at the spectacle of some private grief. The honourable thing to do would be to return to his room and forget he had ever been witness to such inner despair. He turned, but not to forget. He dressed quickly and pulled on a white V-neck sweater over his shirt and flannels. He snatched another one from the shelf. The countess would be freezing. It was an unromantic but typically practical British gesture.

"Oh," she gazed at him like a startled deer.

He smiled reassuringly. "A bit chilly," he said, and gently wrapped the cashmere sweater around her shoulders.

"I . . . Thank you."

He sat beside her and she made a move as if to go. He laid a hand restrainingly on hers.

"Please, don't go on my account."

Beneath his hand, hers was like that of a child. He felt a great wave of protection. She glanced around her fearfully.

"We can't be seen," he said easily. "The only rooms to look this way are mine. No one will invade your privacy for hours yet. Not even me, if you don't want me to."

"Oh, but I do want you to." She blushed. "I mean, it's very kind of you to have brought me the sweater."

She relaxed again, seeming unaware that her hand still lay imprisoned beneath Vere's. For a long time they did not speak. The pearl dissolved into the first flush of dawn. Birds chirrupped and fluttered in the trees above their heads.

At last Vere said, still staring out to where the rising sun was beginning to warm the distant mountains, "Marriages are damnable things, aren't they?"

The little countess nodded, her eyes lowered to her lap.

Overcoming British diffidence with difficulty, he continued, "Sometimes, the more you try to please, the worse it gets."

She raised a solemn face to his. "Yes," she said wonderingly. "Yes. It is like you say. How do you know so much about marriage?"

Vere laughed ruefully. "I married ten years ago."

"And your marriage, too, is unhappy?"

"My marriage is over," Vere said, and it was his first public admission of the fact.

"I'm sorry."

"So am I, but sometimes one faces a situation in which nothing can ever change. Not unless one changes it oneself."

"You will . . . divorce?" The word was hard for the little countess to say.

"I will divorce," Vere said firmly. "It will be the first divorce in a family going back to the Conqueror, but not the first broken marriage. Those happen by the handful in every generation."

"But the scandal?"

"The scandal will keep the public happy for a few days and then will be forgotten."

Countess Szapary smiled wanly. "It is easy for you. You are a man."

In the long silence that followed as the sun rose above the horizon, warming the sea to tints of jade and aquamarine, many things went through Vere Winterton's head.

Until his rash declaration of love to Nancy he had never acted impulsively. He was cool, level-headed and practical. With the clarity of hindsight he saw his infatuation with Nancy for what it was—the leftover longings of a boyhood dream. Nancy had known and she had pointed it out to him herself: as she had pointed other things out. All through his sleepless night he had thought of Clarissa. His only concern, ever since the sunlit afternoon at Molesworth when she had told him that she could no longer fulfil her duties as a wife, had been to protect her. First out of the love he still felt for her, and then out of loyalty as the love, without anything to nourish it, stultified and died.

He, too, had stultified and died inside. He was too fastidious to indulge in light, meaningless liaisons, and as the Duke of Meldon he could not afford to indulge in any other kind. Then Nancy had come and given him some of the inner strength that she possessed and seemed so unaware of.

She had been right about Clarissa. She would be relieved by a divorce. She would suffer no financial hardships and would no longer have to endure putting in obligatory appearances once or twice a year at Molesworth and accompanying him publicly to Ascot and Cowes.

Nancy had aroused the part of himself that he had so carefully smothered. As he sat with the little countess by his side, he experienced emotions that he had not experienced for a decade: tenderness and protectiveness. He had yearned after Nancy and had suffered appallingly when she had refused him as a lover. He was aware that he was no longer suffering. He was no longer yearning for

Nancy. He was experiencing another emotion: richer and stronger and deeper.

"Are you very unhappy?" he asked, and as tear-filled eyes met his, Vere Winterton knew that his future was determined. Szapary had broken two other child-brides before his present one. The first had committed suicide: the second had died an untimely death, hastened by drink and drugs. The third was going to be Duchess of Meldon.

"Come along," he said tenderly, and as he drew her to her feet his arms flipped quite naturally around her shoulders.

It would not do to hurry her. It was enough for the moment that she had not drawn away from him. He had heard rumours that Szapary was already tiring of his young wife. If that was so, maybe the affair could be arranged amicably, man to man. Szapary's blood was blue enough, but Vere doubted if his wealth was as vast as the count would have liked. A sizeable increment might tempt him to release his third wife as he had so mercilessly relinquished those before her.

Later that morning, as Nancy began her first full day as Sanfords' directrice and met for half an hour of discussion with Senora Henriques and then a longer and more formal discussion with first the head chef and then Villiers, Ramon took the opportunity he had long been waiting for. He strolled with deceptive indolence towards the suite harbouring Senator Jack Cameron.

Jack's night had been nearly as sleepless as Maria's. He had been correct in his assumption that Syrie would have brought all that was necessary to reduce Nancy to a semi-comotose condition in order to remove her quietly from Sanfords. They had discussed tactics down to the minutest detail. If Nancy ever suspected that her husband and his mistress had drugged and kidnapped her, then whether Sanford found a new lover or not would be immaterial. She would never remain his wife. It was of the utmost importance that Nancy believed herself to be ill. That on recovering consciousness she would have no recollection of having been forcibly injected. Their plan of action was relatively simple. It was Nancy's habit to have an Irish coffee every night as a nightcap. Maria prepared it and Nancy's routine at Hyannis or Washington was to drink it in bed while she read until she finally felt tired enough to sleep. The fresh cream required for this was always kept in an icebox along with champagne and chilled orange juice. Syrie would visit the Garden Suite and apologize to Nancy. She would feel faint and help herself to a glass of water. She would then inject the soluble morphine-sulphate into the daily quota of fresh cream. That night Nancy would not need to read to lull herself to sleep. She would be deeply unconscious within minutes.

There would be no difficulty in Jack gaining entrance to her suite in the late hours of the night, as Nancy had a fear of hotel fires and the only time her suite was locked was when both she and Maria were absent at the same time. He and Syrie would wear white overalls that Syrie had removed from the staff linen room, and two medical face masks that formed part of Jack's travelling medical kit. If the injection awoke her, as it was bound to do, if only for a few shattering moments, all that Nancy would see and remember would be the masked faces and gowned figures of a nurse and a doctor. Jack's valet had been instructed to revert to chauffeur and be waiting to motor the ill Mrs. Cameron down to the docks and the *Aquitania*. The *Aquitania* would sail only hours later, and Jack was gambling that it would sail before Sanford was aware of Nancy's absence.

"What makes it even better," he said to Syrie with grim satisfaction, "is that Nancy's health isn't all that it should be. Do you remember that fainting fit at the Met and her fatigue these last few months?"

"She doesn't seem fatigued now," Syrie said drily.

Jack wasn't listening. "I wish to God I'd spoken to Lorrimer myself. It might have been useful to know what his diagnosis was. He's tried hard enough over the last few weeks to get in touch with me."

"I thought you'd spoken to him? No wonder he's been jamming the switchboard and inundating us with mail."

"I've more important things to do than waste my time discussing Nancy's health. It's time you ran along and did your party piece."

He held her tightly in his arms, admiring the pretty, feminine face and the brilliant mind that hid behind the wide-set, ice-cool eyes. Her eyebrows were in the Dietrich style, one eye partially obscured by a fall of thickly gleaming hair. He had been very clever to find Syrie Geeson. Syrie knew what he was thinking and a smile haunted her mouth. Jack Cameron had not found her; she had found him. She had used him and would continue to use him. She extricated herself from his arms, smoothed down her severely styled and expensively cut skirt, and with the prepared morphine-sulphate in her clutch bag went in search of her victim.

"Mrs. Cameron is not available," Maria said icily. She had never liked the senator's secretary. That she had always referred to her as a secretary made Syrie Geeson long to smack her across the face.

"I think if you tell her that I am alone she will see me," Syrie said composedly.

"She will not see you," Maria said, "because she is not here. She is with Senora Henriques."

Syrie had no idea who Senora Henriques was, and cared even less. The stillness in the room behind Maria indicated that the maid was speaking the truth. She gasped and clutched at her throat, leaning weakly against the side of the open door. "Oh goodness. I feel so dizzy."

Maria stared, disconcerted. She would have thought Miss Geeson incapable of weakness of any kind.

Miss Geeson showed no signs of recovering. She was sinking gradually, her eyes glazed.

Hastily Maria grabbed hold of her and supported her. There was no alternative but to help her into the Garden Suite and on to a chair.

"Oh God! I think I'm going to be sick."

Maria flew into the bathroom for water.

Syrie had located the wood-veneered refrigerator, but there was no way to reach it before Maria came back and she was forced to sip the proffered drink.

"Could you telephone reception and ask for a doctor?" Syrie asked weakly. "Or perhaps you could telephone Mr. Cameron in Suite 17."

There were two telephones in the Garden Suite—one at Mrs. Cameron's bedside, the other in the green and lavender drawing room that opened out on to the terrace. Both were out of sight of where she was now sitting. Both were out of sight of the refrigerator and coffee percolator and the other essential bric-à-brac that comprised the tiny but well-fitted kitchen. It was typical of Maria that she should have deposited her in what was virtually the servants' province. At any other time Syrie would have seethed at such an indignity. Now she gave grateful and silent thanks.

Maria disappeared and rang reception. She had no desire to speak to Mr. Cameron.

Syrie moved swiftly. The bottle of cream was unopened. Without so much as a tremble of her hands she injected a third of a grain of morphine-sulphate into it, then she shook the bottle vigorously and returned to her chair. The hole in the metal lid was virtually unnoticeable. It would be discarded and never found.

"The hotel doctor is on his way," Maria said without warmth.

Syrie managed a shaky smile. "Thank you. I feel a little better now. Perhaps you could ask him to see me in my own room—Room 25."

Maria shrugged and Syrie took it for assent. Step one had been executed perfectly.

There was only one disturbing doubt in Syrie's mind and it was one she had not mentioned as yet to Jack. It was pointless to do so. If it proved valid and their plans failed, they would have to think of another one, that was all. Jack had been adamant that Nancy *always*, wherever she was, drank a nightcap of coffee, Irish whisky and cream. Syrie believed him, but would Nancy still be doing so if her bed was shared by a lover? She imagined that Ramon Sanford's post-coital relaxation would be accompanied by champagne or whisky on the rocks: not a warm, comforting, cream-laden coffee. They would have to wait and see.

Her hand reached out for the ornate brass knob on the door leading to Suite 17, and stayed where it was. From within came voices: Jack's and Ramon Sanford's. Very slowly and quietly she opened the door and closed it behind her. They were in the main room and she tip-toed stealthily into Jack's bedroom, sitting on the bed and listening to the conversation with interest.

"That's one of the advantages of being totally amoral," Ramon was saying in the lazy, self-assured drawl that drove Jack wild. "I have no scruples in affairs of this kind. I love your wife: you don't and, as far as I can see, never have. Therefore she stays with me and divorces you. It's as simple as that."

"My wife is not going to be publicly ridiculed by you or anyone else," Jack said, breathing heavily, determined not to lose his temper in the face of Sanford's insolent coolness. "She's behaved recklessly and regretted it. She's returning with me aboard the *Aquitania* and our lives will continue as before."

Ramon laughed. "I doubt it," he said, his voice holding a silky softness that sent a chill of fear down Syrie's spine. "I doubt that Nancy will return to an empty house in Hyannis with nothing to occupy her but walks on the beach and endless rounds of lonely golf, while you continue to further your public career and seek sexual gratification where you can find it."

Syrie couldn't see but she could sense the mocking smile on Ramon Sanford's strong-boned face.

"How difficult it must be, only able to choose mistresses amongst a group as vulnerable as yourself. Mistresses who can never discuss their *affaires* with girlfriends or even, heaven forbid, a wider public. I imagine the erotic little circle is composed entirely of the wives of fellow senators and visiting ambassadors." He paused. "And employees, too."

"Damn you to hell!" Sanford was laughing at him and Jack could stand it no longer. "What right have you to come in here and criticize my morals, when yours are as loose as those of a tom cat?"

"Because I do not suffer from the disease that afflicts you and your kind. Hypocrisy." The contempt in Ramon's voice was crushing. "I am not a married man. I have never vowed to love and cherish one woman above all others. When I take that vow I will keep it."

"There's as much chance of you being faithful to one woman as there is of Madeleine Mancini becoming a nun," Jack said savagely.

Ramon's smile was in his voice. "Ah, so you have already noticed the talents of Miss Mancini? What a pity that you are unable to take advantage of them. *That* would not be at all suitable. Miss Mancini is not at all accustomed to conducting her *affaires* with the secrecy and stealth the women of Washington are. I had always been under the impression that you were a man of sound judgment. Now I see that you are not. Neither, more fearfully, are the men who believe in you as a future world leader. However, I've not the slightest doubt that they will realize their mistake in a very short time whether Nancy leaves you or not. What amazes me now, is that you still appear to be labouring under the impression that I am about to spend a month, months or even a year with your wife and then discard her. I have no such intention. Nancy is going to marry me and neither you nor anyone else on God's earth is going to stop her from doing so."

Syrie felt the nape of her neck tingle at the power and passion in the deep, rich voice.

"She's returning with me," Jack said stubbornly, and in comparison his voice held an underlying note of weakness.

"I understand you can charm the birds from the sky when you so desire," Ramon said, regarding Jack as he might a curiosity in a zoo. "That is what has gained you the position you now hold. That, and a certain amount of slick cleverness and a never-ending supply of money. I have never thought of charm as a dangerous quality before, but if it can be switched on and off with the dexterity you exhibit, then I find it an extremely dangerous quality. I wonder how many people really know you, Jack Cameron? Do your political allies? Does the ambitious and accessible Miss Geeson?"

"Get out!" Jack hissed. "Get out before I throw you out."

This time Ramon's laugh was genuine. "Bad judgment again, Senator. You are under *my* roof. It is *I*, not you, who has the power to issue the orders. If it wasn't for Nancy I would never have allowed you over the threshold. As it is, my patience has come to an end. The

Aquitania sails in the morning and you will be aboard her."

Syrie could hear him moving towards the door.

"By the way, what will happen to the loyal Miss Geeson when Nancy divorces you? Won't a wife without an impeccable social background be a little of a handicap in those tight-knit and illustrious Washington cliques?"

"No wife of mine will ever handicap me," Jack said fiercely. "Not even Nancy. If she doesn't come to heel I'll make a laughing stock of both of you."

"And marry Miss Geeson?" Ramon asked, amused.

"Don't be ridiculous. Camerons don't marry coal miners' daughters. If Nancy think she's the prop of my political life, she's been over-estimating herself. I can marry where I want and far more suitably than the daughter of a lace-curtain Irish mayor who's going to lose his next election by a landslide."

The insults as to Nancy's background were lost on Syrie. She heard nothing after Jack's flat statement that Camerons did not marry coal miners' daughters. Of course they didn't. Why then had she believed that some day . . . Sometime . . .

She didn't move. She sat perfectly still and schooled herself to breathe in and out, slowly and steadily. In. Out. Her head was clearing. In. Out. She thought she had been using him, and she had. She wore expensive clothes, had a flat on Madison Avenue and drove her own Pontiac. She had never mentioned marriage because she had known that Nancy was necessary to Jack if he was to gain the ultimate in political power. Yet, womanlike, she had subconsciously believed that he would have married her if the way had been clear. If Nancy had died . . . He wouldn't, of course. A child of three could have seen that. He would have remained a widower for an acceptable length of time and then chosen a suitable bride from amongst his own set. She would continue as mistress and confidante. It was, after all, her role. She would still be the one to wield unseen power. The wife, Nancy or otherwise, would be nothing but an ornamental trapping. It would make no difference: but it did. It made a difference because of the crucifying tone of Jack's voice when he had referred to her as "a coal miner's daughter". That was how he saw her and would always see her. A coal miner's daughter who would never, in a hundred years, be allowed to sit at the same social dinner table as the Cameron family. A coal miner's daughter who had brains that he could put to use and a body that was convenient.

The door closed behind Ramon Sanford and she heard the clink of a glass against a decanter. Slowly she rose and was appalled to find that her legs were trembling. With infinite care she opened the door and slipped out of Jack Cameron's suite. Sanford had disappeared. She began to walk with increasing briskness down the long corridor: through the acres of public rooms and out into the fresh air. She needed to think. Now, of all times, she must not act hastily.

Careless laughter floated from the direction of the swimming pool. Syrie paused, hands deep in the pockets of her dress. Georgina Montcalm and Venetia Bessbrook were sunbathing. Georgina reached a languid hand towards champagne chilling in a silver ice bucket. Almost instantly a white-coated waiter materialized and deferentially refilled her glass. Syrie's eyes narrowed. She hated them and all women like them. Rich, idle women who had never worked in their lives. Where she came from the women worked—hard, back-breaking work from early morning to late at night. Cooking, mending, cleaning. Scrubbing floors out of pails of pan-boiled water. Old at thirty from too many babies, too much worry and too little attention. Syrie had never been ashamed of her background. She had risen above it because she had been born with brains and the kind of ambition that would have elevated her in whatever environment she had been born in.

She had gravitated towards politics because politics was power and power was what she needed to change the living conditions of people like her parents. Now she saw that she had been grossly misguided. Jack Cameron would have made promises for votes, but he would never have cared on any deep level for the hundreds and thousands of small-town Americans who coped daily with the kind of poverty that he had no conception of. She hated these people—the thoughtless rich, the grand coterie who allowed no one into their ranks unless an accident of birth made them eligible. She knew what she was going to do. She was going to exact revenge.

Chapter Sixteen

It had been a perfect day. In the morning, after going over the list of new arrivals with Senora Henriques, she had spent several hours with Salli Nedeco, Zia's dressmaker, discussing details of both her own costume and those of the guests for the fancy dress ball. It was imperative that no two ladies adopted the same costume.

Bobo was going as a Persian princess; Venetia Bessbrook, capitalizing on her Christian name, as a Venetian court lady. Lavinia Meade, for reasons that defeated both Salli and Nancy, was going as a Chinese empress. Marisa Moreno had not needed the services of Salli and her minions, she was going as herself, dressed in the magnificent costume of a matador. Nancy's own costume was that of Anne Boleyn and Salli had made her a magnificent gown of crimson velvet edged with pearls.

She had given detailed instructions for the next ball and had chosen the colour pink as a theme. The decor, the food, the champagne, the clothes: all would be pink. Then, satisfied with her work, she had personally greeted

Prince Felix Zaronski and his magnificent white stallion. The stallion, having been led by a bevy of the prince's liveried aides up the steep narrow road from the harbour, had pawed the ground wild-eyed, its mouth foam-flecked. Nancy decided it was too potentially dangerous to join the peacocks and doves, and after admiring it to the prince's satisfaction, had had it led away to the magnificent, but not often used, stables.

The prince's admiration of his hostess' appearance had been blatant; after his eyes had slowly travelled from the top of her head to the tip of her feet and back again he asked after his fellow guests. On being told that Prince Nicholas Vasileyev was also in residence, the fiery eyes in the high-boned face had lit with new light. The Vasileyevs and Zaronskis were linked by a mutual grandmother. Nancy grinned and wondered if it had been the one born on the wrong side of the royal blanket. On mention of the Szaparys the prince had looked nonplussed. The name meant nothing to one of Romanov blood. On being told that Lady Bessbrook was staying until the end of the month, enthusiasm had returned. He had met Lady Bessbrook on the Adriatic the previous year. Unfortunately she had been infatuated with a nonentity millionaire. Nancy, rightly deducing from his none too flattering description that the millionaire was Reggie, had the unfortunate task of informing the prince that the gentleman was also in residence, adding casually that though the two were still friends, a breach had occurred over the last few months. Of Mr. Luke Golding she said nothing. Unless Mr. Golding found himself another *amoureuse* prepared to pay for his bed and board, Mr. Golding would have to be asked to settle his account and leave. In Villiers' vast experience this would have to be done speedily as he did not think Mr. Golding had the price of a motor fare into Funchal.

After the prince, she had entertained the ebullient,

earthy Miss Polly Watertight of Boston, Mass.

Nancy reflected that she had been leading a sheltered life. That she and Miss Watertight could have shared the same home town and never met showed that her own existence had been cloistered. Miss Watertight was well into her eighties, had a magnificent bosom that she still enjoyed exhibiting and a laugh that could be heard in Funchal.

When Kate Murphy had also arrived, Nancy found her presence irrelevant. It transpired that one of Mrs. Murphy's ex-husbands had also been an ex-gentleman friend of Miss Watertight. Gales of laughter had followed as they had discussed with relish the poor man's faults, failings and the more eccentric of his foibles. Nancy, hardened to the malicious gossip and witticisms of Washington and New York, had blushed to the roots of her hair at the bawdy reminiscences of the two octogenarians, and escaped, ordering that they were to be kept supplied with champagne and not disturbed until they wished to leave of their own accord.

She had spent a full hour with Miss Nina Correlli and found that off-stage the great operatic star was torturously shy. A bellboy had been despatched in search of the Montcalms, inviting them to join Nancy and Miss Correlli for mid-morning iced coffee.

By the time Nancy was discreetly informed that her presence was needed elsewhere, Miss Correlli, faced with the Montcalms' easy friendliness, was thawing out and even beginning to look as if she was enjoying herself.

Senora Henriques told Nancy that the English debutante to whom everything was "blissikins" had lain in her morning bath and calmly slashed both her wrists. When Nancy hurriedly arrived, the smell and sight of blood lingered so that the erstwhile pretty lavender and gold bathroom resembled a butcher's shop.

The girl was now laying on her bed, covered with a

quilt, and Sanfords' doctor was rapidly bandaging the second of her bleeding wrists. The girl's face was so white it was indistinguishable from the sheets.

"She nearly did it this time," the Portuguese doctor said grimly. "Another ten minutes and it would have been too late."

"Does this happen often?" Nancy asked, horrified.

The doctor shrugged. "Once or twice a season. Usually late at night after too much drink and the breaking-off of a love affair."

The bandaging was completed. The maids had finished cleaning the bathroom. The girl's eyelids fluttered open and gazed at the doctor, dull-eyed.

"What do we do now?" Nancy asked. The girl was no older than Verity.

"Give her a sedative," the doctor said unsympathetically, lifting the girl's head from the pillow and placing a small tablet on her tongue, raising a tumbler of water to her lips. She swallowed unprotestingly.

The doctor packed his bag. "She won't do it again. At least, not for a few months. They never do." He nodded deferentially to Nancy and left the room.

"I will see to it that a maid is left at her bedside," Senora Henriques said, preparing to follow the doctor.

"Yes." Nancy continued to stand at the foot of the bed and gaze at the still features before her. "I was to meet Mrs. Honey-Smith for a welcoming drink. Will you please give her my apologies?"

The housekeeper nodded and closed the door behind her. The maid, overawed by Nancy's presence, sat discreetly by the door.

The girl's eyes remained closed. Nancy walked slowly around the bed and sat at her side, reaching out gently with her hand and putting it warmly over the girl's cold one.

Lady Helen Bingham-Smythe: daughter of the Duke

and Duchess of Dentley; accompanied to Sanfords by an aunt who so far had been uncontactable.

"I'm sorry you are so unhappy," she said. There was an imperceptible change in the rhythm of the girl's breathing. "I know you won't believe me, but whatever it is, however bad it is, this time next year you will have forgotten all about it."

A small tear slid down the childlike face.

"If someone told you you were going to die whether you wanted to or not, you would fight with your last breath to live, no matter how unhappy you were."

The eyelids fluttered open once again, this time curiosity replacing the glazed dullness. "I wouldn't. I would be glad."

Nancy shook her head. "I'm dying. There's nothing I can do to stop it and no matter how desperately unhappy I was, I would prefer to live and fight my unhappiness than die. Many people say dying is the cowardly way out. I'm not too sure of that. It seems to me it requires a great deal of courage. But it is the defeatist's way."

She now had the girl's full attention.

"You can't possibly be dying! You're too young!"

"I am, and it's hideous. It's also my secret and yours."

Fingers tightened on Nancy's, as if offering comfort. Nancy smiled. "Now, you wouldn't truly want to change places with me, would you?"

Slowly, the girl shook her head.

"What happened?" Nancy asked, the first battle over. "What is making you so unhappy?"

Unbelievably the beautiful, ethereal Mrs. Nancy Leigh Cameron seemed at that moment to Helen Bingham-Smythe more comforting and maternal than her own mother had ever done.

"My aunt," she said briefly. "I came here to meet Piers. We've been in love for simply ages but Mummy disapproves of him. She said it would be a good idea if I left London for a while. She thought I would forget him." Another tear made its way down her face. "Naturally Piers and I were not going to be separated like that, so we thought that I would come here chaperoned by my aunt and Piers would come as well. It was all going to be such fun."

"What went wrong?" Nancy asked, feeling a certain amount of sympathy for the gullible duchess.

"It was yesterday. Piers had gone into Funchal. At least he *said* he was going into Funchel. My aunt was playing bridge with Lady Meade and the Carringtons. I was sunbathing but then Bobo . . . Do you know Bobo?"

Nancy nodded.

"Well, Bobo asked if I'd like to have a game of tennis so I came up to my room for my tennis things and there they were, in my bed!" Sobs choked her.

Nancy felt a cold murderous rage at the man who had played so carelessly with a young girl's heart, and the duplicity of an aunt who could put herself in the position of chaperone, and not only abuse that but willingly seduce or be seduced by her charge's lover.

"If it hadn't been your aunt, it would have been someone else. Some men are like that. Perhaps your mother was not so unreasonable in trying to break up your relationship as you thought."

"But he *loved* me. We were going to elope . . ."

Nancy gave silent thanks to the unscrupulous aunt.

"Do you like Sanfords?" she asked unexpectedly.

Helen looked surprised. "Oh yes, it's the first time I've ever been away on my own—or nearly on my own. Finishing school was no fun at all. Mummy's quite religious and they were very strict."

"And you like Bobo?"

"Oh yes," the pale face grew quite animated. "She's terrific fun."

"Would you like to stay if your aunt and Piers left?"

"But I *can't* stay without my aunt. Mummy and Daddy would never allow it. And I don't ever want to see her again. I hate her. When I walked in on them she . . . She . . . *laughed.*"

Nancy's eyes glittered. Helen's aunt had spent her last night under Sanfords' roof.

"And perhaps Piers does still love me, really."

"No, he doesn't, but lots of other young men will. Nice young men who wouldn't dream of treating you the way Piers did. I shall contact your parents and assure them that you are under good supervision. The Montcalms are here and one word from Georgina Montcalm seems to work wonders with British aristocracy from the king down. Your aunt and Piers will have to go. And within the next fifteen minutes. I want no tears from you on their behalf. I'll see to it that Sanfords' dressmaker makes you lots of pretty dresses with long sleeves and I shall expect you to enjoy yourself with Bobo and the Montcalms and lots of other people I shall introduce you to. But no more tears. Understand?"

"Yes," a meek little voice said, "and thank you."

Nancy smiled. Her maternal instinct was strong and she had been able to exercise it to the full. If only she had been able to have more children . . . She dashed the thought from her mind. It was one that had crept in unbidden many times since her interview with Dr. Lorrimer. It was almost as if having a brood of children would have compensated her for an early death. It was a ridiculous idea and she had no time for ridiculous ideas. She had to track down the Duke of Dentley's sister and inform her that she was leaving along with the young man whose company she found her in.

Piers Cunningham was good-looking in a flashy, shallow sort of way, his hair slicked and brilliantined, his clothes indicating him to be a gentleman—his manner belying it.

The duke's sister was Nancy's own age, exquisitely coiffured, with small features that had once held a rosebud prettiness and now held very little of either beauty, personality or character.

Her indignation had been loud and shrill. It had abated abruptly when Nancy had coolly informed her that unless she agreed to leave Sanfords quietly and immediately, the Duke and Duchess of Dentley would be informed that she had not only countenanced the meeting of their daughter with a man they wished to separate her from, but that she herself had become the same man's mistress and that consequently their dearly-loved, only daughter had attempted a near-successful suicide.

Neither Piers nor his companion seemed distressed at the news of Helen's attempted suicide. Certainly neither showed enough curiosity to ask after her condition.

When they returned to their rooms, it was to find their cases already packed. Dressed in the clothes they stood up in they were escorted by one of Sanfords' chauffeurs to the harbour and seen safely aboard the *Aquitania*.

Their departure was made relatively unnoticeable by the hysterical exit of the Countess Zmitsky. Sobs, tears, accusations were long and loud as the countess, followed by her retinue, made her way to her waiting Bentley. She was so heavily veiled it was impossible to see her face. Startled guests assumed that the Czech countess had been informed of a bereavement and that this accounted for both her hysteria and her garb. They were wrong. The outlandish black hat with its funereal drapes was to hide her face, but not from grief.

Mysteriously, magically, the countess' false teeth had been spirited away in the middle of the night. No amount of searching or bribery had brought them to light. Sanfords provided many services but not those of a dentist, at least not one capable of replacing a full set of dentures at a moment's notice. The countess had screamed, lain semi-comotose on her bed, rallied herself, beat her breast, beat her maids, all to no avail. The teeth, so essential to a lady of her years, were gone. It would take weeks for her to reach Vienna and her dentist. Weeks before she could emerge in public. Weeks of being hidden behind heavy crèpe veiling. Weeks of celibacy. Half-conscious with grief and rage, the countess was propelled into the back of the Bentley. Her anguished cries could be heard even after the car had disappeared from sight on its speedy way to the docks.

Maria grinned and patted the distasteful bulge in her pocket. She would drop the monstrous objects in the sea. Now only Viscountess Lothermere remained to be taken care of. The viscountess' perfect teeth were her own. Maria was undeterred. God had not blessed her with imagination for nothing.

"Where the devil have you been?" Ramon asked impatiently, kissing her so fiercely it was minutes before she could extricate herself and tell him.

"I've made quite sure none of our guests have duplicated their costumes for the fancy dress ball. I've come up with a theme for the following ball and discussed it with Senora Henriques, who approves. I've greeted one Russian prince and horse, and two ladies of inexhaustible energy."

"Miss Watertight and Mrs. Murphy have arrived then?"

"They have, and how!"

Ramon laughed and bent his head, intent on kissing her again. She averted her head teasingly and said, "I've despatched two guests who didn't wish to be despatched and comforted an eighteen-year-old girl who thought her life was over and slashed her wrists to prove it."

His eyes scrutinized her face carefully. "It's not been too much for you, has it?"

"Not a bit. I've enjoyed myself hugely."

"Then as Sanfords would seem to be running with accustomed smoothness, let's abandon it and spend the afternoon in the mountains."

"But I haven't had lunch yet."

"That's because it's in a hamper in the rear of the Daimler."

The sun was hot, the car unchauffered. In a bliss of contentment Nancy sat beside Ramon as they swept through Funchal's steep alleys and streets full of flowers and trees. In the hot sunlight the mosaic pavements glistened like gold and then they were out on the coast road, Ramon's strong hands manipulating the wheel skilfully around hairpin bends, with breathtaking drops to distant rocks and pounding surf. Judas trees and angel's trumpets flourished thickly, giving way to mountain pines as they climbed higher inland up tracks fit only for mules. Higher and higher amidst rich, dense foliage.

There was no mention of Jack. No talk of divorce. The afternoon was theirs, unsullied by any thoughts but those of each other. They picnicked on the banks of a rushing mountain stream and Nancy slipped off her sandals and squealed girlishly as she paddled in the ice-cold water. Ramon watched indulgently and then, finishing his wine, leapt to his feet and chased her, hopping dexterously from stone to stone until at last his hands caught hold of her and he dragged her laughing on to the bank, her feet and legs sparkling with water, her skirt damp.

His body pinned her down in the grass thick with wild flowers and the hum of bees.

"I love you," he said and his lovemaking left her in no doubt of it.

Hours later, as they walked back to the car, arms circling each other's waists, Nancy asked, "What is the name of this stream, Ramon?"

"The Ribeira de Janela," he said, his hand sliding up to cup her breast.

"Janela. It's a pretty name." Long afterwards, she wondered why she had asked. Why the pretty name had been filed away in her memory. Perhaps, subconsciously, she had known even then. Consciously, she only knew that it was now dusk, that the *Aquitania* sailed at dawn and that Jack had no intention of going aboard without her.

She half expected him to be waiting to see her when she returned to the Garden Suite. He was not there. Maria informed her that Miss Geeson had called much earlier in the day to offer apologies and had been taken ill. Maria's tone indicated that the illness was not to be taken seriously. Nevertheless, Nancy rang Jack's room.

"Is Syrie all right? Maria tells me she was ill this morning."

"She's fine." Jack's voice sounded confident and firm and bore no traces of the loss of control that had bedevilled it for the last forty-eight hours. "I guess your tête-à-tête upset her, but she's over that now."

"I'm glad." Nancy's voice was dry. It would take more than a few idle words to upset a lady of Syrie Geeson's temperament.

"I'm sailing tomorrow. I still wish you'd come with me, Nancy. It would make things much easier. We could come to some arrangement, as long as you were discreet . . ."

"No, Jack." Her relief at his change of attutide was so intense she had to sit down. "I'm staying with Ramon, but I give you my word that I'll do nothing to jeopardize your future."

There was a pause as Jack checked himself. How she

could do one thing without the other was a mystery to him. He was beginning to doubt her sanity. It didn't matter. In a few hours' time she would be unconscious and tucked up safe and secure in his state room aboard the *Aquitania.*

"We'll give it a month," he said charitably. "We should be able to keep things out of the press until then?"

"Yes. I'm sorry, Jack."

"Yes."

The line went dead. They hadn't even said goodbye.

The evening was a gay one. Nicky appeared with a sparkling-eyed Fleur Molière on his arm. His eyes, when they met Nancy's, were amused and reproachful. Later, dancing with her while Ramon glared furiously at them, watching their every move, and ignoring the coterie of guests surrounding them, Nicky said, "I hear I have been supplanted by our host."

"Not supplanted, Nicky."

"So I was nothing but an interlude?" he asked, trying to look injured, and failing.

She laughed. "A pleasant interlude."

Ramon's glower was taking on demonic proportions.

"Whoever nicknamed him the Panther was most astute," Nicky said, whirling her around in a far corner of the ballroom. "I would far more willingly face a horde of wild Cossacks than your outraged lover. The sooner I return you to him the better—for my safety at least."

Vere was dancing with the little Countess Szapary and whenever his eyes met Nancy's the expression in them was warm. There was no ill feeling there and Nancy was relieved.

"Do you have to dance so close to that damnable Russian?" Ramon was demanding as they took to the floor.

Nancy stifled an impish grin and said demurely, "I was only doing as you asked, darling. You said I was to circulate and play Zia's part as hostess and Zia always dances with the guests . . ."

"My mother's guests weren't all in love with her," Ramon said darkly and when Prince Felix appeared later with every intention of executing an admirable foxtrot with his delightful hostess, Ramon's glare froze him on the spot.

Only with great reluctance did Ramon relinquish her to the chaste arms of Charles Montcalm, and even then he watched their every movement as if Charles was a menace to womankind and likely to ravish her on the dance floor.

Costas was once more in command of Madeleine Mancini. Now it was Madeleine who waited meekly at the Greek's side while he recounted scandalous stories to the president of the Chetwynd Cork Company. Hassan had dispensed with her services. He liked passion but drew the line at ferocity. He was once more in Bobo's arms and Bobo was blatantly happy.

Venetia Bessbrook was in the enviable position of being courted by both Reggie Minter and the dashing Prince Zaronski. Luke Golding sulked. His attempts to charm Viscountess Lothermere had failed miserably. Marisa was indifferent to him, as were all the other ladies now they knew he was no longer being sponsored by the generous Lady Bessbrook. Details of his expenses to date had been subtly delivered to his room in the afternoon. There was no way that Luke could pay, and every day he stayed made the sum more preposterous. He damned Hildegarde and his own foolishness to hell, and attempted to pry Venetia away from her admirers. He failed miserably. Venetia had made up her mind. Luke had arrived with her as her companion, and had neglected her. There could be no second chances. No one made a fool of Venetia Bessbrook. As the hours passed, Nancy became more and more aware of her husband's imminent departure.

"Darling, please don't be angry with me, but I do think I should go and see Jack one last time."

It was a waltz. She was held very close in his arms.

"Of course, my love, if you feel you should."

She looked up at him doubtfully. It was unlike Ramon to be so bland.

"You're sure you don't mind?"

"Why should I? You told me you were divorcing him. He seems to have accepted the situation. Saying goodbye to him would only be courteous."

"Ramon . . ." There was something in his voice and his eyes that she had never seen before. She began to feel very unsure of the situation. Why was he suddenly so amenable? It wasn't a side of his character she had ever come across before. Certainly not where Jack was concerned. The last notes of "The Viennese Waltz" died softly away. Lady Lovesy and her insignificant son were descending on them.

"I'll go now," she said reluctantly. Ramon raised her hands to his lips and kissed them. His smile was angelic. Seriously disturbed, Nancy quickly left the ballroom and made her way to Suite 17. Jack had not shown himself in public since his arrival. He had wanted as few people as possible to know he was in residence and not at the side of his wife who was carrying out duties as Sanfords' hostess.

His goodbye was almost as puzzling as Ramon's permission for it had been. There was no belligerence; no accusations. He was calm and controlled—his language once more that of a public figure. He hoped at the end of the month she would return to Washington. He would tell friends, family and colleagues that she was on vacation. She had a sudden overwhelming urge to tell him that she would never be returning to Washington.

That she was dying. That this goodbye was their last. They had shared seventeen years; the whole of their adult lives. It seemed a mockery that it should end as distantly as two strangers parting after a fleeting acquaintance on a train or a ship.

"Jack . . ." she began, but he did not turn to her. He continued to pack his alligator suitcases. He was as remote from her as the moon.

"Goodbye, Jack."

"Goodbye, Nancy."

She stood for another few awkward moments, watching the immaculately dressed stranger pack hairbrush and comb, cufflinks and tie clips. There was nothing more she could say and nothing more Jack wanted to say. The goodbyes were over. She turned and left the room.

The warmth in Ramon's eyes as she entered the ballroom erased any sadness. Quality of time was what was important—not quantity. She had had quantity enough with Jack and it had all been meaningless. With Ramon every second counted. She entered his arms like a homing pidgeon and stayed there until he said:

"Time for bed, my love. I don't want a repetition of last night's exhaustion."

"I'm not in the least exhausted."

"It's still time for bed."

She felt her throat tighten with longing for him and did not protest further.

As Maria prepared to leave the Garden Suite, Ramon stayed her with a motion of his hand. "Mrs. Cameron is tired, Maria. She is going to have an early night. Perhaps you would fix her coffee for her."

Nancy stared at him in astonishment. "But I thought . . ."

He grinned. "I know very well what you thought, but I have business to attend to with Villiers."

"At this time of night?"

"Unfortunately, yes. I also have no intention of leaving you in the ballroom at the mercy of Vasileyev and Meldon and Costas and Zaronski!"

His kisses silenced her protests. Disappointedly she allowed him to leave her. She could not expect to dominate all his time. He had given her the whole of the afternoon and the evening. Presumably, while they had been in their own private heaven high in the mountains, Villiers had been kicking his heels with a mass of paperwork that needed Ramon's critical eye and signature.

She bathed slowly, luxuriously, and then slipped into her five-foot wide bed, looking sadly at the empty pillow where a head of dark curling hair should have been.

Maria brought her in her coffee and the book she had been reading on the voyage out. It was Scott Fitzgerald's *This Side of Paradise.* She smiled. It was an apt title but she did not open it. She drank the Irish coffee that Maria made so excellently, and lay back against her pillows, thinking of Ramon and of the strange, almost mystical, quality of their lovemaking on the banks of the steeply rushing Ribeira da Janela. Her eyelids were heavy. Ramon had been right. She was tired; unbelievably tired. When Maria came back into the bedroom she was soundly asleep.

Jack had already telephoned reception and informed them that his assistant, Miss Geeson, had been taken ill and that as they were returning aboard the *Aquitania* in the morning, he thought it best that she be removed there this evening and that the *Aquitania*'s doctor, and not Sanfords', take care of her. Nancy, wrapped in blankets and unconscious, would be carried from Sanfords and reception would assume she was Miss Geeson. Syrie would leave less conspicuously by a back entrance.

A strategically placed Syrie had informed him that Sanford had left Nancy's suite an hour ago and that Maria had left fifteen minutes ago.

Jack's cases were already in the boot of his hired Bentley. Shelby was even now at the wheel, waiting to take the sick Miss Geeson down to the harbour.

Silently he and Syrie made their way to the Garden Suite. There was music and laughter from the ballroom and a cocktail bar. They passed the Bridge Room and the murmur of subdued conversation. They reached the Garden Suite without being seen—not that it would have mattered if they had been. A man approaching his wife's rooms could hardly be held to be suspicious.

The Garden Suite was in darkness. In the entrance hall he and Syrie quickly donned white overalls and medical face masks. The stronger dose of morphine-sulphate was already in the syringe. They crossed the darkened drawing room and Syrie switched on a table lamp. The bedroom door was open. Beneath the crèpe de chine sheets Nancy's breathing was deep and rhythmical.

"Don't forget she'll regain consciousness, if only for a few minutes," Jack whispered to Syrie. "Whatever you do, don't panic and speak my name."

Slowly he pulled back the sheets. Slowly he lifted the silk of Nancy's nightdress high, so that her right leg and thigh were exposed. Syrie had told him that the injection had to be given in the thigh. Jack had not argued with her. Syrie always knew what she was doing. Their only argument had been over her refusal to give the injection herself. Instead, Jack had bad-temperedly practised injecting oranges and now felt more than competent to render his wife senseless with the minimum of fuss.

He poised the needle over Nancy's gleaming flesh. Syrie closed her eyes. He pushed the needle home and there was a simultaneous scream and then lights blazed and pandemonium broke out. It seemed to Jack that a wild beast had hurtled across the room and grabbed him by the throat. His windpipe was blocked, his eyes were starting from their sockets. He was struggling for air. Struggling for life.

"It's all right, madame! It's all right, madame!" Maria was saying urgently, holding tightly to a hysterical Nancy.

Syrie simply stood, watching complacently as Ramon proceeded to choke the life out of Jack Cameron.

Villiers and two massively built footmen lunged at him, dragging him physically off the semi-conscious senator.

"*For Christ's sake, what's happening? Ramon!*" Nancy felt sick and dizzy and could not move from the bed because firm hands were restraining her. Ramon was struggling to free himself. His face was bleeding from the deep scratchmarks Jack Cameron had inflicted before passing into unconsciousness.

"*Mae de Deus!*"

His eyes were glazed as he threw Villiers from him and sprang once more towards his victim.

Jack lay unaided on the floor, consciousness returning, his hand reaching to his swollen throat. He struggled to his knees and vomited on the Persian carpet. Nancy felt as if she had descended into either hell or a madhouse. The white-coated figure was unknown to her. Another white-coated and masked figure stood motionless, as if none of the life and death struggle were taking place.

"For God's sake get him off him!" one of the footmen yelled in English as Ramon again seized hold of Jack Cameron.

Nancy had struggled into a kneeling position on the bed, her eyes wild as Maria held her with all her strength. Syrie was removing her mask, folding her overall neatly, smoothing down her skirt, making sure the seams of her stockings were straight.

Ramon's fist connected hard with Jack Cameron's jaw, sending him reeling. The smell of vomit hung in the air. The gasps and grunts as Villiers and his two henchmen once more intervened between Ramon and Jack sounded like the noises of nightmare.

"I'll kill him! *Filho de duta*! I'll kill him!"

"No, sir. That would do Sanfords no good at all," Villiers' voice held sweet sanity.

"Ramon! What is it? What is happening?"

Jack was staggering to his feet again. Ramon, his employees' strong hands restraining his arms, kicked his victim viciously with his foot.

"Ask him! Perhaps he can tell you!"

For the first time Nancy realized that the white-coated figure Ramon had been attacking so viciously was her husband.

"Oh my God!" She swayed, held upright only by Maria's arms.

"I'll tell her," Syrie said composedly as Jack staggered to his knees, the mask ripped from his face, his jaw swollen and dislocated by Ramon's frenzied blows.

"Jack had no intention of letting you stay here when the *Aquitania* sailed, Nancy. He sent me here this morning while you were out and I drugged the cream you use in your Irish coffee. The theatricals," she nodded contemptuously at the white coats, "were borrowed from the linen room. The face masks from Jack's medical kit. When you were heavily drugged we were to enter and give you a much stronger dose by injection. Too heavy a dose in the coffee and you might have been aware of the taste. The amount in the syringe would have rendered you senseless for sixteen hours or more—long enough to get you aboard the *Aquitania* and to be out at sea before Ramon realized you had gone. Reception had been told I was ill and was being taken down to the ship. Wrapped in blankets, Jack's gamble was that no one would notice the difference. We knew Ramon had left your room and that he would be unaware of your absence until the morning. That he would not worry about it till much later."

"I don't understand." Nancy gazed bewilderedly at the faces around the bed. "I don't understand."

"He tried to drug you," Ramon said harshly, and held up the syringe in proof. "In doing so he could quite easily have killed you."

"But I'm all right! I'm not unconscious!"

Ramon's laugh was mirthless. "Only because your husband had such a low opinion of coal miners."

Nancy blinked, trying to rally her drugged mind.

"Without knowing it, he insulted his only ally and she came to me. For a certain consideration she told me everything that Jack-oh-so-clever-Cameron had planned to do. There was only sugared water in the syringe. Not an hypnotic drug to induce a state of unconsciousness that could last indefinitely. A 'twilight sleep' as Miss Geeson so accurately described it."

"I don't believe it." Her words lacked conviction. She gazed at the syringe; at the white overall Jack still wore; at the expression of hate in his eyes as he nursed his injured jaw. She faced Syrie and for once believed her smooth, dreadful words. The pain in her thigh was acute. Maria's first action when the lights had blazed had been to pull down Nancy's nightdress. Nancy had no need to lift it to know what she would see. Syrie's voice continued passionlessly.

"Jack didn't think Sanford would bother if you left. He was sure, once away from him, he could handle you. He had underestimated you before and wasn't going to do so in the future. There would have been no returning to Hyannis. He would have kept you in Washington and he would have kept you under close surveillance."

"Or in such a doped condition, you would have been

helpless," Ramon said so savagely that, even though he made no move towards him, Jack flinched.

"But I would have known . . ." Nancy felt as if she were fighting her way through cotton wool.

"No, you wouldn't. When you regained consciousness aboard the *Aquitania, if* you regained consciousness . . ."

Instinctively, Villiers and the footmen grasped his arm as Jack shrank back against the wall.

". . . all you would have remembered was the sight of a nurse and a doctor. That *Filho de duta!*" even the hardened Villiers flinched, "could have spun you whatever story he pleased!"

"He needs a doctor," Villiers said unnecessarily.

"He's lucky. Without you he would have only needed a priest!"

"Jack . . ." Nancy said, her eyes pleading for a denial. There was none. The look he gave her was one of pure venom.

"You'll pay," he said inarticulately. "You'll all pay!" And then he was gone, skirting the room to avoid any possible contact with Ramon.

Syrie shrugged. "I don't think Roosevelt has anything to worry about," she said drily.

"He'll ruin you." Nancy was sitting back on her heels, still on the bed, desperately trying to get her brain to function.

"He'll try. His handicap will be the rather unsavoury scene we have all just witnessed. I don't think he would like it spread abroad and he knows it wouldn't be only my word against his. It would be Mr. Sanford's as well and Mr. Sanford carries quite a punch—in more ways than one. Goodnight, Mr. Sanford. Goodnight, Mrs. Cameron," and as perfectly composed as ever, Syrie Geeson excused herself and returned to her own room.

"You cannot sleep in here, madame," Maria was saying. "The room must be cleaned and disinfected."

"She'll sleep in mine," Ramon said, and shaking off Villiers and the footmen, he strode to the bed and picked her up in his arms. "Tomorrow my solicitors will instigate divorce proceedings." His face was grim. It was as if he were challenging her, as if he knew she had not really meant it before.

"Yes," she said, her arms winding around his neck. "Yes, please do that, Ramon."

Venetia and Prince Felix were leaving the ballroom, laughing and swaying slightly from too much champagne. They halted and stared at the sight of Ramon Sanford striding down the mirrored corridor, Nancy Cameron in his arms, clad only in a rose-pink, lace-edged nightdress. He didn't even glance in their direction; or at the Carringtons and Meades who had also emerged in time to witness the startling scene. Venetia's eyes glazed. The Rape of the Sabine Women had always been a private fantasy. With a man like Ramon Sanford fantasies came true. She wound her arms more tightly around Prince Zaronski's waist. He could quite easily look like an avenging Cossack. Though she envied Nancy, her own evening would be a satisfactory one.

"Who does the man think he is?" Lavinia Meade asked apoplectically. "A feudal chief?"

Sir Maxwell regretfully watched them disappear. He would like to have treated the lissom Hildegarde in a similar fashion, but his doctor had warned him against any undue exertion. The exertion of making love to Hildegarde was immense. It was Sir Maxwell's private opinion that his escapades of the last few days had already robbed him of a good five years of life. He didn't care. It had been worth it.

"Love," he said tolerantly. "It does the heart good to see it."

Sir Maxwell's last act before boarding the *Ile de France* for Madeira had been to write to *The Times* complaining of the indecencies of courting couples in Hyde Park. At this sudden about-turn his wife stared at him in surprise and then suspicion. There were lots of nubile young ladies at Sanfords, but surely Max was beyond temptation? She was filled with doubt and determined to watch him more carefully. One could never be too sure. People did the most extraordinary things. Nancy Leigh Cameron, for instance. She shook her head in complete bewilderment at the behaviour of her fellow human beings and followed her husband to their puritanically separately-bedroomed suite.

Chapter Seventeen

"I'm sorry about the coffee, sweetheart," Ramon said, depositing her in the middle of a vast bed that would have done credit to a Roman emperor, "but I wanted to prove to you what a bastard Cameron is. I knew damn well you didn't intend to divorce him. You're a beautiful lover but a bloody bad liar. Juarez! Coffee, please. Hot, strong and black."

From a room unseen a valet obeyed his command.

"I only let you drink the damn stuff because Syrie convinced me the solution she had prepared was nothing but a strong sleeping draught and because I wasn't going to listen to any more excuses. If I'd told you what Cameron intended to do you'd never have believed me.

"It's a strange thing," he said as Juarez deposited a steaming percolator and china cups and saucers on the bedside table, "but despite everything I rather like the Geeson girl. She's tough and she's not acted too admirably in the past, but she's thumbed her nose to Cameron and that can't have been easy for a girl in her position. No more Madison Avenue flat, no more prestigious lover or large car or limitless expense account."

Nancy made an effort to keep her eyes open and drank her coffee as if it were medicine.

"I'm not too sure where Syrie fits into all this . . ."

"She finally realized that she was being used more than she was using. I think she also finally saw with painful clarity that Cameron will never make it to a senior government post. Under pressure his true character shows through. No amount of gloss and charm and an office full of slick PR men can hide that. Syrie, it appears, is a crusader for women's right. She was out for far more than wealth when she latched on to Cameron."

"What will she do now?"

"She'll return on the *Ile de France*. It's due to dock in a few days' time with your father aboard." He grinned suddenly. "Let's thank our lucky stars *he* wasn't here tonight, or blood *would* have been spilled. If he ever found out what Cameron tried to do to you . . ."

Nancy trembled at the thought.

"Exactly," Ramon said, refilling her cup. "So we don't tell him. Not unless he's so bull-headed about the whole thing that we have to."

"What about . . . ?" Nancy tried to say her husband's name and couldn't. She suddenly felt very sick.

"Cameron left the hotel two minutes after leaving your suite. His bags were already in his motor car, his chauffeur at the wheel. No doubt he's now safely tucked up in his state room and planning on ways to make us, as he so elegantly put it, pay."

"He can't hurt you, can he, Ramon?" She was thinking of Jack's position as a senator. She had seen the expression in his eyes as he had stumbled from her bedroom. The hate had been fanatical. Hatred for Ramon; for Syrie. Hatred for herself. She shivered and

Ramon took the cup from her hand.

"He has no more ability to hurt me, or you, or even Syrie, than a fly on the wall. When it comes to ruthlessness Senator Cameron has a lot to learn. The Sanford side of me may have been British-educated with a penchant for fair play—the de Gama side is more than equal to any upstart senator who can think of no better way of dealing with his wife than resorting to drugs."

He pulled his shirt over his head and turned off all the lamps but one. In the soft light his chest glowed bronze, gleaming with the sweat from his fight, if such a one-sided encounter could be called a fight. Nancy shivered again. If it hadn't been for Villiers and the nameless footmen, Ramon would have annihilated Jack. Even now she could see the hands that were so tender in love, pressing demonically on Jack's windpipe, attempting to squeeze out life in an overwhelming fury of murderous rage.

"Mad, bad and dangerous to know," Lady Caroline Lamb had said of Byron. Ramon was not mad, despite Vere's earlier assumption, and he was not bad . . . though no doubt Jack would never be convinced of that. But he was quite definitely a man who could be dangerous to know. A man who would always look after his own with ferocious tenacity. A man who could look after himself with ease and her with pleasure.

"A penny for them," he said, slipping into the bed beside her.

She turned towards him and sought shelter in his arms. "Byron," she said engimatically, and fell asleep.

When she awoke it took her several minutes to realize that the hideous dream that had assailed her had been reality.

Jack floundering in his own vomit. Ramon, his face

scored by frantic scratchmarks, blood dripping on to the pristine whiteness of his evening shirt. Syrie, calm and composed as though she were a spectator at a play. And herself, disorientated, hysterical, bewildered and finally dazed. She opened her eyes. He was leaning on his elbow and looking down at her. It would not have surprised her if he had kept vigil all through the long night; watching her, awake in case she cried out in the throes of sleep.

"I love you," she said, and as her fingertips connected with the smoothness of his flesh, the tenderness in his eyes deepened to desire. Her arms tightened around him convulsively. His body rolled across hers. The nightmare receded and only love remained.

Every morning, immediately after her half hour with Senora Henriques, Nancy visited Zia. Despite Ramon's protests that she should rest, Nancy insisted on conducting her day as usual. She wanted to be reminded of normality. The events of the previous evening had bordered so closely on insanity that she knew if she dwelt on them she would feel physically ill. The *Aquitania* had sailed. Her old life was over. Her new life, however long, however, short, was just beginning.

When she arrived in Zia's suite she was surprised to find the lavishly tented bed empty.

"Madame," Zia's pretty maid explained, "has insisted on fresh air and though too weak to walk, has been carried to her favourite spot beneath the jacaranda tree."

Nancy suppressed a smile as she crossed the fragrant-scented garden, doves fluttering out of her way. Zia looked even more resplendent when ill than she did in good health. She was sitting beneath a parasol of peacock feathers, dressed in a loose-fitting gown, soft and sensuous and silver. Two heavy ropes of baroque pearls hung waist-length. Her cloud of chestnut hair was piled loosely on the crown of her head. There was a gleam of colour on her eyelids and lips. Champagne and orange juice and petits-fours were within a hand's reach. Her perfume drifted headily on the faint breeze that blew warmly from the distant African coast.

"Darling, Senora Henriques has told me of your scheme for the next ball. Do you think we can coerce Ramon into fancy dress? He would look quite splendid."

"I don't think I could coerce Ramon into anything," Nancy said, smiling. "He'll do what he wants, as he always has."

Zia's answering smile faded. Yes, her strong-willed son would do exactly as he liked. He would not listen to any half truths or vague explanations when she rallied her strength and told him that his *affaire* with Nancy could not continue. She had tried on more than one occasion to break the news, but at the last moment had felt unequal to the task. Chips would be here soon. She needed his support. They were both responsible for the past and for the hideousness that might, after so many years, be brought finally into the light of day.

What would happen then? What would happen to the love Ramon had always borne her? Would she see it wither and die with disgust and incredulity? Would the final victory be Duarte's after all? Her head ached. Perhaps if she told only Nancy? Yes. Nancy would not want to see her father's life destroyed. She was at the height of her beauty. There would be other men for her: other lovers. It would be better that way. Anything would be better than Ramon knowing the truth, and seeing the love that was the mainspring of her life, die.

"Nancy," she said, but Nancy had gone and she realized that she had fallen asleep. She was thankful. It was like a stay of execution. She would wait until Chips arrived. They had always needed each other. Now, as their lives entered their final phase, they needed each other more than ever. She closed her eyes again. The sun was pleasantly warm. Perhaps when she reopened them, it would be to see the *Ile de France* pulling magnificently into Funchal harbour. Even from this distance she would be able to distinguish Chips' compact, forceful body from amongst the crowds of other passengers. She had always been able to seek him out, no matter how great the throng. She had never even had to be told that he was there. Instinct had done that for her. A chemistry of the soul that never let her down. It had been passion that had done that. Passion and lack of restraint and an abandonment of all the values she had been brought up with and held dear.

"If only," she whispered to herself. "If only . . ." She had been saying the words for years. They were the saddest words in the English language. Tears glistened on her still-thick lashes as she closed her eyes and slept.

"Madame come quickly! The English viscountess!"

Nancy turned instantly. The little maid was flying across the lawn to her. They met in a near head-on collision.

"It is terrible, madame! A tragedy! A disaster!"

Nancy forced herself to be calm. Whatever it was it could not be worse than the scene that had met her in Helen Bingham-Smythe's bedroom. The anguished look on the faces around her as she hurried towards the viscountess' lavish suite of rooms gave her cause for doubt.

"A most valued client," Villiers was saying, shaken for once out of his usual composure. "Impossible to make amends . . ."

"I'll kill myself!" the viscountess' French maid was shrieking wildly. "I'll kill myself before I let this happen to her ladyship. How could she accuse me of such a thing? I'll kill myself first!"

Nancy did not feel she could cope with two suicide attempts in twenty-four hours.

"Slap her face and give her some brandy," she said to

Villiers' secretary without pausing in her anxious stride to the viscountess' suite.

"An outrage," the viscount was saying as he paced the sumptuous drawing room. "A desecration! A profanity!"

There was no sign of the viscountess.

"What," Nancy asked, taking a steadying breath, "has happened?"

There was no sign of blood. No sign of violence.

"My wife has been insulted, ridiculed, humiliated . . ."

Nancy marvelled at the string of adjectives. She had never heard him utter more than two consecutive words before.

"May I see your wife, please?"

"See her! See her! Everyone will see her! There's no avoiding it! We've tried everything! Soapflakes, shampoo, even bath cleaner! Nothing will move it!"

Nancy decided that there was no point in waiting for the viscount to calm down sufficiently to be understandable. She marched across the pale lilac carpet and knocked on the bedroom door. She was rewarded by a piercing scream. The scream shook her more than any of the servants' histrionics or the viscount's wrath. Such a scream could never have come from the icily cool, blonde and soignée, utterly detached Serena, Viscountess Lothermere. It came again. Nancy felt perspiration break out on her palms as she ruthlessly turned the knob and pushed open the door.

Two terrified maids were filling a hand basin with soap-sudded water. From the dampness of their uniforms it was not the first time they had done so. Water swamped the floor of the en suite bathroom. Towels lay squandered. The viscountess sat erect on her dressing stool, her eyes glazed. Her hair was a rivetting, shimmering, awe-inspiring emerald green.

Nancy faltered and grasped the door for support. "What the . . . ?"

"It was the shampoo, madame," one of the maids said timidly. "Her ladyship's maid shampooed her ladyship's hair and . . ."

"I shall sue!" The words were cracked and brittle, a travesty of her usual languid speech. "I shall sue!" She seemed unable to utter anything else.

Nancy was ordering a maid to Sanfords' own hair salon for the advice of the resident hair stylist. She examined the shampoo bottle and saw all too clearly that it had been tampered with and that the colour was not the manufacturer's fault. She uttered soothing, calming words to the viscountess. They fell on stony ground.

"I shall sue!"

Serena, Viscountess Lothermere, was like an automaton. Sanfords' appalled hair stylist hurriedly arrived, shampooed and rinsed, shampooed and rinsed. The more he shampooed the more irridescent the green became.

The viscount sought help elsewhere. The *Aquitania* had sailed but the Carringtons had not. Their yacht still graced the harbour. The Carringtons rose to the occasion. Of course they didn't mind curtailing their vacation. Of course dear Serena must be transported immediately to London.

The eighty pieces of luggage that had accompanied the viscountess were packed were trembling speed. The French maid, still in the throes of hysteria, proved of little use. Sanfords' maids dressed her ladyship and searched frantically for a suitable head covering. The cloche hats that the viscountess favoured were unequal to the task of containing the hair that had not only taken on the colour of jungle green, but also the texture. The tiny pill-boxes, so fashionable, were utterly useless, as were the flower-laden picture hats. In the end a deep-crowned, broad-rimmed hat in the manner of Greta Garbo was unearthed and hid all but the merest wisp of verdant green.

"I shall sue," the viscountess said again as, physically supported by her husband and the gallant Victor Carrington, she made her way from her suite to the Carringtons' Armstrong-Siddeley. "I shall sue."

Despite Nancy's orders and Villiers' vigilance, her route was lined by awestruck maids and valets, footmen and waiters. Prince Vasileyev watched with wicked amusement; Countess Szapary with anguished sympathy; Madeleine Mancini, maliciously; Lavinia Meade unbelievingly. Maria watched complacently. Now there was only Mrs. Peckwyn-Peake.

"I shall sue," the viscountess was heard to say as the doors of the Armstrong-Siddeley were briskly closed by a stunned chauffeur.

Maria turned and returned to the Garden Suite. Mrs. Peckwyn-Peake was made of sterner stuff than the countess and viscountess. She would have to think of something truly dreadful in order to drive the formidable American from Minnesota away. She permitted herself a small smile. She would succeed. The prize was worth all the effort. Luis might not be perfect husband material but Maria had decided she was going to marry him. He would need careful watching, but then any man worth having always did. She sang to herself as she began to sew a hem of fine French lace on to one of Nancy's petticoats.

"It's as mad as a wake with no whisky," Seamus Flannery said glumly as he hung over the deckrail of the *Ile de France*.

Chips tossed the butt of his cigar into the creamy waves. "It's a vacation. Even a mayor is entitled to a vacation."

"Not when he needs re-electing," Seamus said like a prophet of doom.

Chips turned up the collar of his astrakhan overcoat.

"The election is sewn up good and tight. There isn't even an opposition."

"There is, and he'll be rubbing his hands in glee at this very moment. I can just hear him asking who it is that pays for the mayor's trips to Europe; or for a first-class state room on a ship that's a floating palace . . ."

"*I* pay," Chips said complacently. "He can dig and dig until he reaches Australia and he'll never find any different."

"Madness," Seamus uttered again.

Chips was uncaring. His political sixth-sense never let him down. He had wanted to come to Europe and he had seen a way of doing it to his advantage. His PR men would talk of his meeting with British members of parliament: would talk of his personal assessment of the work of the League of Nations: would talk of anything as long as it gave Bostonians the clear impression that their mayor was a man of worldly affairs as well as civic ones. And if he did, by any remote miracle, lose the election, then he'd use his European trip to stand him in good stead when he entered the running for governor. It was all a perfect cover-up for seeing Zia and his daughter. Madeira would feature nowhere in official press-releases. He would only spend a week there. It would be enough. His parting with Nancy had been agonizing. She had been distraught—he had been ill. He had handled the whole affair with the delicacy of a bull in a china shop. He wanted her back home. She was the pivot around which his life revolved. Her place was in Boston, Hyannis or Washington. Anywhere as long as it was within a telephone call and a fast motor car ride. Her behaviour on the day she had left Boston had frightened him. It had no longer been his little girl he had been talking to. It had been a woman with tortured eyes and a detachment that had terrified him. The Sanford affair may have been fleeting, but it had hit her hard. It was as if her whole personality had disintegrated and reformed into that of a stranger.

"Can you tell me any reason why a man should want monkeys in his bathroom?" Seamus asked, after an extended silence, when it was obvious he would get no political sense from his hero.

"Living or dead?" Chips asked, sloughing off his despondency at the traumatic goodbye between himself and Nancy and regaining his usual good spirits at the prospect of a reunion.

"Neither. They're painted on the walls where any right-thinking man would have seagulls or fish. God have mercy on my mother," Seamus crossed himself reverently, "but she'd turn in her grave if she could see me in my birthday suit surrounded by a pack of monkeys."

"Progress, dear boy," Chips said indulgently to his loyal aide, who bordered on the ripe old age of seventy. "If Vincent Astor can bathe with monkeys, why shouldn't Seamus Flannery of Hanover Street?"

"Because it seems to me there's a great deal more sanity in Hanover Street. Give me a tin bath in front of a roaring fire any day."

Chips guffawed. "Progress, dear boy, has left you far behind. How would I get votes if I offered the honest citizens of the North End nothing but tin tubs in front of the fire?"

"You'd get a fine sight more than if you offered them monkeys staring at them whenever they took their trousers down," Seamus said darkly.

Chips slapped him on his back and resumed his leisurely stroll along the deck. "So you're not impressed by your venture into the world of the rich?"

"I'm impressed by the bar," Seamus said grudgingly. "Twenty-seven feet, it is. Longer even than Paddy Murphy's."

"The French Line will be most gratified at that

comparison," Chips said gravely, reflecting that it would need a good deal of sawdust on the floor and several gallons of poteen instead of twelve-year-old Chivas Regal to make the transition from the panache of the *Ile de France* to the squalor of Murphy's downtown bar.

"As it seems the only place aboard to meet with your approval, let's adjourn there and reflect on the desperate measures Sean O'Flynn will be driven to in trying to make capital of my absence."

"It's not O'Flynn we have to worry about," Seamus said, mollified at the thought of endless drinking hours. Prohibition had left a mark on him which would never be erased. He still downed his Scotch with the speed of a man who constantly expected to have his glass forcibly removed. "It's the blue-eyed boy exuding honesty and fair play. No more graft. No more patronage. No more helping immigrants in return for votes. He's appealing to a whole new section of the electorate."

"He's wet behind the ears," Chips said comfortably, "and his supporters are a bunch of chowderheads."

Seamus was unconvinced but the Scotch in his glass was as smooth as a baby's bottom and diluted only by ice cubes. If a man had to travel, and Seamus had never seen any reason to, then it was comforting to do so facing a well-stocked bar. He began to discuss how they could best exploit Chips' slum clearance programme, but Chips was no longer listening to him. The last few weeks had been harrowing.

He had expected abuse from Gloria after her banishment to Jamaica Plain. He had not expected her to telephone him every hour of the day, at home and at the office, sobbing uncontrollably. He had refused to see her. He wouldn't divorce her. It wasn't worth his while. But neither would he share his roof with her. Not until it was expedient for him to do so. He had taken her from obscurity and moulded her into a woman fit to be a mayor's wife. She had never once made a *faux pas* in public. Her accent had acquired flat Bostonian vowels that equalled those of a Winthrop. She had carried out her duties perfectly. She was pretty and full of life and the press loved her. She had been as big an asset to him in her own way as Seamus was in his. At civic receptions he was proud of her, enjoying the envious glances of men young enough to be his grandsons. At home he enjoyed her. She made him laugh. She made him feel young. She brought a dimension into his bedroom activities that enabled him to face the end of each day with undiluted pleasure.

He had never said he loved her because he hadn't believed it was true. They had an arrangement, an understanding. Faithfullness on her part had formed its basis. He was too old to suffer the indignity of being cuckolded. Her purpose was to shore up his image. To make sure the electorate saw their mayor as a virile, energetic, vigorous go-getter more than capable of serving another four years in office. In return he gave her social status: a house in Beacon Hill; a mansion in Palm Springs; a thirty-acre retreat in Rhode Island.

It had been a comfortable arrangement, one that had been negotiated in far-away Los Angeles in a bar of dubious reputation and over a magnum of champagne. Later, on their honeymoon, she had said she loved him. He had patted her bottom and been pleased but had not believed a word of it. She would have said the same to Bela Lugosi if he had rescued her from her former life and transported her to a world of furs and jewels and gossamer silk stockings.

No one expected the marriage to last six months; not the gossip columnists, not Seamus, not even Nancy. But it had. Gustily so.

He remembered coming home exuberantly from a meeting and bursting in on Gloria as she wallowed shoulder-deep in perfumed bubbles.

"God, how absolutely super," she had said at news he could no longer recall. He had stripped off his clothes with the eagerness of a seventeen-year-old boy faced with his first mistress and Gloria had squealed with delight as he jumped into the bath with her, water swirling and swamping the rose-pink carpet. There was no coyness, no inhibition, no restraint about Gloria's lovemaking. After the darkened fumblings his first wife had reluctantly allowed him and the nameless string of pliant, empty-headed women that had followed, Gloria had been like a tonic.

Not only did he enjoy making love to her, he actually enjoyed talking to her. It had been an unsought bonus—one that was now denied him. His Beacon Hill home had taken on a museum-like atmosphere without Gloria's sun-gold shingled curls and risqué conversation. No longer did he look forward to leaving City Hall for the regal drive home. He told himself that he had not spoken to her because her adultery with Sanford had placed her beneath his contempt. He was man enough to know that it was not the only reason. It was because he did not trust himself not to weaken if he once heard her voice.

The previous Friday she had ordered her flamboyant white Rolls to City Hall and physically assaulted his outer office, demanding to see him. Seamus and his aides and secretary had seized hold of her before she could hurtle into his inner sanctum. He had sat at his massive desk, his hands clenched on the tooled leather surface, his mouth a thin, almost invisible line, his face grey as he heard her anguished cries.

"Chips! Please! Chips! *Chips*!"

They had taken her away and he forbade entry to anyone, even Seamus, for the next hour. At the end of that hour he had written a letter without the aid of his secretary. He told Gloria she had no need to fear a change in her lifestyle. She could still be his wife. She could reign over their Palm Beach mansion and Rhode Island home just as she had previously done. Only Beacon Hill would be barred to her.

Her answering letter had been hand delivered. There were smudges that looked like tear marks on the back. Her usual flowing handwriting was uneven. He had burnt it unopened. The next morning he had booked himself and Seamus aboard the *Ile de France*, and to the utter stupefaction of his aides and colleagues left the maintenance of municipal order to them.

He was no longer sleeping, no longer eating. He was behaving like a man who had discovered that the woman he loved had been unfaithful. Before he succumbed to that illusion he was going to beat a retreat: back to the woman he did love—the woman he had always loved. It was the only way to clear his mind. To regain logic before he so lost command of himself that he hauled Gloria from her banishment at Jamaica Plain, beat her black and blue, demanded apologies and promises and made love to her with a violence indecent and unhealthy in a man of his advancing years.

The last thing he had seen, as the pride of the French Line slid away from her berth and towards the Narrows, was an unmistakable white Rolls Royce careering to a stop and a hatless, frantic figure running and waving. Her curls had glinted gold in the cold winter sun. As the passengers lining the deckrails shouted goodbyes to relatives and friends, Chips stood mute, his collar high against the bitter wind, his fists clenched deep in the pockets of his coat.

Her hand faltered and fell. She had not been waving goodbye, but beckoning desperately for his return. She stood small and desolate amongst the fur-wrapped throng around her.

He turned abruptly and made his way to his state room

and a bottle of bourbon. She had deceived him once and she was deceiving him again. Her despair was only for the things she thought she stood in danger of losing. His despair was so deep it could not be openly acknowledged, even to himself.

"Then you will marry me?" Luis' long-lashed eyes were urgent.

"I will think about it," Maria said demurely.

"*Mae de Deus*! I'm offering you my hand, not a bunch of flowers!"

"I like flowers," Maria said serenly.

Luis prayed for strength. "Then I'll give you armfuls of them. A roomful."

Maria, remembering Prince Vasileyev's gift to Nancy, suppressed a shudder. "One flower will do."

"One flower, a hundred, what difference does it make? I'm asking you to marry me."

They were far from the hotel, where the gardens overflowed and drifted off into a fragrant wilderness.

"I could not marry a man who would not be faithful to me," Maria said, her eyes lowered so that she could retain her self-control and not throw herself into his arms.

"I shall be faithful until death!" Luis felt physically faint and wondered if it really was his own voice he was hearing. "I promise by the Virgin Mary and all the Saints. Please, Maria. Marry me." Something caught in his throat. "I love you, Maria."

Great dark eyes looked up at him slowly. "And I you," she said softly.

His lips met hers and his fate was sealed. He made her an engagement ring of tiny yellow flowers.

"And the ladies?" Maria asked.

Luis had long abandoned any attempts at trying to deceive Maria as to his relationships with the ladies.

"Countess Zimitsky and the English viscountess have left, there is no one else, I promise you."

Maria suppressed her disappointment at this lie, but was determined not to spoil the evening of her wedding proposal. She wound her arms around his neck and, to his immense satisfaction, let him kiss her with a passion she had previously forbidden.

Minnie Peckwyn-Peake was as aware of Maria as Maria was of her. She had noted not only the way the Czechs countess' eyes slid constantly in Luis' direction, but also how often glances were exchanged between Luis and Mrs. Nancy Leigh Cameron's spectacularly pretty maid. Minnie Peckwyn-Peake was not disturbed. When one door closed another opened. She had watched in admiring amusement as first the Czech countess and then the English viscountess had been obliged to leave ignominiously. By the law of averages she would be next on the spirited little Puerto Rican's list. Minnie waited in pleasurable anticipation. Nancy Leigh Cameron's maid had finally met her match. Minnie was quite happy to relinquish Luis in the cause of true love. Besides, she liked a fighter and the dusky-skinned maid was certainly that. She would not, however, be driven from Sanfords as Luis' other two mistresses had been. Minnie Peckwyn-Peake never left anywhere until she chose to do so. She wondered when Maria would strike. She did not have long to wait. When she returned to her suite after sunbathing with the Michaeljohns and a rather interesting encounter with Mr. Luke Golding, it was to find her maid in tears.

"I can't understand how it can have happened, madame. I've looked everywhere. I've asked the laundry maids and the room maids. Nobody admits to having seen or taken them."

"Taking what?" For a second anxiety clutched at Minnie's heart. She could handle practical jokes but not the theft of any of her valuables.

"Your brassières, madame."

"Brassières!" Minnie Peckwyn-Peake sat on the edge of her majestic four-poster and began to laugh. Her maid failed to find anything amusing in the situation and was near to tears.

"But there's not one, madame, and you're dining tonight with Mrs. Cameron and Mr. Sanford and Prince Zaronski and Lady Bessbrook and the Earl and Countess of Montcalm . . ."

The fashion might be for topless, backless, thigh-splitting evening gowns but Minnie's proportions were large. Those that were unkind said that they were titanic. It took a good half-hour for her maid to lace her tightly into her boned corsets and her mammoth brassières looked more like weapons of war than articles of underclothing. Without them Mrs. Peckwyn-Peake would not be able to appear in public. Instead of being reduced to hysteria Mrs. Peckwyn-Peake seemed positively amused.

"That girl certainly knows where to find the Achilles heel," she said, divesting herself of the tent-like apparel she wore for sunbathing.

"It is brassières that are missing," the maid repeated, wondering if perhaps her mistress had been out in the sun to long. "Not shoes."

Minnie waved her away. The girl was obedient but witless. She wondered where Mrs. Cameron had found her enterprising Puerto Rican and envied her the acquisition.

Her bath run, she lowered her enormous bulk into the blissfully hot depths. When Countess Zimitsky had left amid hysteria and yards of heavy veiling, the culprit had watched from a safe distance. When Viscountess Lothermere had been led, glazed-eyed, to the Carringtons' motor car the same culprit had watched in smiling satisfaction. Minnie wallowed in the foam-filled water. This time the little minx was in for a disappointment. A lack of brassières was not enough to disconcert a Peckwyn-Peake of Minnesota.

"But, madame," her maid was aghast at her mistress' intention of still attending the dinner.

The lavishly sequined dress, worn with its normal foundation garments, was low-necked enough to reveal a magnificent chest on which a cascading necklace of diamonds lay as if on a shelf. Without restraint from beneath, Mrs. Peckwyn-Peake's breasts spread far and wide, the corsetry of her massive hips only emphasizing the eruption that was taking place above.

"Madame, you can't possibly . . ."

"I can," Minnie said, pinning a plume in her hair with a giant sized diamond and picking up her feather boa.

"Madame, please . . ."

Minnie's torso swayed magnificently as she rose to her feet. It was as if the upper part of her anatomy had a life of its own.

"Oh, madame," her maid wailed, but her employer was unconcerned. Head held high, unbridled flesh undulating, she walked as majestically as a Roman empress through the sumptuous drawing rooms and towards Mr. Ramon Sanford's private dining suite.

The footman looked, closed his eyes, looked again and in a voice that was little more than a whisper announced: "Mrs. Minnie Peckwyn-Peake."

Minnie smiled graciously at him, narrowly avoiding doing him an injury with her right breast which had developed a rhythm of its own, and entered the gold and white dining room to be greeted by Nancy and Ramon.

Charles Montcalm paled and demanded a brandy instead of the aperitif offered. Georgina blinked and with enormous effort raised her eyes to those of a bland and unconcerned Minnie.

Prince Felix murmured a word not usually associated with the aristocracy and Venetia was reduced to stunned silence.

Only Nancy seemed capable of speech. Drinks were served. Mrs. Peckwyn-Peake was introduced; conversation rallied manfully. Ramon murmured in an aside that their new guest made Lavinia Meade positively flat-chested in comparison and was rewarded by a sharp dig in the ribs from Nancy.

White-gloved footmen pulled back Sanford-monogrammed chairs for the guests to sit upon and even Nancy's well-bred eyes were rivetted as Mrs. Peckwyn-Peake's bosom descended amply on to gleaming white napery.

"I hope you are enjoying your stay," Nancy managed, a trifle hoarsely.

"I am," Minnie said, a wayward breast toppling a George III salt cellar.

A waiter repositioned it nervously. There seemed no way of telling in which direction Mrs. Peckwyn-Peake's upper half would next venture.

"Despite my loss."

"Your loss?" A frown creased Ramon's brow. Villiers' detailed biography of Mrs. Peckwyn-Peake had not mentioned any recent bereavement. Mr. Peckwyn-Peake had departed this world for the next a good ten years previously.

"Brassières," Minnie said as Charles Montcalm spilled soup on to his trousers and Venetia Bessbrook choked on a crouton.

A hypnotist could not have commanded a more mesmerized audience.

Minnie raised her soup spoon to her mouth, swallowed and smiled benignly. "With the countess it was false teeth. With the viscountess, hair dye. For myself it was brassières."

"I'm afraid I don't understand," Nancy said feebly.

Minnie continued with her soup. She was the only one capable of doing so. Prince Zaronski's spoon was held motionless in mid-air. Even Ramon was transfixed.

"A certain young lady is so much in love that she has very enterprisingly removed all opposition, except for myself."

Ramon vainly tried to think of a man capable of being the lover of the elderly Czech countess, the coolly beautiful viscountess, and the awe-inspiring Mrs. Peckwyn-Peake. He failed.

"But who . . . ?" Nancy began.

Minnie smiled benevolently. "I'm sure you would not want me to be so indiscreet," she said. "I shall speak to the young lady myself and I assure you there will be no further unpleasantries. In fact, I can quite confidently say that by midnight all my undergarments will be safely returned," and with both hands she unself-consciously hoisted her bosom away from the dish of Espada that the waiter placed in front of her.

Chapter Eighteen

"Why the look of utter desolation?" Ramon asked the next morning as Nancy sat on her terrace toying with her breakfast.

She smiled up at him and caught his hand in hers, holding it closely against her cheek before he sat down beside her and poured himself a black, sugarless coffee.

"Maria is leaving me."

Ramon raised his eyebrows quizzically. He was naked except for a towelling robe of dark navy, salt water from his early morning swim glistening in his dark curls.

"She's getting married. To Luis Chavez."

Coffee slopped over into his saucer. "Good God!"

"Is it so bad?"

"It's surprising," Ramon said drily as a clean coffee cup and saucer were placed before him. "I've never regarded Luis as a domestic animal."

"Then do you think I should try and dissuade her?"

"Could you?"

"No, I don't think so. Maria doesn't act on impulse. If

she says she's going to marry Luis, then she means it."

"Then let her. It's about time Luis married. He's been skirting deep trouble these last few seasons."

Nancy's anxious expression made him grin. "Nothing criminal, my love. Only slightly dishonourable."

"But then surely I should tell Maria . . ."

Ramon's grin widened. "Your demure little maid has more cards up her sleeve than an ace poker player. She knows all about her beloved Luis' little failings. What is more, she seems to be curtailing them in an exceptionally talented manner."

"I haven't a clue what you're talking about."

"I know, and it doesn't matter. Is that the magnificent Mrs. Peckwyn-Peake strolling in the garden with London's literary lion?"

Nancy put down her coffee cup and stared in the direction Ramon was pointing.

Luke was slouching, his hands desultorily rammed in his pockets. Without his broad-brimmed black hat and silk-lined cloak, he looked like any other young man out for a pre-breakfast walk.

"His flamboyance seems to have deserted him."

"It did that when he was faced with his hotel bill. I have a feeling that the inimitable Minnie is Mr. Golding's last chance."

"He shouldn't have treated Venetia so underhandedly," Nancy said without sympathy.

Venetia, after considering a reconciliation with Reggie, had turned instead to the more exotic Prince Zaronski. Her zest and sparkle had returned but Nancy knew that Luke Golding had hurt her intensely.

She put down her coffee cup and stared into the distant harbour. The Carringtons' yacht was not the only one absent.

"Where's the *Kezia?*" she asked with surprise.

"Nearing Oporto, where it will pick up my lawyer and

Dr. Oliveira and bring them straight back to Funchal."

She stared.

"Your lawyers are in America. Not very convenient for arranging a rapid divorce." His lean, strong hands encircled her wrists. His face had a hard, uncompromising look that she had learned not to argue with.

"The doctor?" she said helplessly. "Why have you sent for a doctor?"

"Serrado isn't happy with your health and neither am I. Dr. Oliveira will soon be able to tell if there is anything wrong with you. I don't want any more protests of physical fitness. I don't trust them. You'd tell me you were perfectly healthy if you were dying on your feet."

"Syrie," she said weakly, unable to look him in the eyes. "Where is she now?"

"With Charles Montcalm."

"*Charles*!"

Ramon laughed, his hold on her wrists becoming gentle. "That most English of Englishmen is behaving most virtuously, I assure you. He is dictating long letters to Ramsay MacDonald and Baldwin. He has a far more knowledgeable grasp of the political situation in Europe than they appear to have. With the exception of Churchill, and no one appears to be paying too much attention to him at the moment. What Charles is trying to do is set things out in plain black and white for them. He wants to rouse them from their stupor before it's too late. He's a naval man and war is far more of a reality to him than it is to the civil servants and government ministers sitting behind their comfortable desks in Whitehall."

"War?" The blood had drained from Nancy's face. "Surely that sort of talk is irresponsible."

Fresh coffee was served. When they were once again alone Ramon said carefully, "It's no use turning your back on what is happening in Germany and Austria. I know your daughter's marriage makes the whole subject difficult for you, but you have to face facts. In Vienna there have been massive Nazi demonstrations and they have said publicly that they intend to gain control of the country this year. If they do, it won't be without bloodshed. Felix tells me that when the curtain went up at the Burgtheater for the opening performance of George Bernard Shaw's *The Apple Cart* it revealed a huge swastika banner placed by Nazis who had neatly managed to upset the apple cart of the backstage management."

Nancy's hands twisted in her lap. She wondered if Ramon knew her son-in-law was a fanatical follower of the German Chancellor. If he knew that Dieter was a committed Nazi.

"While America is besotted by such fripperies as Will Rogers, Janet Gaynor and Eddie Cantor, Hitler is calmly trebling his army."

"But Austria's Chancellor approved a new campaign for the suppression of Nazi propaganda only a few weeks ago," Nancy protested.

"Then it is failing or the rallies and the Vienna theatre performance caper could never have taken place."

It was suddenly still on the sunlit terrace. On the horizon the *Ile de France* edged into sight. Nancy's thoughts were so full of Austria and Germany and Verity and Dieter that she did not even register its imminent arrival.

"Austria is in chaos, Nancy. Ask Felix. He has a house there but will not be returning to it. In his opinion the fascists will take over the Dollfuss government within months or even weeks and Dollfuss and his ministers will be assassinated."

"Stop it!" She covered her ears with her hands.

Gently but firmly he removed them. His strong-boned face was grave. "I'm telling you all this, Nancy, because I love you and if you have a daughter in Germany you should be aware of what the future might hold. There is already civil war in Austria."

"But Germany is stable!"

"It is Germany that is causing the chaos." In the distance Costas could be heard laughing loudly at the poolside. Countess Szapary was running down a mimosa-clouded path, her face as radiant as if she was meeting a lover. A waiter was carrying a tray of iced daiquiris. Their conversation amongst such surroundings seemed bizarre and unreal.

Princess Louise emerged into the early morning sunlight, Mr. Blenheim escorting her regally. The princess was in black. A black armband encircled the exiled king's arm.

"King Albert," Nancy said, glad to be diverted from the subject. "I'd almost forgotten about him. The Meades have gone into mourning as well. Sir Maxwell was quite close to the Belgian court at one time."

"That's the trouble—and the blessing—of Madeira," Ramon said, watching them as they made their way sedately to a seat that gave a magnificent view of the harbour and mountains. "The happenings in the outside world seem unreal. The King of Belgium is killed in a mountaineering accident at fifty-nine. If half of our guests were in their own countries, they would have immediately assumed mourning. Here, the event seems so distant that only the old brigade behave appropriately. I don't envy the heir to the throne and his beautiful princess. Now is not the choicest time to ascend a European throne."

Georgina Montcalm stepped out on to the terrace.

"You're right about people's priorities," she said, joining them with no fear of disapproval. "Poolside conversation is revolving around Carole Lombard and George Raft's performances in *Bolero.* The insufferable Count Szapary has informed us all that the Earl of

Athlone and his family have been vacationing in the United States for some time and intend visiting Miami en route to the Bahamas. Reggie tells us that Boston has been cut off from New York by a blizzard and both Madeleine Mancini and Bobo are finally agreed on one point: that Roosevelt has more sex appeal than any previous American president. Prince Leopold and Princess Astrid's future is taking a very definite back seat. Presumably because talk of Belgium would lead inevitably to talk of Germany and then to Austria. According to Charles, war clouds are massing over Western and Central Europe and the more they mass, the more merry and carefree we foolishly become. He says he's a lone wolf crying in the wilderness. Venetia thinks he's completely ga-ga but he's not. If I were you, Nancy, I'd haul that daughter of yours out of Germany and back to America. Anywhere in the world would be a better place of residence right now.

"My daughter's husband is German," Nancy said quietly.

"Then haul him out as well. He can't approve of what is going on, can he?"

Nancy rose unsteadily to her feet. "My son-in-law fully supports the new German Chancellor," she said and walked into the shadow of her bedroom.

Ramon's face was grim: Georgina's horrified.

"I'll go after her," she said hastily. "How thoughtless of me . . . It never occurred to me . . ."

Nancy was sitting at her dressing table, carefully applying face powder and lipstick.

"I'm sorry, darling. Was I disastrously tactless?"

Nancy put down her powder puff, her hand trembling. "My son-in-law is a Nazi. I can't believe he would be so unless Hitler was a responsible man."

"Then let's hope Charles is wrong," Georgina said, unconvinced.

"You don't believe he is, do you?" Nancy's violet dark eyes were troubled.

"No," Georgina said truthfully and changed the subject. "The *Ile de France* is about to dock and I'm dying to see aboard. Bobo sailed on her maiden voyage and says the decor is very futuristic and very, *very* French. All blond wood and concealed lighting."

"Oh God," Nancy said. "My father's aboard."

"I thought your relationship with your father was so close as to border on the incestuous. Why the lack of enthusiasm?"

"My relationship with my father has always been that of the good little girl to genial parent," Nancy said drily. "When the good little girl stopped being good the parent stopped being quite so genial."

Georgina raised her eyes skywards at the folly of people who didn't manage their private lives with her efficiency and said, "I'm just going to collect Charles. That poor Geeson girl has been taking notes since eight-thirty this morning. I'll meet you in reception in ten minutes."

Ramon stood at the French windows, his legs apart, his hands on his hips. The sun was behind him and she could not see his face clearly, only the muscled outline of his body and the unruly darkness of his hair.

"I don't want to go," she said. "I don't want to see him. Let's leave together, now."

It was a faint echo of his pleas to her at Hyannis.

"We can't, my love. The *Kezia* is on its way to Oporto."

"We could if we really wanted to!"

He caught hold of her and she clung to him. "Promise me that you won't let anything spoil things for us?"

His laugh was low and husky. "It's I that should be asking you for that promise. Kiss me."

She raised her face obediently and time was forgotten.

Georgina stamped her foot impatiently on the marble floor. In Funchal, Chips O'Shaughnessy descended the gangplank with the air of a man accustomed to being first off ship. Unbelievably there was no one to meet him.

"Where's my daughter?" Chips asked as the Montcalms' Bentley finally careered down over the cobbled streets and Georgina Montcalm pushed her way through the crowds and seized hold of his hand in welcome.

"She's been detained." She didn't elaborate by whom or why. She knew very well who and she had a dark suspicion as to why, but neither were explanations that could be given to a doting father.

Seamus was left to attend to the baggage and Chips, who hadn't seen the Montcalms for nearly twenty years, allowed himself to be escorted to their Bentley and marvelled again at the false impression so many of his countrymen had of the English. When they chose to be, they were the friendliest people in the world. He remembered his wife and his wife's family and revised his opinion. The Montcalms were the exception: not the rule.

"Nice to see you again after so long," Chips was saying to Charles Montcalm and wondering where the hell Nancy was—and Zia. In his imagination she had been there on the quay, waiting for him, her chiffon dress floating in the breeze; her titian hair a fiery nebula in the rays of the hot Madeira sun.

Names were being mentioned. Margot Alleynian; Reggie Minter; Stew Chetwynd, the president of the Chetwynd Cork Company . . .

He made polite noises, his mind elsewhere: on his daughter, on the woman he still regarded as the only love of his life and on his damn fool son-in-law. Cameron, at least, should have been at the dockside. However irrational Nancy's behaviour in New York and Boston, it was important that they presented a united front to people like the Montcalms and the rest of the talkative, gossip-mongering international set that sought refuge from the hectic pace of London, Paris and Rome, at Sanfords.

She was standing in the grandiose reception hall as they entered. Her face was flushed, as if she had been running. Her hair was tousled as if she had just jumped out of bed, a wilful curl straying across her forehead. Her dress was of white silk and simple. Her legs and sandalled feet were bare.

"It's lovely to see you," she said and hugged him fiercely despite their audience of receptionists, bellboys, Montcalms and Minnie Peckwyn-Peake leaving arm-in-arm for her Rolls Royce with a resigned Luke Golding.

"Nancy!" There was a lump in his throat. She looked well and happy and only then did he know how frightened he had been: how terrified of seeing again the pale wraith that had said goodbye to him in Boston. She had needed a holiday; sun; Zia's companionship. They would all return together. He had never been so angry in his life as when he had discovered that Jack Cameron had sailed for Madeira without informing him of his plans. For Nancy's sake, he would avoid a scene with his son-in-law. His daughter and her husband would return to Boston and all the foolishness that had been spoken would be forgotten.

"Zia," he said. "Where is Zia?"

"She's ill, darling."

Chips felt his heart miss a beat.

"Exhaustion, the doctor says. She's been resting for several days now."

"But she knows I'm coming? She's expecting me?"

Nancy patted his arm reassuringly. "She watched the liner dock from her garden. She's waiting for you now."

Chips beamed buoyantly and did not notice the signs of stress on Nancy's face as she said:

"Before you see her, I'd like to talk to you."

"Afterwards," Chips said ebulliently.

"It's very important."

"So is Zia."

Nancy knew that by telling him straight away of Ramon's presence, she would destroy his happiness at one stroke. But it seemed to her that it would be better to do that than let him continue being so heartbreakingly joyful, confident that everything was right in his own particular world.

"Daddy . . ."

"This way, Mr. O'Shaughnessy, sir," Villiers said smoothly and, despite Nancy's protests, swept Chips towards Zia's bronzed-studded door.

Nancy sat down abruptly. Villiers' cavalier manner had destroyed any hope of breaking the news to him gently. A waiter passed with glasses of sherry for the Michaeljohns and Meades who were playing bridge. Absent-mindedly Nancy removed a glass as he passed and sat, sipping it.

Zia might not mention Ramon. They would probably just talk of old times: the North End: Boston: Chips' new lease of life as mayor. She put down her empty glass and telephoned Ramon's suite.

"Mr. Sanford has gone out, madame," his valet informed her.

"Out? Where? To the pool?" Her mind was still on the conversation taking place between her father and Zia.

"No, madame. He has driven over to the Rossmans. He will be back for cocktails."

She didn't say thank you. She put the telephone receiver back on its rest.

He had told her he would leave the hotel until she had broken the news to her father. One heart attack could quite easily be followed by another. The mayor would have to be told the truth that would be distinctly unpalatable to him, but there was no reason to make matters worse by facing him with Ramon unforewarned.

The Rossmans were old family friends. It was quite natural that Ramon should spend the afternoon there. Tessa Rossman had no idea how nearly she had become Mrs. Ramon Sanford. She had no cause for jealousy; no need to feel such sweeping desolation. She returned to the Garden Suite, after leaving instructions that her father be brought to her when he had finished his visit to Mrs. Sanford. The desolation did not ease. It was silly and irrational. Her father would be angry as any man would be angry at having his daughter announce her intention of marrying a man his wife had taken as a lover.

Nancy pushed the memory of Gloria to the back of her mind. Tessa Rossman lingered more persistently. Innocently young, fair hair glistening, eyes shining, adoration for Ramon in her every expression and movement. She leaned her cheek against the coolness of her dressing table mirror. She was behaving like a child of Tessa Rossman's years and not a sophisticated, beautiful woman of thirty-five. Ramon loved her. She knew it as surely as she knew that she loved him. Nothing could come between them. Not her father, not her husband, not a hundred Tessa Rossmans.

She lay down on herbed and tried to rest as she waited for her father. The sun shone brilliantly into the room but the inescapable feeling of desolation did not melt in its warmth. Instead, as the minutes lengthened into half an hour and the half an hour into an hour, it intensified and solidified and she was suddenly sure that this was the end. No more happiness. No more Ramon.

Cursing herself for a fool, she rose and mixed herself a Martini.

Her father had always done exactly as he pleased and so would she. Except, a small voice said as she stepped out into the heat of the terrace, except when to please himself would have been to destroy his parents. The memory of her grandparents floated vividly to the surface of her mind. To protect them, Chips had relinquished Zia. She downed her Martini and stared meditatively out at the jade and amethyst sea. No such sacrifice could possibly be called of her. It was 1934 now, not the 1890s. Lives could no longer be ruined because of a lack of marriage lines or illegitimacy or adultery.

She fought the temptation to pour another drink and sat down, closed her eyes against the glare of the sun and steeled herself to wait.

Chips' face was sheet-white. Zia had received him in her lilac, sun-filled boudoir, the large French windows thrown open, flowers and doves spilling into the room, making it difficult to see where the room finished and the garden began. She had not trusted her strength to sustain her in any other place but her bed. Her negligée was deep mauve, her peignoir a confection of matching lace. Her maid had taken special pains with her hair and her perfume filled the room, carrying him back across generations with effortless ease. He had kissed her; held her. The maids had left them alone. Then she had told him; very simply and very quietly. For one hideous moment he thought he was going to be sick. Guilt swept over him in crashing waves. He had ruined Zia's life. He was ruining his daughter's. No; it wasn't him. It was Duarte who had ruined their lives. Duarte, who, from beyond the grave, continued to exact revenge.

"There must be a way . . ."

"No." The long column of her throat was still lovely, her fine-boned features as beautiful as ever. "They love each other, Chips, and I know my son. I've seen the way he looks at her: the way his eyes light up when she enters the room. He will never give her up. Never."

"You want me to tell her, don't you?" It was a

rhetorical question which needed no answer. He moved away from the bed and towards the open French windows. In his vanity he had thought he had been the final victor, but it had been an illusion. No one had ever crowed in victory over Duarte Sanford. Duarte had simply been doing what he had always done: waiting, watching and biding his time. Now, years after his death, he had avenged himself through his son. The room was very still and quiet but Chips had to restrain himself forcibly from covering his ears against the hated laughter that had mocked him for so many years. He turned and Zia's eyes were anguished.

"Ramon never saw the side of Duarte that you and I did, Chips. If he knew what had happened he would demand justice."

"But if he loves Nancy . . ."

"Ramon is Portuguese," Zia said simply. "He is my child but there is none of my blood in him. He is wholly his father's son."

"Then I must pray that Nancy is wholly my daughter and that she will find the strength that I had to find so many years ago." His eyes were brilliant with tears. "God in heaven, Zia. How can one thing, one mistake, destroy so many lives?"

"The sin was mine," Zia said, and her flawless skin had taken on a transluscent quality. "If I had been able to live with it, no other lives would be ruined. No blood would ever have been shed."

"No!" The rage had gone from his voice. He sank to his knees beside the bed, taking her hand in his. "No sin was ever yours, Zia." He kissed her and with the bowed shoulders of an old man he left the room and went in search of his daughter.

All the words she had rehearsed vanished at the sight of

him. When he had entered Sanfords he had been jaunty and zestful, full of his usual pep and full-blooded love of life. Now he stood at her door, an old man. There were bags under his eyes, deep haggard lines running from nose to mouth. His springy white hair seemed to have thinned and lay flat and lifeless. His suit, hand-stitched by Boston's most exclusive tailor, looked as if it had been made for a bigger, broader man. It seemed to Nancy that, in the brief time that he had entered Sanfords, he had physically shrunk. His skin had taken on the greyish tinge of the severely ill. His eyes were dull and defeated.

She rushed across to him, forgetting her set little speech of how she had her own life to lead; of how she was a mature woman of thirty-five; of how the past was past and only the future mattered.

"My God, Daddy. Are you all right?"

He nodded and reached out for her blindly. For the first time in her life he clung to her and she was the support.

"What happened?" She could hardly form the words, she felt so fearful. "Is it Zia? Has she had a relapse?"

"No." He couldn't bear to release her. Afterwards, when the things that had to be said were said, she might never again come into his arms. Might never again even speak to him.

He drew in a deep, shuddering breath and Nancy pushed herself away from him, staring at him, appalled.

"Something's happened. You look as if you've seen a ghost. Should I get a doctor?"

He shook his head mutely.

"A brandy? There must be something I can do!"

"You can listen," he said wearily, and with his arm around her shoulder he began to walk heavily towards the sunlit terrace and the jazzily painted wicker chairs and the glass-topped table with its welcoming bottle of iced champagne.

"You can listen about ghosts and you can get rid of that bloody lemonade and get some honest to goodness American bourbon."

She had wanted a private, intimate reunion with him. In view of the news she had to break, she had given Maria the day off and dismissed her Sanford servants. Now she picked up the creamy-white telephone receiver and shakily asked for a bottle of bourbon. She was amazed to find that her hand was trembling. She returned to the terrace and they sat silently, only feet apart, until the obnoxious champagne had been replaced by a honey-gold bottle of Jim Beam.

Her father poured himself a glass that reached to the brim and drank heavily. Still neither of them spoke. She had geared herself for a confrontation with him. Now the tables had been turned. He was the one about to do the confronting.

He said at last. "Zia tells me Ramon is here."

"Yes."

She knew by the tone of his voice that Ramon's presence was not the cause of his almost physical disintegration. He drank more bourbon and refilled the glass.

"Zia tells me that he followed you here from New York; that he wants to marry you."

"Yes."

She was powerless to say anything further. The subject that she had so feared broaching to him was now serving only as a lead-in to something worse. Something she could not possibly imagine.

He opened his mouth to speak again and fell silent, staring down into his glass, swirling ice cubes endlessly.

Nancy clenched her hands in the effort to remain silent. She was terrified that if she spoke he would lose his nerve and that she would never know what had so disastrously changed him in the space of one glorious, sun-filled afternoon. Seeing him drain his glass, she was terrified that he would become too drunk to tell her anything. At last, when she thought she could stand the silence no longer, he said, not looking at her:

"You can't marry him, Nancy."

She nearly sobbed with relief. If that was all the Grand Guignol was about, she had been over-reacting as much as he had. She had known he would say that. The dark, nameless fear that had held her in its grip relaxed its hold.

She said gently, "I'm sorry you feel like that, Daddy. I love Ramon and I'm going to marry him." She didn't mention Jack. It was as if Jack had become as irrelevant to him as he had to her. He shook his head with a finality that was deathly.

"No, Nancy. You can't marry Ramon. Not now; not ever."

The fear was back; dark and tangible, sitting on her shoulders like a medieval demon.

"Why?" she asked, and could barely hear her own question.

"Duarte Sanford," he said, and his voice held none of the rhetoric and vigour that mesmerized his electorate. Instead it was flat, almost expressionless, as if all passion had been spent. "Duarte Sanford was evil."

Her hands fumbled for a glass and the bottle. Bourbon on top of Martini was not the best combination, but she did not care. Her father's whole demeanour was so alien that she knew she was going to need all the alcoholic help she could get to survive the next few moments.

"For years his blackmail made me politically impotent, and for years he made Zia's life a living hell."

The bourbon was comforting. So far so good. She knew all this already. Duarte Sanford had not been amongst the world's most charming men. He had been cold, sadistic and spiteful. Duarte Sanford was dead and she was not marrying him. She was marrying his son and

Ramon was not cold or sadistic. Ramon was . . .

". . . so I killed him."

The glass slipped from her hand to the floor and shattered.

"How long was I to wait? I had no more *time* to wait! Until he died I could do nothing." His face was ashen. "I saw Zia that summer. He had broken her as brutally as a child wrenching a rose from its roots. He had tortured her both mentally and physically. I swore I would kill him."

This time, as he raised his glass, the bourbon spilled on the front of his shirt. He still did not look at her. The world had stopped revolving and had finally steadied. Bizarrely, it was still the same; sun, sea, mountains, trees. Two people on a terrace: a bottle, glasses.

"How?" she asked through cracked lips. "When?"

"In 1928. I returned to Boston and I spoke to . . ." He hesitated. "I spoke to someone who made crime their business."

"The man who took the photographs?"

He nodded. "I don't have to tell you how, Nancy. Charlie came over here in the fall. When he returned to America Sanford was dead."

"Oh God," she said. "Oh Christ!" and rushed into the bathroom to vomit.

She sat on the edge of the bath shivering convulsively. Bourbon and Martini did not mix. Her father was a murderer. She should never drink on an empty stomach. Her father had killed Duarte Sanford.

He stood in the doorway, his hands hanging loosely at his side, his tie undone, his top two shirt buttons missing as if he had wrenched them off in an effort to breathe. He looked as ill as she felt.

"So you see," he said, "you can never marry Ramon Sanford. Zia and I have lived with the knowledge but you could not possibly live with it. Not as Ramon's wife. Not without telling him. And if you told him . . ."

"If I told him he would kill you," she said, and her voice was as flat and drained as his had been.

Of course Ramon would kill him. Zia had known that. No wonder she had collapsed. The prospect of her son marrying the daughter of his father's murderer was enough to make any woman run screaming for the madhouse. Especially if, as Chips had indicated but left unsaid, she had acquiesced in that murder. If Ramon should ever discover that . . . If he should discover that his mother had not only played a part in his father's death, but was actually still in love with the man who had caused it . . .

Nancy trembled for Zia Sanford. The trembling continued and would not stop. She wrapped her arms around herself, hugging herself for a warmth that did not come. Blood for blood. That would be Ramon's code. His mother had known that. How had she lived with the knowledge? How was she to live with it? She fought off waves of nausea; the trembling intensified.

"Nancy . . ."

She brushed his hand away savagely, galvanized into movement.

"Don't offer me *sympathy*! Dear God! What am I supposed to do? Say I'm sorry you're a murderer, but I still love you? Say, never mind, I'll forget it just as conveniently as you and Zia did? Say, Ramon was only a fleeting flirtation and of course I don't mind not marrying him? Well I bloody well won't! I *do* mind. I mind so much I'm dying by inches!" She began to laugh hysterically. "Quite literally dying by bloody inches, in a way you and your precious Zia can never imagine. So she was unhappy, was she? And you wanted to be mayor? And Duarte Sanford enjoyed little games of cat and mouse that were inconvenient to both of you? What a shame. What a damn awful, mother-fucking *shame*!"

He groped for the bed, her language devastating him in a way nothing else had ever done.

"But of course there's no problem, is there? You simply tell me and I behave like a good little girl and say that of course I wouldn't dream of telling Ramon the truth about his darling mother and her helpful lover and everything goes on as before. Only one tiny sacrifice is involved. I have to break off my relationship with Ramon without even being able to tell him why! God in heaven, what do I say? That I've changed my mind? Sorry, I don't love you any more? It was all a mistake?"

He stumbled to his feet and she saw him through a haze of rage and tears and lashed out wildly at him, knocking him back on the bed.

"You and your precious Zia! If she'd loved you as I love Ramon then no man on earth could have taken her from you! Do you think if I'd been wearing Ramon's ring, I would have allowed myself to be seduced by charm and flattery and money? No woman gives herself unless she wants to and it's about time you faced up to the fact that back in those far off days in Boston, Zia bloody well wanted to!"

"No . . ." He was clinging to the gold orb that crowned the bedpost.

She was merciless, crazed with grief, knowing that her world had come to an end and hating the people who had wrecked it with their selfishness and vengeance.

"You were no better! When she did come to you, what did you do? You allowed Duarte to blackmail you into relinquishing her. Have you ever truly asked yourself why? Was it only for Patrick and Maura's sake? From what I know of my grandfather he never gave a rap for what anyone thought of him. His back was broad enough to take any amount of scandal and I don't believe he ever gave a damn if he was socially accepted or not."

"Your grandmother . . ."

"She had Patrick to lean on! Dear God, I wish I had a Patrick to lean on! I did have! After all these lonely, barren, crucifyingly empty years I did finally have someone. His shoulders were just as broad as Patrick's. He could have stood with me against a world of gossip and scandal and you've taken him away from me! You've destroyed the only thing of worth I've ever had."

"That's not true . . ."

"You didn't defy Duarte Sanford because *you* couldn't stand the shame of being publicly branded a bastard! It was *you* who came first. *You*, you were thinking of. You've always been selfish and the monstrosity of it is, that you've never seen it. You've lied to yourself as you've lied to so many others. Why did you marry my mother? You didn't love her. You didn't even pretend to love her. You married her because she gave you an entry into a world you craved for and that you now verbally despise because it is politically expedient to do so. A world not only of wealth but of breeding. A world where money came from land that was tenanted when America was still the happy hunting ground of buffalo and undisturbed Indians! A world of titles and royalty. You lapped it up, didn't you? Cowes and being invited aboard the king's yacht. Parties attended by the Kaiser and the Tsar. Chips-bloody-O'Shaughnessy. A second generation Irish Catholic who would have been refused entry into the Yankee clubs back home in Boston. So you never applied, did you? I understand a refusal often offends! God, what my mother must have gone through. I never loved her properly because of you. I was always so besotted by you. You overpowered her so that she seemed insignificant, yet without her you would have been nothing; just another socially unacceptable Irish Catholic who happened to have money." She was panting. She had never known she could feel such destructiveness.

"How *dare* you try to play God? Sending an employee to commit a murder as another man would send an employee to fetch a ledger. You weren't even man enough to kill him yourself. You had to get someone else to do it for you." She began to sob. Great, tearing sobs. "Ramon won't send a third party when he knows what you did. He'll kill you himself with his bare hands." Her face streamed with tears. "Only he'll never know, will he? Because you know damned well that I'll never tell him! Oh God. I hate you for what you've done to me. I hate you. Hate you . . ."

He staggered to his feet, swaying. She made no move towards him. Slowly he groped his way towards the door. It clicked behind him. She was alone. The sun continued to stream into the room in a blasphemy of light. She had always been alone. All through her marriage to Jack she had been alone. As far as the future stretched, no matter how many people surrounded her, she would be alone. Ramon had been an interlude—a peep into a world that was half dream, half miracle. That world had now come to an end. She closed the blinds and shut out the sun. Only one thing remained to be done. To tell Ramon that the dream was over.

Chapter Nineteen

She lost all sense of time. Maria returned, took one look at the still, motionless figure on the darkening terrace and went about her duties silently. She had been with Nancy in Boston when the mayor had collapsed and Nancy had locked herself in her room for days afterwards. She had heard rumours of the row at City Hall, of how Nancy had caused the mayor's collapse. It was inconceivable to her. Nancy had never done an unkind thing in her life and she adored her father. Yet now, within hours of the mayor's arrival, Nancy's radiant happiness had fled. Her face was marbled white; her eyes unseeing. She looked like a woman doomed and Maria dared not intrude on her unnamed grief.

There was to be a small and select cocktail party to welcome the Maharajah of Sakpur. The maharajah was far more regal than his fellow potentates. There was no outrageous and bewitching female matador on *his* arm. The maharani was petite, her beautiful kohled eyes lowered demurely as if she were a concubine and not a wife. The maharajah's retinue had been so numerous that several maids and valets of existing residents had found themselves in the midst of an enforced upheaval. Rooms had been changed and complaints had been vociferous. Senora Henriques had dealt with it all calmly and efficiently, but had resorted to asking for help from Mrs. Cameron. Mrs. Cameron, Villiers had told her, was with her father and not to be disturbed. Senora Henriques had suppressed her surprise.

In the last few days Nancy had proved that she was far more than titular hostess of Sanfords. She had spent hours studying the mechanics of the running of the hotel: had organized what she termed a "time-saving" plan, by insisting that for two days all tasks performed by every member of the staff, from Villiers and the head butler and maitre d'hôtel, down to the chamber maids and bellboys, be meticulously timed. She intended to use the result to institute an even more streamlined service than the one in existence. She had never before been too busy or occupied to attend to anything, however trivial, if it concerned the running of the hotel.

Lady Maxwell Meade's maid had been tearfully removed to a smaller room. Her next-door-neighbour, Bobo's laconic American maid of all work, had merely shrugged her shoulders and moved without complaint. One room was as good as another. In the end, by juggling with the quarters of the Michaeljohns' valet, maid and chauffeur, Senora Henriques had managed to vacate a block of rooms for the maharajah's turbaned and exotic household. Only Prince Vasileyev's excitable retinue of Russians had proved intractable. Faced with emotions on such a grand scale, Senora Henriques had baulked. The Indians and Russians would have to co-habit on the same floor. They eyed each other with hatred and suspicion and Senora Henriques retreated, hoping fervently that the maharajah's visit would be a short one.

Maria had glimpsed him on his stately entrance, and been suitably impressed. His coat had been of scarlet, his many buttons an alternation of rubies and diamonds. His gigantic walnut-brown head had been swathed with saffron silk intertwined with Tyrian purple.

Maria paused at Nancy's vast wardrobe of evening and cocktail dresses. Nancy liked to select her own clothes but time was running short. She glanced at her again, but could not bring herself to break Nancy's awesome withdrawal into some private world,by asking such a mundane question as to which dress she preferred to wear. The maharani's sari had been eye-searing cerise edged with gold. Prince Felix would be present and that meant that Lady Bessbrook would also be in attendance. Lady Bessbrook favoured sizzling reds and orange chiffon for after dark. The Montcalms would also be there to welcome the maharajah. Maria tried to remember what Georgina Montcalm favoured in the way of evening dress. Usually she dressed with elegant understatement, cream or ivory silk or soft-hued muted pastels. Maria made her mind up and withdrew a starkly plain black organdie dress by Patou from the sea of colours. The black would not only be a perfect foil for Nancy's pansy dark eyes and flawless skin, but would set her stunningly apart from the riot of colour around her.

The telephone rang and Maria answered it. Its shrill ringing had not stirred Nancy into movement. It was the mayor wishing to speak to his daughter: at least he said it was the mayor. To Maria, the trembling voice bore no likeness to Mayor O'Shaughnessy's boisterous tone.

"The mayor, madame," she said timidly.

Very slowly Nancy turned her head in Maria's direction. The rest of her body remained statue-like, her beautiful long-fingered hands hanging over the narrow arms of her wicker chair, as if broken at the wrists. The thick-fringed eyes were limpid pools devoid of expression. For the first time in her life Maria felt frightened.

"He wishes to speak to you, madame."

Nancy still did not speak. She simply turned her head away and continued to stare sightlessly over the now sunless sea.

Maria returned to the telephone, picking up the diamanté-encrusted receiver and saying with an authority she did not feel: "Mrs. Cameron is not available at the moment, Mayor O'Shaughnessy."

The line clicked and went dead. Maria let out a sigh of relief. She had expected a battle with the forceful mayor. A shouting insistence that his daughter be put on the line. He was acting out of character—as was Nancy. She returned to the terrace and said hesitantly, "There is only another thirty minutes until cocktails in the Orchid Room, madame."

A slight motion of Nancy's head indicated that she had heard. Maria returned to the bedroom, checked that Nancy's cosmetics and perfume were all within hand's reach, and topped up the cooling perfumed bath water. There was nothing more she could do.

For a long time the black pit into which Nancy had fallen had suppressed all positive thought. She could not allow herself to think. To do so would be to endure a pain so unspeakable that her conscious mind shrank from the task. The hours passed and step by infinitesimal step she allowed thought to replace numbing oblivion. It needed every particle of her courage to allow herself to face up to reality.

Theoretically she had a choice. She could continue loving and living with Ramon and keeping her father's terrible secret just as Zia had done: or she could tell him and stand by whilst he destroyed her father either by civil justice or personal vengeance. She had no way of knowing if she chose the latter whether he would still want her, or whether the sight of her would be such a painful reminder of her father's crime, that he would repudiate her utterly.

Practically, she had no choice at all. She was incapable of living with such a monstrous revelation. Bleakly she wondered why they had found it necessary to tell her. Why they couldn't have continued with their own private hell and spared her. As twilight deepened to dusk, she assumed that it was because of the word "marriage." Presumably the prospect of having grandchildren with one grandparent responsible for the death of another, was too much for even Zia's iron nerve. Zia had insisted that she be told and had known that by doing so the marriage would be prevented. Just as she knew her son, Zia knew her lover's daughter. She had known that she would never expose him and see him suffer for his crime.

There was no choice at all. She had to do what Zia and Chips had known she must do. She had to tell Ramon that their *affaire* was at an end. All because one far-off day Duarte Sanford, a man totally European and with a life-long hatred of America, had been instructed by his father to enlarge his business knowledge by experiencing the New World at first hand. She could imagine how reluctantly he had made contact with the *nouveau riche* O'Shaughnessys. How distasteful it must have been to his aristocratic sense of breeding and refinement to meet with a man whom his father had set on the first step to riches. A man who had been born a peasant. How the de Gama in him must have rebelled at such an encounter. She wondered how Patrick had received the arrogant and condescending son of his life-long friend. Probably with concealed amusement. Duarte Sanford's opinion of him would not have caused Patrick to lose a second's sleep. But Duarte Sanford's open contempt would have struck at the very core of her father's being. He was the king in his own particular kingdom of the North End. His father's wealth, as well as his own ambition and overpowering personality, had seen to that. Educated at the Boston Latin School and Harvard, he had mixed with sons of millionaires—but with one difference. He could still remember back to a time when he had run the cobbled streets with bare feet and patched trousers. Over the years, inches by inches, he had fought for what his classmates had taken for granted: social acceptability. Even when he was mayor and a millionaire several times over, he had been refused entry into one of the prestigious Yankee clubs. She could remember his rage: his demonic frustration, his yelling of:

"I'm an American, aren't I? Goddamn it! I'm *mayor* of this city! How dare they refuse me permission to sit among their musty leather chairs and drink their second-rate bourbon on the grounds that I'm Irish and a Catholic? I'll show them what an *American* with Irish ancestry can do! How can a man be refused entry to some piss-hole Yankee club simply because his religion is different and his background isn't that of the Pilgrim Fathers? What does a man have to do in the land of the free to be equal?"

It was after that humiliation that he had gone to Europe. With his English, blue-blooded wife as an entry card, he had assaulted European high society like a man climbing the Eiger. Nancy afterwards wondered if the insular society of Edwardian England had ever been the same again. Eccentric, they said of him. It was the only description the reticent English could summon to describe Chips' rash vulgarity, overwhelming bonhomie, and irresistible charm. But that had been long years after Duarte Sanford's arrival in Boston. Then, full of swagger and bounce, he had been faced for the first time with condescension and contempt. Duarte Sanford would have left him in no doubt as to where a second-generation Irish immigrant rated in the eyes of a Portuguese nobleman, with an ancestry going back to the Middle Ages.

The antipathy between the two of them must have been immediate. Zia the catalyst. Even Duarte, accustomed to the sophisticates of Paris and Lisbon, must have been dazzled by Zia's exotic, effortless beauty. He must have seen immediately that in Boston and in the world Chips inhabited, Zia was as rare as an orchid on a winter's day. That Zia, for Chips, was irreplaceable. She could imagine Duarte Sanford, olive-skinned and dark-eyed, his black hair slicked and shining, his moustache magnificent, his dress impeccable. Dove-grey velvet suits and silk-lined top hats, ebony canes and jewels on his fingers and in the folds of his neckties. He must have descended on nineteenth century Boston like European royalty. His carriage drawn by a team of perfectly-matched greys, his manner as alien to the local populace as theirs was to him. Foreigner or not, no Yankee club would have closed its doors to Duarte Sanford. Rather, they would have welcomed him with open arms. He was the epitome of what they most admired. He had breeding, refinement—the embodiment of a sense of history.

How Chips must have hated him—seeing in him all the things he secretly longed to be. How Duarte must have longed to put the bumptious upstart who lorded it over a miserable square mile of overcrowded houses, pubs and waterfronts, into his place. Zia's fate had been practically pre-ordained.

Nancy's anger had left her. Whatever Zia had done she had paid for and the price had been high. Never, perhaps, higher than it was at the present moment.

Maria told her that her father was on the telephone. She had no desire to speak to him; not until after her break with Ramon. Then there would be all the time in the world for him to beg her forgiveness, to offer useless anodynes for her grief. From where she sat she could see the juniper trees that lined the rocky road to Camara de Lobos. Headlights flashed brilliantly between the trees as a corner was taken at suicidal speed. No chauffeur ever drove like that. No chauffeur ever drove to Camara de Lobos. Madeira's guests were content to traverse only the mile-long stretch of road from the harbour to the hotel. Ramon had returned. She made her decision.

Maria was shaken out of her inertia by Nancy running into the bedroom, sandals flying in the direction of the bed, her dress following, a trail of French lingerie scattering the floor to the gold-cherubed bathroom. Even before Maria could reach for a giant-size, inches-deep towel, Nancy had soaked herself, rinsed and was stepping out of the bath. With respect for the black organdie dress, talcum powder was dispensed with and Maria lavishly sprayed eau de cologne in its place.

Meanwhile, Nancy was already applying her hand-made Paris cosmetics. The merest hint of rouge to highlight her exquisite cheekbones, a gloss of scarlet on her lips, a barely discernible touch of colour on her eyelids, and a generous application of mascara to accentuate the incredible sweep of her lashes. She pushed away the jewels that Maria had laid out on the dressing table to complete the dramatic starkness of Patou's evening creation. Instead, Nancy looped her mother's heavy rope of pearls and slipped them over her head. As she slid her sheer silk-stockinged feet into peep-toed sling-back evening pumps, Maria complemented the eau de cologne by spraying her with matching perfume. Nancy took one brief look in the full-length triple mirror, and before Maria could reach the door and open it for her, she flung it open herself and fell headlong into Ramon's arms.

"Where's the fire?" he asked with lazy amusement, as

she attempted to control her breathing.

"I'm late." She felt as if she had just run an Olympic mile.

"It's your privilege," he said easily. His dark eyes appraised her. "You look incredible. Shall we desert our guests and lock ourselves in with a bottle of champagne?"

"Later," she was managing a smile. His hold on her wrist felt like a burning brand.

"I take it this afternoon was not as bad as you anticipated?"

"No." The words were strangled in her throat.

He didn't notice. The near-black eyes, so piercing that nothing missed their gaze, were untroubled. He slipped his arm around her waist and kissed her behind her ear.

"I'll give myself only another ten seconds of self-control. If we are not in the Orchid Room by then I shall make love to you where we stand."

She felt faint. His touch seared her because she knew it was the last time they would ever walk together, his arm around her waist, two people with an evening of good food and wine and conversation ahead of them. With the prospect of dancing in a fairytale, chandelier-lit ballroom and later on a deserted, moonlit, fragrant-scented terrace. With whispered words of love heightening the anticipation of the moment when they would at last be alone: when the music would fade and the laughter recede and they would make love with a fusion of body and spirit that transcended anything either had ever experienced of earthly happiness.

Incredibly, she managed to smile and even whisper an impish: "You're a second too late", as the great gold-embossed doors were flung wide and they made their entrance. She had made her decision and it was to ensure that the evening and night ahead would contain enough happiness and joy to last her for the rest of her life. Her senses were heightened to a pitch that bordered on intoxication.

They parted and circulated, her eyes constantly leaving those of her guests to watch him, to imprint his every gesture indeliby on her mind. He moved with the lean grace of the jungle cat he was nicknamed after. She saw the expression in the women's eyes as he greeted them, and knew the emotions he was arousing as he smiled his devastating smile. Then, like her, his glance would leave his guests. Their eyes would meet and his expression was bold and black and blatantly erotic. She felt shameless, her thighs damp with longing. She didn't see the hand-stitched, faultless cut of his white dinner jacket, or the exquisite lace of his evening shirt. She saw only his naked body: a body she knew as intimately as she did her own, the ripple of his muscles in moonlight, lamplight and sunlight. The curling pelt of the hair on his chest, wet and tasting of salt when he emerged from the sea, damp and delicious beneath her fingertips in the aftermath of lovemaking. His skin, honey gold, darkening through tones of olive as it merged into the magnificent mass of his pubic hair.

They were separated by laughing groups, each the centre of a chattering, star-studded coterie that would have warmed the heart of any gossip columnist.

"He's as handsome as a blooded stallion and twice as dangerous," Bobo was saying to an Englishwoman with a spray of red roses on her shoulder and five or six diamond bracelets encircling her arm. Their eyes were on Ramon.

Nancy's soft lips curved and her smile was that of a woman who had conquered the unconquerable. What Bobo said was true, and he was hers and would have been for ever. No one would be able to take that knowledge away from her.

"They say that Princess Marinsky is distraught and

has taken to her room . . ."

Nancy had moved out of earshot and so was unaware of the princess' decline.

"That's the trouble, darling. He's never had to ask for anything in his life. Ramon simply takes." The Englishwoman licked her bottom lip slowly. Bobo recognized the expression in her eyes and wished her luck. She would need it if she hoped to seduce Ramon. To Bobo's knowledge no woman ever had. Ramon was the seducer. A natural predator who put every husband immediately on his guard—and with good reason.

Bobo blew an answering kiss across the room to Hassan who was hemmed in by the sultan and the maharajah.

Nancy Leigh Cameron was achieving a world record. Bobo wondered if she was aware of it, and also how much longer it would last. Ramon showed none of the usual signs of boredom which afflicted him after the first few weeks of an *affaire.* It was all very intriguing. Not least the arrival and quick departure of Senator Jack Cameron. Bobo could not see Jack Cameron playing the part of a compliant husband. American herself, she knew how important the public image of happy family life was to a man in Jack's position. She had expected a quick curtailment of the *affaire* and Nancy's return to Washington. When the liner docked in New York, reporters and photographers would flock and Jack would explain blandly how his wife had taken a winter vacation and of how, missing her intolerably, he had been driven to cross the Atlantic and to bring her back with him. The public would love it. Jack would kiss Nancy for the photographers' benefit and millions of romance-starved women would drool over the story as they drank their morning coffee.

But Nancy had not returned with Jack and, even while her husband had been in residence, she and Ramon had done nothing to hide their feelings for each other. It had left one conclusion to be drawn. It was one so breathtaking that even the worldly Bobo had gasped at the implications.

At dinner they were joined by Nina Correlli, who had struck up a rather odd friendship with Margot Alleynian's angular twenty-one-year-old son, and Lady Helen Bingham-Smythe who was escorted by Reggie Minter. Nicky was there and his eyes travelled meaningfully to her mouth. She sent him a pleading look of admonition as Ramon also saw and uttered a word in Portuguese that none of his guests fortunately understood.

Later, in the ballroom, he danced with her and her alone, performing rumbas and tangos with an innate sense of rhythm that his guests could not hope to emulate.

Nancy laughed and followed him step for step, her body moving to the music with a freedom Lady Meade found indecent.

"If I'm all Portuguese, you're all Irish," Ramon said, his hand hot on her waist. "Where have all your Bostonian restraints gone?"

"Into the Charles river," she answered gaily.

Georgina Montcalm decided it was too late to ask Zia to counsel Nancy and urge her to be more discreet. Too many people now knew of the *affaire* between her and Ramon. No one seeing them together could imagine they were anything but lovers. Every glance, every touch was an open declaration. They seemed oblivious of the gossip they were causing. It was almost as if they were flaunting their *affaire*. In weeks, days even, London and Paris and Rome would begin to buzz with rumours. Then they would never be able to leave Madeira without having to face a barrage of reporters and flash bulbs. Even if they remained, the world's press would print their own version of the affair, each more scandalous than the last.

Nancy Leigh Cameron, scion of America's new aristocracy, darling of the Democrats, favourite subject of society columns from California to Massachusetts, would find herself a social outcast. Adulterous relationships might be the norm among the section of society that had the time, leisure and disposition to indulge in them, but they were not relationships that were publicly acknowledged. A divorce could still hold a newspaper's front page for three days at a time. Georgina, like Bobo, began to wonder if she had underestimated the relationship. It was the only explanation for behaviour that bordered on social suicide.

Count and Countess Szapary danced past them in a foxtrot that the count executed with military precision and blatant lack of enjoyment. The little countess' face was flushed. Nancy turned her head, following the direction of the sparkling eyes. She was not surprised to find that the countess was looking rapturously in Vere's direction.

He smiled when he saw Nancy's eyes on him and moved his shoulders in a gesture which said: "I can't talk to you when I never see you."

Madeleine Mancini's entry temporarily silenced the room full of sophisticates. Her dress was split thigh-high and made of leopard skin. Her finger and toe nails were enamelled a deep black. Her lipstick was black; her eyes so heavily lashed that she resembled a panda. A very sexy, very man-eating panda, not the cuddly sort imitated by the toy manufacturers. Costas escorted her and threw his arms exuberantly around the maharajah in greeting. Nancy wondered if there was anyone that the big jovial Greek did not know.

They were dancing to a tango. Expertly Ramon swung her low, his body bending over hers as he said softly, "Do you know what I am going to do with you tonight, my love?"

Before she could gasp a reply she was upright again, his cheek pressed against hers, their hands joined as he proceeded to tell her in the minutest detail.

Her face flamed and he laughed. "Not all of your Bostonian upbringing is in the Charles river. Tonight we will make sure that what remains is drowned for ever."

Desire licked through her, lighting her with a radiance that was incandescent. For years afterwards Kate Murphy said she had never seen any woman as beautiful as Nancy Leigh Cameron was that night.

She was not alone in her opinion. Not a man in the room remained unstirred by the magical luminosity she exuded. Even Charles Montcalm lost track of his conversation with Lord Michaeljohn and stared wonderingly after her for so long that Georgina had to tap him on the arm three times to bring him out of his reverie.

The music slowed to a waltz. Countess Szapary's head barely reached Vere's shoulder. Nicky's eyes still sought Nancy's but, nevertheless, his hand slid indecently low over Fleur Molière's delicious bottom.

Nancy closed her eyes as Ramon gently but firmly waltzed her out of the glittering, flower-decked ballroom and into the coolness of the night air. When she opened them she could see the moon high over the dark silhouette of the mountains.

"I love you," he said, and she hugged the very timbre of his voice to her heart.

They did not re-enter the ballroom. They danced until the terrace gave way to grass and then, hands clasped, they ran like children to the wide-open French windows to the Bridge Room. The hem of her dress was damp, her black satin pumps grass-stained. She was uncaring. He swung her up in his arms and strode with her through the empty lounges and down the softly lit corridor to the Garden Suite. They did not see Maria or hear her silent departure. They had re-entered their private world and there were no intruders.

She did not sleep. As dawn broke and Ramon lay exhausted at her side, his breathing deep and regular, his hand still cupping her breast, she lay awake treasuring every fleeting moment. Her fingertips traced his hairline and the smooth curve of his jaw. Once, in his sleep, he murmured her name. She smiled and her arm tightened around him.

Inexorably the light in the room paled and the first shafts of sun filtered through the shutters. She lay perfectly still, willing him to sleep on, fearful that any movement might waken him. He looked curiously vulnerable. His face had lost its hardness and there was no trace of the deep furrows that formed between his brows when he frowned, or the grim, almost brutal lines that transformed his mouth when his volatile temper was roused.

His hand tightened its hold on her breast and as his eyes flickered open he automatically moved to roll across her.

"No . . ." She slipped from his grasp. If he made love to her now she was lost.

He was immediately wide awake. "What's the matter?"

She was standing by the bed, barefoot, tying a serviceable white towelling dressing gown tightly around her waist. She was unaware of it, but it emphasized her femininity in a way that not even the finest of her French negligées did.

"I have to talk to you."

"Then come back to bed."

"No. What I have to say can't be said in bed."

His eyes narrowed and he sat up, reaching to the

bedside table for cigarettes and matches. When he had inhaled he said simply:

"Well, I'm listening."

Her mouth was so dry she thought she would never be able to utter a word. Her fists were clenched tightly in the depths of her dressing gown pockets. Her eyes located a point on the wall some six inches above his head, and she stared at it fixedly, saying with a rush, "I'm leaving Madeira with my father."

"The hell you are!" He leapt from the bed and as she cried out and backed away he gripped hold of her shoulders.

"Just what happened yesterday afternoon?"

"Nothing. It's just that I realize now that . . . That we can't possibly continue like this. Jack needs me . . ."

"Jack Cameron would kill you if it was advantageous for him to do so!"

"No. I . . ."

He shook her like a rag doll. "Look at me," he blazed, as her eyes fought desperately to avoid his. "Look at me, for Christ's sake! Are you going back with your father to join Cameron? Are you? *Are you*?"

"No . . . No . . ."

She could feel hysterical sobs rising in her throat and fought them down. She had to remain calm. She had to remain lucid.

"What did O'Shaughnessy say to you? What did he blackmail you with?" He had stopped shaking her and his left hand had wound itself through her hair, pulling her head back cruelly so that she was forced to face him.

"Nothing. Please, Ramon. You're hurting me!"

The hand relinquished its grip by the merest fraction. "Tell me what he said to make you agree to leave. Tell me, Nancy, or I swear to God he'll be lucky to die from a heart attack!"

"Nothing," she repeated helplessly. "He didn't say

anything. He's ill and he's old and he needs a rest. He says my private life is my own. He's reconciled to the fact that I'm not returning to Jack. Truly. Ramon, please! Believe me!"

"*Then why?*" he repeated through clenched teeth. "*Why are you leaving?*"

"Because . . . Because I'm tired. It's been fun, Ramon, but I'm a city girl at heart. I'm homesick for Boston."

Her hair felt as if it was being torn from its roots. His face was only inches from hers, a mask of fury.

"Of course! I should have guessed! That's why you used to bury yourself at Hyannis for nine months out of twelve. You just had to be near those bright lights, didn't you? The non-stop night life that rocks miles and miles of sand dunes and gives the gulls no peace! Whatever lies you tell me, Nancy, make them credible ones!"

"Oh God! Stop! *Please!*" He was forcing her down on her knees in front of him.

"So it was fun, was it? And now you're tired and want to go home. Is that the truth? *Tell me. Tell me!*"

Her eyes glazed with a fury that equalled his own. "Yes! If you want to know, that's exactly the truth. I'm tired of being trapped here. I'm tired of having no other lovers. I'm tired of you!"

He let go of her as suddenly as if she had been poisonous.

"I don't believe you, Nancy. It's something *he* said." His rage was being replaced by something far worse. There was inexpressible agony in his eyes, pleading.

She moved away from him. Her voice was perfectly controlled. "I'm sorry Ramon. You're wrong. My father has nothing to do with my decision. It's merely convenient that he will be returning home soon and that I can join him. I would have left anyhow."

"You love me!" He spat the words.

She laughed, a harsh brittle laugh. "Well of course I

said I loved you. We were sleeping together, weren't we? I believe it's quite acceptable vocabulary under those circumstances."

"You bitch," he said viciously. "You incredible, unbelievable, smooth-talking little *bitch*!" His skin seemed to have tightened over his cheekbones. She flinched and backed away from him. His eyes were filled with loathing.

"Don't worry, I shan't hurt you. I shan't lay a finger on you. Not ever again."

He was dressing, pulling on his trousers, leaving his evening shirt open, not bothering to fasten the buttons. It was as if he couldn't leave the room quickly enough. He slung his jacket over his shoulder and said tightly, "Thank you for an interesting few weeks. I'll have Villiers repay you financially for your services. You deserve it. A more accomplished little whore I've yet to meet!"

The door slammed behind him.

"Oh God," she sobbed and sank down on her knees beside the bed. "Oh dear, dear *God*!"

Chapter Twenty

Three hours later she crawled to her feet and became aware, for the first time, of Maria's presence. Shakily she drank the endless cups of black coffee that Maria poured and then numbly she dressed.

"Tell my father I wish to see him."

"Yes, madame."

Her face was anxious as she returned to Nancy and said: "The mayor is with Mrs. Sanford, madame."

Nancy's eyes were lacklustre, her skin pallid. She said on a note of surprise, "I'm going to be sick," and rushed to the bathroom.

It was reaction, she told herself afterwards, as Maria brought her a slice of dry toast and a glass of Perrier water. If her father was with Zia it was all for the best. She could see both of them at the same time. The queasiness lingered. She felt distinctly unwell.

"Don't you think you should go back to bed, madame?" Maria asked. "I will change it now. Immediately."

The silk sheets were still rumpled from the previous night's lovemaking. Nancy averted her head. "No thank you, Maria. I'm going to see my father. Will you begin to pack my bags, please."

She had no idea what ship her father was returning on, or when. The *Ile de France* was still in harbour but en route for South Africa. She didn't care. He would be leaving soon. It was election year, and an extended absence would be ruinous for him.

She wore a simple tailored grey skirt and white silk blouse. To hide her eyes, still puffed and red from weeping, she put on a pair of large, dark sun spectacles.

They were beneath the jacaranda tree. She could see them break off their conversation in mid-sentence at the sight of her; could see the lookof fear that flitted across Zia's fine-boned features; the tortured anxiety on her father's face. She was unsympathetic. They could teach her nothing about suffering.

"My dear . . ." Zia's hand faltered as it stretched towards her.

"Nancy . . ." Her father's voice was unsteady.

She said unemotionally, "Champagne and orange juice and petits fours for the doves. Nothing changes at Sanfords; does it, Zia?"

"My dear. I'm so sorry. Truly I am."

Nancy shrugged her slender shoulders. She had come nearer to loving Zia Sanford than she had her own mother and she had been destroyed by her. She would not allow her to see how deep her hurt had been. How deep her hurt was. That, at least, could remain private.

She said to her father, "When do we leave?"

"I . . . It's not that easy, Nancy."

He looked an old man. She felt pity and crushed it. She could not afford to pity him yet. She could afford no emotion whatsoever if she was to survive the next hours and days.

"What do you mean?" Her voice was curt, rigidly under control.

They gazed at each other helplessly and then Chips said with difficulty: "I meant to tell you yesterday, Nancy. Only it wasn't possible. Not with . . . Not with the other things that had to be said."

She could feel her heart beat wildly and irregularly. "Then tell me now."

Dear God, what other hideous secrets of the past were to be sprung on her? Rape? Incest?

"Verity and Dieter are on their way here."

She felt the breath escape from her body and afterwards wondered how she'd remained standing.

"A family party," she said at last. "How nice. How very thoughtful of you to invite my daughter to witness my humiliation and misery. Is it to serve as a lesson to her for the future? Do not commit adultery or you may end up like your mother?"

"Nancy, Nancy." His eyes were blinded by tears as he groped to hold her.

She stepped backwards. "Not yet, Daddy. There's a long way to go before I fall back into the old pattern of seeking to please you at any cost."

"I never knew you had."

"That makes it all the more terrible."

They faced each other like two protagonists.

Zia said faintly, "The Mezriczkys made their booking before your father arrived."

Pastel-petalled franciscea bloomed thickly at their feet. A lizard darted quickly into the undergrowth.

"How long?" she asked bleakly. "How long till they arrive?"

"One week, perhaps two. They were not definite in their dates."

Her iron control began to crack at the seams. "Two weeks! After all that has happened you expect me to stay on here for another two weeks? Seeing him every day! Seeing the contempt in his eyes! The loathing! Have you any idea what I had to say to him to convince him that our *affaire* was at an end? Have either of you any idea of anything but the need to protect yourselves?"

"Nancy, darling . . ."

Nancy's eyes flashed as she rounded on Zia. "*You* couldn't have lived seeing yourself diminished in his eyes, could you? Why do you think that it's any different for me? If you had to have a sacrificial lamb, don't make a feast out of it. I've broken off our relationship. I've told him I won't marry him. No one will ever know you were both responsible for Duarte's death."

"Zia had no part in it," her father began agitatedly.

"She knew," Nancy said starkly. "Isn't that being an accessory? I'm afraid Portuguese law isn't my strongest point."

"We know the sacrifice you have made for us," Zia said, and her words were a mere whisper. "We're truly grateful, Nancy. Ramon worshipped his father. If he ever knew. Even suspected . . ."

She looked ghastly. Nancy fought down the impulse to comfort her. She said instead, her voice flat and empty, "Ramon will never know."

Zia began to cry. Her father put his arms around her. Nancy turned away. They were old and they were frightened and she was not making things easy for them. After a little while she said, "You must see that I can't possibly stay here. Not even for Verity."

"You must." Chips' desperation was naked. "You wrote to her, telling her that you were leaving her father after eighteen years of marriage. She must be nearly out of her mind. You can't allow her to travel all this way and find you gone."

She was trapped. "Ramon," she said helplessly. "I can't live still seeing him."

"Ramon will leave," Zia said, with a shadow of her old confidence. "He only stayed here for you. Because you were happy here."

"We were both happy here," Nancy corrected and, unable to bear looking at them any longer, turned on her heel and walked quickly over the sweet-smelling grass to the open doors of the hotel.

"Unpack everything," she said wearily to Maria. "We shan't be leaving for another two weeks. My daughter and her husband are on their way here."

"Yes, madame."

Maria had always enjoyed being employed by Mrs. Cameron. Now she was beginning to think that the relative orderliness of her own house would be a welcome blessing.

"Senora Henriques has asked to see you, madame."

It was the night of the grand fancy dress ball. There were final arrangements to make. Hildegarde had announced her intention of dressing as the late Tsarina and the grand duchess had sworn blood and a public assassination if she did so.

"Thank you, Maria." She had forgotten all about her regular, mid-morning rendezvous with Senora Henriques. The housekeeper's irritation at being kept waiting vanished when she saw Nancy's pallor and the way the sun glasses remained in place, even though they were in the shadows of her study.

"I'll speak to Hildegarde myself," she said as they sat at the giant-size desk. "Salli has an oriental costume that Hildegarde will not be able to resist. Unfortunately, it's more apt for a belly dancer than our theme of historic royalty, but anything is better than the grand duchess' wrath. Is that the list of music?" She scanned it quickly and nodded. "Good. José has done as I suggested and included plenty of Viennese waltzes. Is the gypsy band here?"

"Yes, madame. They arrived last night from Lisbon."

"Lovely. Genuine gypsy music will please our large Russian contingent. Has chef done as I asked and provided a light dinner for this evening?"

"Yes, madame. There is also the supper menu, and he has done as you asked, and arranged that hot soup, cutlets, quail and cold dishes are available all through the evening. He likes the English idea of serving devilled kidneys, eggs and bacon, and other savouries in the supper room from two o'clock onwards. Yourself and Mr. Sanford will receive . . ."

The slim gold pen fell from Nancy's hand and rolled across the polished surface of the desk.

"I think perhaps the head of the stairs instead of the door of the ballroom."

"I'm sorry, Carlota." Without being aware of it, Nancy had used the housekeeper's Christian name. "I shall not be receiving this evening with Mr. Sanford. Or in the future."

"But Mrs. Sanford is far too weak. The doctor has seen her this morning and her condition seems to be deteriorating, not improving."

"Mr. Sanford will receive the guests on his own."

Senora Henriques was aghast. "That is simply not possible. There *must* be a hostess."

"Of course there must," Ramon said from the doorway and his voice had a silky, almost bored note. "As Mrs. Cameron has performed her duties as hostess with such accomplishment in the past, I see no reason why she should not continue for the duration of her visit. Her . . . *services* . . . are inestimable."

He lingered over the word, taunting her with his eyes. She felt bright spots of colour flare in her cheeks.

"My services have terminated," she said icily and was grateful to God that there was no throb of passion or pain in her cool, perfectly controlled voice.

She saw his eyes flame with momentary anger. His white shirt was open at the neck. He looked as if he had just come in from a game of tennis. The anger was immediately quenched. He said lazily:

"Until my mother has recovered you will continue to act as hostess. Good day, Mrs. Cameron. Good day, Senora Henriques."

His eyes flicked over her with insolent indifference and then he was gone. Her hands shook as she retrieved her pen. "I would like to add the following to the supper menu," she said unsteadily. "Mousse of chicken, mayonnaise of turbot, lobster patties, turban of chicken and tongue, tomatoes à la tartare, quenelles of pheasant, baba au rhum, viscotins of pears and apricot choux. Please make sure there is plenty of iced coffee as well as champagne and hock and spirits. Perhaps you would also remind the waiter that Lady Bessbrook drinks only pink champagne."

"Yes, madame."

Senora Henriques now knew why Mrs. Cameron was so unlike her usual self. Mr. Sanford's soft spoken words had been like the lashes of a whip. She was sorry. If it hadn't been for the inconvenience of her being a married woman, Mrs. Cameron would have made a perfect mistress for Sanfords. She picked up the extended supper menu. "I will take it to chef now. The flower arrangements are already being attended to and an extra quantity of vodka for the gypsy band has been ordered from the cellars."

"Thank you, Carlota." She sat behind the giant desk for five minutes and then rose resolutely and made her way down through the terraced gardens and the wilderness beyond to the rocks and the sea and the soothing, undemanding company of Giovanni Ferranzi.

* * *

Her first picture was complete. Giovanni eyed it and felt rising excitement. It was strong and passionate. Primitive art at its best.

"I go to Rome at the end of the week," he said as he cleaned his brushes and put away his palette and his knives. "I would like to take your painting with me."

"Whatever for?"

"To show to a friend of mine—a dealer."

"I wouldn't want to sell it," she said, amazed at the prospect.

"Then I will not sell it. But still I will take it and return it."

This time they walked back up the steeply winding pathway together.

"I have an exhibition in Rome and must be there for the opening. But I will be back."

"If I am not here when you return, would you see that my daughter receives the painting?"

"Of course."

He knew what she meant. That it was possible she would be dead. Looking at her in the harsh light of the sun, Giovanni could well believe it. She looked truly ill.

Vere was sitting on his terrace. With blessed relief she saw he was alone. Unbeknown to her, he had been waiting for her return for hours.

"May a neighbour come calling?" he asked cheerfully as she stepped out on to her adjoining balcony.

"With the utmost pleasure."

He picked up his bottle of Scotch and his glass and joined her. She sat at the glass-topped table while he retrieved a second glass from her room and then silently half-filled them both with neat whisky.

"I'm both friend and family," he said at last. "Surely I should rate as a confidant?"

"Is it so obvious that I'm in need of one?"

"Blatantly."

"Some things are too terrible to tell anyone."

She remembered Clarissa. He knew about such things but he had kept his secret and she must keep hers.

"Is it Sanford?" he asked sympathetically.

"Yes, our *affaire*—our relationship—is over." She drank the whisky and shuddered. She had never drunk it before without soda. "God, how I hate those words, Vere. They're so flippant and trite. They don't conjure up love at all."

"Most people involved in them don't feel love," Vere said drily.

She managed a laugh, thinking of Bobo and Venetia and Nicky and Luke Golding.

"No. They seem to be entered into rather as a matter of course, don't they? A new Daimler a year, a new mink, a new lover."

"Sanford's a fool."

"No." She shook her head of dark hair, her eyes tragic. "It wasn't his fault, Vere. It wasn't even mine. If I said it was fate, it would sound melodramatic and idiotic, but I'm beginning to have a quite healthy respect for fate."

"What will you do?"

"Leave. I'd go tomorrow if I could. Even if it meant leaving on a tramp steamer or a rowing boat, but my daughter is on her way here. I must stay until she arrives."

"An uncomfortable position to be in," Vere said with English understatement.

"Especially as Ramon still insists I carry out my duties as hostess."

"Refuse."

"I can't. I can't refuse him anything it's possible to still give him."

Vere was out of his depth. He felt that someone should beat some sense into Sanford, or else knock the stuffing out of him. Unfortunately, he knew that he was not the man to do it. He was not a coward but he knew that he would only come out the loser in such an encounter, and so gain nothing, not even satisfaction.

"What about you, Vere? I haven't seen you to talk to for so long. When do you return to England?"

"Not yet, not for a little while. I have some unfinished business to take care of." His blue eyes had livened, the well-bred features almost animated.

"It wouldn't have anything to do with Countess Szapary, would it?"

"How did you guess?" He was genuinely shocked. He had behaved with the utmost discretion. He abhorred tittle-tattle and had no intention of focusing gossip on his beloved Alexia.

Nancy laughed. "Eyes across a crowded room can tell the observer an awful lot, Vere."

There was a slight flush of embarrassment on his cheeks. He was wearing white flannels and white shirt with a cashmere pullover. His blond hair looked as if it had never been disturbed by human hand and his immaculately clipped moustache glittered gold in the rays of the late afternoon sun. He looked very correct, very English. She couldn't imagine Vere, in whatever situation, using violence on a woman. He would never have forced her to her knees, pulling back her head until she thought her neck would break, blaspheming and calling her a bitch. But then, she couldn't imagine Vere making love, not with the passion and raw sexuality that was second nature to Ramon. She closed her eyes. She wanted him so much it was a physical pain.

"Are you all right?" Vere's voice was concerned.

She opened her eyes and forced a smile. "Yes. Just a little tired. It's the grand fancy dress ball and there have been a few hitches. Both Helen and Fleur wanted to go as Mary, Queen of Scots. Helen because her family own more of Scotland than is decent, and Fleur because the queen was also dauphiness of France."

"I heard the uproar over Hildegarde's intention of assuming the identity of the late Tsarina."

"If it had been Countess Szapary, then I'm sure no one would have objected. I imagine that Hildegarde's avant garde approach would have inevitably caused offence. After all, a lot of our guests still remember her with deep affection."

"I remember her with awe," Vere said. "She was very beautiful, but totally without warmth. Except where her family were concerned."

The sun disappeared behind clouds and the terrace was plunged into shadow. For a few minutes they each thought of the terrible deaths of the close-knit family who had last ruled Russia, and then Nancy said:

"I must make sure that all the costumes have been delivered to their rightful owners. Patriotism seems to be in full flood today. A French court costume inadvertently delivered to an Italian guest could well result in bloodshed."

Vere remained on the terrace. He had already approached Szapary and told him he wanted to marry his wife. The count's lizard-like eyes had sharpened and he had refused adamantly. Alexia was his only treasure. He had no worldly wealth apart from her. Vere had interpreted his words as the count had intended and said that he was more advantageously placed. In fact, he was so advantageously placed that if the count would agree to a divorce and allow Alexia to sail back to England with him aboard the *Rosslyn*, one hundred thousand pounds in cash would be available to recompense him for his selfishness.

Vere had never felt more acutely embarrassed in his life. He hadn't the faintest idea how much money he should offer for Alexia. There was no precedent for such a transaction. When, a hundred years ago, the Americans had bought slaves, presumably they had known the going price. There could be no going price for a wife as perfect as Alexia.

The count had scoffed, but Vere was shrewd enough to see that it was the amount he was derisive of, not the offer.

"Two hundred thousand."

The count had stroked his jowelled chin thoughtfully, but still shook his head. No expression flitted over Vere's face. He knew Szapary would hold out for ever if he thought more was forthcoming. It wasn't that he only rated his darling Alexia at two hundred thousand pounds, but he was damned if he was going to line Szapary's greasy paw with more of Molesworth's money than was absolutely necessary. There was Clarissa to think of as well. He would have to provide handsomely for her, and the divorce itself would be costly.

From where they stood they could see the flower-shrouded drive that led to Sanfords' grand entrance, and an Armstrong-Siddeley Atlanta saloon draw up.

"Nice motor car," Vere said as if they had been discussing nothing more important than the weather. "I believe the Danish royal family favour them."

Hands in his pockets, he turned and began to stroll in the direction of the tennis courts.

Szapary blinked, rapidly assessed the situation and hurried after him. "Alexia's happiness was always my first consideration. If she loves you and you love her . . ."

"Two hundred thousand pounds," Vere said agreeably, and the count nodded.

Vere knew he could have dropped the price by fifty thousand, and Szapary would still have been grateful. He hadn't done it. It was bad enough that he was prepared to sell her like a chattel without knowing for how little, if pushed, he would sell her for.

He had not yet asked Alexia to marry him. He had had no need for he knew what her answer would be. Even now, he would not ask. He would simply tell her. Alexia was physically unable to make a decision of her own, however simple. To another man, this childlike quality and utter dependence would have been an irritant. Vere welcomed it. He could spoil her, indulge her, and whenever she looked at him her glowing eyes showed only absolute adoration. After the years of emasculation he had suffered at Clarissa's hands, Alexia was like an angel from heaven. She made him feel masterful and dominant and resolute. They were qualities he would need when first facing Clarissa. Already he had written to his lawyers in London and within the next few weeks his letter to Clarissa should catch her up somewhere between Hyderbad and Nagpur. She had no reason even to return for the divorce and Vere doubted if she would want to. A convenient weekend in Brighton with a lady recommended by his lawyer and, given sufficient time, he would be free to marry again . . . to marry Alexia.

The gowns had all been carried off by their appropriate owners' maids. The Russian gypsy band looked magnificent in high-necked silk shirts, their breeches tucked into gleaming boots, the flower arrangements were breathtaking and even the chef declared he had never been so pleased with a buffet table. Nancy sighed with relief and prepared to return to the Garden Suite to bathe and to change into her own costume.

Senora Henriques coughed discreetly. "There is just one tiny alteration to tonight's arrangements, madame."

"Yes?"

Senora Henriques disliked inflicting pain. She said as indifferently as possible. "Mr. Sanford has informed me that there will be an extra guest. Miss Rossman."

"I see. Yes. Of course. Has Miss Rossman a costume? If not, perhaps I should have a word with Salli?"

"I understand Miss Rossman is to attend as an English rose."

Nancy even managed a smile. "How apt. I'm sure she will look charming. Excuse me now, Senora Henriques. I never realized before how complicated Tudor costumes are. It's going to take me twice as long to dress as usual." She smiled again and hurried from the room. Senora Henriques watched her with admiration. She had seen the split second of utter devastation when she had heard Tessa Rossman's name and yet Nancy's innate social skills had carried her through the crippling moment unfalteringly. She was glad she would not be in attendance at the ball. Although she had seen previous ladies treated so casually by Ramon Sanford that it amounted to callousness, she had never before felt pity for them. She felt intense pity for Nancy Leigh Cameron. She liked and respected her. She sighed and went back to her account books, glad that she no longer involved herself in *affaires* of the heart.

She had chosen to go to the grand ball as Anne Boleyn. She liked the costume of the period and felt a certain amount of sympathy for the girl unlucky enough to have caught the eye of a king. They had the same colouring—dark hair and creamy skin—and like Anne Boleyn, she was destined for an early death. The choice, as far as Nancy was concerned, was perfect.

The dress Salli had made for her was of heavy crimson velvet with a low-cut, square décolletage that showed off her smooth shoulders and perfect, high-rounded breasts even more alluringly than the plunging-fronted dresses of Patou and Schiaparelli. The full, heavy sleeves were slashed to reveal cloth of gold and the skirt fell open to reveal matching material underneath. The bodice and neckline were trimmed with pearls, as was the crimson velvet coif that framed her face and transformed her into a queen.

"Madame, it is magnificent," Maria said rapturously.

It was, but Nancy could take little joy in her appearance. She had only minutes left before walking alone to the head of the great staircase to join the waiting and forbidding figure of Ramon.

She lingered at her dressing table, dreading the commitment of the walk down the sumptuously decorated corridor.

"Is anything the matter, madame?" Maria asked.

Nancy's eyes met hers in the mirror.

"No," she said, and rose to her feet, feeling rather like Anne Boleyn must have felt when she rose to face the long walk to the axe. "Nothing."

She was well prepared for the evening ahead of her. After all she had endured a rehearsal, and survived. The evening when Ramon had entered with Tessa on his arm seemed light years away. Because of the undisguised nature of their subsequent reunion with him, she knew she would be the focus of all eyes when, after dutifully greeting the guests, she was left unescorted and Ramon would once more lavish his attention on Tessa.

He was dressed in a glittering military uniform, white breeches tucked into gleaming knee-high black boots, a gold-braided, fur-edged cape swinging negligently from one shoulder. He looked magnificent.

She smiled stiffly and took her place at his side. There was no answering smile. His face was grim and uncompromising.

The liveried footmen and toastmaster took up their posts, the great doors at the end of the long salon were thrown open and, in order of precedence, their guests approached. Mr. Blenheim, much to the grand duchess' disgust, had chosen to abandon his *nom de plume* and resplendently and majestically appeared as himself. The

Grand Duchess Nadejda Livada had attempted no disguise. The theme was royalty and she was royal. There the matter ended. Nicky looked almost as devastating as Ramon and instead of merely brushing the back of her hand with his lips his mouth was hot and ardent on her skin.

Prince Felix had donned Russian military dress and was ablaze with medals and decorations and loops of gold braid.

As an English duke, Vere had dressed as if for court, his sobriety a startling contrast to the Russians' splendour. He wore his full complement of orders and decorations and even in Madeleine's eyes looked splendid.

Costas had abandoned Greek nationalism and transformed himself into Henry VIII. His doublet was of royal purple embroidered with gold, and to scandalized and admiring applause, he revealed a magnificent codpiece that glazed even Madeleine's eyes. His wide-shouldered jacket fell in ample folds, lavishly edged with fur and, as he strutted and postured, it was possible to believe that the outrageous Greek had a generous dash of Tudor blood in his veins.

Lavinia Meade had forsaken her Chinese empress costume and replaced Zia as an awesome Catherine the Great. Luke Golding, revived by the paying of his hotel bill by Minnie Peckwyn-Peake, exchanged bets with Reggie Minter as to whether Sonny Zakar would carry out his promise and inform her of her heroine's sexual proclivities.

Polly Watertight descended on the amazed throng as the most unlikely Pocahontas in history.

Marisa wore the skin-tight trousers of a matador and, dressed like a man, looked more womanly than ever.

Petite Madama Molière made an enchanting Mary, Queen of Scots, and refused to believe Charles Montcalm when he told her that the lady in question had been nearly six foot tall.

Hildegarde sported the jewel in her navel that the erstwhile Mr. Blenheim had intended for Marisa. Sonny had found comfort elsewhere. An ex-king was too stiff competition for a law-abiding American film producer.

As a Venetian court lady, Venetia Bessbrook looked exquisite. In flowing robes and headdress, Hassan looked like a desert sheikh.

Lady Michaeljohn had chosen to represent Queen Victoria, but sadly she did not have the chest for it. Georgina Montcalm had simply worn one of her usual loosely flowing creations and encircled her throat with a five-stringed pearl choker to indicate that she was Queen Mary.

Princess Louise had made a pathetic attempt to pass as the dazzling Empress Elizabeth of Austria, and Mr. Chetwynd had defiantly worn knee chaps and a stetson and pronounced that an American cowboy was royal enough for him.

Jewels sparkled and shone from ears, throats, chests, arms, wrists and even, in the case of the maharani, toes.

Everyone had raided their safety boxes in an effort to outbid each other in royal, or pseudo-royal grandeur.

As before, when Tessa Rossman entered, she stole the show by wearing only the simplest of white organdie dresses, her only adornment a wreath of red roses encircling her golden hair.

Nancy wondered if the stunning simplicity was her own idea or Ramon's. When they had shaken hands, Tessa had smiled at her with such sweetness that it was impossible for Nancy to feel any of the emotions she would have liked to feel. It would have been so much easier if she could have disliked her heartily, but it was impossible to dislike Tessa Rossman. Her initial shyness gone, she was gay and charming, her unsophisticated manner a welcome change after the conversation of some of the more pretentious guests.

Helen Bingham-Smythe was radiant as a not-very-convincing Lady Jane Grey and Nancy was pleased to see that Reggie Minter was still in attendance. She was focussing her attention anywhere and everywhere but on Ramon and Tessa Rossman. Her duties were over. She had stood with him and greeted the guests. Then, as eyes swivelled incredulously, he had turned his back on her and taken Tessa Rossman by the arm and led her out on to the dance floor for the first waltz.

The waltz ended and Ramon did not relinquish his hold on Tessa. Nancy would have had to be deaf and blind to be unaware of the sensation they were causing. She stood talking to the Montcalms, a fixed half-smile on her face as she pretended to listen to Georgina, the words flowing over her unheard. Before, when she had seen him with Tessa, the agony had been bad enough. Tonight, it was unspeakable. Now everyone knew and she could feel a hundred pairs of speculative eyes on her. And it was all of her own doing. Tessa could still have been immured at Carmara de Lobos. She could still have been in Ramon's arms. If . . . If . . .

Nicky was at her side. She allowed him to sweep her on to the dance floor. She felt like a puppet. Georgina spoke to her and she responded. Nicky asked her to dance and she accepted.

"I love you," he said, whirling her round effortlessly.

"Yes," she answered automatically. Ramon and Tessa were now with Prince Felix and Bobo. Ramon's hand still lingered around Tessa's waist. She was laughing. He was smiling. In the deep tan of his neck his black curls clustered, damp with light perspiration. She saw him unhook his short, fur-trimmed cloak and toss it lightly over one of the gilt chairs.

"Will you marry me?"

"Yes . . . I beg your pardon?"

Nicky laughed. "I knew you weren't listening to a word I was saying."

"I'm sorry. My thoughts were elsewhere."

"On Sanford?"

"No." Her eyes told him she was lying.

"I said I loved you and I want you to marry me." His honeyed eyes held hers. "Why else do you think I lavished every single one of my family heirlooms on you?"

"As a gesture," she said and smiled.

Nicky saw the sadness behind the smile and continued, undeterred.

"As you know and I know, I would have been appalled if you had scooped them into your handbag and high-tailed it for the nearest liner."

This time her smile was a genuine. She had wondered what would have happened if she had not returned his king's ransom.

"I intended to both give them to you and to retain them. The devious Romanov blood runs deep."

"Just how would you have managed to do both?" She could feel the heat of his hand through the velvet of her dress. The French windows that ran wall-length on the south side of the ballroom had been flung open in respect for the unusually heavy materials and furs being worn.

"By marrying you."

She faltered and lost her step. "Are you serious?"

He raised his warm brown eyes heavenwards. "*Ma chère amie*, I do not go around lavishing my worldly wealth on ladies for whom a single jewel would be sufficient. I love you. You are entrancing, mysterious, delightful, sophisticated, cultivated and so sensual that you disturb my days as well as my nights."

"And Madame Molière?"

"Was a very welcome and imaginative gift. She is also very firmly married to her wealthy American and intends to stay that way. Flirtations and *affaires* are a way of life for Fleur. They are a pleasure, like eating and drinking and gambling. They are not to be taken seriously and neither is she. She would bore me to tears within a month. You, *ma chère amie*, would not bore a man in a lifetime."

Across the throng of dancers Ramon's eyes met hers. They glittered with pain and fury. Nancy felt the knife in her heart twist so savagely that it was all she could do to prevent herself from crying out loud. He loved her. He still loved her. He was suffering just as she was.

"I am also married," she heard herself say to Nicky, when a mass of waltzing dancers blocked Ramon from her view. "And I do not intend to divorce and marry again."

"That was not what I understood, *ma petite*." He looked pointedly in Ramon's direction. Nancy could not trust herself to follow his gaze.

"It is the truth," she said simply. The music ended. He retained his hold on her.

"I will not give up so easily, Nancy."

"And I will not change my mind."

They were still in the centre of the ballroom when Vere strolled across to them, exchanged pleasantries with Nicky and, when the music struck up again, whisked her away with expertize but not the panache of the Russian.

"I'm beginning to feel like an elder brother must, extricating a too beautiful sister from unwelcome attentions."

"Nicky's attentions are at least honourable," Nancy said, glad of his comforting presence.

Vere raised his brows. "A marriage to Sanford would have been explosive enough. Marriage to a Russian revolutionary would be even more disastrous. The old order will never be restored in Russia. Stalin's grip is like a vice."

"Thank goodness for democracy and Roosevelt," Nancy said drily.

"According to Charles, democracy and Roosevelt may not be enough. He seems to think this German-Austria fracas will spread."

"Charles' trouble is that he simply can't wait to put his destroyer to sea and use it for the purpose it was built for," Nancy said, with a lightness she was far from feeling. "I'm sure when Dieter arrives he'll be able to put Charles' mind at rest. Lady Michaeljohn was only saying yesterday that Hitler was to be applauded for making Germany such a bulwark against Bolshevism."

"He may be rejuvenating his country, but I prefer a little British understatement myself. His frenzied speeches leave me cold."

Vere's eyes met Alexia's and Germany and Hitler were forgotten.

Nancy's back was to Ramon but she could tell his eyes were on her, watching, seeing who she danced with—who she would leave with.

She danced next with Charles and then Luke Golding. She entered the supper room on Sonny Zakar's muscled arm and was glad of his wit as a raconteur. It was impossible not to laugh at Sonny's outrageous anecdotes of the Hollywood stars. She drank twice as much champagne as usual and was unaffected by it.

She overheard Lavinia Meade, Bobo, Venetia Bessbrook and even Madeleine Mancini say that Tessa Rossman was as sweet-natured as she was sweet-looking. Time had given her perception. She had endured and survived the first moments when the world at large had been aware that her *affaire* with Ramon was at an end. She had managed to remain composed as she greeted Tessa, and behave as normal, despite her inner agony, as he danced, laughed and talked with her.

Even without her father's and Zia's dreadful revelation, they could only have had a few brief months of happiness together, and then Ramon would have needed someone else. Better that it was a Tessa Rossman than the promiscuous Princess Marinsky or the avaricious Lady Linderdowne. Tessa would make Ramon a good, loving and faithful wife. What sort of husband he would make for Tessa, she had no idea. Ramon as a husband seemed so unlikely as to be unbelievable. Yet he had wanted to marry her. Had *demanded* that he marry her. She blinked away weary tears. To leave the ballroom alone would only call attention to herself. To leave with another man would only confirm Ramon's suspicions. She turned to Charles. Even Ramon could not imagine that there was anything but friendship between her and Charles Montcalm.

"I have a blinding headache, Charles. Would you be an angel and escort me to my room?"

"Of course." Charles drained his glass and took her arm. Both he and Georgina had been watching her anxiously all evening. Her manner had been superb. If she was a publicly cast-off mistress, she had not behaved like one. She had conducted herself with utter assurance; laughing softly and not too often, with the hint of huskiness that even he found arousing. He could not imagine the effort it had cost her to appear so relaxed and carefree.

"Never let your guard down," her father had said once. She never had. Not in public. Her years of social training had stood her in good stead. It would have been blatantly rude to leave without wishing Tessa "good-night".

Tessa blushed prettily and said nervously, "I was wondering if perhaps you would visit us at Camara de Lobos, Mrs. Cameron? Mummy and daddy would love to meet you. We don't have a very large pool and the tennis courts aren't as good as Sanfords' of course, but . . ."

Nancy could see the heroine worship in the girl's eyes and knew the crushing disappointment that would follow if she refused.

"I would love to," she said and wondered how the

words ever passed her lips. "Perhaps we could visit when my daughter, Verity, arrives on Madeira. She is the same age as yourself and will be arriving within the next week or so."

If she moved the merest fraction of an inch, she would be in physical contact with Ramon. Her eyes were fixed firmly on Tessa's heart-shaped face. She must not look at Ramon. Whatever she did, she must not allow his burning gaze to draw her eyes.

"That would be marvellous." Tessa's cornflower-blue eyes glowed. "It's been such a privilege meeting you, Mrs. Cameron."

Nancy smiled. "I hate formality. Please call me Nancy. Goodnight, Tessa. Goodnight, Ramon."

Still she averted her eyes from his. She could feel his sharp intake of breath. Could feel the barely controlled tenseness of his body. It occurred to her that Hildegarde knew nothing about acting in comparison to herself. Even Garbo could have learned a few lessons from her performance that evening. Charles took her arm; they were leaving the room. Ramon had not spoken, not even to wish her goodnight. The lights from the chandeliers dazzled her; she felt dizzy and then a rushing blackness drowned her as she stumbled and fell.

Charles was too taken by surprise to catch hold of her. She crumpled at his feet, her face ashen, her dark hair fanning glossily on the pale beige of the carpet.

"Nancy, my dear girl!" He dropped to his knees, raising her head and shoulders in his arms. He had known that she was suffering but had not imagined the intensity of it. She had been publicly humiliated and now he was left with her, limp and unconscious, in his arms. He would rather have been left facing the enemy fleet single-handed. A maid ran towards them and Charles greeted her with relief.

"Can you carry madame?" the little maid asked him.

"Yes. Of course."

He lifted her in his arms and knew why Vere and Vasileyev had fallen under her spell. Her skin was satin-smooth, her mouth as soft and vulnerable as a child's. She smelt deliciously of the wild white roses that grew in such profusion in Sanfords' garden. She stirred slightly and his arms tightened his hold on her as Ramon burst from the ballroom, his face anguished.

He moved to take her from Charles Montcalm, but the earl's patience had worn thin. "You've done enough damage for one night, Sanford! You're the cause of this with your disgraceful disregard for other people's feelings. I suggest you remove yourself and go back to Miss Rossman."

"Don't be a bloody fool!"

The little maid waited nervously while they glared at each other.

Nancy's eyes fluttered open and Ramon said hoarsely: "Nancy?"

She turned her head away, her voice muffled by Charles Montcalm's chest as she said, "Please take me to my room, Charles."

"Certainly, Nancy," and then coldly to Ramon, "goodnight Sanford," and he strode down the corridor, Nancy's head against his shoulder, her arms around his neck.

Ramon's eyes were brilliant with pain and fury. With a snap of his fingers he summoned a bellboy and said curtly, "Doctor Oliveira has arrived. Please send him immediately to Mrs. Cameron in the Garden Suite."

"Yes, sir. At once, sir." He scurried to do as he was bid and Ramon turned once more to the ballroom, the abrasively masculine lines of his face grim and harsh, hiding his pain.

Maria thanked the earl profusely and speedily undressed Nancy, slipping a silk nightdress over her head. As she turned down the lace-edged sheet, there was an authoritative knock on the door. Nancy's heart began to beat wildly, torn between hope and dread. When Maria opened the door to a dark-suited stranger carrying a doctor's bag, she sat down wearily on the edge of the bed, near to tears. It was Dr. Oliveira. The man Ramon had summoned from Oporto in his anxiety for her health.

He was short and stocky with a beaming smile and glossily slicked dark hair. A white carnation was sported jauntily in his lapel.

"I intended to see you tomorrow, Mrs. Cameron," he said, crossing to the bed, "but I understand that you have just had another attack of faintness. Allow me."

He was gently pulling down her eyelids, examining her nails, feeling her pulse.

"Dr. Oliveira, please. There's no need."

"There is every need, Mrs. Cameron. Healthy young women should not faint for no just cause."

His bright black eyes were shrewd. "Certainly you are anaemic and, I think, a little more. Tomorrow I would like to give you a detailed examination."

His voice brooked no argument. She said wearily. "There's no need to examine me, Doctor."

"Nevertheless . . ."

"I know what is wrong with me, Doctor." Her voice was flat and tired. "I have aplastic anaemia. It was diagnosed some while ago by Dr. Henry Lorrimer of New York."

The doctor was no longer beaming. "I see. Was Mr. Sanford hoping for a second opinion?"

She shook her head. "Mr. Sanford is unaware of my condition." She pushed her hair away from her face. "I do not wish him to be told of it. Mr. Sanford is not my husband, nor is he family."

"Mr. Sanford is very concerned about you."

Her smile was bleak. "No longer, Dr. Oliveira. I think you will find Mr. Sanford will be quite happy to hear I have anaemia and will not pursue the matter further. I am sorry you have had to travel so far unnecessarily."

"I do not think my visit has been unnecessary, Mrs. Cameron. With your permission I would still like to conduct an examination."

"No, Doctor. I'm sorry. I came here to be away from doctors and reminders of my illness. There is nothing to be done. I'm sure you understand."

He nodded, his eyes thoughtful.

"And you'll honour my request that Mr. Sanford is not told the truth?"

"I will tell Mr. Sanford that you have anaemia. I will not tell him to what degree. I will also speak to you again. Goodnight, Mrs. Cameron."

The door closed quietly behind him and Nancy sank back against the pillows. Her one desire was to leave at first light, yet she could not. She could not leave until she had seen Verity. She was again on the treadmill that she thought she had broken free of. She was living for Verity: staying and suffering because Verity would expect her to be here on her arrival, and would be hurt and uncomprehending if she was not. The Nancy Leigh Cameron who had been a woman in her own right had been nothing but a chimera. She was once again Nancy Leigh Cameron: mother. Her daughter's happiness coming before her own.

Tomorrow she would be Nancy Leigh Cameron: daughter. She would go to her father and lyingly tell him that he had not destroyed her happiness. More truthfully, that she still loved him and that she was sorry for the cruelty of her words.

She closed her eyes. One thing she would never revert to was Nancy Leigh Cameron: wife. Jack had sailed out of her life for ever.

Her eyes remained closed but sleep did not come. Against her lids she saw only images of Tessa Rossman in Ramon's arms. For the first time she realized what a truly terrible gift imagination could be.

Chapter Twenty-One

The next morning she was sick again. She retched till only bile remained and even then her stomach heaved and her throat gagged.

Maria, so seriously disturbed at the train of events between her mistress and Ramon Sanford, had informed Luis that she could not leave Mrs. Cameron's employ until her mistress was once again happy and well. Luis failed to see why Mrs. Cameron's happiness should have any bearing on theirs. Maria had been adamant. Senator Cameron's arrival and abrupt departure had unnerved her. The mayor's arrival had astounded her. Mrs. Cameron needed her. Therefore Maria would stay with her. Later, when Mrs. Cameron's complicated private life righted itself, she would hand over to a replacement and join Luis at the altar of Igreja de Santa Isabel in Lisbon. The wedding had to take place in Lisbon because Luis' parents and numerous brothers and sisters, nieces and nephews, lived there. Maria was indifferent to where they married. She had no family. Her only allegiance was to Nancy.

Nancy shakily left the bathroom and shuddered at the sight of her breakfast tray. At Maria's insistence, she once again ate half a slice of dry toast and drank a small quantity of Perrier water. She dressed in a pair of pearl-grey trousers, her white silk blouse with her monogram discreetly embroidered on the breast pocket, slung a black cardigan over her shoulders and, equipped with the dark glasses that had become standard equipment, went to meet Senora Henriques.

The ball had been a success. The gypsy band had played with vigour and by three in the morning Prince Felix Zaronsky and Prince Nicholas Vasileyev had taken to the floor with a display of Russian dancing that had drawn cheers which carried as far away as Funchal. At four o'clock Kate Murphy and Polly Watertight had taken to the floor. The two octogenarians had executed on energetic can-can that had surpassed even the Russians' performance. Kate Murphy's ribald and unexpurgated version of "Eskimo Nell" had reduced even the strait-laced Princess Louise to tears of scandalized laughter. At five o'clock Hildegarde had decided that a belly-dancer should dance and had done so with an eroticism that had aroused envy in the breast of every woman present and lust in the more private parts of their companions. At six, when the other ladies fortunately had retired exhausted to their beds, Madeleine had decided that it was her turn for the limelight and had executed a striptease that the conoisseur of the art, the Sultan of Mahore, had declared superlative.

At seven o'clock the recumbent figure of Sir Maxwell Meade had been carried to his suite. Sonny and Costas had gone for a naked swim in a freezing sea and Mr. Chetwynd, still wearing his stetson, had been found *in flagrante* with the insatiable Hildegarde.

Nancy went through the list of requested reservations

and deleted the unsuitable. The suitable included an English marquis, single and chased by husband-hunters the length and breadth of Europe; a Knight Commander of the Indian Empire; Lance St. John Colbert, a playboy only a little below Ramon on that particular Richter scale; Yolande Yale, recuperating from the disastrous finale of her sixth marriage and Joseph Fenway, a long-time political opponent of her father. Joseph, despite his name, had a Protestant background going back to the Pilgrim Fathers. He was the patrician of all Back Bay Bostonians, the class who most bitterly opposed their roistering, Irish Catholic mayor. If he arrived while Chips was still in residence, it would give a bite to the conversation and be just the tonic her father needed. Joseph Fenway was a man with all the advantages that had been denied to Chips. His religion was uncontroversial—his background flawless. He could count three ex-United States Presidents in his family tree and no doubt, with a little effort, could have come up with a handful of Secretaries of State as well.

Lady Bessbrook's request that Mr. Golding be removed from her adjoining suite was duly sanctioned, and a simultaneous request from Mrs. Peckwyn-Meade that Mr. Golding be installed on her floor, granted.

The menus were approved. The repairs for the damage caused by the gypsy band when they had returned to their quarters and consumed awesome quantities of vodka, were put in hand. Mrs. Honey-Smith's complaint that her maid was being annoyed by one of Sanfords' footmen was also dealt with.

Business concluded, Nancy avoided the pool and by her usual route began to make her way down to the rocks and the sea, and Giovanni.

Costas met her at the door. It was still only ten o'clock. If he had been swimming in the sea at six o'clock, it was impossible that he had been to bed. He looked as exuberant as ever. His open shirt revealed a mass of tightly curling grey hair that would have done credit to a yak. A gold chain with an ornate St. Christopher medallion hung around his strongly muscled neck. Both his wrists were encircled by heavy-linked gold bracelets. On Luke Golding or Reggie Minter they would have caused raised eyebrows and murmurs as to whether their owner was quite, one hundred per cent, pukka. On Costas no such conclusions could be drawn. His heterosexuality was unquestionable and would be so even if he took to wearing perfume.

In the shade of the hotel a card table had been set up by party-goers who had still not slept. The poker-playing foursome included an Old Etonian, a self-made millioniare from Wapping, a Detroit financier and an East European royal. Money, Nancy observed to herself as she continued through gardens purple with the haze of early flowering jacarandas, was a great leveller of class. Only members of the old school, like the grand duchess, and Princess Louise, remained aloof from people of unequal birth. If a man had several million pounds then he was as welcome at a card table as the most blue-blooded of aristocrats.

Giovanni welcomed her with a blank canvas. She sat before it for a long time and then made her first bold stroke. There would be no joy in this painting. Only darkness and confinement and unutterable dread.

"How many are there?" Chips asked Zia when her maids had solicitously installed her in her peacock-feathered throne.

"Ten. On average, I'm receiving three a day."

Chips clenched his jaw. His white hair sprang thickly back from his forehead, giving him the appearance of an aging lion. The lines from nose to mouth were deeply etched, but in Zia's eyes he was still a handsome man. And in Gloria's too, apparently.

"Burn them."

"No. Anyone who sends cablegrams with this frequency and frenzy deserves to have them read."

The first had arrived even before Chips. It had been addressed to herself. The contents had shaken her.

"I love him stop please send him back stop".

The second said: "Tell him I am sorry and will never do it again stop".

The third: "Please please tell him I love him stop It isn't the money I want stop It is him stop".

The fourth: "I know he loves you stop Don't ask him to divorce me stop Gloria stop".

The fifth: "If he doesn't come back I'll die stop No one invites me anywhere now or speaks to me stop Please tell him I'm lonely stop".

The sixth: "Tell him I'll divorce him if that's what he wants stop".

The remainder were addressed to Chips. He held them unopened in his large hand.

"What was it you had to forgive her for?" Zia asked.

"The usual. An *affaire.*" Strangely enough it no longer seemed important that the offending party was Zia's son.

"Only one?"

For the first time in his life Chips lost his temper in Zia's presence. "Of course it was only one! What sort of a woman do you think my wife is?"

Zia suppressed a smile. She had elicited the response she had needed to make her decision.

He wished to God she had never given him the cablegrams. He didn't trust himself to open them. Whatever they said was irrelevant. He was going back to Boston and he was taking Zia with him.

"I've always enjoyed the Beacon Hill house, perhaps because Beacon Hill has always been so staunchly

Republican that I gained pleasure simply from invading their private citadel. However, I don't expect you to live in a house that two former wives have lived in. We'll start afresh. Perhaps Dorchester. There's some nice property there and it's still within easy access of City Hall . . ."

"I'm not going back with you, Chips."

". . . I know you like the sun but there's the house in Palm Beach . . ."

"I'm not going, Chips."

He stared at her.

She smiled gently and took his hand. "Time has passed us by. We're nearly fifty years too late."

"It's never too late! We've loved each other for the whole of our lives!"

"But they've been separate lives, darling. We've never had to live together, sharing the daily irritations; growing bored by over-familiarity." She gave a soft laugh. "No wonder we remained in love. We only ever saw each other at our best, or dreamed of the other and attributed to the dream every quality we could possibly desire."

"You *have* every quality I could possibly desire!" he said, feeling a sudden desperation.

"You *think* I have, darling. I certainly haven't one, and it's one you have overlooked. I'm not remotely political—not any longer. My interest in American or world politics is strictly on a dinner-table level. I have no hankering for Boston and the thought of Palm Beach fills me with horror. My home is here: in Madeira. Alone."

"I don't believe you." His voice lacked conviction.

Zia knew that he did and did not bother to protest. She said instead, "The Morrison-Whitneys were in Madeira last July. They said you were looking like a man of forty and that Gloria was exceptionally bright and unbelievably pretty."

Chips' jaw clenched.

"They said that though it was a surprising marriage, it

seemed to be a very successful one." She paused, and then continued gently, "One *affaire* isn't enough to end a marriage. If it was, no one in the country would ever celebrate a silver wedding."

Chips made a sound between a grunt and a snort.

"She's young, darling. It's very easy to make mistakes when you are young. I, of all people, know that." She rose to her feet unaided. The early blossom had sprinkled her hair like confetti. "She loves you, Chips. Don't turn your back on her."

Slowly she made her way across the grass to the open French windows of her boudoir.

Chips remained beneath the jacaranda tree, the cablegrams in his hand. Only after several straight bourbons did he open them.

"Please come home stop Gloria".

"I love you and I am sorry stop Gloria".

"I am lonely and I need you and it is horrible without you stop".

"Goodbye sweetheart stop Gloria".

For one insane moment he thought it was a suicide note. Frantically he checked the date it had been sent. If it had been a suicide note he would have known by now. Other cables would have followed: from Seamus, from the Police Department. He gave a trembling sigh of relief that was short-lived. Perhaps it *was* a suicide note but she had not yet committed the fatal act; or not been found. Perspiration broke out on his forehead. Gloria would not commit suicide. Gloria had guts and a love of life that infected all around her. The sweat rolled down the back of his neck. He remembered the tiny figure at the docks, waving frantically for him to return. Jesus Christ. Gloria couldn't kill herself! She was only twenty-three. If she killed herself it would all be his fault. He would have nothing to return to. No one. He broke into a run.

There had to be a liner returning to Southampton.

From there he could cross to New York on the *Manhattan* or the *Aquitania* or the *Mauritania*. Anything, just as long as it floated.

He ran all the way to his suite to give orders for his cases to be packed. He ran all the way to reception to ask that a cable be sent to Mrs. O'Shaughnessy, reading: "Coming home stop Love you stop Chips".

He ran all the way to the Garden Suite to tell Nancy that he would not be staying to greet his grand-daughter.

There was a ship leaving at dusk. Leaving Nancy incredulous and uncomprehending, he spent the rest of his time with Zia. She did not escort him to Sanfords' grand entrance when he left. Their last goodbye had been a private one.

"But surely you can wait another two days," Nancy protested for the fourth time.

"No, I can't. I have to get back. Give my love to Verity. Don't allow that husband of hers to go around singing the praises of Hitler and do try and forgive me."

"I already have."

He hugged her tightly. To her amazement she saw that he was crying.

"I've ruined enough lives, Nancy. Zia's, your mother's, yours. I can't ruin Gloria's as well. Goodbye, sweetheart." He kissed her forehead and brushed his tears away clumsily.

"Goodbye, Daddy."

The Sanford Rolls slid away down the drive and towards the docks. She felt utterly deserted. If she had pleaded with him to stay, would he have done so? What would he have given up for her? The bleak answer was very little. He was returning to his young and, presumably, forgiven wife. Zia's life would continue as it had for the past countless years. Only hers had been disrupted.

Ramon insisted again that she play hostess to his host.

She wore a black crèpe dress with a short-waisted, mandarin-necked gold jacket. He seemed to derive some sadistic pleasure from forcing her to remain at his side. Or was it masochistic? After all, in his eyes *she* had terminated the *affaire*. She was the one who had laughed at the word love and made light of all the beauty and magic and sacredness of what had passed between them.

"Let me introduce you to Lance St. John Colbert," Ramon was saying, the cruelty in his voice naked as he gripped her elbow in a pincer-like grip and steered her through the chattering groups. "Lance enjoys a good time. You should get on together very well. You'll have your fun in bed without the inconvenience of love."

"Ramon, please . . ."

"Or is Charles Montcalm more in your line? I believe seducing the husband of a best friend always adds extra zest to sexual activities."

"Ramon, you're hurting me . . ."

He was smiling, nodding in various directions, saying as he did so, "I admire you, Nancy. I really do. To present such a façade of respectability in public and be such a whore in private must require great talent."

Sparks flared in her eyes. "I never once pretended to be anything but what I was—your mistress!"

His voice was like silk. "That was here—away from the world press. What I admire is the ingeniousness you must have employed to conduct your clandestine *affaires* in the very heart of New York and Washington."

She tried to wrench her arm away but his grip was vice-like.

"How dare you call me a whore! I gave up my husband for you, my home . . ." She stopped in mid-sentence, horrified.

His eyes had narrowed to mere slits. People were turning to look in their direction, but they were oblivious.

"*Why*?" he demanded fiercely. "For a little *fun*? For a few weeks' *diversion*?"

She was so pale he thought she was going to faint.

"Let go of me," she gasped. "You said you would never touch me again! Don't sully your fingers by laying them on a *whore*!"

She spun around. A glass of Oeil-de-Perdrix cascaded down Bobo's silk lamé. She was aware of staring faces: bodies. There was a stunned silence as she ran from the room.

"What extraordinary behaviour," the newcomer said to Margot Alleynian.

"Incredible," her compatriot agreed. "You expect that sort of thing from the Latins but not the Americans. And not *that* American."

"Should I go after her?" Georgina asked Charles anxiously.

His reply was too hurried to be in good taste. "Leave well alone. I don't know what's going on and I don't want to know. Sanford looks on the border of dementia and Nancy . . ." Words failed him. He took his third whisky in five minutes from the tray of a hovering waiter. He was beginning to drink far too much. Warfare was tranquil in comparison to life at Sanfords.

A deep, scorching rage enabled Nancy to survive the next two weeks. She no longer appeared as Sanfords' hostess. No power on earth would induce her to do so. She no longer attended the dinners, cocktail parties and balls. She painted and, occasionally, when dark had fallen and the pool and surrounding places were deserted, she swam. Unknown to her, from Zia's terrace, Ramon watched hour after hour after hour. His hands clenched in tight knots behind his back, his only companion a bottle of whisky. It was a week before Villiers informed him of Nancy's habit of swimming between seven and eight in the evenings. From then on he stationed himself in the unlit snooker room and watched through the cold glass as she swam relentlessly up and down, up and down, until exhaustion forced her to climb, shivering, from the sunless water.

He continued to see Tessa and his fondness for her increased, but it was not love. Love was what he felt for Nancy. Love that had been flung back in his face.

There had been no other men. Surveillance on the Garden Suite was tighter than on the White House. He didn't understand it. All his life women had been his for the asking. Night after night he fought the temptation to stride down to the pool and either take her by force or drown her. Sometimes he felt that only by committing both acts would he ever again achieve peace of mind.

Nancy's sickness continued. Her breakfast tray now only contained dry toast, black, sugarless coffee and the ubiquitous Perrier water.

Maria's pleas that she see a doctor went unheeded. The fatigue and the nosebleeds had stopped, as had her period. Presumably Dr. Lorrimer had omitted to mention the inconvenience of morning sickness. Nancy bore it stoically. By ten or eleven she felt well enough to paint. A few hours' nausea was a small price to pay when suffering from an incurable disease. As a child she had seen a great aunt die of cancer. She knew when she was lucky.

Giovanni disappeared to Rome with her paintings and her second canvas was followed by a third. The Szaparys left: Alexia aboard the *Rosslyn*, the count, looking more than satisifed, aboard a liner bound for Durban.

On 7 April, ex-Prince Hubertus and ex-Prince Friedrich of Germany appeared in public, wearing the uniforms of Nazi Storm-troopers. On 11 April Sir Gerald du Maurier, the great actor and manager, died. On 14 April the Meades sailed away and, even to Georgina's eyes, Sir Maxwell's yellow silk handkerchief appeared crushed and limply pathetic. On 16 April Verity and

Dieter, Count and Countess Mezriczky, finally arrived, the count wearing the same controversial uniform as the sons of the ex-Kaiser.

Nancy's shock was overcome by pleasure at seeing her daughter. She hugged her but Verity's slim body remained stiff and unresponsive. Nancy remembered that Verity disliked public displays of affection. Chips' Irish blood had by-passed his grand-daughter.

"Darling, you look marvellous," she said, drawing back and taking a good look at her only child.

She did. Verity had never been an overly pretty child. Her hair had been straight and her features had always seemed too large for her small, pointed face. In company she tended to be awkward and diffident. Ever since she had been a toddler, Nancy had taken great care to ensure that plenty of contemporaries were invited to their Hyannis home as playmates. Verity had accepted them without enthusiasm. The children had more often than not played amongst themselves while Verity watched disinterestedly. As Verity had grown older, Nancy spared no efforts in trying to overcome her shyness. She had seen to it that she could swim, ride, play tennis and dance. The introverted toddler became a withdrawn and unparticipating pupil at Dorchester High School. She had refused adamantly to attend any of the city centre schools. Chauffeur-driven, she disappeared daily outside Boston's city limits and returned as uncommunicative as ever. Nancy suffered for her. She had never been afflicted by shyness and sensitivity on the scale that Verity was. Jack intended that, after her post-graduate year, Verity should go on to Wellesley. By now, her straight hair was no longer such a handicap. She had long ago given up attempting to curl it and wore it in a long, unfashionable, bob. Strangely enough it suited her. Over the years her features and face had adjusted so that though her appearance was starkly different from the frothy, giggling girls of her own age group, she had evolved a style of her own. She also had an innate imperiousness that resulted from her efforts to overcome her shyness. The aloof attitude set her apart, just as her unusual looks did. Boys were intrigued, often awed, by her. At her seventeenth birthday party Nancy had finally let out a sigh of relief. Discarding frills and flounces, Verity had dressed simply and with stunning good taste. She looked far older than her classmates and spent more time talking to her parents' acquaintances and family friends and their visitors who were staying at the Cape. She had no shortage of dance partners: she betrayed no sign of her shyness. Rather, she seemed amazingly self-assured for a girl between school and college.

It was the Halloways who brought Count Dieter Mezriczky as their guest. The girls' heads swivelled. Local boys paled into insignificance.

The count was in his early twenties, blond-haired and blue-eyed. His manner was as withdrawn and detached as Verity's and consequently just as intriguing. Every girl present felt a personal challenge to arouse interest in the pale, bored eyes. He did not drink and, to their disappointment, he refused to dance.

When Nancy hurried from the supper room, where she had been ensuring that fresh supplies of food were reaching the table, and out into the lamplit garden, she was amazed to see her daughter and the count standing apart from the other guests, their heads close together, deep in discussion.

Her first reaction had been one of pleasure. Her daughter, who for so many years had seemed destined to be a wallflower, was obviously not going to suffer that fate. She was fast acquiring poise and confidence, and had captured the undivided attention of their most eligible guest. When, one month later, Verity announced she would not be going to Wellesley, but marrying Dieter instead, Nancy's pleasure had turned to horror.

Even Jack had returned from Washington, an unheard-of precedent.

Verity, the quiet, silent little girl who had suffered so acutely from shyness and lack of confidence, was transformed. She was still quiet. Nancy couldn't remember her raising her voice once as they sat up night after night, pleading with her, persuading, bribing. Verity was immovable. She was not going to Wellesley. She was marrying Dieter. For the first time, Nancy became aware of her daughter's stubbornness.

In the end it was Jack who had capitulated. They could become engaged on her eighteenth birthday and married on her nineteenth. Nancy had choked back a cry of protest. Verity was still a child. Dieter was her first romantic attachment. To permit an engagement was lunacy.

"I'm not waiting two years," Verity said calmly as her father rose to leave the table around which they had all been sitting. "I'm marrying him now—this month."

For once Jack Cameron had been speechless.

"You can't." It was Nancy who spoke, firmly and authoritatively. "You can't marry without our permission and we won't give it. We love you too much to see you ruin your life by marrying the first boy you fall in love with."

"Dieter isn't a boy: he's a man." Verity, too, rose from the table. "If you don't give permission I shall live with him anyway."

Jack blustered. Nancy hung on to the remnants of her self-control and reasoned. Verity was adamant. Neither of her parents doubted a word she said. It was no hysterical, girlish threat.

The marriage had taken place in St. Stephen's Church. As if to lay the lie to rumour and speculation as to its almost indecent haste, Jack had seen to it that it was the wedding of the year.

As her friends' daughters entered colleges, went dutifully in laughing groups to Boston's Convent of the Sacred Heart, held tennis parties and swimming parties, Nancy stood shell-shocked on New York's crowded pier and said goodbye to her daughter. Verity was remarkably composed. Nancy envied her her self-control. She couldn't see the beloved face for tears. Dieter, as always, was punctiliously polite. There would be a welcome for them any time in Germany.

Germany. Nancy's self-control abandoned her as they boarded the *Bremen* and Jack ushered her into the back of their waiting Rolls. Germany. It was another world. She began to cry helplessly.

"She doesn't even know the language! She's seventeen, Jack. *Seventeen*! How could we have allowed her to do it? She'll be wretchedly homesick. She'll be lonely. No friends. No family."

She groped in her crocodile-skin handbag for a handkerchief. "She's too young to realize what she's doing. It's just an adventure for her. Perhaps she never wanted to go to Wellesley at all? Perhaps this is just her way of escape?"

She gained no comfort from Jack. He sat, his face as immobile as if it were carved from stone. An engagement after two weeks of meeting: a wedding scarcely two months after. Christ. The whole of the eastern seaboard must believe his daughter to be pregnant.

"I'll pick up Shelby and the Lagonda at the apartment. I have to be in Washington for tonight."

"Yes." She stuffed her handkerchief back into her handbag. He didn't ask if she was staying in New York or returning to Hyannis. He didn't offer her any comfort. He was too busy nursing his bruised pride.

She had returned, desolate, to the Cape. Her days were spent playing solitary rounds of golf on a course buffetted by stiff Atlantic sea breezes and bounded by marshes and clumps of low-lying brush and wiry weeds. After a light and plain lunch she would button up her windbreaker, don a headscarf and walk for miles along the beach, oblivious of the wet breezes blowing in from Nantucket Sound. It was shortly after Verity's departure that she began to suffer from unaccountable attacks of fatigue. Then, dutifully accompanying Jack on one of his public appearances at the Metropolitan Opera House in New York, she had fainted. And subsequently seen Dr. Lorrimer.

Verity's light brown hair was pulled smoothly away from her forehead, circling her head in Brunhilde-style plaits. If she had been dressed in German national costume she could not have looked less American. Her eyes were bright, her face fuller than when she had left New York. There was no trace of homesickness or regret at her hasty marriage. It was hard for Nancy to realize that Verity was still only seventeen as she said, after Dieter had kissed her hand, clicking his heels in a manner that embarrassed Nancy, "Well, Mother. Don't you think it's time you returned home?"

"I beg your pardon?"

The Mezriczkys' gold-embossed luggage was being transferred to their suite. Nancy had been about to say how marvellous it was to see them. Verity withdrew grey leather, gauntlet gloves and began to move away from reception and towards the public rooms. Her suit was severe with wide shoulders and narrow skirts with modest side-slits. It was a Paris original and the material had been specially woven. The emerald on the third finger of her left hand was so large that it seemed impossible that it should not weigh her hand down.

"When are you returning home? After your letter I naturally wrote to father. He said your age and attendant condition were responsible for your behaviour but that he was coming here to take care of you. Where is he?"

Nancy tried to stifle the slow, burning anger that Verity's unexpected attitude was arousing in her.

"Your father certainly tried to take care of me," she said acidly. "At the present moment he's presumably back in Washington."

Verity raised her eyebrows. Nancy felt the sickness that usually only assailed her in the morning flood over her like a tide. This was not what she had endured weeks of pain and humiliation for. She had expected hugs and kisses and a joyful family reunion. A full-length mirror caught them both as they paused at the entrance of the large salon. Verity's severe suit and heavy features made her look several years older than she was.

Nancy's bare sun-tanned legs, white, silk, halter-necked sundress and dazzling, thickly lashed eyes, made her look years younger. A stranger would have assumed them to be sisters.

She halted and said, holding Verity's eyes through the mirror, "As to my age, I hardly think even you can imagine I'm so ancient that it can affect my health."

A dull red flush stained Verity's cheeks. Nancy immediately regretted her words. Verity had acquired an assurance and an impeccable manner of dress, but she would never be as beautiful as her mother. Her words had ben unforgivable. She took her hand.

"There's a cold lunch waiting for us in my suite. You must both be tired and hungry. How is your home? Can you speak German yet? Why were you so long in arriving?"

Verity carefully withdrew her hand from Nancy's grasp and accompanied her silently.

Dieter said, "We travelled to Vienna first and stayed longer than we had anticipated."

"Oh," Nancy smiled brilliantly. They were not to know what that change of plan had cost her. "Prince

Felix Zaronsky is here. He has a home in Vienna. He tells me it is a beautiful city."

Too late, she remembered that Felix was not returning to his Viennese home because of the civil war and Nazi intrusion.

What on earth was Dieter thinking of, appearing at an hotel like Sanfords in full Nazi uniform? Surely he knew that Sanfords' guests were international? That he was bound to arouse antagonism? She would have to have a quiet word with him. She shrank from the thought. Accomplished hostess as she was, she had to search desperately for words when faced with her impressive-faced son-in-law. Even when talking to Verity, it was like talking to a stranger.

Perhaps when they were alone—when Dieter was no longer with them—they would be able to resume the ease of their old relationship? Verity's shyness, though now under control, was still a part of her personality. She would not feel free to discuss her new home while her husband was with them. Especially if some aspects of German life were unflattering. Reassured by this thought, Nancy led them into the Garden Suite.

The conversation became even more stilted. Dieter's boredom was obvious. Retrieving erring mothers-in-law was obviously not in his line. Nor was Madeira. When Nancy asked him how he liked the mass of sub-tropical flowers and the purple haze of the jacaranda blossom, he had said merely that he preferred Munich and the mountains. His own country had the most magnificent scenery in the world.

"Is it very pretty?" Nancy had asked desperately.

Dieter had looked at her pityingly. "Germany is not pretty. It is majestic."

"Of course."

He had declined the wine and showed no intention of leaving her alone with Verity. In the end it was Verity that said she had a blinding headache and was retiring to her room. Nancy was ashamed at the relief she felt.

"I've arranged a small dinner party for this evening. On the terrace, here. I've invited Reggie Minter, the son of the tinplate magnate, and Lady Helen Bingham-Smythe. She's your age, Verity, and very sweet. She's recovering from a broken love *affaire* and would appreciate a friend."

How she had ever imagined that Verity could provide friendship for Helen, she didn't know. Verity had never provided friendship for anyone. Her own head was beginning to pound.

"I've also invited Bobo James and her current man-friend and Prince Zaronsky and Lady Bessbrook. They are all close friends and I want you to meet them."

Verity kissed her coolly on the cheek. Dieter shook her hand with the formality that never deserted him, and Nancy's eyes were drawn to the swastika on his breast.

When they had gone she lay down on her bed and put an eau-de-cologne-soaked handkerchief across her forehead. A year ago her daughter had been a rather introverted schoolgirl. Now she was as much a stranger as Dieter. She had asked when she was returning to America and had referred to her mother's age with barely-concealed insolence. There had been a brief moment when Nancy had had to restrain herself from slapping her daughter's face.

Presumably, Dieter's influence was paramount and he disapproved of wives who left their husbands. Jack's letter would also have been no help. She could quite well imagine how Jack would have depicted the situation. What she needed was time alone with Verity. Time to explain gently and lovingly that she had her own life to lead; but not with the man she had left Jack for.

"*Hell!*" she said aloud, and to no one. "Bloody, bloody *hell!*"

* * *

The Mezriczkys had been invited for welcoming cocktails at seven o'clock with Ramon Sanford. A gold-embossed card, delivered by a bellboy and signed by Villiers, requested Nancy's presence as well. Gritting her teeth, Nancy dressed with consummate care. No plunging, backless Parisian creation to offend her priggish son-in-law. Instead, she chose a full-length, plain black sheath dress of crèpe de chine with a white crèpe de chine jacket. With unnutterable relief, she saw that her son-in-law had abandoned his uniform for conventional evening dress.

Ramon's son-bronzed face was set in the hard, uncompromising lines that now seldom left it. He received the Mezriczkys courteously but exerted none of his usual charm. He barely acknowledged Nancy. Tessa was with him and she chattered happily to Verity although Nancy could see that her daughter was giving her very little encouragement. Marriage had not altered her incapacity for making friends.

Tessa was beginning to look slightly crushed and uncomfortable and Nancy rescued her by intruding on them by saying: "Please excuse us, Tessa. The Montcalms are old family friends and haven't seen Verity since she was a child."

Why, in God's name, she thought as they approached Georgina and Charles, did she feel an affection for Tessa Rossman that she did not feel for her own daughter? Perhaps slow, mental instability was also a sign of her deteriorating condition. She could think of no other reason.

As the Montcalms and Mezriczkys exchanged politeness, Nancy was aware of an undercurrent of hostility. Introducing Dieter to Charles Montcalm had been a mistake. It was as if each knew instinctively the political ideals of the other.

Another few minutes were spent introducing her

daughter and son-in-law to the exuberant Polly Watertight. The expression on Dieter's face was one of distaste. With a shock, Nancy saw an exact replica of it on her daughter's.

Ramon's arm was around Tessa as he moved with assured ease from group to group, studiously avoiding any further contact with the Mezrickys.

"You're making an utter fool of yourself, Mother," Verity suddenly said as they moved away from the unabashed Polly towards the Michaeljohns. "It's patently obvious that Sanford barely knows who you are, let alone loves you."

Nancy felt as if she had been struck across the face. The Michaeljohns were upon them and she could not reply.

The half-hour struck. The privileged few who were dining with Ramon and Tessa drifted together. Other twosomes, foursomes and sixsomes made their way into Sanfords' opulent dining room. Nancy's party strolled with happy anticipation of a pleasant evening, towards the mauve and green decor of the Garden Suite.

Chapter Twenty-Two

The staff had set the table on the balcony, and had swung gaily coloured fairylights from the palm that flourished in Nancy's corner to the two jacaranda trees that gave Vere shade.

"What a lovely idea, eating out of doors. It's like a picnic," Venetia said enthusiastically as they were seated.

"A very *civilized* picnic," Hassan said drily. "Not like your incomprehensible English sorties to the countryside with only ants and bugs and rain for company."

Everybody laughed—except Dieter and Verity.

Venetia laid her hand lightly on Hassan's exquisitely suited arm. "Darling, your trouble is that you're simply not happy away from sand!"

Again there was laughter. Nancy saw Dieter almost physically flinch with distaste as Lady Bessbrook addressed her friend's lover.

The hors d'oeuvres were slices of roasted grouse, woodcock livers, and water chestnuts accompanied lavishly by champagne.

It should have been a pleasant, easy, casual meal. Instead, it was the hardest dinner Nancy had ever held. Verity's heavy features never lifted. She spoke when she was spoken to. She barely touched her food or champagne. She never once laughed. Nancy tried desperately hard to believe that it was somehow Dieter's influence, but beneath the table their hands would touch and when she looked at him, Verity's eyes held an expression that was one of adoring worship. The tiny expressions of marital devotion were returned. The Mezriczkys were to all talents and purposes a devoted couple.

Nancy found herself looking again and again at the face of her son-in-law. His colouring was the same as Vere's. Blond hair, blue eyes, light skin. But there the similarity ended. One was immediately drawn to Vere's quiet, understated English charm and equally repelled by Dieter's almost indecent Nordic good looks.

"I understand Syrie has left for Washington," it was Verity: speaking to her without being spoken to for the first time.

Ridiculously, Nancy felt flustered. She hadn't realized that Verity had known of Syrie's visit to Sanfords. "Yes, darling, she returned some days ago."

"But *not* to Washington." Verity's voice was flat and colourless and unrelenting. "I understand you spoiled things between her and daddy and that she's had to go back to Chicago."

Nancy tried to speak but the words wouldn't come. She had never imagined that Verity had known of her father's *affaire* with Syrie. It was the sort of truth she had gone to endless lengths to protect her from. In her innocence she had thought Verity would have been devastated by such knowledge. Now, in public, she mentioned it as casually as if she were referring to Garbo's performance in

Queen Christina.

"I didn't spoil anything," Nancy said quietly, "and I think the remainder of this conversation is best conducted later, in private."

To her immense gratitude, Bobo had immediately grasped the situation and Venetia, Felix and Reggie and Helen were helpless with laughter as she described the departure of Viscountess Lothermere.

Chicken halibut, dauphine potatoes, and cucumber salad replaced the crawfish. Rhein wine replaced the sherry. That, at least, should please the apparently unpleasable German.

Bobo was giving her own version of the banned *Ulysses* and Helen Bingham-Smythe's eyes were round and unbelieving.

Nancy was glad of the respite. What had happened? How could Verity possibly make it so cruelly plain that her loyalty was with her father and Syrie? Had her own behaviour in leaving Jack and Hyannis aroused such resentment that this was its only outlet? She shook her head and tried to clear it. If Verity had known of Jack's *affaire* with Syrie, she had known before she had arrived in Madeira. Before she had even received her letter from Hyannis. She had accepted it and not even felt bound to tell her mother what was happening. She hadn't *cared* whether Nancy was being hurt or not. Cold water seemed to drip down Nancy's spine. She was being ridiculous. Of course, Verity would have cared. They had always been close. Jack had scarcely been a visitor. Verity would have kept the knowledge to herself to spare her pain.

There was more laughter. Sherbets with rum punch followed the chicken and wine and then the moment that Nancy had subconsciously been dreading, arrived.

"When is Hitler going to toe the line?" Reggie asked Dieter in a friendly manner. Tact had never been one of Reggie's virtues. Venetia tried to talk too loud and too quickly about something else but Dieter's voice cut across hers.

"The Führer is a law unto himself."

"How convenient for the Führer," Bobo said idly and helped herself to a grape.

"There's nothing wrong with Hitler," Reggie said a trifle too hurriedly, seeing too late the spark of anger in Dieter's pale blue eyes. "He's simply whipping Germany into shape with typical Prussian thoroughness."

"He's not Prussian," Bobo corrected with the same affected languor.

"Isn't he? I thought all Germans were Prussians." History had never been Reggie's strong point.

"Germany has been humiliated enough," Dieter said icily.

Nancy closed her eyes. It was going to be a repeat of his Hyannis monologue. The one she had tried so hard to believe in.

"I know the lies of your country. They still believe we started the war in 1914. It is not true. The Versailles Treaty crushed us. It was vengeful and unjust."

"But the Weimar Republic . . ." Venetia began.

Dieter rounded on her, his eyes pinpricks of brilliant blue light. "The Weimar Republic was dominated by degenerate homosexuals and was destined to fail. Germany will determine its own future. It will never again be a pawn to be moved around the chessboard of Europe by the United States and the British."

"I say, steady on, old man," Reggie admonished.

"No. Please continue. I find the subject completely fascinating," Bobo said, resting her chin on the back of one hand. "I keep hearing so much about the new Germany and understanding so little." She reached for another grape. "If Hitler's new Germany is so marvellous, why have all the Jews who can afford to been emigrating?"

"Germany is for Germans—now Jews!" The words were spat out with a viciousness that damped the previous gaiety.

"Not even German Jews?" Bobo's voice was barely interested. She was examining her grapes with great care.

"There are no such things as German Jews or Polish Jews or Czech Jews. Only Jews."

"I see. How simply you put it. Silly of me not to have seen that before."

Again Venetia tried to turn the conversation elsewhere but Dieter, silent for so long, was now impossible to stop.

"Fascism is the greatest creed that Western civilization has ever given to the world!"

"A creed that abhors modern art, modern music, Jews, Masons and Catholics?" Felix said contemptuously. "That closes art galleries and opera houses if the paintings or music have been created by Jews? That makes Jew-baiting such a national sport that they sell all they possess, beg and borrow in order to leave a country that has been their home and their parents' and their grandparents' and their great-grandparents' home? That has defiled Vienna's Ring, the most magnificent boulevard in Europe, so that the Viennese can no longer sit in peace and sip their beer and coffee in sidewalk cafés and stroll and talk and enjoy the beauty of their city? There is no beauty left in Vienna now. The Nazis have destroyed it. Fascism is as destructive as Communism. Both creeds are an abomination."

There was a stunned silence. Prince Felix Zaronsky, gay, laughing, and carefree, had never before displayed such vehement feeling over anything other than a pretty woman or the fall of a dice.

He's like Nicky, Nancy thought, desperately trying to defuse the situation and failing. He's like Nicky. On the surface a pleasure-loving playboy and below the surface a passionate revolutionary. Her suggestion that they go inside for coffee was ignored.

"Is it true about the Jews?" Helen asked. "Is it true that they are having to leave their country?"

"They don't *have* a country!" There was foam at the corners of Dieter's mouth.

Verity said carelessly, "What is all the fuss about? They are just Jews and so must be got rid of."

"Verity, you can't mean that! You don't understand . . ."

Verity faced her mother unflinchingly. "I understand perfectly, Mother. Jews are nothing but pigs and should be treated as such."

Bobo rose slowly to her feet, the scraping back of her chair drowning Nancy's inarticulate cry.

"*I* am a Jew," she said, as if she were saying that she was cold or warm or sleepy or happy. "A hundred and fifty years ago my great-grandfather grew tired of having his *shetl* invaded and embarked for America with my great-grandmother and my grandfather. Along with hordes of Irish, Scots, Poles, Italians. America is a wonderful melting pot. You would never have known if I hadn't told you, would you? You would have continued to eat with me, to drink with me and talk about something you know nothing about. I doubt, with your background and upbringing, if you have ever in your life known a Jew socially. You hate an abstract idea and have turned it into a terrible reality. There's no need for you to leave the table to avoid contaminating your racial purity by eating with me. The revulsion is mutual. Goodnight."

She turned. Her silk lamé dress clung as tightly as her curves would allow, her skirt so narrow that every step was a work of art. Her dignity was breathtaking.

"You will excuse us?" Reggie's discomfort was acute. Helen's face strained and white.

Felix took Nancy's hand and kissed it. "Goodnight, *ma chère.* You can't choose your son-in-law. Let the knowledge be a comfort to you."

Venetia kissed Nancy on the cheek. She stared at Verity for a long second and then accompanied her lover, who had shown such an unexpected side to his character.

"*Une animale curieuse*," Nancy heard her say to Felix as they disappeared through the door of her salon. She knew Venetia was referring to her daughter.

Hassan alone remained. He blew a wraith of cigar smoke upwards and leant back in his chair, regarding Dieter and Verity as he would two animals in a zoo. At last he turned to Nancy.

"Thank you, my dear Nancy, for a most entertaining and informative evening. It is one that has changed my life."

For one wild moment Nancy wondered if the dark-skinned Hassan was going to embrace racial purity too.

"I always said I would remain a bachelor until I met a woman worth more than rubies. I have. Goodnight."

"I hope there won't be a repeat of tonight," Verity said, taking a cigarette from Dieter's initialled, gold case. "A Jewess is bad enough, but a black . . ."

"Get out!" Nancy was on her feet, her eyes blazing and her face ashen. *"Get out! Out of my sight! Out of my room!"*

Dieter stood and moved his hand towards Verity's shoulder.

"Leave my daughter with me. I want to talk to her!"

"I don't think so, Mother. Not tonight . . ."

"Stay where you are!"

Verity blanched at the ferocity in her voice. Ugly spots of colour were staining Dieter's unblemished skin.

"*Heil Hitler*," he shouted and as he gave the Nazi salute Nancy knocked the offending arm so violently that he lost his balance and fell crashing against the table. Half empty bottles of champagne and brandy and grapes and cutlery fell around him.

"Get out! Out! OUT!"

There was a trace of chicken on his jacket and his hands were smeared with crushed grapeskins.

"Jew lover!" he hissed as he struggled to his feet, his eyes ferocious. "Immoral, decadent, American bitch!"

He slammed the door behind him so savagely that it rocked on its hinges.

Nancy rounded on her daughter. *"Tomorrow morning you will go to Bobo and apologize!"*

"I will do no such thing."

"Bobo is a friend of mine. She gave up an evening with far more exciting company, just to welcome you here. Do you realize the things that you have said? The colossal *rudeness* you exhibited. The *ignorance*?"

"No ignorance at all, Mother. Nothing was said that wasn't true."

Nancy's legs would no longer support her. She sank on to a sofa. Verity remained seated a few yards away, coolly smoking.

"When did you become a Nazi?" she asked at last.

"I've always been one. I just didn't know the right word for it."

"You haven't. You were a nice, normal little girl. You used to go swimming, sailing, enjoy clambakes and strawberry festivals."

"No I didn't. I endured them."

"You were shy."

"I was never shy." The grey eyes, so different from her own and Jack's, regarded her with something like contempt. "I was simply bored. I had nothing in common with those dreadful girls at Dorchester and those terrible daughters of your friends. I had nothing in common with anyone until I met Dieter."

Nancy stared across the room at her. What had she done? Where had she gone wrong? How, in simply loving her, could she have created this charmless, unpleasant, unloving, unlovable, intolerant creature that called Jews pigs and was able to say without the slightest discomfiture that they should all be got rid of? Verity knew nothing about Jews. By accident, not design, their social circle had never included Jews.

She remembered Bobo's withering assessment of Dieter. People like Verity and Dieter had no need to know Jews to hate them. They were unreasoning, unthinking. They were Nazis.

She made one last attempt. Very quietly, very slowly she said, "What do you think we should do with Jews, Verity?"

"Burn them," Verity said and blew a cloud of cigarette smoke into the air. When she rose to her feet and left the room, Nancy did not detain her.

The waiters entered to clear the table and Nancy dismissed them. Maria hesitantly entered and was also dismissed. She remained sitting on the sofa, staring into space. She could see Verity at eight years old when it had been her birthday party, quietly watching while the others played. Verity at ten, never part of the crowd, always alone. "A strange little girl," friends had said affectionately. "She'll grow out of it". Verity at fourteen, receiving her mother's goodnight kiss but never proffering one. Always contained; always unemotional; always an enigma.

There was a knock on the door. She did not bother to answer it. Even when she saw it was Ramon she was too numb to react other than to give a surprise, "Oh!"

"I've just heard a condensed version of what happened, from Venetia and Felix."

His voice was grim. She couldn't see the expression on his face because she couldn't bear to look.

"I'm sorry," she said. She couldn't move. She should be offering him a drink, asking him to sit down. It was his hotel and his guests and her daughter and son-in-law had insulted one of them on a scale that was unprecedented.

"Why have you to be sorry?" he asked harshly, striding across to the drinks trolley and pouring himself a whisky. "You're not a Nazi, are you?"

"Don't be ridiculous." She began to cry.

"Nancy . . ."

"Just ask them to leave."

Her hands covered her face. She was sobbing uncontrollably. His arms were around her, his deep voice urgent. "Come back to me, Nancy. Let's stop hurting each other. Let's love again."

"I can't! Oh Jesus Christ! I can't! *I can't*!"

His arms fell. He stood looking down at her for a long time but she did not turn to him. Even now, when he knew what she must be suffering over her unspeakable daughter and detestable son-in-law, she still did not need him.

"I'll see that they leave tonight," he said, regaining his lazy drawl. "As I will."

When she knew he had left the room, she stumbled towards the bed and lay across it, crying, crying, crying.

She didn't remember sleeping. Six months ago she had had a husband who, if not faithful, she did at least respect. The sight of him masked and bloody and with the damning syringe in his hand had destroyed that illusion for ever. She had had a daughter she had loved unreservedly. A daughter she had thought of as compensation for the hollowness of her marriage. A daughter she believed had loved her as totally as she had been loved. Now she knew that the shy, undemonstrative little girl had been not shy but simply cold. There had been no demonstrations of affection because none had been felt. Her father had been the idol of her life and had come crashing off his pedestal in one terrible, brief conversation. He was a murderer. He had killed—not with his own hands—but just as effectively. The sickness was worse that morning. Maria had abandoned all immediate plans of marriage. Something was terribly wrong with Mrs. Cameron and she could not leave her until she regained her strength. Despite the heat of the sun, Nancy felt cold as she slipped on her dark glasses to hide puffed and blue-shadowed eyes and went in search of Senora Henriques. She dreaded facing the housekeeper after the debacle of the previous evening, yet it had to be done. She pulled her cardigan closer around her shoulders.

Senora Henriques smiled and made no mention of the disturbance that had taken place in Mrs. Cameron's suite. She flicked efficiently through the list of new arrivals and departures: the necessity to arrange a birthday party for Lady Helen Bingham-Smythe who would be eighteen the following week; the dismissing of a light-fingered footman; the engaging of two still-room maids from Oporto. Black coffee was served to them and after the third cup Nancy began to feel a semblance of normality.

"Mr. Sanford has asked me to inform you that Count and Countess Mezriczky have decided to curtail their visit and join the liner on which they arrived. It sails this evening." Her voice was expressionless. "Unfortunately, Count Mezriczky had a bad fall late last night and broke two ribs. The doctor has strapped them and I believe the count is reasonably comfortable."

Nancy poured herself another coffee and wondered what obscenity Dieter had uttered to provoke Ramon to such an act of violence.

"Mr. Sanford also asked me to give you copies of the newspapers from London that were aboard the liner. Will that be all?"

"Yes. Thank you, Carlota."

She poured herself a fourth cup of coffee and opened a copy of *The Times.* A small paragraph on an inside page had been ringed in red to draw her attention.

Senator Jack Cameron has announced his intention of instituting divorce proceedings against his wife, the former Miss Nancy Leigh O'Shaughnessy. Senator Cameron is citing Ramon Sanford, the millionaire playboy and head of the wine shipping house of Sanfords . . .

Nancy could not read on. A less literate paper simply carried the headline: *"Senator seeks divorce from Panther-Loving Wife".* A photograph of Ramon had been superimposed upon one of Nancy when she had attended the Arts Ball. It was the best the press could do. To their chagrin there were no photographs of the couple together in existence.

She rang for fresh coffee and leaned her head against the high back of the leather chair.

She now had no reason to stay. She should ring for Villiers and ask him to make her a booking on the first available liner. Though not the one carrying Dieter and Verity back to Europe. The coffee arrived and she nursed the cup in her hand.

Where would she go? Not back to Washington or New York or Hyannis. Not back to America at all. England then, and Molesworth? Vere would welcome her but his domestic life would be nearly as chaotic as her own. He would be divorcing Clarissa and devoting all his attention to Alexia. She would be *de trop* at Molesworth—especially if she brought to it her own private scandal. Private no longer, she thought, looking distastefully at the garish newsprint. One inhabitant of Molesworth seeking a divorce would cause headlines enough. Two would reduce the press to gibbering incoherence.

There was Paris, Rome, Venice. She shrank from the thought of lonely hotel rooms and meaningless days. Here at Sanfords she had a purpose. She had friends: Bobo and Venetia and Georgina. None of them showed any signs of leaving. Charles had returned to his naval duties and in Georgina's eyes had not expressed sufficient regret at having to do so.

Ramon had said that he was leaving. It had been nearly four months since she had stood in Dr. Lorrimer's hatefully opulent office. There could not be much time left for her. She would spend it at Sanfords. She would paint and help Senora Henriques and try not to think of Ramon.

Summoning the remains of the strength that was fast deserting her, she rose to her feet and crossed to the open French window, intending to take her usual route to the rocks and her painting. The easel and oils would already be waiting for her: as would a wicker basket of refreshment a little more suitable than the cheese and rough red wine that Giovanni favoured.

He was striding purposefully towards her office. She backed away quickly and rushed to the door, opening it with trembling hands. What did he want of her? To tell her himself of the Mezriczkys' departure? To be angry with her? To be kind? Whatever it was, she could not bear it. She could not bear to be in his presence and not to touch him. He was leaving. He had said so the previous evening. Perhaps that was what he was coming to tell her. Whatever it was, she hadn't the courage to stand only inches away from him and listen to the deep timbre of his voice, see the strong movement of his hands, feel the powerful nearness of his body. She had endured unspeakable horrors in the past few days—she could not endure that.

When she entered her suite, panting as if from a long run, it was to find Zia sitting on the terrace in a gown of loosely flowing shining silk. A rope of pearls encircled her waist and hung in a long single strand, almost ankle-length. At the end was a huge sapphire and she was toying with it, letting it fall as Nancy entered.

"Ramon tells me he is going to leave Madeira," she said in her deep velvety voice. "I came to ask you if you would stay."

"Yes, I'll stay. I don't seem to have anywhere else to go."

She very seldom felt nauseous through the day but now the sickness came in full force.

"Excuse me," she said to a startled Zia and hurried quickly to the bathroom.

Zia rose to her feet in consternation, intent on following her. Maria forestalled her. "Mrs. Cameron will be all right in a few moments' time. It is the sickness."

"The sickness?" Zia's sea-green eyes were baffled. "Is Mrs. Cameron ill? Why didn't she tell me? Has she seen the doctor?"

"Babies don't need doctors," Maria said practically.

Zia swayed on her feet.

Maria watched her closely. It had been no casual slip of the tongue. Mrs. Cameron was pregnant and seemed to have no intention of doing anything about it. There had been no reconciliation between her and Ramon and yet Ramon Sanford was looking as tortured and haggard as Nancy. True, he continually had the little English girl at his side but she knew from his valet that he was drinking heavily in the privacy of his suite: that his nights were sleepless: that his gaiety and mocking laughter were shed with his evening clothes. It was all very mysterious and Maria could not begin to understand it. Something had happened between them and pride was keeping them apart. A reconciliation had to take place—especially now the baby was on its way. Zia Sanford might be able to do what she, Maria, could not.

"Brandy," Zia croaked. "A glass of brandy, quick."

Maria watched interestedly as the elegant Zia Sanford clutched with trembling hands at the brandy glass, gulping the liquid down as if it were medicine. Without the beautifully-applied cosmetics there would have been no colour in her face.

"I must lay down, rest."

Maria helped her to the door. Outside the three aides who had escorted her from her own room to the Garden Suite took one look at her and practically carried her back to her flower-filled *boudoir.*

Mrs. Sanford had suffered a relapse. Her heavy velvet drapes shut out the sunlight and the cooing of the doves. The champagne and orange juice and petits-fours were abandoned. Medicinal brandy took their place. She would speak to no one: not the doctor, not Villiers, not even Ramon.

Ramon, believing his mother's condition to have been caused by the announcement that he was leaving, revised his plans. They were plans he would have found virtually impossible to execute anyway.

Nancy felt guilty. If Zia hadn't attempted the long walk to the Garden Suite, she may never have collapsed. Daily she went to see Zia and daily she was told that Mrs. Sanford was not receiving visitors.

The visit to Camara de Lobos could no longer be put off. To her everlasting relief Ramon was not present. Just Tessa and her quiet, charming parents and Reggie Minter and Helen. It was, all in all, a pleasant day. The Rossmans lived comfortably but quietly. The villa was not the usual showpiece to display Gauguins and Picassos and Oliver Messel decor in an attempt to establish the owner's wealth. The Vermeer in the main salon was an original and was there only because Mrs. Rossman had fallen in love with the picture. In an alcove nearby were four flower studies by an artist Nancy had never heard of and at the top of the balustraded staircase was a large crayonned picture of an owl—a childish signature in the corner said "Tessa Rossman, 1922".

A week after Zia's collapse Giovanni returned. He wanted to see the work she had been doing in his absence. He nodded his head, eyes glowing, rubbing his blunt-fingered, peasant hands together, almost rapturously.

"They are good. Good. Carreras, my dealer, wants to mount an exhibition. He offered twenty-five thousand dollars for your painting. I told him it was not for sale. He wants to know who painted it, where you are. I said nothing. Soon, soon . . ."

"Twenty-five thousand dollars," Nancy repeated in amazement. The money itself was negligible to a woman cushioned from birth by millions of dollars, but the millions had been earned by her grandparents, her parents, by investment and securities. Twenty-five thousand dollars for something *she* had done? It was incredible. She sat down on the rock, weakly.

"Twenty-five thousand dollars?" she said again, unbelievingly.

Giovanni grinned and nodded. "You must work hard. You will need at least six pictures. Six *good* pictures."

He was amused by her incredulity. "We must work," he said.

She nodded. Work was her only solace. For a few brief, blissful hours she was able to forget Ramon and enter a world where only colour and light and texture were important.

After half an hour or so Giovanni startled her by suddenly speaking. It was an unwritten rule that while working no conversation ever took place.

"Artists are a rare breed of people. They see things not obvious to the eyes of others."

"Yes." She assumed he was talking in the abstract.

"Yourself, for instance."

"Me?" She halted, her brush poised in mid-air.

"I see the change in you and I wonder why you have not told me. Me, to whom you tell everything."

"Because I was happy about the painting. Excited at the thought that anyone should want to exhibit my work. I didn't want to spoil anything by talking about my daughter and her political beliefs."

This time it was Giovanni's brush that remained poised.

He said carefully, like a man about to confront a fifteen-year-old girl with an awesome truth. "That sundress reveals your breasts. Have you not noticed the difference in them?"

Nancy stared down at herself in surprise. Her figure *had* changed. Her breasts were fuller and heavier than they had been. The previous afternoon a new Shantung dress had been discarded and replaced by an old favourite, shaped more loosely. She had not thought about it twice. She was leading a relatively inactive life. Reading on the terrace; sunbathing with Georgina. There were no hectic walks along Nantucket Sound to disperse the excess pounds of fat. No energetic rounds of golf on the Hyannis links. It was natural enough that she would put on weight.

"I used to walk a lot," she said. "Miles and miles every day. Madeira is not a country for walking. There are no long beaches—only mountain cliffs dropping sheer to the sea. There are no golf courses and though I do play tennis, I haven't had the energy for it lately."

"*Mama mia!*" Giovanni exclaimed and laid his brush down. "You have told me many things in the hours we have spent alone down here. Now it is my turn to tell you something, but not about myself. Never that. If the world wants to know about the life of Giovanni Ferranzi it will have to be learned through my paintings. There will be no biographies, no tiresome interviews with philistine reporters."

Nancy suppressed a smile. "What is it you want to tell me?"

On the rocks a few feet away from them the sea pounded in sprays of surf. Above them creepers and shrubs and massive palms provided a solid background of greenery. From the angle at which they were sitting not even Sanfords' rose-red roofs gleamed through the foliage.

"That you are with child," Giovanni said.

She laughed. "Giovanni, I'm thirty-five years old."

"My mother was still having babies when she was a decade older than that."

"But I can't have children. I wanted more after Verity but the doctor said it was not possible."

Giovanni shrugged dismissively. "Doctors, what do they know? A different man, a different result. It is that simple."

She was no longer laughing. Unthinkingly her hand had cupped the heavy fullness of her breasts. The sickness every morning, the menstruation that had ceased. She gazed down at her breasts and saw the pale blue veins beneath the honey-gold of her skin. The veins that had not been visible since she had been pregnant with Verity. Wonderingly, she ran her hand over her belly. Beneath the soft silk of her dress she could feel the change: the rounding, the fullness.

"When?" she asked dazedly aloud, and knew the answer. When they had picknicked in the mountains and made love by the banks of the icily rushing Ribiera de Janela. How many weeks ago had that been? Six? Eight? So many things had happened that she had lost all track of time.

"I can't be! It isn't possible!"

Giovanni did not bother to contradict her.

She stared unseeing at the canvas before her. A baby. Ramon's baby. The brilliance of the sun seared her eyes. She was trembling violently. She had been given a respite. She was pregnant and she was going to carry the life within her to full term. She *must* carry it to full term. The brilliance of the sun seared her eyes. She felt weak with wonder and joy.

"Oh God," she said pleadingly to the Deity she had doubted. "Let me have the baby! *Please* let me have my baby!" and she took the canvas from the easel and replaced it with another. There was no more darkness in her mind. Only hope. Her next painting would be as full of joy as her others had been of grief.

Giovanni drank from the neck of his wine bottle, and returned to his work. Perhaps she would allow him to be the godfather . . . He would like to be godfather to a child of a woman like Nancy Leigh Cameron.

Chapter Twenty-Three

Dr. Oliveira finished examining her and nodded, puzzled. "Certainly there is a baby. Perhaps, under the circumstances, you would prefer it if there was an early miscarriage?"

Nancy stared at him. "I don't understand you. Are you saying I will miscarry?" Fear was naked in her eyes.

He said gently, "A woman in your condition cannot carry a baby full term, Mrs. Cameron. Whatever life is left for you will be shortened considerably by the attempt."

"But I *must* have the baby. I *must*!" Her eyes were fanatical.

He sighed and said carefully, "The choice, of course, is yours. I can only give you my advice. So far the symptoms of your disease have been slight. There have been fainting attacks and nosebleeds. However, with the added strain of pregnancy, your illness is going to be more apparent."

She twisted her hands tightly in her lap. "In what way,

Dr. Oliveira?"

"Your tiredness is going to increase; as is the feeling of cold you experience and keep so silent about."

Subconsciously Nancy touched the hem of the light cashmere shawl she had begun to take everywhere with her. The little Portuguese doctor's eyes were sharp.

"Your hair will lose its lustre; your nails become brittle."

"Is that all?" There was relief in her voice. "It seems a small price to pay to carry a child."

Dr. Oliveira's eyes were kind. "I am not an expert on blood diseases, Mrs. Cameron. I shall, of course, write to your New York specialist. He will be able to give me much more information. That is, if you insist on attempting to carry the baby."

His eyes held hers steadily. "My personal advice is for an abortion. Especially under the rather unusual circumstances."

She turned away from him and stared out over the sea. He was not talking about her illness. He was alluding to the parentage of her child. He knew the father was Ramon; as would everybody else. She would have to leave the island.

"I intend to have the baby in Portugal," she said with calm determination. "I would appreciate it if you could attend me there through my pregnancy and birth."

Dr. Oliveira spread his hands wide in resignation. "If you insist on carrying the child I will give you every assistance possible. However . . ." His sharp, black eyes were bleak. ". . . you must understand clearly, Mrs. Cameron, that although there is the possibility that you will carry the child and that it will be healthy, there can be no possibility of a recovery for you from the birth."

A small pulse beat in her throat. Her twisting fingers were stilled.

"You will hemorrhage, Mrs. Cameron. It is inevitable."

"And die?"

He nodded.

Her smile was haunting in its sadness and sweetness. "I think, Dr. Oliveira, that I would prefer to die giving life than die slowly, day by day."

Dr. Oliveira nodded. She was steadfast in her decision and he accepted it. He doubted if she would carry the baby to full term but miracles had happened before. Mrs. Cameron carried with her her own brand of magic and magic and miracles went hand in hand. It was possible. He would do his utmost to see that it became a reality.

"Whereabouts in Portugal do you intend to stay? It would be advisable to be within easy reach of Lisbon or Oporto."

Already his mind was on blood transfusions: on the possibility that he might have been wrong in his prognosis. That if she was fed with the right haemotinics, if she had a transfusion immediately she started to hemorrhage, that her death would not be inevitable.

"Lisbon," she said, her twisting fingers once more relaxed in her lap. She had thought about where to go all the previous night. She had dismissed Ireland as being too damp and Switzerland as being too popular with members of her own set. She wanted peace and seclusion. The answer had been obvious. She would have the baby in Lisbon. Ramon's Portuguese blood had always dominated over his American blood. He would have wanted his child to be born in Portugal. The Sanford family home was in Oporto. If Ramon journeyed to the mainland, Oporto was the city he would return to, not Lisbon.

Dr. Oliveira rose to his feet. "Then I will attend you in Lisbon, Mrs. Cameron."

She smiled at him, shook his hand and, pulling her shawl lightly over her shoulders, walked out into the garden.

She no longer dressed lavishly for Sanfords' cocktail parties and dinners, for she no longer attended them. Occasionally she would dine with friends: Felix and Venetia and perhaps Costas and the now seemingly tamed Madeleine. The sultan and Marisa often spent an hour sitting on her terrace over daiquiris before joining the pleasure-loving throng in the public rooms. Marisa had managed to accomplish what Nancy thought impossible—to present bull-fighting in a new and acceptable light.

"I hate it," Nancy said one evening as they sat in the dusk, fireflies flirting around the lamps, iced mint juleps making a refreshing change from the endless flow of champagne. "It's like fox hunting. A cruel sport."

The sultan had laughed. "I thought you were half English. How can you disapprove of their national sport?"

"It's only the national sport of a certain section of English society. *My* section. My American upbringing has disastrous results as far as my mother's relatives are concerned. I never have and never will partake in a fox hunt."

Marisa had made a rude noise. "Fox hunting is a sport that requires no skill or courage; except for sitting a horse and a child of ten can sit a horse. In bullfighting a matador risks his life." Her eyes flashed. "When I have thrust the banderillas in the bull's neck and I dismount for the kill, I stand in the sand of the ring and it is only the bull and myself. And then . . ." Her tiny body was tense, erect, as if she were once again in the bull ring. ". . . and then I plunge my sword into the back of his skull and the bull is dead and I am alive!"

Nancy shuddered.

Marisa said impatiently, "Every bull that is ever born is eventually killed by man. Bulls bred for the ring live in glory and die with honour, not like the emasculated lives of bulls bred for beef. There is no glory or bravery in *their* deaths. The fighting bull lives freely and wildly: for four, five or six years—not a brief two-year span of bulls that are bred for food. Then, when he dies, it is fighting. Showered with flowers. Applauded by hundreds. If *I* were a bull I would much, much rather be a bull reared for the ring than a pathetic, domestic animal, reared only to be slaughtered for meat!"

A knock at the door startled her. She had promised Sonny she would have a drink with him and was dressed in a gold embroidered kaftan that had been a gift from the sultan. She remembered Villiers. She had no need of his list. She had only to ask him to book her a passage to Lisbon.

Maria opened the door and Ramon strode into the room, his entrance almost a physical impact.

Maria did not need to be told to leave. She scurried through the still-open door. Had Mrs. Sanford told her son of Mrs. Cameron's condition? Holy Mary, what had she done? She hurried to find Luis and seek comfort in arms that she knew now never held another woman.

She sat down on her dressing table stool, the strength flooding from her legs. He remained standing; legs apart, a deep frown furrowing his brow. There was a slight tic at the corner of his jawline. He was dressed for dinner; in a white tuxedo and a shirt so lavishly embellished with *point de venise* lace that it would have looked effeminate on a lesser man. On Ramon it looked magnificent. The intricate ruffles that fronted it and circled his wrists emphasized his raw masculinity. His cuff links were large diamonds. The ruby glowed like fire on the little finger of his left hand. His usual easy, almost insolent negligence had been replaced by a tenseness that unnerved her. He looked like an animal about to spring.

Her heart was beating so fast and irregularly that she thought she was going to faint. She sat perfectly motionless, her hands folded in her lap. She must give an appearance of calm; she must remain controlled. There would be plenty of ships enroute to Lisbon. This time tomorrow she would be aboard one. This was the last time she would have to suffer such an encounter. The last time she would see the father of her child.

"Marry me," he said and there was no pleading, no asking, in his voice. It was a harsh command: an order.

She could not bring her breathing under control. Motionless, she was beginning to pant.

"I can't. I'm sorry." She sounded as if she were refusing a dinner invitation.

His eyes were terrible. "Agree to marry me or I leave this room and ask Tessa Rossman!"

"*No*!" The agonized cry flew from her lips before she could prevent it, her hand clutching wildly at her palpitating heart, her eyes desperate.

He was across the room, kneeling before her, his hands imprisoning her wrists, his eyes glazing.

"Why not? For the love of God, Nancy, why not? I don't *believe* what you said to me about our *affaire*. That it was simply fun and that you were now bored. I *refuse* to believe it. I *will* not believe it! I'll go to my grave and I will not *believe* those things you said to me! There have been no other men. I know, because I've had you watched every minute of every day. You love me, Nancy. I *know* it!"

"No . . ." The cry came from the very depths of her soul. "No. I did mean it. Truly."

He was on his feet, towering above her, demented with rage and incomprehension and longing.

"I don't believe it, Nancy. I . . . do . . . not . . . BELIEVE . . . it!"

She said nothing. Speech was beyond her.

"Damn you to hell!" he shouted savagely. "Tessa Rossman is worth a hundred of you! You've done me a great favour, Nancy. Thank you!"

He was leaving her.

"Ramon . . ." she gasped, but the door had slammed. Her whole will was bent on the effort of remaining seated, of not rushing after him. Seconds passed and merged into minutes. Her inner battle was over. She was still in her room. She had not run, crying his name, through Sanfords' marbled halls. It was a Pyrrhic victory.

She cancelled her arrangements for drinks with Sonny and ordered Maria to start packing. Villiers came and was shocked at her appearance. She was shivering, her skin bloodless. There was a liner leaving for Lisbon in the morning. The state rooms were all occupied but a single cabin could be obtained. She went to great lengths to ask about connections from Lisbon to New York. Ramon must not suspect that Lisbon was her final destination. Villiers meticulously informed her of sailing dates and times and offered to make the arrangements. She declined. She would do so herself in Lisbon. She thanked him and dismissed him. He had the distinct impression that she was barely aware of his presence.

The next morning she rose early, said a brief goodbye to an astonished Georgina, Bobo and Venetia and left a note for Prince Vasileyev. Then, at ten o'clock, accompanied only by Maria, she discreetly left Sanfords by a side entrance. Her gold-monogrammed luggage was piled neatly in the rear of the Rolls.Dark glasses hid her face.

At ten-thirty, Villiers sought a private audience with Mrs. Sanford. He was refused, as everyone else had been for the last week. He insisted. He even, to the stunned amazement of the staff, grew agitated. At ten forty-five he was admitted. At eleven o'clock Ramon was summoned to his mother's bedside.

Nancy was the last to board the *Helena.* Maria had hurried below to supervise the unpacking of the case containing Mrs. Cameron's requirements for the short, four day voyage to Lisbon. Nancy remained on deck. Anchor chains were hauled. Engines throbbed. The sleek liner began to move slowly away from Funchal's dockside and towards the open Atlantic.

Sanfords' rose-red roofs gleamed enticingly. Words learnt in childhood were recalled to memory. It seemed to her that Sanfords was "the sheening bright city built on a hill, barred by high gates" in *Dialogues of Mortality.*

She remembered Eroton's question: "Barred from all, Phraetes?"

"From all, Eroton, who do not desire to enter it more strongly than they desire all other cities."

"Then it is barred indeed and most men must let it go."

She had let it go. She had not desired to enter it and remain more than she had desired to spare her father from destruction.

The figures around the harbour were smaller. The bullocks and carts and white straw-hatted Madeirans like toy animals and people. Madeira rose from the depths of the sea, its perfume still lingering, carried on the breeze. Mimosa and bougainvillaea, hibiscus and strelitzia, birds-of-paradise and her favourite pastel-petalled franciscea. The jacaranda blossom drowned Funchal in a lilac haze. Flame trees were now in flower, their fiery blossom brilliant against the lush green foliage and the purity of white lilies. Madeirans said that their island was the original Garden of Eden. It had been hers, briefly.

Her hand gripped hold of the deckrail. A Daimler was racing crazily down to the dockside, flower sellers scattering hurriedly, bullocks breaking into a run to avoid being mown down. He leapt from the motor and raced towards the *Kezia*, deserted apart from its crew, ever since the abortive arrival of his lawyer.

More people began strolling to the deckrails to watch with curiosity as the *Kezia* began to ease away from its berth. It would have been prudent to wait until the *Helena* gained open waters. There was a mass of smaller shipping in the harbour and it was customary to give a liner the size of the *Helena* a clear passage. The *Kezia*, for all its magnificence, was smaller and sleeker than the *Helena*. From the far side of the harbour it headed not to open sea, but with increasing speed diagonally in the path of the liner. Now the rails were crowded with apprehensive passengers.

The captain blew warning blasts, all to no avail. The *Kezia* never wavered. She was heading at right angles, straight into the *Helena*'s path. The liner's engines were silenced. Until the *Kezia* continued on her erratic way, she had no way of outmanoeuvering her.

"Remove yourself at once," the *Helena*'s captain called angrily through a hailer.

"You are about to be boarded," the *Kezia*'s captain returned. Already a dinghy was being lowered into the water. The crowd's apprehension had turned to excitement. There was to be no collision. Their lives were not in danger.

"It's Sanford!"

"Who?"

"Sanford!"

Nancy hung on the deckrail. Had he lost his senses altogether? Was he going to kill her? Carry her off? He leapt agilely from the rocking dinghy to the hastily lowered rope ladder, shouldering his way through the restraining hands of the *Helena*'s crew as if they were no more than annoying flies.

"Nancy!"

The crowd around her parted, goggle-eyed. "*Nancy*!"

He was holding her so tightly that she could not breathe. His voice held something that, if she had not known Ramon better, she would have interpreted as a sob and then his mouth was on hers and there was no denying him.

Her lips parted willingly beneath his. She could not live without him. Whatever the cost, however high the price, she had to have him.

"Come on!" He was dragging her in his wake, male passengers applauding loudly—female ones sighing enviously.

"But Ramon . . ."

"*Come on!*"

The ladder seemed to stretch into infinity.

"I can't!"

"You can, or I'll put you over my shoulder."

There were cheers as she made her perilous descent. A handful of the *Kezia*'s crew helped her aboard the dinghy. Ramon leapt in beside her.

"*You bloody fool*!" he said angrily.

Of all the things she had expected, this was the least.

"Why didn't you tell me? How *dare* you go off to have my child as if it were nothing to do with me?" The *Kezia*'s crew hung on to every word.

"You don't understand . . ."

"*I do bloody understand*! I understand that you and my mother and your damn fool father have nearly ruined our lives! He never killed my father or even caused him to be killed! My father died of a cerebral hemorrhage. I should know! I was there!" He was gripping her wrists so tightly that she thought he must be stopping the flow of blood. "Your father's inept accomplice merely loosened the screw on his Lagonda. His Lagonda *did* crash. Because my father, like myself, enjoyed driving himself. Ever since, your father has believed he was responsible. He wasn't.

Every wheel on the Lagonda was still in place. I might add that I'm bloody glad he *did* believe he killed my father. He *could* have!"

"But he didn't?" She was crying with relief.

"Of course he didn't! Now, for God's sake, stop crying and kiss me!"

It took five minutes for the dinghy to reach the *Kezia*; another three for her to climb the swaying ladder to the blessed safety of the deck. Eight minutes and she had come to the most important decision of her life. She would marry Ramon and she would keep her secret. Their child would be born in wedlock. Nothing was going to spoil their newfound happiness. If she told him the truth now, he would be devastated. The months of her pregnancy would be spent futilely chasing from consultant to consultant and all to no avail. She had grown and matured in the months since she had stood in Dr. Lorrimer's claustrophobically hot surgery. She had discovered a strength of character she had never before suspected she possessed. She had learnt to live with her knowledge—treasuring each new day that dawned; grateful for pain as well as joy. Grateful for anything that denoted she was still alive and in love. The burden was hers and she would not share it. Her baby would be born and would have a father. In time, perhaps Ramon would marry again. There was Tessa Rossman, with her fair hair and sweet smile. Tessa would make a gentle and loving stepmother. The future was indeterminable. All that mattered now was that she was once again with Ramon, loving and loved.

Zia was a reborn woman. "Darling, isn't it wonderful news?" she exclaimed, walking across the grass of her garden to meet them with a spring in her step that had been absent for weeks. The champagne and orange juice and petits-fours were once again in evidence.

"I do think it would be hypocritical for you to remain in the Garden Suite and Ramon in his, under the circumstances. And I *do* want you to stay here until the baby is born. At least at Sanfords you can be sure of *some* privacy."

"Maria," Nancy cried, her hand flying to her mouth. "She's still aboard the *Helena*."

Ramon laughed, his arms tight around her waist where she had longed for them to be. "Then she'll just have to remain there until the *Helena* docks in Lisbon. I'll see to it that she's brought back immediately."

"But she *hates* travelling by sea."

"*Mae de Deus*!" Ramon said, his eyebrows flying upwards. "Luis was in my office this morning, ranting and raving and swearing he was following her at the earliest opportunity. If I don't stop him they'll be able to wave to each other as they cross in mid-ocean!"

"American divorces don't take too long, darling, do they?" Zia was saying as she crumbled the petits-fours and scattered them to the doves. "Not that I *mind* if the baby comes before you and Ramon are married. I don't mind about anything any longer." Her smile was soft, indecently radiant for a woman of nearly seventy. "I've already written to your father. There is nothing to spoil his future happiness now. His conscience will at last be clear and he will have his Gloria. Tell me," she sat in the shade of her parasol of peacock feathers, "what is Gloria like?"

"You'd better ask Ramon," Nancy said demurely, and was rewarded by a gleam in his eye that promised a volatile chastisement and even more volatile reconciliation.

Nancy abandoned her role as hostess. As her happiness

increased, so did her tiredness. The vast suite of rooms she occupied with Ramon opened out on to tropical gardens and her days were spent lying in the shade on a chaise longue, receiving a few visitors and close friends, and painting.

Ramon, ignorant as to the mysteries of pregnancy, remained unsuspecting and joyful, watching her hour after hour as first one canvas and then another was completed.

"They are good," Giovanni said with stark simplicity, at the end of May, when she nervously displayed the six finished paintings to him for the first time. "Very good. Carrera will be pleased. I'll take them to Rome tomorrow."

"Oh no! Not so soon!"

Giovanni raised bushy eyebrows.

"They need working on . . ."

"They are completed," Giovanni said with finality. "There is no need to be nervous. I, Giovanni, have told you that they are worthy of exhibition. Do you doubt me?"

"No . . . It's just that . . ." She lay back weakly. "I'm frightened, Giovanni. What if no one likes them?"

"Do *you* like them?"

Nancy looked long and hard at the six canvasses. She had put her heart into them: her hopes and fears.

"Yes," she said simply.

"Then it is enough."

At the end of May, Bobo and Hassan married in Paris and returned to Sanfords for their honeymoon. In Rome, Leopold Carrera mounted a small, exclusive exhibition. The work was that of a new, unknown artist. The paintings received guarded praise in the art columns of Italy's national papers. They received a good deal more when two of them were privately purchased and hung alongside such masters as Chagall and Labisse in a Florentine palace. When a national bank in Amsterdam approached the artist through Carrera, commissioning a painting for its new multi-million pound office, both the art critics of *The Times* and *Le Monde* took note.

Nancy was staggered. "I can't believe it," she said to Ramon, spreading out the newspapers, reading and re-reading the letter from Leopold Carrera. "He wants me to go to Rome. He wants me to acknowledge the paintings."

"*I* want you to acknowledge the paintings," Ramon said. "I also utterly forbid you to sell the other four without allowing me to see them first. I think Sanfords should have the privilege of acquiring one of them."

"I'll do all the paintings you want," she said, her face flushing with pleasure.

"You're not going to have time," Ramon said drily. "Not with world famous corporations inundating you with commissions."

"One corporation."

"Two," Ramon corrected. "This came at lunch time." He handed her a telegram from Carrera.

She gasped. "New World Oil! Why on earth do they want one of my pictures?"

"Because, sweet darling, they are obviously outstandingly, amazingly good. As I shall see for myself in a few days' time. We're going to Rome and you can personally silence all the rumours as to who the artist really is. Even you must have realized that the signature 'Nancy' would cause speculation."

"Yes . . . No . . . I didn't think it would matter. I didn't think anyone would *care* who had painted them." She hesitated and then said slowly: "And I didn't want to sign them with Jack's surname. He stifled me for so long. I could never have painted if I had remained with him. He would have laughed, ridiculed. Those paintings weren't done by Nancy Cameron. I shan't alter the signature; not until we are married."

His hands grasped hers tightly. "I love you," he said, his black eyes holding hers, sending a shiver of delight down her spine. "You're a neverending source of delight and surprise. What are you going to do next? Sculpt? Write? Compose?"

"Make love," she said, and slid into his arms.

In June, Georgina Montcalm returned reluctantly to her duties as a leading light in the upper echelons of British high society and African lilies clouded the hills around Funchal.

In July Vere wrote to say that Clarissa had agreed to an undefended divorce and hydrangeas turned the island from green to blue.

In August, Sonny's film starring Hildegarde was released and the world acclaimed her a star, second only to Garbo.

In September, yellow-petalled cassia flowers filled Ramon and Nancy's rooms and Reggie Minter announced his engagement to Helen Bingham-Smythe.

In October, allemanda bloomed and Jack and Nancy Cameron's divorce was made absolute.

"But we'll have to go to Lisbon for a civil wedding," Nancy protested as Ramon kissed her magnificent stomach and told his son that he would not be born a bastard. "The church won't marry us. All the priests in Funchal are Catholic."

"True." His eyes darkened thoughtfully.

Nancy was eight months pregnant and, despite her fatigue, more beautiful than ever. Her hair and nails had suffered as Dr. Oliveira had said they would. Maria had been reduced to tears in her efforts to restore her hair to its former shining glory. With resignation Nancy submitted herself to hour-long sessions of assiduous brushing, of daily applications of wheatgerm oil, conditioning her hair beneath hot, steaming towels. Maria's tireless ministrations saw to it that Nancy's rapidly declining health was not apparent in her looks. Her brittle nails she wore short, as always. It was how Ramon liked them. One of the first things he had noticed about her had been the softly buffed nails, naked of brilliant enamel. She could feel, daily, her strength decreasing and was filled with a strange serenity. Each day that she held Ramon, loved him, feasted her eyes upon him, was a gift from the gods that no one could take away from her.

Dr. Oliveira had urged strongly that she should sail to Lisbon for the birth. There were no facilities on Madeira. She would be able to receive no blood transfusions. Nancy had refused. Dr. Lorrimer had written fully and extensively: blood transfusions would only delay the inevitable. She told the agitated Portuguese doctor that she would remain on the island.

Ramon, for reasons of his own, agreed with her. He did not like the idea of her travelling to Lisbon when she was so far advanced in her pregnancy. Not even for the purpose of getting married. The journey would be strenuous and the press would be at the wedding in stifling force.

Nancy was now so weak that he carried her daily from her vast bed to the chaise longue beneath the shade of the trees. Dr. Oliveira viewed him with frustration, wishing he would grow anxious about his wife's condition and give him some excuse for breaking his vow of silence. Ramon remained unperturbedly unconcerned. Pregnancy was a mystery to him. He saw nothing odd in Nancy's weakness. If Zia had any doubts she kept them to herself. Nancy was, after all, thirty-five. After Verity's birth she had been told she would never carry a child again. It was not to be expected that her pregnancy would be without difficulties.

Ramon dismissed the idea of marriage in Lisbon and grinned. "We'll get married aboard the *Kezia.*"

"You're mad." She was laughing helplessly as he swung her bulk around in his arms.

"I'm not. Captains at sea can perform marriages. We'll put to sea and Captain Enrico can marry us. Afterwards, when the baby is born, we can have as many civil ceremonies as we like, if it will make you feel any happier."

"I couldn't possibly feel any happier," she said, as he lowered her gently to the ground and she took his face in her hands. "It isn't possible to be any happier than I am at this minute."

His kiss was long and tender and gradually they gravitated to the bed and she removed her kaftan and he lay naked against her, his arms round her, his hands warm and strong on her stomach as the baby kicked and moved with restless energy.

Bobo was summoned from Paris to be matron-of-honour. Helen Bingham-Smythe sailed in from London to be a bridesmaid. Tessa Rossman was overcome at being asked to be a second bridesmaid.

Champagne by the crateload was transferred to the *Kezia.* Sanfords' chef moved aboard to prepare a banquet, the likes of which had never been seen before. Her father's congratulatory telegram was ebullient; Vere's touching. Costas arrived in person, but without Madeleine. His new companion did not look a day over eighteen. The Bessbrooks cancelled their vacation and arrived for the ceremony, as did Sonny and Georgina Montcalm. Charles, ensconced in Malta with his fleet, was unable to attend but sent his best wishes in a way that

Georgina assured Nancy was quite effusive for Charles.

Charles was not given to superlatives. Georgina confided to Nancy that she only knew he loved her because of the way he treated her: not because he told her so. He didn't. He thought such declarations unseemly and rather vulgar.

Prince Vasileyev arrived with a pretty Italian fiancée and Giovanni Ferranzi abandoned his work in his villa on the outskirts of Rome and astounded everybody by announcing his intention to attend a public ceremony.

The *Kezia* was bedecked with flowers and looked like a floating garden and on 18 October, ten months after she had first met him, Nancy Leigh Cameron, née O'Shaughnessy, married Ramon Sanford.

"I shall be glad when I can get close to you again," Ramon complained as they danced to the strains of Cole Porter.

Nancy giggled. "I must have looked the most ridiculous bride. I felt like a hippopotamus. There was no way I could hold my bouquet of roses in front of me. They simply rested on Junior."

"You'd have thought he would have had the sensitivity to have stayed still while his parents married," Ramon said wryly. "He was bucketing around under that white silk dress so that every eye in the place was riveted on him."

"He's not bucketing about now," Nancy said. "He's unusually still."

"His timing is very bad."

"Yes." A slight frown furrowed Nancy's brow.

Their guests were wining, dining, dancing and laughing.

"Ramon . . ." Her voice was hesitant.

"Yes, Mrs. Sanford."

"Ramon, I'm not sure, but I think Junior is about to make his appearance."

He stopped dancing and looked down at her with horror. "He can't. He's not due for another month!"

A spasm crossed Nancy's face. "I know, darling, but I don't think anyone has told him that."

The music changed to a foxtrot. Bobo and Hassan were kissing and giggling as if they had just married and were not already in their third month of marital bliss.

"You must be mistaken. You've drunk too much champagne."

Nancy gripped hold of his hand hard. "I haven't and he is."

"Is what?"

"Arriving."

"Christ!" One look at her face as another wave of pain crossed it told him she was telling the truth. He moved to lift her bodily.

She pushed him away gently. "Don't be silly, darling. I can walk. Babies don't come in five minutes."

"Let me get you back to Sanfords," he said urgently.

A tipsy guest gaily threw a wreath of flowers over his neck. Costas' new girlfriend was gesticulating nervously with a foot-length jade cigarette holder. Venetia was pouting at Felix's refusal yet again to dance, and taking Sonny's arm with the declaration that *she* wanted to have fun!

No one noticed the disappearance of the bride and groom. Ramon's face was distraught as he hurried her, her white veil swirling high in the breeze, down the gangplank and into the back of his Hispano-Suzia. Nancy smiled at his concern and then gasped as another pain crept round from the centre of her back and gripped hard on her stomach muscles.

"*Mae de Deus*!" Ramon's face was agonized. "I didn't realize what it would be like. I was going to have gynaecologists flown in . . . nurses . . ."

Nancy gripped his hand hard. "It's too late, darling. If the chauffeur doesn't hurry I'm going to have the baby here."

His face was grey. "Can't you tell Junior to wait? Can you still walk?"

They were at Sanfords' entrance. The pains were coming every five minutes. Verity had taken twenty-four hours to appear. Ramon Junior seemed intent on making his appearance in twenty-four minutes.

"*The baby's coming*!" Ramon shouted to a startled Maria and ran for Doctor Oliveira, too agitated to even think of telephoning him.

Nancy gasped as another pain gripped her. As it receded she said quickly to Maria, "Help me out of my dress and into a nightdress. There isn't much time. Oh . . . !" They waited together, Maria clasping her hands. The pain ebbed. The white silk wedding gown was practically ripped off and tossed carelessly to one side.

Maria had only just managed to slip a nightdress over Nancy's head when another pain came—a pain so intense that she cried out loud.

Dr. Oliveira, Zia and Ramon came running into the room.

"Out!" Oliveira said to Ramon.

"Like hell," Ramon responded, and took hold of Nancy's hand as she lay prostrate on the bed.

Dr. Oliveira knew better than to argue and besides, there wasn't time.

Zia crossed herself and withdrew. Her first grandchild. Chips' grandchild. She hadn't prayed for years. She went back to her suite and did so with the fervour of a true Catholic.

"My bag," Oliveira said urgently to Maria. "Put towels on the sheets, quickly girl!"

This time the pain had taken on a new dimension. Her

knees were drawn up, her nightdress around her sweating stomach. Ramon's hand was her lifeline. She gripped it with all her strength. When the pain became intolerable she fastened her eyes on his. Black, agonized eyes in a strangely white face. Where had all his honey-gold flesh gone? Why did he look so frightened? Did he know? Had he guessed?

Another pain came, ferocious in its intensity. Her nails dug into her palm. She tried to speak to him, but only a strange, animal cry emerged. She could see Dr. Oliveira's face, taut and anxious. He had never expected her to carry the baby to full term. She had done so, triumphantly. The pain came again, but this time it was different. The baby was pushing down hard, splitting her apart.

"Pant!" Dr. Oliveira was saying. "Pant!"

She panted. She could do nothing else. She was being torn in two. There was a rush of liquid and the baby slithered, howling, on to the bed. Ramon's face was ablaze with joy. He seized her shoulders, lifting her up so that she could see the miracle that kicked and yelled between her legs, tiny hands clenched, eyes screwed up, black hair plastered flatly to its head.

"It's a girl!" she said weakly. "It's a girl. It isn't a he after all."

"Perhaps you'll leave while I attend to Mrs. Sanford and the baby," Dr. Oliveira said tartly.

"I'll do no such thing! This is my wife and my child and I'm staying! Isn't she beautiful, Nancy? Isn't she unbelievably, amazingly, *thunderingly* beautiful?"

No one but a father could have said that. She still wasn't bathed, the umbilical cord still sprouted from her tummy. To Ramon she was the most wonderful thing he had ever seen.

Nancy fell back against the pillows. It was three o'clock. They had been married only hours. Her sweating body was sponged down, a clean nightdress slipped over her head.

"What is the baby's name?" Maria asked tremulously, tears of relief and joy on her cheeks. She had never seen a baby born before. It had been the most wonderful moment of her life. She would have lots of babies when she married Luis; babies like this one, strong and healthy with dark eyes and black hair.

"Janela," Ramon said, and the love in his eyes was so exquisite that Nancy knew nothing could ever surpass it.

Janela: a baby conceived by the banks of a mountain stream. Born in love. Janela: it was a beautiful name. A beautiful baby. She smiled and lay back against her pillows, overcome with exhaustion. The dream had finally come to an end. She had been given all that she had asked for. She had carried her baby and given birth to it and now her strength was ebbing. She felt no fear, only a deep, all-pervading joy. How long had it been since she had stood, lonely and alone, in Dr. Lorrimer's office? Ten months? A year? She had thought then that her world had come to an end. Instead she had been on the threshhold of all that had given it meaning. She had found a love that would sustain her through all eternity. She had discovered talents she had barely known existed. She had given birth to a child Ramon would love to the end of his days.

He was holding the baby now, his strong handsome face alight with wonder and unbelievable tenderness. The late evening sun glinted on the two dark heads. Father and daughter; looking at each other for the first time; forging a bond that would be unbreakable. She felt calm and fulfilled, supremely happy. She wanted to keep her eyes open, to gaze and gaze at them, but she could not. Her life blood surged, heavy and hot, between her legs, seeping into the delicate sheets, spreading and staining. She did not call for Dr. Oliveira. She no longer had the strength. She was sinking into drowsy warmth and a darkness that was welcoming. Ramon would grieve for her as passionately and intensely as he had loved her. Then, as he finally came to terms with her death and his grief became a part of his life, he would marry Tessa. The last flicker of a smile curved her lips. Tessa, with her gentleness and kindness, would love Ramon and Janela. None of them would ever forget her. She was part of them and they would be part of her for ever.

As if from a vast distance, she heard Dr. Oliveira's cry of alarm and felt Ramon's hand grasp hers. She wanted to comfort him and could not. She could no longer see him. Her fingers moved imperceptibly in his. A smile fluttered at the corners of her mouth. She whispered his name and then, leaf-light, her spirit soared and drifted away and only the fragrance of jasmine remained.